A BOY, A GIRL, AND A GHOST

A BOY, A GIRL, AND A GHOST

ROBERT J. MCCARTER

Little Hummingbird Publishing

For Mom

Cover photography © Robert J. McCarter

Version 1.0, October 2019

ISBN: 978-1-941153-23-9

Find out more about this book at: ShuffledOff.com

Visit Robert's website at: www.RobertJMcCarter.com

Published by:

Little Hummingbird Publishing

P.O. Box 23518

Flagstaff, AZ 86002

www.LittleHummingbird.com

Little Hummingbird Publishing is a division of Arapas, Inc. Find more about Arapas at: www.Arapas.com.

 Created with Vellum

PART 1

A Boy and a Girl

1

SATURDAY, JUNE 11, 1977

I'M STARTING TO BE ABLE TO SEE HIM... THE GHOST, THAT IS. Not just a flash of light out of the corner of my eye, like I see all over the graveyard, but square on. He's very skinny with sunken-in cheeks and a mustache. His mouth moves, and his brown eyes look so earnest. He's trying to tell me something, something important. But I can't hear him.

It all started a few weeks ago. I've been having a good year, probably my best year. Chemo ended last November, the leukemia is officially in remission, and I even got to attend a lot of tenth grade.

It was a Saturday night, school had just let out, and Mom had made meatloaf for dinner, with mashed potatoes and gravy. Dad went on and on about the Shakespeare festival and the replica of the Old Globe Theatre that had just been completed. He was so excited, and to the tell the truth, so was I. He had been taking me to plays since I was old enough to sit still for two hours (well, three, let's be honest Shakespeare's plays tend to be long).

"The Globe Theatre, here in Cedar City, Utah," he chuckles, playing with what was left of his mashed potatoes with his fork, mounding them up higher and higher. "Do you know what that means, Aaron?" He doesn't wait for me to answer, his grey eyes sparkling behind his glasses. "It means our little Cedar is going to be something. A lot more people will come to the festival. We'll be on the map."

Cedar City is in Southern Utah on Interstate 15, an hour north of St. George and the Arizona border, and a long ways from Las Vegas or Salt Lake City or anything at all resembling a real city.

Cedar City was founded in the mid-1800s as an iron mining settlement. It's a small town with about 10,000 people and wouldn't be much at all without the university.

"It means," I offer, "your little bookstore will get busier selling stuff to those tourists." His shop is on Main Street just a couple blocks from Southern Utah University and in our little downtown area. He teaches English at the university and runs Cedar Books and Such.

"Yes it will, son. Yes it will." He gets this distant look in his eyes as if he is seeing all those people entering the shop, asking for the odd book, going away happily clutching their purchases.

I catch my mom's eye, she is leaning against the kitchen counter with her arms crossed, smiling. It is an entirely mundane conversation about normal things, having nothing to do with Cancer (in this house "cancer" has a capital "C" like it's a living thing and deserves to be referred to with a proper noun).

"Good day?" Mom asks me later as I am heading up to bed. Her pink lipstick is slightly smudged, her blue eyes drilling into me. She had started this ritual when I was eleven, when the leukemia first hit. I think it's her way of acknowledging the tenuous nature of my existence and being a nurse, she understands it better than most.

"Yeah, good day. You know how I love meatloaf." I gave

her a big smile which I saw echoed on her face. People have always told me I have her eyes and her smile, which I take as a compliment. Because when my mom smiles, you can't help but feel some happiness.

"Good. Get some rest, church in the morning."

I want to protest, but don't bother. It would do no good. My mom always wants me to go to church and I never want to go. It's a thing.

I trot up the steps into my room and flop onto the bed. I crack open Richard Bach's *Illusions*. I am fascinated by the book's view of our world as not real, as an illusion. Not a stretch, I know. If this world is illusion, then my Cancer is too. But the book doesn't hold my interest, I feel a restlessness I can't explain.

I shut the light off and pull the sheet up; my window is open, but my room tends to stay hot in the summer. I stare at the glow-in-the dark stars on my ceiling. I'm up in the second floor with my ceiling the sloping roof of the house. I've got a dormer and a window, but it's mostly roof. When I was eight, my dad put the stars up after much asking and whining. I know I'm a bit old for them, but I still really like them.

When I finally fall asleep, I have this dream of when I was a little boy. I don't remember who had died, but my mother took me to the Cedar City Cemetery when I was very young, maybe four years old.

The cemetery sits on the north edge of town and is an oasis of tall trees and grass in the desert. It is surrounded by a wall made of reddish sandstone blocks, which is taller than me at that point. I touch the rough surface as we pass through. I remember liking it, jumping on the grass with joy, only to receive a tight-lipped frown from my mother. What is not to like about all this grass with the oddly square pieces of stone placed at regular intervals. It is a park of some kind. It has to be.

I keep jumping and playing, I can't help myself. Among the gravestones, I see the strangest people. There are three of them, and they move so gracefully between the granite stones, as if they are floating.

One sees me and waves. I wave back. He's a chubby man and smiles at me, motioning to his friends to come look. All three of them, the chubby man, a little girl, and a boy wave at me.

"Mama," I say. "What is wrong with them? I can see through them."

Her mouth moves and she blinks hard, looking carefully over the headstones where I'm looking. "Aaron," she says to me, "I don't see anyone. What are you talking about?"

"Them," I say, pointing and then waving back. "There is a girl my age. Can I go over there and play?" They all look so excited when I wave to them, I just know they want me to come over.

My mom looks me over for a few moments, her face so serious. She then takes my hand and leads me away, and never takes me down to the graveyard. I remember seeing the three of them and their sad faces as they watched us go from behind that sandstone wall.

I woke up all in a sweat. I had forgotten all about it, and as I boy I never thought they might be ghosts. Now, I know that is what they must have been.

———

I SNEAK DOWN THE STAIRS DRESSED, BUT WITHOUT MY SHOES on. I know which stairs creak, carefully stepping over those. It is almost midnight and the dream will not leave me alone. I feel compelled to go.

At the front door, I stop and listen carefully, the smell of meatloaf still hanging in the air. I can hear the tick-tock of the clock in the living room, the sigh of the breeze outside, and nothing else.

I slowly pull back the dead bolt, freezing as it clicks home, sure it was loud enough to wake my parents. Nothing.

I ease the door open, the creaking of the hinges making my heart bang in my chest. I make a mental note to oil them. I ease out the door and slowly close it, put my shoes on, and walk quickly away from my house.

I want to ride my bike—riding feels more natural to me than walking—but I don't want to risk anymore noise. I walk down the deserted streets of my neighborhood, get on Main Street, a few cars still ambling along, and head north to the graveyard. It's cool, in the lower fifties, and I pull my sweat jacket tight, more scared than cold.

I stand there for a moment on the sidewalk in front of that low wall, my hand brushing at the rough sandstone. I had been by it a thousand times and never seen ghosts except for that one time when I was like, four. I am not sure what I expect. Did I really think the dream was trying to tell me something?

Guilt plagues me. I'm not really the kind of kid that sneaks out of his house in the middle of the night. But I'm not exactly normal either. I have suffered years of illness, doctors, treatments, and overprotective parents.

I follow the wall until I come to one of the narrow roads that lead into the cemetery. It's lined on both side with massive cottonwood trees, their leaves swaying in the darkness above me, the sound of it comforting.

I have people here. My friend Charley who died in a car wreck a couple of years back and my uncle Don.

The thought of my uncle, my mother's brother, sticks with me. He was this big burly man who would envelop you in his hugs but had this kind way about him. He had this lilting southern accent that I loved, one that my mother seems to have trained herself out of. He was a long-haul truck driver and died about two years ago. He got the flu and just never got better.

My mom and I came to his grave and placed flowers regularly the first few months after he died, but she suddenly stopped. Since I'm there, I decide to pay my respects. I click on my flashlight and walk back into the graveyard, take my second left, turn right at the fir tree and walk back until I find his modest granite headstone.

Donald Evan Walters
August 1, 1938 - May 16, 1975
Beloved father and husband

I sit down with a sigh, clicking the flashlight off and letting the darkness come back. The lights of Main Street aren't that far, and I can hear the low hum of the traffic on the highway, but it feels good to just sit here with just the breeze and headstones for company.

I'm young, turned sixteen last month, but the Cancer has made me look hard at my own mortality. We all die, right? How smart is it to be afraid of the most inevitable thing?

I imagine my uncle Don, what is left of him, lying below the ground. They call them headstones, so I figure the marker is where his head is, so I lie down on the grass with his headstone at my head, so I am positioned just like he is.

I stare up through the trees at the star-filled sky and take a deep breath, letting it slowly escape in a long sigh. I miss my uncle. When I was a boy, he would play with me so hard, rolling around on the grass with me, laughing. When I got sick he didn't treat me differently, he'd still joke with me, slap me on the back, tickle me. Most folks seemed to be afraid to break me, but not him.

It's while I'm lying there that I catch this flash of motion out of the corner of my eye. It's not much, nothing I can identify, but I'm sure I've seen something.

I sit up and look around. Nothing. My eyes have adjusted to the dark and if someone was there I am sure I would have seen them. I slow my breath, my heart pounding in my ears, and listen. Nothing.

I think about lying down, but I don't feel so safe anymore. I'm about to get up and leave when I see it. A flash of white out of the corner of my eye. I swivel my head to the right, but I don't see anything.

"What the hell?" I mumble.

I get to my feet and slowly look all around, and there it is again. Another flash of white that looks vaguely like a person. I look directly at it and, again, see nothing.

I bite my lip and slowly move my eyes back so they are facing forward, and there it is. My sense of it is rather vague, like trying to see something clearly out of your peripheral vision—you can't. It's this whitish human-looking form standing placidly.

I keep my eyes forward and point to it, realizing my hands are shaking and I am sweating despite the cool air. "Are you real?"

After I speak, what I see changes. It's not a person standing still, it's a person wildly waving their arms. My dream comes crashing back and I'm convinced it's a ghost.

I run home as fast as I can.

2

SUNDAY, JUNE 12, 1977

I HELP OUT AT MY DAD'S BOOKSTORE. I LOVE IT. IN FACT, IT would be fine with me if I could just quit school and do that. It's simpler. I know my place. I know what to do.

With the leukemia, I've missed so much school it's hard for me to fit in and I tend to keep to myself. Everyone has all this shared history that I've missed. I'm not a jock, or an egghead, or a stoner. I don't have a place there. At the bookstore, I do. Behind the counter ringing people up on Dad's ancient cash register, or in the stacks filing books, or helping people find what they want. I know what to do. I know who I am.

Cedar Books and Such is on Main Street. Almost everything in Cedar City is. It's just one of those small western towns that are like that. Our narrow space is sandwiched between two tourist shops that sell what my mother would call "bric-a-brac." We sell some of that too, postcards, posters for the nearby national parks, and games kids can play in the car. A few doors north is the Cedar Theatre.

The front of the shop is glass with a raised platform, I think it used to be some kind of clothing store originally.

We've got best sellers and some bric-a-brac displayed up there. There is also a back door that opens to the parking area behind the Main Street shops. The back of the shop is a hallway to that back door, a bathroom on one side, and our supply room and office on the other. The counter and the register are at the back of the store up against the storeroom wall.

Main Street is wide, with two lanes in each direction, a turn lane in the center, and room for street-side parking. Much of older Cedar City is this way, laid out in a logical square grid with roads wide enough to accommodate a growth in traffic.

Across the street on the corner of Main and Center is the brick and columned post office, it's a beautiful building and gives Cedar that "Leave it to Beaver" kind of vibe. To the left, rising up is an iron-rich hill, the dirt reddish-brown, covered in low bushes, reminding you we are in the high desert.

The "historic" section of downtown really only goes a few blocks to the north and a few blocks south of Center, with old buildings filled with food and wares to attract the tourists. The rest of Main Street, both north and south of this section, is anything you can imagine, from motels to groceries to restaurants to tire places to fast food to where you buy paint.

This historic area is just a blip, almost an extension of the university, and I imagine if this new Shakespearean theatre is successful and the festival grows, it will become even more so.

Iron isn't king in Iron County anymore, like it was for the birth of Cedar City, and it's not agriculture that took over when iron production didn't take. Now it's Shakespeare and tourism. Cedar City is close to a host of national parks, including Bryce, Zion, Cedar Breaks, and the North Rim of the Grand Canyon.

It was those tourists that spawned the Shakespeare festival, and it is the festival that will bring more tourists.

And if you think about it, it's quite the trick. Little Cedar City in Southern Utah, a long ways away from anything, is becoming a focal point for some of the English language's greatest theatre.

I get paid a little to work at the bookstore, which is nice, but I get books too. Every month, Dad lets me take a book to keep (I can borrow anytime as long as I take real good care of them). The day after the incident at the graveyard I go to the stationary section and grab a nice thick journal. It's about five by eight inches and has this blue cloth cover.

"Can I get my monthly book early?" I ask him, showing him the journal. He's got his glasses on and he's behind the desk in the storeroom that he does the business stuff at. It's got a desk stacked with papers, a couple of filing cabinets, an adding machine, and a phone. It is surrounded by boxes of books and other things we sell and special orders waiting for customers to come pick them up.

He glances up, looking over his bifocals at me, his eyebrows coming together. "Something I need to know about?" he asks.

I shrug. I was worried about this, that my sudden desire for a journal would start a line of questioning. "Just got some things to write down."

His grey eyes linger, studying my face, and then he shrugs and grunts, his attention back to the paperwork in front of him. That is his "yes."

I've turned around and am leaving when he adds, "Take two or three if you need. I get them pretty cheap."

I look back at him, but his head is down. He's encouraging me to journal—this worries me. I resolve to figure out a way to do it where my folks can't read it. If I'm going to be writing about ghosts, and things that might make them think I've lost it, I need privacy.

After work, I go to the library, to the science section, and start browsing a book on cryptography.

———

BILLY CHADOW IS MY BEST FRIEND. HE'S BIG WITH HEALTHY layers of muscle and fat. I'm envious.

I was always pretty skinny, but since the Cancer came a knocking, I am very thin. Since remission hit, I've been doing better, but I would love to be a little fat—it would mean my body was working normally.

"No way," he says. Dad had let me take off from my duties at the bookstore—he's adamant I need plenty of "kid time"— and I had biked over to Billy's and brought him here. I tell him just about everything, although it took some figurative arm twisting to get him to ride over here with me.

Billy's eyes dart from my uncle's grave to me and back. "You're shitting me, right?" His hand goes to his messy red hair, his green eyes are wide.

The cottonwoods block most of the hot summer sun and I can smell the spruce trees that are grouped right next to Uncle Don's grave.

"No shit," I say. "Just the real deal, B."

"Aaron, I swear to god if you are shitting me I will pummel you good. You ain't sick no more, so I won't hold back." He stares at me, his eyes totally serious.

I step up and touch the gravestone. "I swear on my favorite uncle Don's grave that this is the truth. I saw a ghost. It saw me and reacted when I spoke to it."

"Shit," Billy says, slumping to his knees on the freshly cut green grass. "So is that what happens to all of us when we die? We are stuck in the fricking graveyard moaning and stuff? I gotta know, A. I gotta know."

When Billy calls me "A" instead of "Aaron," I know he believes me. It made me happy that he did, that it wasn't some big production, just his usual overuse of the word "shit." And I understood his question. We had been best friends since forever, so he had witnessed each step in my illness. He had pondered mortality with me.

I sit down beside him and say, "I don't know, B."

"Can you see anything now?" he asks.

I stand up and defocus my eyes a bit and slowly rotate around, keeping my eyes pointing straight ahead. I sit back down and say, "No, nothing."

We sit there silent for the longest time, lost in our thoughts.

"Maybe," he says, his voice going low, "they only come out around midnight. Hungry spirits looking to feed off of fresh human brains."

"Shut up," I tell him, poking him in the arm. He's been obsessed with zombies since his big brother snuck him into a showing of *Night of the Living Dead* a few years back. That and too many *Tales from the Crypt* comic books.

"Well then what?" he asks.

I shrug. "Maybe I can't see them when it's light. Could be that's it."

He nods, looking serious, and whispers, "Can you come back tonight? I'll meet you down here."

———

I DON'T KNOW IF IT'S THIS WAY FOR OTHER KIDS, BUT MY mom seems to want to keep me a child, while my dad wants to push me forward, see me grow up.

Over Sunday dinner, my mom is fussing over me. A few months ago I might have needed it, but I'm healthy now. I can take care of myself.

"You know the Millers are just across the street," she says over dessert. Vanilla ice cream. "Janet will be there all day if you need something while we're both working tomorrow. I called her and—"

"I'm fine, Mom," I say. "I feel good, really I do."

Her forehead crinkles and she stares hard at me, her blue eyes giving me that "look." The look that says, I almost lost you several times and I'm afraid it could happen at any moment now. I get it. This Cancer has been hard on all of us. But, I don't like it.

"Seriously, Mom. I'm good. I'm gaining weight, riding my bike. I'll be at the bookstore for a while and then Billy and I have plans, you don't have to worry about me."

The crinkling on her forehead gets deeper. I shouldn't have mentioned Billy. She doesn't exactly approve of him. She doesn't think he's good enough for me. I'll admit that Billy and I are different—I'll overthink things, he'll act on impulse and get in huge messes. We actually balance each other out pretty good.

"And what are these plans?" she asks.

I couldn't exactly tell her we were meeting at the graveyard at midnight to try to see ghosts. "Umm… Well…" I stammer.

My mother crosses her arms and leans back in her chair. We're at the round oak table just off the kitchen, a big window looking out on our backyard. "I'm waiting," she says.

I let out a big sigh. "Nothing big, Mom. He's got some new comics, we're going to sit around and read them."

Her pink lips twist into a frown and she slowly shakes her head. Billy's love of comics is yet another of the ways he's not good enough for her.

"I just wish—" she begins, but my dad cuts her off by touching her arm.

"Laura," he says, "I read them when I was a kid. They didn't ruin me."

I breathe a sigh of relief, but I see by the brief flaring of my mother's nostrils that my dad is going pay for his comment.

I see him puff up his chest, like some bird getting ready for a fight. "In fact," he continues, looking at me, "why don't you and Billy come by. I've been thinking it might make sense to have a small rack of comics in the store. Something for the younger folks. You two could help me out." He ends the speech with a broad smile. My mom is suddenly in the kitchen doing dishes.

And that's what I mean by the difference between them. My mom seems to want to control me, like I'm a baby. My dad encourages me to find my own way.

I thank him and head upstairs to write in this journal until it's time to go try to see the ghost.

———

FOR THE MOST PART, I LIKE THE DARKNESS. AFTER I SNEAK out of the house and walk towards Main Street, there are plenty of streetlights, but once I get into the graveyard, it's pretty dark.

People fear what they can't see, but it somehow makes me feel powerful. Walking slowly and quietly without a flashlight, I'm hidden. It would be hard to see me. Hard to do anything to me. Yes, the dark can be scary, but I think of it as armor. I have a flashlight, but it is a last resort, only to be used when absolutely necessary.

The word nyctophilia just might apply to me. In some ways, I prefer the dark to the light. Weird, I know.

I know the way, and there is enough of a glow from surrounding lights that I easily find my uncle's grave. It's about 11:30 and I'm early. I was falling asleep so I decided to leave early.

The graveyard is full of trees and grass, the cottonwood trees tower a hundred feet tall, at least, and line the roads that cut through the cemetery. Interspersed are a few spruce and fir trees, and I feel more comfortable among them. Cedar is high enough to support them, and they invoke the higher, cooler climes of the land just to the west. Up at Cedar Breaks are groves of bristlecone pine trees, twisted, hardy trees that dangle over the edge of the cliffs, cling to sandy soil, drink in scant water, and yet survive. And the bristlecones are the oldest living things on the planet, the ones up the mountain from us are 2,000 years old.

Uncle Don is buried under a dark green spruce, and as I lie there, I almost feel connected to the spruce and fir that dominate the higher altitudes and to the rare bristlecones that live longer under the harshest of conditions.

Sneaking out of the house the first time was hard. The second time was a bit easier. I still felt this guilt, but there are some things that parents just won't understand. Some roads they can't help you travel down.

Besides, I wasn't out here doing anything dangerous. People are afraid of graveyards and the dark. But this is Cedar City. There is nothing nefarious going on around here.

And yes, I relate to the bristlecone. I want to be the bristlecone. I know it's full of ego, this comparison, but I've lived under the harsh conditions of leukemia and chemo, it has twisted me and changed me, and with two strikes against me, I feel like I'm clinging to the edge of a precipice and could fall at any moment.

Despite (or maybe because of) the stresses and their extreme conditions, the bristlecones survive. I want to think that I will survive despite (let's be clear it won't be "because of") the Cancer.

I am willing to be stunted, twisted, enjoy a tenuous existence under harsh conditions like the bristlecone, but I want to survive.

These thoughts are running through my head when I hear yelling out on Main Street. I sit up, look, and see a car stopped and two people standing in the harsh light of the headlights yelling at each other.

He looks like a jock, with his letterman's jacket and his hands shoved into his jeans.

She's tall and slim, and doing most of the yelling.

They're about a half block away from me and there's lots of trees between us, so I can't see a lot of details or hear everything, but I get the gist.

"I am not like that," she shouts, bringing a cigarette to her lips and sucking in.

He laughs. She slaps him hard, turns on her heel, and starts walking right towards me.

I suck in a breath. How does she know I'm here? She can't possibly see me, can she? Who is this girl, would she tell my parents I'm out like this?

I shake off the thoughts rampaging through my mind. It's a coincidence... she can't know I'm here.

"Helena, please!" the jock yells, taking a step towards her. They are out of the headlights, so it's harder to see them, but I can see enough.

She comes to the low wall bordering the graveyard and hops right over it. He comes up to it, his head swiveling around, but he doesn't proceed. I almost laugh out loud. The big jock is afraid to go into a cemetery.

"Come on back. Let's talk about this," he says.

She stops, I see the glow of the cigarette as she takes a long drag. She slowly turns back to him. "No means *no*, you asshole."

"I just thought..." he begins, his voice trailing off as he looks down.

"What?" she yells, taking a step back towards him. "You thought because people whisper rumors about me that you can do whatever you want? That one lousy meal is the price of me?"

"Look... I'm sorry. Don't..."

"Don't tell anyone? Is that what you are trying to say. Don't tell anyone how the mighty Jeff Tate almost raped me and would have if I hadn't socked him in the nuts. Don't call the sheriff and report you? What don't you want me to do, Jeff?"

While they talk I sneak closer, cloaked by darkness. I feel bad for eavesdropping, but I don't want to miss a word.

I know Jeff Tate, and I too have heard the whispers about Helena Monfort. She is a grade ahead of me, having just finished her junior year in high school. The whispers said she was a good time and not too picky.

I can see Jeff's face now. His eyes are wide and his mouth is moving silently. I bet if there were more light he would be beet red. "You listen to me, Helena. You breathe a word of tonight and I will ruin you. You're nobody. Who's going to take your word over mine?"

"That's it, Jeff?" she says. "I am just quaking in my boots. How you gonna ruin me? You only asked me out because you thought you'd get lucky. My grades suck, my reputation is terrible, and I don't have many friends. What the hell can you take from me?"

He's quiet for a few breaths, his eyes hard. "Your father," he says. "That job he's got at the new warehouse. I can make that go away."

"What?" she says, her hands shaking as she lights another cigarette.

"He's a fuckup just like you. It wouldn't be hard. A few words to my father, and he says a few words to your father's boss, and he's out on his ass. All because…" he lets the phrase hang there all heavy and sinister.

Helena is fuming, I can see her shoulders rising as she breathes hard, the cigarette dangling at her side.

"Now be a good girl and get back in the car," Jeff says, pointing to his Dodge Charger.

She takes a couple of deep breaths and a long drag of the cigarette. Jeff shifts from foot to foot, nervous.

"You see this," she yells. I can clearly see her outlined by the light coming from the Charger and the streetlights. She's flipping him the bird.

He stops shifting on his feet and crosses his arms, his face getting hard while she sticks the cigarette in her mouth and raises the other hand with its middle finger outstretched, shaking both hands at him to emphasize her message.

"Is this sinking in?" she yells.

"Goddamn it, Helena. Just get in the car. Let me drive you home. I won't try anything, I promise."

She lowers her hands and for a moment I think she's going to go with him. She flicks the cigarette to the ground and stomps it out, turns on her heel and heads into the darkness of the cemetery right towards me.

My heart leaps into my throat. I've been witness to all this. I hadn't wanted to eavesdrop, but I was there, and I couldn't help myself. What am I going to do? A thought leaps into my mind. Hide! I don't like it, but I do it.

I scoot behind a taller gravestone and crouch down. Jeff is pacing now, out on the street in front of his car. She's mumbling as she marches quickly into the graveyard. I don't hear much, just the occasional curse. Her walk is more like a march and she doesn't seem to be paying much attention to where she is going.

A car door slamming and the screech of tires announces Jeff's departure. She pauses and turns back to where he was. "No means no, you fucking asshole!" She then turns back towards where I am hiding and resumes her muttering and march.

After a couple of steps her foot catches on the edge of a gravestone and she goes down hard. I hear the grunt and the air escaping from her lungs. She curses some more and then starts to cry.

I feel like such a coward, behind my shield of granite, squatting on someone's grave, watching this girl cry her eyes out. She doesn't move, she's just lying sobbing and then she starts pounding the grass with her fist.

I have to do something. I've faced chemo, Cancer, and the very real possibility of death, but somehow this moment here feels harder. Revealing my presence, potentially becoming the object of her anger.

She's not the kind of person I would make friends with. She's too rough, too loud, and she smokes. I find the habit disgusting, and somehow think that people that fall into it must be weak.

But she's a human being. She's in pain. She needs help.

I take a deep breath and stand straight up. That's not enough, she can't see me. I click on my flashlight, pointing it at the ground at my feet and clear my throat. Still not enough. "Umm... I..." I stammer. "Do you need some help?"

She stops sobbing and slowly pushes herself up, her head swiveling around.

"Umm... my name is Aaron," I say. "Aaron Wade. I was... well... Do you need some help?"

She gets herself into a sitting position and is fumbling with her now crushed package of cigarettes, her hands shaking. I take a couple of steps towards her and can smell cheap perfume. I don't like it much. I've gotten real sensitive to synthetic smells since I got sick.

"Who..." she begins, her voice shaking. "Did you? I mean, did..." She looks up at me briefly but not for long. She's back trying to get a cigarette out.

"Here," I say, sitting on the cool grass next to her. I set the flashlight down so it provides some general illumination but doesn't blind anyone. I take the pack of cigarettes from her, my fingers brushing against her. She's cold. It's cooler tonight, down around 50 degrees, and she doesn't have any kind of a jacket. I hand her a cigarette, take off my sweat jacket and put it around her, sitting back down in front of her.

She's fumbling with a lighter, I help her with that too, lighting the cigarette for her. When she was fighting with Jeff, she seemed so strong, so tough, so mature. But now she's just a scared girl.

As she inhales and blows smoke out, it seems to calm her.

"Thank you," she says.

"Sure."

"You saw all that," she says, her hand vaguely pointing out towards the street.

"Yeah."

She nods and picks up the flashlight and shines it in my face. I look away, the light is too bright.

"What are you doing?" I ask.

She doesn't answer, but asks, "How old are you?"

"Sixteen last month." She sets the flashlight back down. "How old are you?" I ask.

"I turned seventeen a month ago."

I look at her again. The light is terrible, but I thought she was older. By her actions and the kind of situation she had gotten herself in. But that's probably just my delayed teenage years speaking, and then I feel self-conscious. She's only a year older than me, tall, beautiful, and taking life on. I'm a scrawny sixteen-year-old who still loves to ride his bike and has mousey brown hair—although for me, having hair at all is a victory.

She finishes the cigarette and brushes at her face, smearing mascara. She takes out a piece of gum and pops it into her mouth, chewing noisily. With a deep breath, she gets up and brushes herself off.

"Aaron, was it?" she asks.

"Yeah. Aaron Wade."

She nods and extends her hand. "I'm Helena Monfort." Her handshake is strong and she's a good four inches taller than me. She's slim with tight jeans, a sweater, and long black hair. "I'd appreciate it if we keep this incident between ourselves." She says it sweetly, but I get her message. You keep my secret, I'll keep yours. I find it odd that she doesn't ask what I'm doing in the graveyard in the middle of the night.

I find it odd, but I like it.

I shake her hand longer than I probably should, but I like the feel of it. Her breath is now an odd cigarettey/minty combo.

After the handshake, she looks around as if she's disoriented.

"Here, take this," I say, giving her my flashlight. "Head that way and you'll hit Main."

Her gaze follows where I am pointing and then she turns around and looks at me again. "Thanks, Wade. You're okay, you know that?"

I shrug, I have no idea what to say.

I watch her as she walks off. She strides confidently, as if she has somewhere important to go. She walks like a boy, but has the body of a woman. The realization stirs something deep inside me. I am sorry to see her go.

I'm left there staring in the direction she went, left with only the strange smell of cigarettes and mint. I realize I'm starting to like that smell.

———

"IS IT A GHOST?" BILLY ASKS EXCITEDLY. "ARE YOU SEEING it right now? What does it look like?" He's chattering away and I'm still standing there looking in the direction Helena went. She walked to Main Street and headed south. I didn't move, but my head swiveled so I could watch her go, watch that walk.

Not long after I lost sight of her, Billy showed up.

"They're not after brains are they?" he continues. "Cause if you think about it, a ghost is dead, and it walks. So, you know, the walking dead. You might consider them zombies, and zombies love to…" He trails off, his nervous rant ending. He's scared—he talks a lot when he's scared.

I shake my head turning towards him. I had completely forgotten about the ghosts and why I came at all. "No, I don't see any ghosts."

"Well, maybe you need to do what you did last time," Billy says.

So we go to my uncle Don's grave and lie there. Billy won't lie down, but states, rather earnestly, that someone has to guard. But I don't see any flashes of light out of the corner of my eye.

He's chatty, asking me questions he should know the answer to. "Your mom and uncle were from Florida, how'd they end up here in Utah of all places?"

I shrug, my shoulders rubbing against the grass below me. "Uncle Don was a trucker. After Dad got the job at the university and Mom and Dad settled here, he did too. He wanted to be close to his family."

In a way it was nice, remembering Uncle Don. He was such a happy man, and had a bit of a southern drawl, unlike my mother who trained herself out of it as soon as she left Florida.

My aunt and cousin left Cedar after Uncle Don died, went to California to be with her family. I really miss them all.

I stand up, suddenly feeling sad, and stare straight ahead, like I did when the ghost seemed to have seen me, but nothing. After about thirty minutes of this, Billy is glad to call it a night and we walk home.

If truth be told, my mind wasn't on ghosts, it was on a girl.

3

MONDAY, JUNE 13, 1977

I WAKE UP TIRED, LIKE I HAVEN'T REALLY SLEPT. AFTER I snuck back into my bed it was 1 a.m., but I laid there for a long time thinking—and not about ghosts.

It's actually a nice change of pace. I've spent many a night awake in my bed, staring up at the glow-in-the-dark stars on my slanted ceiling thinking about Cancer and Death (Death is a proper noun around my house, just like Cancer, although it is talked about a whole lot less).

Instead I laid there thinking about a girl, how she moved, how her dark hair rested on her shoulders, how her face looked, briefly lit by the lighter she used, how her hand felt in mine.

I'm not dumb. I know that girls are what most teenage boys spend their days (and nights) thinking about. But for me it's new, it's different. I think it means that I really am healthy.

I drag myself downstairs at 7 a.m.—having breakfast with the folks before they go to work is a summer requirement (provided I am healthy, of course).

My mom is dressed in jeans and white blouse, scurrying around the kitchen. My dad has his face buried in a newspaper, the *New York Times*. We've got a little oak table in there big enough for the three of us. I scoot into a chair and pour some Apple Jacks into a bowl and smile. I love the sound cereal makes when you pour it into a ceramic bowl. All chaoticy and musical.

"You okay, son?" my father asks, his newspaper now in his lap.

"Yeah," I say, suppressing a yawn. "Just tired. Didn't sleep that great."

Well, my mom is on me about a second later, pressing that back of her hand to my forehead, feeling the lymph nodes in my throat.

"Any bruising?" she asks. "Do you feel okay? Sore throat?"

I push her hands away. My mom is a nurse. And when you get sick, like I did, it's a curse and a blessing. The curse is she knows way too much. Each little thing that might be related to my leukemia is a world-class disaster. The blessing is, she knows her way around hospitals, knows doctors and nurses, knows how to get you taken care of.

"Mom, I just didn't sleep well. I'm fine. I swear."

She pulls her pink lips into the smallest of smiles, but her blue eyes don't follow suit. They are sharp and serious. "Of course," she says, straightening up. I love my mom, I've done really well in the parent lottery, and we've been down this road enough that we all know how she can be. I smile at her, grateful she's taking my word for it. But I feel a stab of guilt—I'm tired because I snuck out of the house in the middle of the night.

"Just take a nap before you go to the bookstore, okay?" she says.

"Sure, Mom."

After they leave, I grab the big telephone book. It's not big because Cedar City is big, it's big because it covers this whole area of Southern Utah. None of the little towns are big enough for their own phone book.

I flip to the M's and scan down: Molina, Monahan, Monfort. There is only one, Monfort, Kyle. My palms start sweating and my breath catches in my throat. I have an address. I have a phone number. I commit the information to memory and put the phonebook back in the kitchen drawer exactly how I found it. I don't want anyone to know I used it. I don't want any questions.

———

I LIKE THE HUM OF MY BIKE TIRES AGAINST THE PAVEMENT. I like the feel of the wind in my face, the sense of motion and power. For me, my bike feels like freedom. A car would be a lot better, but right now a bike is great.

I take the quiet neighborhood roads from our house and parallel Main Street going south. The bookstore is that way and I'm due soon. But, Helena Monfort lives that way too, and I end up cutting through the university and going farther south than I need to.

I'm beginning to think something is wrong with me. I feel this need to see her, so I think I'll take a chance and ride by her house. Even if she's not there, I'll find out something about her. But what if she is there? What if she thinks I'm some crazy love-sick kid and she laughs at me? What if she yells at me like she did Jeff Tate? I couldn't stand that.

But I *have* to see her!

It's insane, but then I remember the time Billy was in love with Nancy Keagan when he was twelve. He'd come to my chemo treatments and babble on about her incessantly. I used to think it was about him trying to distract me from the nasty stuff that was being pumped into my body. Now I know better. He couldn't help himself.

But I chicken out at the last moment and avoid her house and am sure that I must be insane. But as I keep pedaling, sweating in the heat of the summer day, I keep thinking. As I reach the bookstore, I come to the conclusion that while I may be insane in this regard, it's actually (really unbelievably) normal.

My dad takes off after I arrive at the store at around 1 p.m. and I'm in charge. When I'm not dealing with customers, I flip through a few novels in the romance aisle with titles like *Heart in the Sunlight* or *Love's Puppet*. Romance! This further confirms that this insanity I'm feeling plagues us as a species.

I've got this hardcover in my hand. It's got a man with long flowing blond hair with his fluffy shirt open revealing his large, hairy chest. He's taking the hand of a woman in a period dress with an abundance of cleavage showing. I'm standing behind the counter, just about to put it down (it's all gotten rather boring—I don't have the right chromosomes for these kinds of books) when the shop bell rings.

I feel my face flush at someone seeing me reading one of these "bodice rippers." When I look up, I almost pass out. It's Helena Monfort.

"Hey, Wade," she says, casually nodding her head towards me. I like it how she calls me by my last name. No one does that. It feels special.

She immediately looks away from me and starts making a show of browsing through the bookstore. I say "show" because it feels like that to me. She's there and she's all I can see. All I can think about. My heart is pounding in my chest and I'm real aware of every inhale and every exhale. It's like time slows down. She goes from aisle to aisle picking up a book in each one and flipping through it. Even in sections she'd hardly be interested in: business, children's books, etc. That's the "show" part of her entrance.

I stare at her. I can't help myself. Now that I can see her in the light, I can see what she actually looks like. In a word, beautiful.

She's tall and slim with womanly curves and this boyish walk. She has long black hair that cascades over her shoulder, landing on the white T-shirt and sweat jacket she's wearing. Her jeans are tight and the way her flesh moves underneath them is the kind of thing that I am sure drives many a man to write poetry.

Her body is distracting in a way that is still so disconcerting to me, but it's her face that I can't stop looking at. Her eyes are a light brown, but in certain light they look golden sometimes and coppery other times. Amber is the only word I can think of to describe the color. She has high cheekbones with a few scattered freckles on them and a slightly turned up nose. Her lips are full and expressive. It doesn't look like she's wearing any makeup. God know she doesn't need to.

She makes her rounds through the store and ends up standing in front of the counter, a smile on her lips. I'm still sitting on the stool and we are eye to eye. I don't think I've moved since she entered the store, except to watch her.

"Nice book," she says, eyeing the large-chested man and woman on the cover.

I feel heat in my face and neck. I must be beet red. I hastily put the book down. "I... It... Well, you see... Umm... someone just returned it."

She smiles slyly and nods. I close the book and shove it under the counter.

She's here. She's standing right in front of me. What do I say? Where are my words?

"So, I just wanted to thank you for helping me out last night." Her smile widens as she takes off the blue sweat jacket (which I belatedly realize is mine) and sets it on the counter. She puts my flashlight on top of it. She then looks around the store. "I'm glad your old man is not here. Last night is our secret, right?"

"Umm... Yeah. Of course. Totally." I groan inwardly. I

sound like a moron. But where the hell are my words? How do humans survive this, anyway?

Lines briefly form on her smooth forehead. "You okay, Wade?"

"Yeah. Fine. Just didn't get enough sleep last night, you know."

She smiles again. "I do at that."

We stay there, eye to eye, just the counter separating us. I smell her minty/cigarettey breath—she's chomping on some gum.

I smile and then she smiles. Then I feel subconscious about smiling and stop. Then she stops. It's like our faces are trying to find a configuration that doesn't feel awkward. She's still standing there. She's waiting for something. But what?

"Need any books?" I ask. "I can give you the family discount."

The little frown on her face tells me this is not what she was waiting for. Duh.

"No thanks. Listen, I've got to get off to work now. It was nice seeing you again, Wade." She turns and walks towards the door.

"You too."

She turns back, smiles at me again, and leaves.

I feel like one of Billy's zombies just ripped my guts out. This was a test and I just failed it. I know it.

———

TOO RESTLESS TO SLEEP, I SNEAK OUT AGAIN TONIGHT. JUST me and the stars in the graveyard. I don't know, I am finding it comforting to be on the cool green grass under the heavens, lying there above my uncle Don's remains cocooned in darkness.

It feels safe.

And yes, part of me is hoping that by some miracle Helena Monfort will show up again. Foolish beyond words, I know, but there it is.

But after a while even that all goes away and I'm just there. Stars. Grass. Uncle Don's remains. Lovely darkness.

That's when I see him again. The ghost. A flash of white out of my peripheral vision. But I know what to do this time.

I take deep, slow breaths and rise to my feet. I lock my eyes so they are pointed straight forward and slowly rotate around until I can see him as clearly as possible. Looking directly doesn't work, not at all. But if I am careful, I can see him out of my peripheral vision.

Tonight, he seems clearer to me, more formed. I see the complete outline of a tall, thin man. I point and say, "I see you."

He moves his hands—it looks like he is shaking his fists in excitement. I feel my heart thudding in my chest, but I stay put this time. I don't run.

"I can't see you well at all. Only out of the corner of my eye."

His hand waving stops, and he raises one hand to his head. I'm not sure why. My sense of him, while better than the first time, is still pretty vague.

"Are you a ghost?" I ask.

He waves his hands around again.

I lose my focus and sink back down into the cool grass, zipping up my sweat jacket. Thoughts of Helena come drifting back to me. The fabric smells faintly of her distinctive minty odor. She was the last one to wear this.

What the hell am I doing? I am the healthiest I've been in years and here I am obsessing over a girl who probably never gave me a second look. She came by the store only to make sure I don't tell her secret—that Jeff "the football star" Tate

tried to force himself on her. And I'm hanging out at the graveyard in the middle of the night seeing ghosts.

This can't be normal.

I sit there, staring at the grass feeling sorry for myself for a
good five minutes. But that is enough. I stand back up, find him
in my peripheral vision, and say, "Okay. You're a ghost and I
can kind of see you. What the hell do we do now?"

Even with my vague sense of him, I can tell my new ghost
friend is excited. He is waving his arms, kicking out his feet,
putting on quite the display. I have to laugh. It seems I have a
new friend.

4

THURSDAY, JUNE 16, 1977

I'VE BEEN TOO BUSY TO WRITE FOR A FEW DAYS, BUT I'VE been keeping up the same pattern. Sneaking to the graveyard every night. Billy almost got caught sneaking back into his house that first night he snuck out and has been too chicken to try again. Which is kind of okay. I like being there alone.

I've been having breakfast with the folks, napping, and then working at the bookstore for most of the afternoon. Billy and I hang out here and there.

I've also done my best to forget about Helena. Billy has helped. He's completely obsessed with Barbara Bach—she will be playing a Russian spy in the next Bond movie, *The Spy Who Loved Me*, coming out next month. He goes on and on about her, rather endlessly.

Today he sneaks in a copy of *Playboy* featuring Barbara Bach into the store—he stole it from his older brother. We look at it (and her) behind the counter when the store is empty. I thought it would help with the Helena thing (which I still haven't told anyone about, not even Billy). I can't say that it does.

I mean, I like seeing those pictures, but it makes me feel funny in some many ways. It makes me excited, of course, but I feel dirty too. Like I shouldn't be seeing this woman naked, like there is something wrong with it.

Billy was always the one coming up with the pictures of naked women. First it was tribes in Africa in *National Geographic* where the women just don't bother to wear much. Then *Playboy*, but these pictures are very different. The women pose and act sexy. These pictures are supposed to make you want them.

"That's enough," I say, moving from behind the counter.

"What?" Billy asks. "There can never be enough of sweet Barbara. Shit, man. Did you see this one, with the fur coat? I mean… shit!"

I sigh and start shelving a few books. A history on Shakespeare—with the festival we have a big section on the bard. A travel guide to Utah. A new bodice ripper, which are popular.

"What's wrong, Aaron?" he says. "I suspect you're about to get all holy on me, but spit it out anyway."

"Shut up, Billy," I say. "It just doesn't seem right. Staring at those pictures of women like that. We don't know them. It's not real."

He snorts. "As real as either of us losers are going to see any time soon."

I pause, my fingers caressing the pages of Richard Bach's *Illusions*. It's selling well and we have it right at the front of the store.

"Those girls are illusions, Billy. Nothing real there."

He moves from around the counter and stomps through the store. "Barbara Bach is real. She's beautiful and a star and a freaking Bond girl for god's sake. And she's more real than that damn ghost you go see every night. Talk about illusions." He's out the door and gone.

I was left there thinking maybe he was right. The ghost

could be my brain doing something weird. I once overheard my mother tell my father that leukemia can get into your brain and if it does, it's bad... real bad.

And while I know I have exactly zero chances with Helena, I'd rather feel her hand in mine again than stare at naked pictures of women I would never know.

That *Playboy* made things worse. It made me want a real girl in my life. It made me want Helena that much more.

————

THERE ARE A LOT OF GHOSTS IN THIS GRAVEYARD. MY estimate is around twenty or thirty. There are a lot more gravestones than that—it's somehow comforting they're not all ghosts—but I had no idea there would be so many. Each night I've come down here, my ghost friend has come more and more into focus. I can almost see him straight on. And less focused, I can see other ghosts in the background.

Some look human. Some are more ephemeral in their shape—these make me feel uncomfortable. Some are just wisps of white flashing to and fro, seen only out of the corner of my eye.

I know that I may be losing it. That, like Billy said, none of this may be real. Maybe my brain got messed up with all those chemo treatments or the leukemia's gotten in. Maybe I'm going schizo. I don't know. But what keeps me coming back is this: What if the ghosts are real? I saw them as a kid, clear as day. I am starting to see my ghost friend clearer and clearer.

That possibility is important to me. Having had leukemia and a reoccurrence (two strikes, as I call it, but not around my parents) makes me want to believe. Keeps me sneaking out and coming back.

And the ghost wants something. I don't know what it is, but boy does he want something. I think he's trying to talk to me, but for some reason I can only see him, not hear him. We've decided, my ghost friend and I, that it will just take time. Soon I will be able to see him clearly and hopefully hear him too.

I'm sitting on my uncle Don's grave writing in my diary when I notice a flash of light. My progress seeing the ghost is agonizingly slow, so I've taken to bringing my diary and writing in it down here. It's peaceful and quiet. My ghost friend doesn't mind.

When I see the light, I put my diary down and turn my flashlight off, my heart leaping into my throat. What if it's my parents? What if they've found out? I try to calm myself and just watch. It's someone out on Main Street that has just cut into the graveyard. The person is moving slowly and carefully winding their way across the grass, their flashlight searching back and forth.

I'm not sure of it at first, but then it becomes clear. The person is headed my way. Shit!

My brain does flip-flops, trying to figure out what to do. Should I run—no, if they are not coming here, movement would just give me away. Should I stay—that would be stupid and just ensure that I get caught. I'm stuck in indecision as the light gets closer and closer.

"Wade?" the person whispers. "I saw your light. I know you're here. Where are you?"

It's a female voice, and at first I think it's my mother and that freaks me out. But the voice is deeper than hers and rougher, and my mother would never call me Wade.

"Helena?" I ask, turning on my flashlight and shining it at her.

She covers her eyes and says, "Get that damn thing out of my face." I lower my flashlight, but it was on her long enough for me to get a good look at her. She's dressed in a colorful skirt and a white top that shows off plenty of cleavage. The outfit looks familiar, but I just can't place it. My heart speeds up even more.

She walks over and sits down next to me with a sigh, setting her flashlight on the ground, providing some general illumination. I do the same, staring at her, unable to speak. She doesn't talk either, she digs in her old brown purse and pulls out a cigarette and a lighter.

She doesn't look at me as she lights up and takes a long drag, blowing the smoke up at the night. I have no idea what to say, no clue what she's doing here, so I don't say a thing. Despite the cool night, I'm all sweaty now that she's sitting by me and start worrying that I stink bad or something.

"Long shift," she says after she finishes with the cigarette, grinding the butt out in the grass and leaving it there. I want to say something about littering, but keep my mouth shut.

"Shift?" I ask, finally getting a word out.

"Yeah," she says, nodding back out towards Main Street as she pops a stick of gum in her mouth. "I work at La Familia a few nights a week. Saw a light, knew it had to be you."

The outfit makes sense—it's what the waitresses wear. I'm still stunned that she's here. That she would even think about me. I want to say something cool or impressive, but instead I say, "Don't they serve alcohol there? Aren't you seventeen?"

She shrugs. "With the right makeup, I look twenty, easy. The owners are friends of my father's. Besides, this is Cedar City, no one cares."

I nod, suddenly desperate to see her in makeup that makes her look twenty. I hold up my flashlight and say, "Do you mind? I'm curious."

She shrugs again so I cast a little more light on her. She's got black eyeliner on with blue eyeshadow and a touch of red on her high cheekbones. Her freckles have been covered up—I miss them. She definitely looks older, which doesn't seem like that good of a thing to me. I lower my flashlight and say, "I like you better without makeup."

In the dim light I can tell she's staring at me, but she doesn't say anything about the comment. Instead she asks, "What are you doing here, Wade? Why do you hang out in the graveyard in the middle of the night?"

I don't say anything for a while, and she seems fine with that. She leans her head up and stares at the stars. I'm not sure what to tell her, I don't want her thinking I'm a nut job, so I go with the truth—at least some of it. "I'm sorry, Helena, but I don't know you well enough to tell you that."

She's staring at me again for the longest time. I'm afraid I did something horrible, that she'll never speak to me again. She finally says, "You're a weird kid, Wade. You know that?"

I'm sure I've screwed it up. "Umm... I..." I stammer.

She gets up and brushes herself off and asks, "You going to be here tomorrow night?"

"Ahhh... Yeah. Probably. Why?"

"So we can do something about you knowing me well enough to tell me your little secret." With that she turns and walks away.

I can barely breathe.

5

FRIDAY, JUNE 17, 1977

BILLY CHADOW LIVES IN A BIG TWO-STORY HOUSE ABOUT A mile and half away from mine. It's painted a cheerful green and has pansies in red, yellow, and purple lining the sidewalk that leads up to the front door.

I'm a bit nervous—Billy and I don't fight that often and when we do I feel so strange. He's been a constant in my life for so long that any distance from him feels awful.

My dad says that the true test of a friend is how they are in bad times. I've seen a lot of bad times and Billy has always been there. By that test he's the truest of friends, I can't let the little things get in the way.

I walk right in and the smell of bacon and the sound of screaming girls wafts over me. I smile.

The Chadows are Mormons, like many in Cedar City, and like many Mormons they have a lot of kids. I wave at the twins —the source of the screaming—who are chasing each other around the big living room. I wave at Mrs. Chadow who is in the kitchen cleaning up from breakfast. She smiles, her round cheeks red, and waves me up the stairs. She knows I'm here to see Billy.

I feel very comfortable in the Chadows' home. It, and they, are so different from my own family, but in many ways they are my family too. Not just because of my friendship with Billy, but because of the kind of people they are and the amount of time we've all spent together.

As I hit the second floor, I see Billy's older brother, Abe. He's got Billy's red hair and green eyes, but is tall and willowy, unlike most of his family, which tends to be short and stout. He is the source of the *Playboy* that Billy and I fought over.

"Hey, scarecrow," he says to me. He's heading from the bathroom into his own room. I've always been kind of in awe of Abe. He's quite a bit older than Billy and I and always seems to have it together. He's currently in college.

"Hey, beanpole," I say to him. We are both skinny.

He stabs his thumb at Billy's room. "He's bent, not sure why. But tread carefully."

I nod and knock on Billy's door as Abe disappears into his room.

"Go away," he yells. The sound is muffled by his door and the cacophony of his twin sisters screaming makes it hard to hear him.

"It's Aaron," I shout. I want to make sure he can hear me.

There is a long pause before the door slowly opens. "What do you want?" he asks.

"Just let me in, okay?"

He nods and opens the door and I walk in. Billy's room is its usual mess. Bed unmade, clothes everywhere, comic books strewn about, smelling of stale sweat. On the wall are a bunch of posters: the movie posters from *Logan's Run* and *Jaws*, a Kiss poster, and a poster of Farrah Fawcett posing in her red bathing suit. Farrah Fawcett was the girl of his dreams before Barbara Bach.

He slumps down onto his bed and picks up a Spiderman comic, not looking at me.

"I'm sorry, B," I say. "I know Barbara is special to you and I have no right to make light of that." In truth, I think his crushes are a little silly, but I am finally starting to understand them—how irrational a boy can get about a girl.

He nods, his eyes meeting mine. "What the hell got into you anyway?"

I carefully pace around his room, avoiding the Legos and pieces of an erector set. I've been holding back on Billy and that feels odd.

"It's a girl," I say.

Billy is suddenly at full attention, his eyes wide, his posture straight. He's paying attention. "Shit…"

"I… I… Listen, Billy. I can't tell you all the details, but I gotta talk to someone about this. Can I trust you?"

He's blinking rapidly, his eyes locked on mine. I'm sure he's hoping for something a lot more juicy than I have to tell. "Yeah. Shit yeah, you can trust me."

"Just between us, Billy. You gotta swear."

He stands up holding his hands in front of him so I can clearly see there are no crossed fingers. "I swear, A. What is said in this room is sacred. I will tell no one."

I sink to the floor, most of my energy gone. Billy joins me down there, clearing away some dirty clothes. "Her name is—"

I'm cut off by the door to Billy's room opening and two ten-year-old girls' faces poking in. They've got the Chadow green eyes and their wild red hair is contained in a ponytail. Jill and Jane, Billy's twin sisters. Now that I think of it, the screaming had stopped a few minutes ago.

"Hi, Aaron," Jill says. They are identical twins, but I've known them forever and can tell them apart.

"Good to see you," Jane says, her voice rising an octave, just like Jill's had. They both, as of recently, have decided that they "like" me. It's rather uncomfortable.

"Get out!" Billy yells, levering himself up and lunging for the door. The little girls' faces disappear before Billy slams the door. He's standing there panting. Looking at me. "The suspense is killing me. What the hell is her name?"

I swallow hard and bite my lip. "Helena Monfort."

Billy's eyes go wide and he sinks to the floor, his back still pressed against it. "Shit!" A grin spreads on his face. "You lucky bastard. Do you have any idea how jealous I am of you right now? Shit. Helena Freaking Monfort. She's a class-A babe and world-class trouble. Shit, man. Spill. You gotta spill everything now!"

"It's not that exciting." He gives me this look like he doesn't believe me. "Okay, it is exciting. Oh my god! But nothing has happened, and I mean nothing. But, I think we are becoming friends."

Keeping his back pressed firmly to the door to ensure privacy, he says, "Start from the beginning, tell me everything, leave nothing out."

I take a deep breath and tell him what I can. I leave out how we met but tell him the rest.

———

I'M CHUCKLING AS I LEAVE BILLY'S, GET ON MY BIKE, AND head for the bookstore. I love Billy, he's the brother I never had, but I don't trust his advice concerning women. He kept urging me to "make a move." He told me that "a girl that hot needs a confident, assertive man."

I told him, firmly, that we were just friends, that all I wanted was to be friends. He didn't believe it. I don't either, but I can't speak aloud anything else. It feels too scary.

I do my shift at the bookstore, but I'm distracted. For once in my life, I am not content to be among the books. I read the first chapter of *The Shining* while things are slow, but even though I love Stephen King, for some reason I can't get into it. I long for the girl, I want to see the ghost.

As I'm sitting behind the counter, the twin mysteries of my life keep me restless. Why can I see the ghost? When will I see the girl?

My dad notices when he comes in. It's just after four and he's done teaching for the day. The bookstore is so close to the college that he does his office hours here, a parade of students coming through in the late afternoon and early evening most days.

"Thanks, Aaron," he says as he comes behind the counter and lowers his briefcase to the floor. "You can go."

I don't move right away. I'm still sitting on the stool—I am not used to having time I don't know what to do with. At least not while I'm healthy. When I was sick, I would read and read and read, and then sleep and sleep and sleep. Now I can't wait for the night to come. I know the ghost will be there, and I can hope that Helena will be too.

"You okay, son?" he asks.

I shake my head and get off the stool. I look around, the store is empty. "Can I ask you a question?"

He nods and sits down on the vacated stool, adjusting his wire-rimmed glasses.

"Umm... Well..." I stammer, not knowing what kind of consequences my question will have. But my dad has always been open and honest with me. When I got sick, he's the one that laid it out, talked about odds, didn't pull any punches. I was eleven at the time, and it was a lot. Over the years, I've come to appreciate and rely on his honesty.

"What is it, Aaron?"

"I'm just wondering how you knew Mom was the one? You know, back when you first met."

His eyes widen and his brow furrows as he looks carefully at me. He then looks away. It wasn't the reaction I was expecting. I thought he would smile, tell me a brilliant little vignette about something she did. My belly tightens as I watch his face cycle through emotions.

"My love for your mother snuck up on me," he says. "As you know, a mutual friend set us up on a blind date while I was a teaching assistant at University of San Francisco and your mother was in nursing school. I liked her right away and that like slowly grew into love."

I'm disappointed. "So, not like in those books?" I point to the romance section.

He chuckles and shakes his head. "No, not at all."

I nod, not sure what to do with the information. It's not what I expected, and as I think about it now, it's not what I wanted. But as I mulled it over, I realized it could be exactly what I needed to hear. Maybe Helena only likes me now, maybe that like can grow into something else.

"Thanks, Dad," I say, smiling as I grab my backpack and go back to the storeroom to retrieve my bike.

As I am carefully wheeling it towards the door, my dad asks the question I feared, "So do you want to talk about this girl?"

I force a smile on my face and say, "Nope, but thanks anyway."

I know I've let the proverbial cat out of the bag, but I needed something to counterbalance Billy's gung ho, go-get-her talk.

I was happy as I rode home. There was hope for friendship turning into something else, and even if I didn't see Helena tonight, I would see a ghost.

It's turning out to be quite the summer.

———

IF YOU HAVEN'T BEEN TO UTAH, YOU MIGHT THINK IT AN uninterrupted expanse of hot, dry desert with a few cactus and scrawny bushes clinging to sandy soil.

And it is, but that is not all it is. Cedar City is at nearly 6,000 feet elevation and nestled against the Cedar Mountains that contain Cedar Breaks National Monument and Brian Head Peak at over 11,000 feet. Stray too far from Cedar City and Cedar Valley (everything around here is named "Cedar") to the north, south, or west, and you'll find your classic desert, but with much more interesting geography than you're probably imagining. Go to the east and in less than twenty miles, winding up Cedar Canyon, you'll be at over 10,000 feet in elevation and at Cedar Breaks National Monument.

It gets hot here, July can get into the nineties, and it's dry and desert-like, but the elevation and the mountains keep Cedar much more livable, much more friendly.

———

I CAN SEE HIM STRAIGHT ON NOW, MY GHOST FRIEND, THAT is. I can see him clearly. His mouth moves, but I can't hear what he's saying.

He's tall and very thin. He's wearing jeans and a button-down shirt covered in a white smock with black smudges. He has a thick, old-fashioned mustache that twirls up at the ends. It makes me think he's been dead a long time. And he glows. I shine my flashlight on him and while I can't see him as clearly, no light reflects off of him. It's like he's producing his own light.

There are other ghosts, some around him, but he's the only one I can see clearly. The rest are white smudges, glimpsed out of my peripheral vision. But they all seem to be interested in me.

I don't know why, but tonight things have changed. I started to see the flashes of the ghosts as soon as I entered the grave-yard and they gathered around me. When I got close to Uncle Don's grave, there my ghost friend was with a big smile on his lean face.

He has brown eyes and black hair. He has a habit of biting on his lower lip. He gesticulates broadly when he speaks.

If only I could hear him. If only I was sure this wasn't all in my mind.

6

SATURDAY, JUNE 18, 1977

"I THINK I'VE GOT THIS FIGURED OUT," HELENA SAYS AS SHE slumps to the ground next to me and lights a cigarette. The night is overcast and it's darker than usual in the graveyard. They mowed the grass today so it smells all fresh and green.

"What?" I ask.

"This," she says, pointing her cigarette at me and then pointing back to herself. She's got her "La Familia" outfit on and we've both got flashlights on the ground producing some general illumination.

My ghost friend is there, smiling as he looks her up and down.

"Sorry," I say, I'm still confused.

She exhales, cigarette smoke floating up into the air, the scent of it mixing with the smell of the grass. "Long shift," she says. "I'm not being clear. Let me back up. You know the game called 'Truth or Dare'?"

"Yeah."

"Well, I propose we play 'Truth or Truth.' Right here, right now. You ask me anything you want, and I'll tell you the truth.

And then I can ask you anything I want, and you tell the truth. But, I won't ask you why you're here in the middle of the night hanging out with the gravestones. You decide when you tell me that—once, you know, you think you know me well enough."

I'm stunned. Who the hell is this girl? The idea of being able to ask her anything is scary and exciting at the same time. And I can't even imagine the kinds of things she'll want to ask me.

"Well?" she asks. "What do you think of my brilliant plan?"

I still don't speak. This means that she's been thinking about me. This means she wants to get to know me better—even if it is only to find out my secret. "Umm… Sure," I finally say. "How… how do we do this?"

"One more thing," she says, grinding her cigarette butt out in the grass. "When we are here, when we are playing our game, everything shared is confidential. Absolutely secret. You can't share a word of it with your best friend, your mother, or even your priest. I can't either."

I start to hear my heart pounding in my ears. My ghost friend's eyes are a bit wide, but his head is nodding. I look around and he's the only ghost that is close. Does he want to play too? But I still can't hear him.

"Are we agreed?" she asks, extending her hand.

"Agreed," I say, shaking her hand and notice that the ghost has put his hand in there too.

"Sweet!" she says after the handshake is over. She pops a piece of gum in her mouth and starts chewing loudly. "So, shoot, my man."

I bite my lip. What the hell to ask her? What I want to ask is how she feels about me, why she's hanging out with me. But that is just too scary, the potential for disaster is way too high. "Ladies first," I say. I know I'm chickening out, but I really need her to set the tone.

She purses her lips—I'm pretty sure that's what she's doing.

I know she's staring at me, but in the dim light it's a bit hard to read her face. She's silent for a few breaths and then says, "What's it like? Having leukemia, that is?"

I suck in a breath and blink. The ghost is looking at me real hard now, surprised—how could she have known? "How… you know about that?"

She shrugs. "Small town, kid-o. I asked around about you. Took me about three seconds to find that out."

She asked around about me? I feel strange, like I'm not really in my body. Billy's words echo in my head: *class-A babe and world-class trouble*. No one has ever asked me about that. They worry and fret. They get scared and stay away. They get all pity-filled and saccharine. But they don't ask me what it is like. And this is her opening question. What the hell have I gotten myself into?

"You are serious about this game of yours," I finally say.

She nods and smiles. "I am."

I sigh and wrap my arms around me. Suddenly my sweat jacket is not warm enough for the chill of the night. "It's not as exotic as it sounds. At first it was… well, I was just tired. I got sick a lot. Bruised easily, these tiny weird purple marks on my skin. Ran low-grade fevers all the time. Kind of like having the flu for way too long.

"My mom, she's a nurse, so she was all over it and took me into the doctor as soon as symptoms showed up. Still, it took about a month to diagnose. At first, they thought it was the flu or that I was anemic. Then when they found it out, that's when it got tough."

"Why?" she asks.

"It changes everything. It's this whole different world with language and terms and treatments and everything. I had acute lymphoblastic leukemia or 'ALL' for short.

"There is a vast difference between having a flu you can't shake and having capital-C Cancer with a name and treatment plans and survival rates. The diagnosis changes everything. How you go about your life, what you spend your days doing, and worst of all, how people treat you."

She's quiet, but I can tell she's watching me closely. I look up at the ghost and he looks sad, his head slowly nodding. As if he knows what a disease like this can do to a family, as if he wants me to keep talking. And it feels kind of good to talk to someone about it who wasn't there.

"The chemo was worse, though," I say.

"What? Worse than the leukemia?"

I nod. "Way worse. Try being so nauseous that you want to puke every hour of every day for months. Try having all your hair fall out and feeling like if you sneeze you might crack a rib. I know the chemo saved my life—twice now, I've got two strikes—but it was a bitch to go through."

"Two strikes?"

"Yeah. First occurrence when I was eleven. Reoccurrence when I was fourteen, a little over a year ago. Each time cancer occurs your odds of survival get worse. Two strikes."

She takes a deep breath and slowly lets it out. She starts to dig in her purse, for another cigarette, I presume, but then wraps her arms around her chest. "That sucks, Wade. I'm sorry."

"Thanks. I... Well, it's not so bad talking about it. No one really does want to talk about it, you know. I think they're afraid I might freak out, or the words will somehow make it more real."

I feel something shift in regards to Helena. I mean, she's beautiful and all. She seems kind of wild and mysterious. But she's different. She hangs out in a graveyard with a kid she hardly knows, she screams at boys in the road that don't treat her right, she has secrets to keep, and she has the guts to ask me something no one else has ever bothered to ask me about. She's beautiful, yes, but she's fascinating on so many other levels.

"Wade," she says.

"What?"

"You need to talk about this. Anytime. I'm here. Seriously, I mean it."

I nod, but I can't speak, I'm holding back tears because of her kindness, and I sure as hell don't want her to see me cry. She lets the silence be for a few minutes, which I like about her too. So many people can't abide by silence and have to rush in to fill it.

"I owe you some truth," she finally says. "Whenever you're ready."

I close my eyes and take a deep breath. What I want to know most, I don't dare ask—how she feels about me. And judging from the question she asked me, I could ask that question, or really anything. What do I want to know most about her?

I look up at sky above and find a small patch of stars peeking through a break in the clouds. You can really see them in Cedar, not too much light pollution, good air. A thought pops into my head, so I just blurt it out while still looking at the heavens. "Do you believe in god?"

I hear her shuffling around and look back at her. She's got another cigarette out and is lighting it, her hands shaking. I feel bad, like I did something terrible with my questions.

"You don't have to answer it if you don't want to," I say.

Even in the dim light I see her face go hard and I feel like my stomach just dropped into the ground. "Don't do that," she says, her voice low. "I set the rules, I will follow them."

I want to apologize, but keep my mouth shut. I figure she'll not like that either.

"Why do men do that?" she asks.

"What?"

"They see a woman experiencing an emotion and they try

to get out of the way, try to stop it. You just did it. Why do men do that?"

"Because it scares the hell out of us," I say.

She laughs, smoke coming out of her mouth and engulfing me. I cough. "Just don't treat me like I break easy, okay?" she asks.

"Okay," I say.

It's silent as she smokes her cigarette. When she's done, I look straight at the ghost, who's now sitting on the grass near us. Except he's not exactly sitting—he looks like he's sitting, but I can see that the grass is not pressed down and he's not really touching the ground. It's weird and makes me wonder again what it's like to be a ghost.

"So, do you believe in god?" I ask.

I watch the ghost closely. He smiles, but it's a small whimsical thing. He holds his hands out, palms up, and shrugs. Kind of like he's saying, "I'm a ghost, what do you think?"

"I used to," Helena begins. "Our family was religious, I mean religious enough. We went to temple on Sunday. We didn't have a lot of money, but we tithed anyway. We did our best to do the right thing." She bites hard on her lip before continuing. "Then my mom got sick. She had always been high strung. I knew she was different than other kids' moms. Always worrying, always scared or freaked out about something."

I shrugged. "That's a mom for you."

"No, Wade, not like this. She would throw milk out a week before its expiration date afraid it would make me sick. Once when I scraped my knee playing and got some dirt in it, she dragged me to the ER. If she couldn't find me, she would freak out, standing at the front door screaming at the top of her lungs or calling everyone we knew. It wasn't the normal motherly stuff, it was something else.

"When I was very young, I didn't know she was different.

But when I was five or six, I figured it out. I started doing whatever I had to do to keep her safe."

I nodded. I knew what it was like to grow up early.

She took a deep breath and sighed, reaching into her purse again and then shaking her head and wrapping her arms around her chest. "As the years went on, it got worse and worse. She started hearing voices, she hardly slept, she could barely function. Then one day when I was ten, she lost it. She thought I was part of some conspiracy, that I was trying to hurt her. The voices told her she had to do something about me.

"It was a bad day. When my dad came home, she had me backed into a corner with a knife in her hand. She had decided that killing me would stop the conspiracy. Keep her safe."

"What happened?" I ask.

She groans. "Nothing good. To make a horrible story short, my dad got the knife away from her. He called someone, they took her down to a facility in St. George and loaded her up with meds. Except they didn't do such a good job. At some point she must have stopped taking her meds and convinced her caregivers that she was still taking them. She ended up hanging herself."

She digs into her purse and pulls out another cigarette. She smokes it while a thick silence hangs between us. The graveyard closes in and the dark seemed oppressive. The chirping of the crickets grating, the rattle of the leaves jarring.

The sound of a car passing slowly on Main Street jolts her out of it. "And that, my friend, is why I don't believe in god."

"I'm... I..." I stammer, unsure of what to say. "I'm so sorry, Helena. Man, that sucks."

She nods. "But hey, we're really getting to know each other tonight, aren't we?" She tries to laugh, but it comes out all weird, too high pitched and forced.

"Thank you for telling me. Really. I don't even know what to say."

"Sure. Just two friends sharing their personal horror stories in Cedar City's lovely cemetery at—" she looks at her watch, shining her flashlight on it "—one twelve a.m."

"Can I ask another question?" I ask.

"Sure," she says, grinding out her cigarette.

"Why are you here? Why are you hanging out with me?"

The question just hangs between us, almost tangible. Like her cigarette smoke, or my ghost friend. Something not quite real.

She sighs and stands up, brushing her skirt off. "Let's save that for another night, okay?"

"Sure," I say, but my heart is thumping in my chest again. Did I insult her? Does she not want to answer the question?

"See ya, Wade," she says as she turns and walks away.

"Bye, Helena."

I look at the ghost, he's watching her, slowly shaking his head.

"Do you have a clue what just happened?" I ask.

He turns and says, "No." I can't hear him, but he's close enough that the movement of his mouth makes it clear and that glow of his means that I can see him really well in the dark.

"Women," I say. "Now there's a mystery."

He smiles and nods.

After I sneak back home, it takes me a long time to get to sleep. I lie there in my bed the ever-complicating picture of Helena Monfort occupying my mind.

7

SUNDAY, JUNE 19, 1977

HELENA COMES BY THE STORE TODAY. SHE'S GOT ON THE usual tight jeans and a Led Zeppelin T-shirt with the arms ripped off. My dad's behind the counter with a student and I'm puttering around the Southern Utah section. It's after four, and I don't really need to be there, but I'm restless from last night. I'm wondering if there might be something in these books about the cemetery, something that might help me not worry about my sanity and the fact that I can see ghosts.

Helena's mom went crazy. Helena's mom heard voices. I see ghosts. I don't want to end up locked away. I don't want to hang myself.

I've got "Ghosts of the Southwest" open and am scanning through when she walks in. She smiles nervously and walks right to me.

"You okay, Wade?" she asks, all serious.

I'm taken aback. Why is she worried about me? "Yeah, you?"

She shrugs. There are smudges of dark under her amber eyes, she looks like she didn't sleep well. "Just want to make sure

I didn't freak you out too bad last night. Hell of a tale to tell in the... you know..." She's speaking quietly and looks up to my dad as she trails off.

I glance at him and he's noticed Helena, looking at her over his glasses. He throws me a little grin before turning back to his student.

"I've been... Umm... I feel bad for you," I say. "That's gotta be so hard."

"Yeah," she says with a sigh. "And leukemia—twice—is a freaking picnic."

She puts her hand on my shoulder and squeezes. I look at it, to make sure this is real. That she really did touch me. Part of me thinks it's totally lame to be excited by such a small thing, but my body seems to have a mind of its own. I suddenly feel hot and the store seems too small.

She doesn't touch me for long. I miss that feeling when it's gone.

"Listen," she says, eying the door. "I just wanted to check in. I've got to dash. Won't be around tonight either, but maybe tomorrow."

I nod and blink. I can still feel the warmth of her hand.

"Seriously, Wade, are you okay?"

I give her a smile, one I hope is not too weird, and say, "I'm good."

She turns to go and I say, "Helena."

She turns back, a smile on her face. "Yeah?"

"I'm glad we're friends," I say.

Her smile gets real big and she nods. The way her black hair flows over her shoulders fascinates me yet again. "Me too... me too."

———

WE HAD CHICKEN FOR DINNER TONIGHT, BATTERED AND

fried. Mom doesn't do that often and I love it when she does. I even ate all my salad I was so happy.

As we're finishing up, my father asks, "So, who was that girl I saw you talking to in the store? I don't recognize her, is she a new friend?"

My stomach turns over all the food I just ate, and I cover my mouth with a napkin to hide my surprise. Of course he's curious.

"Honey," Mom says, putting the back of her hand to my forehead. "You feeling okay? You're a little flushed."

My father bites back a laugh and says, "He's fine, dear." My mom looks at him, her eyes narrow, but his eyes flick up towards their bedroom in his "I'll tell you about it later" look.

"What's this about a girl?" Mom asks.

I feel like I'm being interrogated or something. It seems kind of bright in here and the grandfather clock in the living room is ticking so loud I can hear it. "She's… a friend. Just a friend."

"Really?" Dad asks, his right eyebrow arching up.

"Yeah," I say. "Friends."

"And what is this young lady's name?" Mom asks.

"Helena. Helena Monfort."

My mother shoots my father a look. Her eyes are a bit wide —she's concerned.

"What?" I ask.

"Nothing dear," she says, her face coming back into its normal configuration.

"That was something," I say. "I know it was. What aren't you saying?" I'm not usually like that with my parents— demanding answers. But all the energy I have from being asked about her twists around on me and it just comes out.

My mom opens her mouth and I think I'm going to get a lecture about the "tone" I used, but she closes her mouth and sighs. "She has a bit of a history, son. That's all."

I nod. "Yeah, and so do I." I get up, the noise of the chair scraping back against the linoleum seeming to be too loud. "And I know all about her history. We're friends. Friends talk about that kind of stuff."

I leave, not looking back, and take the stairs two at a time up to my room. I flop onto my bed and try to sort out what I'm feeling. All the emotions are just so strong. God, is this what normal healthy teenagers are always going through? If so, I'm kind of glad to have missed some of it.

My parents are up later than usual, and since I know Helena won't be at the graveyard, I go to bed early and sleep.

While I'm sleeping, I dream again of that day at the grave- yard where I first saw ghosts.

8

MONDAY, JUNE 20, 1977

MY PARENTS CLEARLY TALKED LAST NIGHT—ABOUT ME AND Helena. Over breakfast of oatmeal and toast, they are a unified front.

"We think it would be nice if your Helena came over for dinner," Mom says.

I cringe at the "*your* Helena." It's not like she's mine. It's not like she's likely to ever be mine.

"Yes, son," my dad adds. "Since you two seem to be such good friends, we'd like to get to know her too."

I shovel a bunch of oatmeal in my mouth and point at it, indicating it would be rude to talk with my mouth so full and buying myself some time.

We are all in new territory. Cancer, doctors, and chemo— we know how to deal with that. Girls—now that's something new. I don't know how to deal with it and their idea is to invite her to dinner—yeah, I don't think they have a clue either.

Because if she isn't just my friend, which they most assuredly suspect, inviting her over like this is an invitation to mess things up for me. On the other hand, if she is just a friend… Well, what would it hurt?

I almost choke on the oatmeal. Of course it could hurt, it could ruin everything, but how can I get out of this?

"How about Saturday?" Mom asks. "Your dad can barbeque, I'll make a pie."

It's Tuesday today, so that at least gives me some time. I shrug and stare into the lumpy mass of oats.

"It's settled then," Dad says. "Can you ask her today? Let us know?"

I nod and pray for breakfast to be over.

———

MY GHOST FRIEND HAS A NAME. LIONEL MALAK.

Holy shit, my ghost friend has a name!

The inspiration came when I was doing my shift at the bookstore. I keep thinking about him—cause I really didn't want to think about inviting Helena to dinner—and it occurs to me that I don't need to be able to hear him to understand him. People communicate all the time without words.

Restless, I sneak out of the house early tonight and go to Uncle Don's grave. When I get there, my ghost friend seems nervous and sad, he has his hands out and shakes them.

"Sorry," I say, getting his meaning. "I couldn't make it last night."

He nods.

"Listen, I figured out a way for us to communicate."

He brightens up and nods again. He so has something to say.

"You'll spell it out for me and I'll write it down." He looks confused, which makes sense, I didn't explain it well at all, I'm just too excited. "Okay, okay. I'll ask you questions to find out what letter is in the word and you'll signal your answer. Okay?"

He nods and smiles. There are some flashes of white, so I can tell other ghosts are gathering around us. We have an audience.

"Let's start with your name. First letter. Is it a consonant?"

He nods.

When I had been researching cryptography for my diary, I had come across the binary search algorithm. With it you divide your choices in half, and if your guess is wrong you find out if the answer is above or below your guess. It's much quicker than going through each choice every time.

"Is the first letter an M?" He nods no. "Show me with your hand if it's higher or lower." He points his thumb down. So I know it must be B through L and have eliminated half the possibilities with one guess.

"G?" He nods and looks disappointed. "When I'm wrong, let me know if it's higher or lower—it'll go faster this way." He points his thumb up.

"J?" He points his thumb up and we are down to K or L.

He smiles when we finally get to L. It goes like this, and despite using the binary search algorithm, it's still kind of slow. But we finally get there.

"Your name is, Lionel Malak." I've been writing the letters in my journal, and when I look back up at him, he seems so happy. And I am too. I just had a direct communication with a ghost. It's real comforting to me—I've been on death's door three times. Twice with pneumonia and once with a MRSA infection (basically a nasty staph infection). Being able to see and communicate with someone who has already died is, as you would imagine, comforting.

Unless, of course, this is all in my head. Paranoid schizophrenia could also explain this.

As I contemplate this, Helena flops down on the grass next to me and lights a cigarette. I had been so involved that I hadn't seen her approach. She's dressed in her La Familia outfit and her cigarette/mint scent washes over me.

"What's that?" she asks, grabbing my diary. "I… What the hell language is this written in? I can't make out a thing."

"It's encoded. I don't want my parents reading it and flipping out."

"Encoded?" she asks, puffing her smoke up towards the heavens.

"Yeah. It's a simple letter shifting algorithm. Not hard to break, but enough to keep prying eyes out."

She looks at it hard and hands the diary back. "Cool. Maybe you can teach it to me someday."

"Sure. It takes some time to get used to, but I can write real fast this way now."

After she finishes her cigarette, she says, "So back to Truth or Truth?"

I nod.

"When we last left," she continues, "you had asked why I was hanging out with you. Do you still want to know?"

I swallow hard and nod.

She sighs. "It's simple really, and I hope in that hormone-infested male brain of yours you can keep it simple."

I know I'm not going to like what she has to say. "Go on."

"You're a weird kid, Wade. You hang out at night in a cemetery. You were kind to me when I needed it. You tell a girl she looks better without makeup. You've seen some hard shit in your life and that makes you…" she trails off, her eyes going to the sky. It's clear tonight, the stars a bright canopy above us. "Well, it makes you someone I want to get to know."

I nod. It makes sense. I wasn't expecting her to profess undying love, but those hormones she spoke of had most certainly been doing a number on me.

"Listen," she says, leaning towards me. I look into her eyes and somehow resist the urge to examine her cleavage in that La

Familia outfit. "I don't make friends easy or often." She snorts and continues. "I don't do well with girls, in general, and boys, well—they tend to be rather focused on what kind of relationship they want."

She leans back and sighs, looking back up to the stars for a bit. "My turn," she says. "And I will remind you that you are required to tell the truth."

I'm sweating now. This game is the kind you love *and* hate, both with great vigor.

"Your hormone-addled brain wants us to be more than friends, doesn't it?"

God it's hot. I swear I'm about to explode, I feel a trickle of sweat crawling down my back. Sounds seem real loud again and my heart is thumping in my ears.

"You have to answer, Wade."

I want to run away. I want to disappear. I want to be anywhere but here… You know what? That's a lie. I long to be in her presence. I long to touch her. "Yes," I say, it comes out loud, too loud, but I can't stop talking now that the energy has found a release. "I would love to be more than just friends. It scares the hell out of me, but I don't know if I want anything more than that. You are smart and fascinating, and probably the most beautiful woman I've ever met." Suddenly I'm standing, my voice is loud and my hands are thrust towards the heavens. "Yes, yes, yes, YES! The answer is yes."

I look down at her and her eyes are wide and her mouth is open as she stares at me.

My face flushes hot and I sink back down to the grass. "But," I begin, "that is probably just the hormones talking."

She stares at me for a moment more and then laughs hard. The sound is deep and husky and rings out over the granite stones marking the final resting places of the dead.

"Damn, but you are the weirdest kid," she says when she stops laughing. "Damn!"

I shrug and stare at the grass, I can't meet her eyes.

"Thank you for telling me," she says. Her voice is gentle now. "I have something more to say, can you look at me?"

I look up and meet her eyes. It's pretty dark, but I can see compassion on her face. She's not smiling or laughing or mocking me.

"Friendship, Wade, is what I need. Hell, I can get a date any time I want one. Finding a friend, that is much more rare. Much more valuable. Understand?"

I nod, but still can't talk.

"I'm tired," she says, getting up and brushing herself off. "How about tomorrow night? I don't have to work and could hang out longer."

"That'd be great," I say, finally finding my words.

9

TUESDAY, JUNE 21, 1977

THE HELENA GRILLING CONTINUES OVER BREAKFAST THIS morning. Mom and Dad are very disappointed that I forgot to ask her to dinner. A promise is required before I get away. I don't want to do it—the potential for disaster is huge—but I guess I'll have to.

I spend the rest of the morning with Billy. We're up in his room hiding from his twin sisters reading comics. They aren't allowed to have locks on their bedroom doors, so I'm sprawled on his bed and he's leaning up against his door. The girls have tried to sneak in three times already.

"She just wants to be friends," I say. I'd been trying to read the same panel of *The Incredible Hulk Unchained* four times. My mind just isn't there.

Billy looks up, his green eyes meeting mine. "Sorry, man. That truly and epically sucks." I love it that I don't have to explain it all to Billy. He knows I'm talking about Helena.

"But she still wants to hang out. She really *does* want to be friends."

His eyes widen. "No shit? It wasn't the 'oh please be my

friend' blow off?" His falsetto voice for the "oh please…" part makes me laugh. He gets up, risking a breach by the twins, and starts walking around on his tiptoes swinging his hips awkwardly and says in his best (read terrible) falsetto, "Oh Aaron, you are such a nice boy. I don't want to risk what we have. Can we just be friends?" He grabs some dirty clothes and shoves them under his spider-man T-shirt, building up two lumpy, and rather disgusting, masses.

He looks ridiculous, but I'm not laughing anymore. What he said sounds too close to what Helena said.

"Oh Aaron, you may be the smartest and kindest boy I've ever met, but I'd rather some dumb stupid football player stick their tongue down my throat."

"Okay, Billy. That's quite enough."

"I have a great big chest," he says, pushing up the clothes under his shirt. "So I need a man with a mighty chest too. A man with more brawn than brains. A manly Neanderthal of a man."

"I am warning you… You better shut up," I say.

But he doesn't listen, he continues. "But god how I value you as a friend. Boyfriends may come and go, but a true friend, like you Aaron Wade, lasts a lifetime."

He continues on, but I'm not listening anymore. I'm out of his room and running down the stairs. I tear out the front door not even saying goodbye to Mrs. Chadow and get on my bike and ride. Hot tears run down my cheeks and the wind from my pedaling makes them ice cold despite the eighty-something degree temperature.

God how I hate this. Billy's little rendition hit close enough to home to hurt. Helena wants to be friends, I know it. I know she is being honest about that. But it still feels horrible. These emotions I am feeling are so big. It feels like I'll die if I can't "be" with her. Friendship is not enough, not nearly enough. I must touch her. I must have her. I must possess her.

I snort and suck in air, I've been riding hard, streets and houses passing me by with me hardly seeing them. I am thinking like that Neanderthal from Billy's little performance. This is not me. I am more logical than this. I am more rational than this.

I end up at the graveyard and slow down, my breath coming in ragged gasps. I need someone to talk to about this. Billy is out—I think he's jealous. Actually, any of my old pre-leukemia friends are out too. They'd be as much use as Billy. My father is out—he would probably love it, but I would die of embarrassment talking to him about this. And my mother? No need to even go there.

Who can I talk to? I need an adult, someone who has survived this. Someone who can provide some perspective.

Lionel.

He's a ghost, he's an adult, and he certainly can't tell my secrets. I pedal to Uncle Don's grave and look for him, but I don't see him. Actually, I don't see any ghosts.

Maybe they are not here. Maybe I can't see them in the daylight. I did that one time as a kid, but maybe it's different now.

I get off my bike, letting it fall onto the grass as I slump next to it. I wipe the remnants of tears off my face and wipe at the snot on my nose.

I don't want to be friends. I lie down flat on the grass, shielding my eyes from the bright sun above.

"You okay, boy?"

My heart leaps into my mouth and I surge up into a sitting position. There is a man dressed in a suit standing there. He's short and rotund with a deep frown on his face. The frown is out of place, it doesn't seem to be the normal configuration.

"Yeah… I'm fine," I say, but my tone does not agree with my words.

"Well, you don't look so fine to me." He speaks in a

southern accent and I notice he's got cowboy boots on with his suit.

I sigh and shake my head. "Just having a bad day, mister."

He nods, and much to my surprise, lowers himself to the grass next to me. With his bulk he does it slowly, a sigh escaping his mouth when he's finally down. "This here your kin?" he asks, pointing at Uncle Don's gravestone.

I nod.

"I'm here visiting kin. My aunt Tilly is buried back that way a bit. I've come to town to wrap up her affairs."

I watch him closely. He's older than I first thought, his black hair losing the battle against the encroaching grey.

"But where are my manners? My name is Edward Lopez, but everyone calls me Big Ed." He nods and smiles, that smile looks right there on his face.

"I'm Aaron Wade."

"So tell me, Mr. Wade, what are you doin' here? I see your uncle's been gone a bit." He points to the gravestones. Uncle Don died in 1975. "I suspect you've got something else on your mind, and if a kind ear will help, then I am here for you."

"I couldn't, Mr. Lopez." I feel my cheeks flushing.

"Understood," he says with a groan, slowly levering himself up to a standing position. "But if you change your mind, I'll be at my aunt's house. It's not far from here." He points to the northwest. "I'm on the corner of 400 West and 940 North. You know where I'm talking about?"

I nod but can't meet his eyes. His kindness is so unexpected and I'm just so embarrassed by all I'm feeling.

He slowly walks off and I'm left stewing in my emotions, wishing my could-be-a-hallucination ghost friend was around.

———

I THINK I NOW UNDERSTAND WHY THEY CALL THIS KIND OF

infatuation—the kind I am in the throes of in regards to Miss Helena Monfort—a crush. It's because the feelings are crushing. There is a weight to them that makes it hard to breathe, or think, or be a rational human being.

I'm not stupid. I know it's the hormones, and I know the hormones are about the propagation of the species. A biological imperative. But, god does it suck.

But, on the other hand, this is an entirely normal problem for a teenage boy to be having. In the midst of all this, I am still aware of that, glad that I am healthy enough to have this completely normal teenage problem.

But the day crawls by, I have an awkward dinner with my folks where the question of Helena having dinner comes up again, and I am so glad once the house quiets down and I can sneak out.

It's about 11:30, the moon a bright sliver in the sky, the air cool, but not cold. I make my way to the graveyard. My feet want me to fly, Helena said she would have more time to hang out, but I resist. I consciously slow myself down. I have a brain, I can think, I can rise above the chemical stew coursing through my veins.

I can, can't I?

I walk in the dark, my flashlight still in my backpack along with my journal. The graveyard is just so peaceful on nights like this. I appreciate it and for a moment forget about her.

"Boo!" a voice shouts, shattering my calm.

I jump back, my heart pounding hard, my breath coming fast as adrenaline courses through my veins.

A throaty laugh comes out of the dark. I look and see Helena. She's squatted behind one of the larger gravestones on the way to Uncle Don's.

"Shit, Helena. You almost scared me to death."

"Sorry… I got here early and was bored."

"So you thought it would be a good idea to scare the shit out of me?"

She stands and I can tell she's dressed in jeans and a sweater. No La Familia getup tonight. "I didn't do that literally, did I?" she asks. "I mean, if you need to run home and change your undies, I'll understand." She's laughing again.

"Shut up," I say, making my way to Uncle Don's grave. I smile because this is the kind of thing Billy might have staged— if he had the guts to sneak out of his house and face the grave- yard at night again. It's the kind of things friends do—mess with each other. It feels good—she really wants to be friends, but also feels kinda bad for the same reason.

The ghosts are gathered around Uncle Don's grave. Lionel, once again, the only one I can see clearly.

"So, it's time," I tell her as I drop my backpack to the grass. My eyes are adjusting, and although I can't see her face clearly, I can see the question on it. "Time to tell you why I am here."

She claps her hands together once, like a kid about to get a present. "It's summer solstice today, very auspicious. So I guess this means we know each other well enough now."

I shrug. "I hope so. You may run away screaming once you I tell you. You may think I'm crazy. But I am hoping you can handle it."

She shoves her hands into her pockets and nods. "I can handle it, Wade."

I sigh and start pacing in a little circle. "I am experiencing something," I begin. "It all started the night before we met. I had this dream, of when I was a little boy and my mother brought me here. I was young, four or five, and I saw these transparent-looking people. I waved at them and they waved back. My mom couldn't see them."

I pause my pacing, stopping right in front of Helena. I know this is a risk, that with her history, with her mother, any sign of me being mentally ill could send her running. But if we are to be friends, then I need us to really be friends.

She doesn't say a word, she just stands there, her breath shallow, as she stares at me.

"After the dream, I snuck out of the house and made my way down here. I told Billy about it and he was meeting me here the night we met."

She let out a big sigh, her shoulders relaxing. "You had a bad dream, you were just down here walking it off. You didn't see…" Her voice trails off as she studies my face. "You didn't see anything that night, did you, Wade?"

I don't answer but nod my head.

"Don't fuck with me, Wade," she says as she digs a cigarette out of her purse and lights up. "I told you things… private things… don't… don't…" Her hands shake as she brings the cigarette to her lips.

"We're friends, right?" I ask.

"Yeah," she says, tilting her head up and blowing out a long stream of smoke.

"Friends speak the truth to each other, right?"

"Yeah…"

"I swear that I am telling you the truth. I saw flashes of light out of my peripheral vision that night. I've been coming back and each time I can see this one ghost clearer and clearer. I can't hear him, but I can see him now. He's standing right there." I point to the left of Helena. Lionel has his hands in his pockets and a worried look on his face.

Helena begins to pace, away from where I said the ghost was. She quickly finishes the cigarette and lights another, her pacing increasing. "Do you… do you think he's real? That ghosts are real? That you can see them?"

I sigh and feel weak, the energy flowing out of me like a burst balloon. "Truth?" I ask.

"Truth," she says.

I pause, thinking about it. She asked me not to treat her like she broke easily. She says she's my friend. I really tell her the truth. "I don't know. I am worried about it, worried that there is something wrong with my brain. Leukemia can go there sometimes, and they pumped so many chemicals in my system, that…"

I hear her sniff, like she's crying or something and she stops her pacing and comes up to me and places her hand on my shoulder. I look up and can see the moonlight glinting off the tears running down her cheeks. She takes a deep breath and I'm terrified of what she is about to say. "I'm glad you told me." Her hand squeezes my shoulder. "You shouldn't have to carry something like this alone."

I almost collapse in relief. She's not running away. She's being my friend.

"Have you told anyone else besides Billy?"

"No. God no! Who the hell would I tell and not get myself locked up?"

Helena sucks in a breath and her hand leaves my shoulder.

"Sorry, Helena. God I'm sorry… Your mom… Shit, but I really have worried about this."

She nods, lights another cigarette, and resumes her pacing. After she's done smoking, she walks back up to me and says, "This is what we are going to do. We are going to start with a hypothesis and then we are going to test it."

I stand there gape jawed. She must have noticed it, because she says, "I'm not stupid. I go to my classes. I study."

"Of course," I say. It makes sense, it's just not the kind of thing you expect to hear a girl that looks like her say.

"So, our hypothesis is that you are really seeing this ghost."

"Yeah," I say. "His name is Lionel Malak."

"Wait. What?" she asks.

"I know his name. We spelled it out last night."

"Lionel…" she began. "Isn't that the guy that ran the little print shop? Not far from your old man's bookstore. It was less than a year ago that he died. I remember seeing the cop cars out front and hearing rumors of something awful."

"Yes. Yes. That's it," I said. "I knew the name was familiar. He was… he was murdered, wasn't he?" Lionel's movements catch my eye. He's shaking his fists vigorously. "You were murdered?" I ask him.

He nods and says "yes," his mouth movements making the word clear even though I can't hear him.

"He's here?" Helena asks, her voice thin.

"Yeah. He's always here."

"Shit," she says, reaching into her purse again but then pulling her hand out, wrapping her arms around her chest and pacing again. "Shit. Shit. Shit."

"The hypothesis. How do we prove—or disprove—it?" I ask.

She's biting on her thumbnail as she paces.

"There's got to be a way, Helena," I say. "I gotta know."

"You can see him?" she asks.

"Yeah."

"He can see you?"

"Uh huh."

"Can he see me?"

I look to Lionel who is nodding his head. "Of course he can see you."

"Okay," she says, stopping, facing me, and holding her hands behind her back. "How many fingers am I holding up."

I shrug. "I don't know."

"Have your ghost look, dummy."

Lionel moves behind her and holds up three fingers.

"Three," I say.

"And now."

Lionel holds up six fingers. "Six."

She takes a deep breath and lets it out slowly. "And now?"

"One."

Her hands come to her face as she rubs it. "Three out of three, Wade. Holy fucking shit! Three out of three. What are the odds?"

"Umm. One in ten chance, three times. That's one in a thousand." I feel this warmth spreading through my body. I want to dance around the graveyard singing "I'm not crazy," but resist the impulse. I think I've tested Helena way enough with my weirdness so far tonight.

"Hmm… That's not good enough," she says.

"What?"

"Look, we want to be absolutely sure. We want the odds to be one in a million. How do we do that?"

I look at my fingers and start running odds. "If Lionel showed me exactly how your fingers are positioned the odds would be two to the 10th power. Or 1024 to one. We do that twice in a row, that would be a million to one."

"Okay, then," she says, holding her hands behind her back. "But let's do it three times."

I nod and look at Lionel. He's got the index and thumb up on his left hand and his index and middle finger on his right hand. I tell Helena.

She nods. "One down."

"All four fingers on both hands," I say.

She nods. "One more."

I laugh as Lionel shows me the middle finger up on each hand. "Now you're just giving me the bird."

"Holy mother of…" Helena says as she sinks to the grass. "You're not crazy, Wade. You are really seeing a ghost."

"Thank god," I say as I flop down on the grass next to her.

We are silent for a while, lost in our own thoughts. I can hear her breath we are so close. I can smell that cigarette-mint breath of hers. I am becoming very fond of that odd scent.

"But why can you see him, what does he want?" she finally asks.

I look around and find Lionel a few yards away. "What do you want?" I ask him.

He moves close, a look of pain on his face. His mouth moves, but I don't know what he's saying. "I'm sorry, I still can't hear you," I tell him.

He holds his index finger up and I see him take a deep breath. He then pantomimes a knife being plunged into his chest as he falls to the ground. When he sits up, I ask, "You were murdered?"

He nods his head vigorously.

"Do you know who did this to you?"

He shakes his head.

"Do you want us to solve your murder?" Helena asks.

He gets up and jumps up and down, a wry smile on his face.

I look to Helena. "That's it. He wants us to solve his murder."

PART 2

A Ghost and a Murder

10

TUESDAY, JUNE 21, 1977

(continued)

EVERYTHING IS DIFFERENT. EVERYTHING HAS CHANGED. MY head is buzzing as I walk home.

I can see ghosts. I'm not crazy. Helena is… here it gets a bit tricky, but this thing with her feels doable now. The crushing weight of the infatuation has lifted somewhat. We now share something that bonds us together. Something unique.

It's not what my hormones want, but my heart is happy. She is now a *real* friend.

As I walk the sidewalks of my neighborhood, I can't help but smile about it all. It's very late, nearly 3 a.m., and I'm not walking alone. Lionel is with me. Something changed for him tonight too. After Helena left, he accompanied me out of the graveyard. He's done that before, but this time, he just kept walking as I reached Main headed south.

"What's happening?" I ask him. He just shrugged.

"Is it because you finally got through to us? That you know we will try to figure out what happened to you?"

He nods, but it's tentative. I get the impression that he doesn't quite understand what is going on either.

As I quietly sneak into the house, I get the second shock of the night.

"Good morning, son," my father says. He's sitting in a rocking chair in our living room, a book open in his lap. The living room's got vaulted ceilings, a few floral-print couches, and quite noticeably lacks a TV. We don't own one. My dad doesn't believe in it.

My heart is thumping loudly in my ears and I feel my face flush red. I don't say a word but walk in and sit on the brown couch. Lionel has a worried look on his face and stays in the hallway.

"Do you mind telling me where you have been?" His voice is freakishly calm and that is a bad sign. It means he is furious. He doesn't yell when he's mad, he gets even quieter.

I just sit there looking at my hands. I feel sick to my stomach and know this is going to be bad.

"I need some kind of explanation," he says smoothly.

I'm freaking out. What the hell can I tell him that won't end up with me getting a mental health evaluation?

"You know," he says leaning forward, looking at me over the rim of his glasses, "in some ways I consider this a good sign."

"What?" I ask, meeting his eyes.

"If you were getting chemo, if you were sick, you wouldn't do something like this. You are well enough to violate your parents' trust. There is a *bit* of a silver lining there."

I look back down at my hands.

He sighs and gets up and paces the room. There are tall bookshelves lining the walls. His hands linger on some of the rare books. A copy of *Huckleberry Finn*, I believe.

"Here is what we are going to do," he says, squatting in front of me. "You and I, we are going to talk about this, right now. Or we are both going to sit here and wait for your mother to get up and I'll turn this matter over to her."

It's a threat, pure and simple. My mother would not be quiet or the least bit logical about this. I know I'm better off letting my father decide what my punishment will be.

"I was down at the graveyard," I say.

He sucks in a sharp breath, stands, and slowly moves back to the rocking chair and lowers himself into it. I've decided to stick with the truth—in as much as I end up telling him. I don't know how much he knows, and even with that reaction it's not out of the realm of possibility that he knows exactly where I was. That he followed me. That he knows much of the truth already.

"And why were you at the graveyard?"

"I've been… I've been visiting Uncle Don's grave."

He nods slowly. "And why?"

"A little over a week ago, I had this dream of when Mom took me there. I was really young and I remember seeing these people that Mom couldn't see among the gravestones. Transparent people. I waved at them and they waved back. Ghosts, you know."

"And this inspired your visit?" he asks.

"Yes. My first one. With all I've been through… well, I wanted to know if I could see them again."

He nods and I hold my breath. I'm waiting for him to ask me if I see ghosts now, but he doesn't. I don't think his logical brain thinks it's even in the realm of possibility. "And why do you keep going?" he asks.

"Helena," I say.

He's quiet for the longest time, slowly rocking in the chair, his fingers steepled and pressed to his lips. I feel sick and need to pee real bad, but I sit as still and as calm as possible. The smell of the bowl of potpourri next to me is strong and I feel nauseous.

He's making assumptions, and while I feel the need to let

him make them, I feel bad about it. I'm not exactly lying to him, but I have definitely hidden the truth from him.

"These nighttime outings have to stop, obviously."

"Yes, sir," I say.

"And you and I are going to sit down and have a long talk about how a man should treat a woman. We are going to make sure you are conducting yourself properly and respectfully where she is concerned."

The thought strikes horror into my heart, but I nod in agreement.

He rubs his chin and continues to stare at me. "But," he finally says, "I think we can keep this between the two of us. This would worry your mother deeply, you know. I don't think she would understand."

"Thank you," I say.

"If your mother is to be told, I'll handle it. I have your word, don't I? You will not sneak out of the house anymore."

"You have my word," I say, meeting his eyes.

11

WEDNESDAY, JUNE 22, 1977

MY MIND IS MUSH OVER BREAKFAST, IT SEEMS TO HAVE LESS structure than the oatmeal I am eating. I pile on the brown sugar in the hopes of waking myself up.

After my little talk with Dad, it took me a while to get to sleep, and then it seemed only minutes before my alarm went off. Must have breakfast with the folks, missing it would be more suspicious than my current zombified state.

My mother is eying me. I know she's about to ask about my health. "I just didn't get much sleep, Mom," I say, trying to head her off.

"Neither of us could," my father offers. "We had a nice chat in the living room in the wee hours. Some father-son bonding time."

My mother's right eyebrow raises and she smiles. "That's nice. And that explains the voices I thought I was hearing last night."

Lionel isn't around this morning. I remember him coming into the house with me, I remember him watching as my father started his lecture, but I didn't see him after that. Weirdly, I didn't even think of him. The whole being caught thing drove him out of my mind.

I poke at the white goo in my bowl, wondering where he went. What do ghosts do all day (and night) long?

"Well, gentlemen," my mother says as she kisses me on the forehead and then kisses my father on the cheek. "I am off, you boys be good."

She leaves quickly, her flowery perfume lingering.

"I'll need you at the bookstore by 11:30 today," my father says.

My usual time is 1 p.m. I groan, I don't want to go to the bookstore today, I want to crawl in bed and sleep. At first, I think he's punishing me for my nighttime outings and that pops the thought of Helena into my mind. If I can't go to the grave-yard at night, when will I see her? I do know her phone number, but the thought of her father answering strikes terror in my bones for some reason. Going there even more so.

"I've got a faculty meeting at lunch. I'll be there to unlock the shop, but I need you to open up."

"Sure, Dad. No problem." I say it with a smile, but he's looking at me and hard. I know he's trying to figure out what's going on in my brain.

"And I want you to do something nice for your mother," he says.

"What?"

"Do something special, something she would like, surprise her."

I now look at him hard, trying to figure out what's going on in his head.

"She worries about you," he continues. "You going out of your way and being thoughtful will not only delight her, but help her realize you really are healthy now."

I nod. I'm not a complete idiot, I totally get how hard my Cancer has been on my parents. They've had to give up a lot just to keep me alive. It's a nice thought now that it's penetrated my sleep-deprived brain. "Okay, Dad. That's... that's really a good idea. I'll think of something awesome."

He smiles widely and pushes his glasses up all the way onto his nose with his index finger.

He gets up quickly, noisily gathering his newspaper. "Thanks for cleaning up, Aaron." Now I know he's punishing me.

———

I STUMBLE THROUGH THE MORNING AS I SLOWLY WAKE UP. The coffee my parents left helps some. It's so bitter, though, I wonder how they can stand drinking it, but as its effects kick in, I begin to understand why.

I debate taking a nap, but after cleaning up I head down to the graveyard on my bike. I need to know what happened to Lionel. I go to Uncle Don's grave, but I can't see him. Maybe it's the sunlight, maybe it's my sodden brain—I don't know.

I call for him, but feel like an idiot for talking to the empty air. I get off my bike and go sit on the grave. I close my eyes tight and rub my face. I'm just so tired. When my hands are covering my eyes, when I can barely see the light of the day, I see the flashes of light.

Shit! No way.

I drop my hands and look around—nothing. I close my eyes and cover them—flashes of light out of my peripheral vision. Amorphous white shapes that vaguely look like people. Just like I've been seeing every night. Just like when I first started seeing Lionel.

I can see the ghosts during the day, but only with my eyes closed. And I'm freaking out about it. If I am not seeing the ghosts with my eyes, then how am I seeing them?

"You do seem to frequent this establishment," I hear a voice say. It's deep with the melody of a southern accent.

I suck in a breath and open my eyes, blinking against the light. It's the big man, Edward Lopez, except no suit this time, just jeans, a button-down shirt, and cowboy boots.

"Oh… hello, Mr. Lopez."

"It's Big Ed, son. I told you that, didn't I?"

"Yes, sir," I say with a nod, standing up. I don't want him to have to try to sit down again. He moves with a fluid grace, as if he were a dancer, or as if he's made of something delicate and is easily hurt.

"I like it here, too," he says, rubbing at his chin which has several days of growth in black and white. "Most folks avoid the cemetery like the plague. But I find it peaceful. Induces a sense of perspective."

I nod but don't comment further. He seems like a nice man, like someone who would be a good listener. But I don't know him. I don't know anything about him.

"I can't just sort all day long," he says, his big finger stabbing out to the southwest. "Aunt Tilly, she weren't so good at throwing things out. The chaos gets to me, so I come down here to walk it off. And stop by and ask her some questions."

"Questions?" I ask. "Isn't your aunt dead?"

He chuckles. "That she is, Mr. Wade. Dead as an armadillo who couldn't cross the road fast enough. But why the hell would that stop me from telling her what I think?"

I stand there blinking. Can he see the dead too? Can he hear them? My stomach flutters in a potent combination of excitement and fear. "Does she answer you…" I say, my voice quiet so he can pretend he didn't hear me if he wants to.

He laughs, it's a great booming sound. "Hell no, son. She's dead, she don't talk back. And frankly, that is fine. It's the first time in my life I've gotten more than a few words in where

Aunt Tilly is concerned. I am kind of evening things up, conversation wise."

I feel stupid for having such a hope. That there was someone else that could see the ghosts too. Someone else that could help me sort this out.

"But it's interesting, though," he continues, his hands shoved deep into the pockets of his blue jeans. "Going through all her things. I am beginning to piece together what her life looked like. She being so far west here, we didn't get out to visit her often, and she stopped traveling a decade ago."

"Are you a detective or something?" I ask.

"Well aren't you perceptive? Why yes, young man, I am. I served for twenty years with the Bowie County Sheriff's Department and then became a private investigator. Can't help but solve puzzles when I find them."

I look him over again. He's stout, there's no other word for it, with a round face and red cheeks. In a few years, once the grey progresses more, he'll make a great Hispanic Santa Claus. Thoughts of Lionel come rushing into my mind. Here's a detective. I have a murder to solve for my ghost friend. But it all seems just too convenient. I want to say something, but find I don't have the courage.

"Well, I best get back to it," he says as he ambles off. "Maybe I'll see you around here again, Mr. Wade."

———

"I'M SORRY, A," BILLY SAYS AS SOON AS HE COMES INTO THE store just after 1 p.m. He's talking kind of loud, his eyes locked on mine. I point to the three customers looking at the Cedar City section and he flushes red and mouths "sorry."

"I was being an ass yesterday," he says in a whisper when he gets up to the counter.

"Yes, you were," I say with a smile. "But that doesn't

matter." I proceed to tell him what has happened since I saw him: Helena and Lionel and how we "proved" he was real. My dad catching me. Meeting a detective in the graveyard.

Billy's reply to the data dump is eloquent as usual. "Shit... Shit... Shit..." He's shaking his head, his voice still low. "I mean... holy shit!"

"So, are you up for solving a murder?" I ask, the grin on my face is huge. After so many summers puking my guts out, I am happy as a clam to have something interesting to do.

"But... How..." he stammers. "Where do we start?"

"Remember that print shop?" I ask, he nods. "It was just three doors down. It happened right in our neighborhood. We start by going to the library, looking at old newspapers, finding out what we can find out."

We would have talked more, but the tourists were ready to check out and it was time for me to go back to work.

———

In the library, Billy looks as out of place as I'd look riding a bull at the rodeo. He's stiff and awkward and has no idea where anything is.

"They got newspapers here?" he asks in a hushed whisper. My shift is over and we've come down here to start our research.

I nod. "They keep some on file and the rest they put on microfiche." He's looking at me like I just told him aliens are running the government. "Tiny pictures... they have these plastic sheets with tiny picture of each page you blow up on a reader."

He nods like it means something to him, but the library is not his place, it's mine. I love it. It's not much as these things go, just a single-story brick building on Center Street not far from the university. It's got narrow windows that run from floor to ceiling and let light into the stacks of books. I love searching the card catalog, thumbing through random books. At every turn is a new story, something new to learn, so much to know.

It's like the bookstore, but more sacred. The information is free to use, open to all. As a society, who would we be without the open sharing of knowledge? Without libraries?

We walk up to the research desk. Mrs. Reynolds greets us. She's a petite woman with glasses and flat brown hair going to grey. "How can I help you, Aaron?" she asks. She knows me, I spend a fair amount of time here when I am healthy.

"Looking for newspaper articles from the winter of 1976, when Lionel Malak died."

She raises one eyebrow and looks from me to Billy. Billy's got his head down and is staring at his shoes.

"And what would you need with that info, dearie?" she asks. Her voice goes up half an octave.

I was afraid of this, but I don't see any big reason to sneak around about it. I just want to read the newspaper. I take a deep breath and tell the lie Billy and I prepared. "Just settling a bet, Mrs. Reynolds. Billy here thinks he was hit over the head. I remember it being a knife." I lean over and lower my voice further. "There's money on the line."

She snorts under her breath and says, "That'll be on microfiche. I don't remember exactly when it happened, so you'll have to search yourself." She sweeps into the back.

"Do they have a comics section?" Billy asks, his head swiveling around as if he's looking for a way to escape.

———

AFTER THE FIRST HALF HOUR OF SEARCHING THE microfiche, I send Billy on his way. He is just slowing me down, interfering with the peace I always feel at the library. I spend the next few hours reading every article about Lionel's murder. I take copious notes in my journal, encoded of course.

On my way home I go by the graveyard, get off my bike, and stare at Uncle Don's grave. It's weird how the space has changed for me. It's not just about my uncle anymore, but tied up with Helena and Lionel and me seeing ghosts. Ghosts that are real.

I look around, making sure no one is here, and then close my eyes tight and cover my eyes with my hands. Sure enough, more flashes of white out of my peripheral vision, but no Lionel.

I sit down, take my journal out of my backpack, and write an unencoded message to Helena. I explain to her that I can't come out at night anymore and that I have news on our "quest" and that she should call me. I sign it "W."

I tear out the page, fold up the note, put an "H" on it, and tuck it into the grass near the gravestone.

I debate going by her house, but the butterflies in my stomach make me think better of it. I will if I don't see her soon, but it's not something I want to do yet. The thought of meeting her father, for some reason, makes my knees weak. I tell my knees that we are just friends, but for some reason they are not buying it.

12

THURSDAY, JUNE 23, 1977

I SLEPT LIKE THE DEAD LAST NIGHT, CATCHING UP FROM THE extra late outing with Helena the night before. I find myself thinking of her as I wake. Small things really. The way her eyes narrow when she laughs, her cheeks rising up so high. How her hair moves, flowing so smoothly across her shoulders and back. How she walks so confidently with those curves of hers, as if she is unaware of how her presence affects those around her.

I find myself aroused and feel rather embarrassed about it. We are just friends, goddamnit, just friends. My body shouldn't be feeling this way about her body.

I think of Billy and what he does under his covers with his *Playboy*s. His "conjugal" visits with Barbara Bach. He never uses the word masturbation, but there is no doubt that is what is going on. He says it calms him, makes him happy, that the "hormones of a young man in his prime must be obeyed. Release must be achieved."

I have a grasp of the basic biology, the propagation of the species and such, but having been sick for so much of my teen years, this experience is new. The knowledge didn't properly prepare me for the chemistry of it. This feeling is like an itch that can only be scratched in one way.

I am trying to be logical about it, think about it clearly. Somehow, I think it would be a disservice to her and our friendship to "release" while imagining her. That it would somehow change things between us. I also don't know if I can stand this feeling, this desire, without something to mitigate it.

All these thoughts, as well as the associated chemicals, are running through me when there is a knock on the door.

"Breakfast, Aaron," my mother says cheerfully. "You are coming down, aren't you?"

Adrenalin dumps into my system and the chemistry of my body shifts. All thoughts of "release" or "conjugal visits" are dismissed.

———

It's Thursday and I still haven't asked Helena over for Saturday dinner. I head things off when I get downstairs by saying, "I didn't see her yesterday, I don't know if she can come on Saturday."

After putting a plate of eggs, bacon, and toast in front of me, my mother purses her lips and looks at me in that way of hers. It's a narrow-eyed appraising look that I've never liked. It's like she's trying to figure out what's going on in my head. And, frankly, I don't want her to know that.

"Maybe you can call her," she says, pointing to the kitchen phone.

I shrug. "I don't have her number." The lie slips out easily, making me feel super guilty.

"Hmm, I thought you two were friends," she says. I'm not looking at her, my attention fully on the scrambled eggs in front of me, but I know she's staring at me with that "look." It's a probing thing, as if she's looking for a weakness, a way in, a way to change something about me.

"We are," I say, taking a bite of the bacon and staring out the window into our little backyard. In it is a swing set that didn't get nearly enough use. It somehow seems sad out there, like it is not fulfilling its purpose, not having a good life (for a swing set, that is).

My mother plops the phonebook down in front of me and then sits down and starts eating her own breakfast. I look up to my dad, hoping for an ally, but his head is buried in his newspaper.

"I think we should give the swing set away," I say, changing the subject.

"What?" Mom asks. My father's head appears above the newsprint.

"You know, find some people with kids who need it. It just seems so lonely. I never got to use it much."

The energy in the room changes. It's no longer about pestering me to invite a girl over for an excruciatingly embarrassing meal, it's now about Cancer and the price that we all paid, how much of my childhood was merely about survival, not doing kid things like swinging.

"It's a good idea, son." My dad has put his paper down. He is fully engaged in the conversation.

"Well... I..." my mom begins. She's all flummoxed. I'm not sure why, but my properly rested brain has come up with a great idea.

"How about I come to church with you on Sunday," I say to her, briefly catching my father's eye. He asked me to do something nice for her and we both know she'll love this. "Maybe we can ask around, find a good home for it."

She's got a frown on her face and then her brow furrows and she nods, a smile creeping onto her pink lips. "That would be nice, Aaron."

My mother goes to the Lutheran church. That was her church when she was a kid, but she was kind of lapsed until I got sick. Since then she always goes—provided I'm healthy enough. My father wouldn't be caught dead in a church. He's an atheist, although not very loud about it. Cedar is a small town in Southern Utah, an area dominated by the Mormon religion. You don't run around and openly proclaim yourself as an atheist.

I catch my father's eye and he's smiling. I'm sure he's not thrilled about me going to a church, but he knows how happy it will make my mother.

The rest of breakfast is quite pleasant, not one more word about Helena.

———

THE MORNING AND THEN MY HOURS AT THE BOOKSTORE GO by at a crawl. I miss Helena, I'm dying to talk to her about what I found out in the newspapers. For once, I don't really want to be in the bookstore. I want to be out in the world trying to find out what happened to Lionel.

It's a strange feeling for me. This sense of purpose. Not that I haven't had a huge purpose before. I have, it was survival. It was all about me. Now it's about someone else, something else besides my Cancer. It's a feeling I like.

It's about 3 p.m. and my dad is settled in with a petite blond going over some homework. She's pretty, and I think at this point in my hormonal life I would have really noticed her, but looking at her makes me want to see Helena all the more. The student is giving off the "vibe" to my dad—it's clear to me that she likes him, but he seems entirely oblivious. Which fits. My dad is a standup guy, he's devoted to my mother.

I say my goodbyes and head out the door and step onto the sidewalk.

"Got your note."

I can't help but smile. Helena's got my note in her hand and is leaning against the red brick of the building.

"Hey," I say, my smile getting so big it must surely classify as "goofy."

"What's with you?" she asks, pushing herself up from the wall.

"Just glad to see you," I say. "We tell the truth in this relationship, right?"

Her eyes narrow and it appears she's giving me her version of the "look." Do all women do this?

"Well I'm glad to see you too," she says. "I've been poking around about Lionel. I've got some good stuff."

"Me too," I say. "I was at the library yesterday and have the basics of what happened."

We both stand there for a breath. I'm staring at her, she's staring at me. I don't know what this moment is, but my memory of this morning and my body wanting hers comes rushing back. I look down and feel my cheeks flush red.

"What!?" she asks, her fist bumping my shoulder.

I look up briefly and shake my head.

"Come on, Wade, what was that look about?" she says. "I don't break easily, we are friends, you can tell me."

I look around, there are a few people headed down the sidewalk towards us and driving on the street. "Not here."

I look around and think, the university is just a couple of blocks away with open spaces and fewer adults.

"Let's find a quiet spot," I nod towards the university.

———

WE FIND A SPOT ON THE GRASS UNDER A BIG SPRUCE TREE IN sight of the construction of the Adam's Shakespearian Theatre, a replica of Shakespeare's Globe Theatre. From the outside it looks like it's complete, but judging from the sawing and the banging, they are still working on the inside. They don't have much time, opening day is in a week.

"What's going on, Wade?" she asks once we are sitting on the grass. "What was that look?"

This spot is up on a slight rise, with fir and spruce trees all around. It feels safe, most people bustling by won't even notice us here.

I bite my lip and try not to fall into those amber eyes of hers. "How much truth can a friendship handle?" I ask.

The "look" comes back briefly before she says, "A lot. A true friendship can handle the truth."

"And do we have a 'true' friendship?"

She shrugs. "This is not the kind of thing I have a lot of experience with. I told you, I have trouble making friends."

I sigh and pick at the grass.

"Just spit it out, Wade. It's Truth or Truth with us, okay?"

I look up and decide to just tell her. She stuck around after finding out I see ghosts. Surely she can handle this, the most obvious of truths. "I understand we are just friends. I get that. But..."

She nods and sighs. "God, I thought this was going to be serious."

"It is," I protest.

"It's hormones," she says. "But go ahead, finish telling me, I can handle it."

"I... I was thinking of you this morning and... Umm..." My face is burning and must be the color of an apple. Helena is just staring at me now, not saying a thing. "I felt... you know... hormones..." I trail off, my attention going back to the grass.

She sighs and punches my shoulder gently. "You got a boner," she says. It's not a question.

My heart is thumping away and I nod, but don't look up.

She chuckles. "Jesus H. Christ, you got guts, Wade. You got guts. Most boys can't admit the truth for anything. Not if they think it might not get them what they want."

I look up and she's smiling.

"You don't care?" I ask.

"Do you think this is something you have control over?"

I shake my head.

She shrugs. "No biggie. I shall choose to take it as a compliment. What you do in the privacy of your own bedroom is *your* business."

I breathe a sigh of relief. Who the hell is this girl? And do I have to always tell her this kind of stuff?

"Before I forget," I say. "My dad noticed you when you came into the bookstore the other day. My parents want you to come over for dinner. This Saturday." Might as well get all the embarrassment out at once.

Her eyes darken and she looks down. "Oh," she begins. "Saturday doesn't work."

"Okay," I say, surprised to find myself disappointed. "What about Sunday?"

She shakes her head. "Family day. My dad and I always spend it together. We hang out, watch baseball, I get most of the cooking done for the week."

I nod my head and then something occurs to me. She told me about Sunday but not Saturday. "So what's going on Saturday and why don't you want to tell me?"

She's bites her lip and stares at the grass.

"Truth or Truth, right?" I ask.

She nods, her eyes meeting mine, a sheepish smile on her face. "I have a date."

Sometimes I hate this truth thing. While the weight of my "crush" has lessened since that night with Lionel, I still feel it. And knowing that she's going out on a date stirs something in me I don't know that I've felt before. Whoever this boy is that is taking her out, I want to hurt him and hurt him bad.

"Please don't be upset," she says.

I shrug and say, "It's fine. I understand."

"But…" she says, prompting me for more.

"But, my biochemistry ain't so fine with it."

She takes a deep breath and lets it come slowly out. "You going to the opening?" she asks, nodding towards the theatre.

"Yeah," I say, welcoming the interruption. "They're doing *Romeo and Juliet*, my dad got tickets. All three of us are going."

"Well… be sure to go to the green show. It's going to be big. I'm working it."

"Working it?" I ask.

"You'll see…" she says mysteriously.

———

BIOLOGY. NONE OF US CAN TRULY ESCAPE OURS. WE ARE these, supposedly, rational thinking beings encased in this soup of biochemistry. Fear, Lust, Passion, Shame. All of them their own cocktail of hormones and endorphins and neurology. They bounce us around, fighting our logic with their chemistry.

In many ways, now that my hormones have kicked in, I think I understand something about being human—this seems to be our challenge. Finding a balance between the logical and the biochemical. We don't want to give in to every urge, and we can't always deny the chemistry.

Balance. Except that is not what being a teenager is about. There is no balance whatsoever.

Helena and I chat about nothing for a while. Our little interchange has actually managed to chase thoughts of solving a ghost's murder out of our heads. We are just trying to find a place back to being okay.

"You're a weird kid, Wade," Helena says as she gets up. This is becoming something of a signoff for her.

"And you're a fascinating woman, Helena," I say. It just slips out, but don't I need something to throw back at her?

She stops brushing her jeans off (tight jeans, I might add) and studies me. The "look" again. The disparity between our comments is obvious. She called me weird and a *kid*. I called her fascinating and a *woman*.

She's quiet. I just smile and watch her. I, honestly, could watch her all day long. She could do the most mundane of things and that would be enough for me.

"Tell your folks I'll be there on Saturday."

"What? I thought you had a date?"

She shrugs. "I'll break it. If he's worth a damn, he'll wait for me." She squats down and looks at me. "I said friendship was more important to me than dates. I guess I ought to live up to that statement."

I just blink, staring into the depths of her beautiful eyes. "It's going to be awkward as hell," I finally say.

"No shit, Sherlock."

"Thanks, Helena."

She smiles and then frowns. "We didn't talk about our ghost." She looks at her watch. "And I've got to go."

"Tomorrow?" I ask.

"That should work." She rises back up and says, "God, you're such a weird kid, Wade." She turns and walks away.

"And you are such a fascinating woman!" I shout after her. Part of me thinks that she called me weird again so that I would call her fascinating (and a woman).

And the word fits. I am utterly fascinated with her.

13

FRIDAY, JUNE 24, 1977

"HE WAS KIND OF A LONER," HELENA SAYS. WE'RE BACK under that tree on the grounds of the university in sight of the Globe Theatre replica. It's midafternoon and she's telling me what she learned about Lionel. "Some of the girls at La Familia remember him. He'd come in to eat Monday, Wednesday, and Friday at 6 p.m. like clockwork. He had a different dish for each day of the week and would order it every time. Nice enough guy, easy to take care of, good tipper."

"He wasn't married?" I ask.

She shakes her head, her cigarette-mint scent becoming a bit more pronounced.

"Did anything odd happen around when he died?" I ask.

"Yeah," she says, chewing her gum a bit before continuing. "The Friday before he died, he didn't come for dinner. He only ever missed on holidays."

I nod. It could be important. "He was killed on a Sunday evening," I said. "He was in his shop late, working, running some brochures for the Shakespeare Festival."

"What did the police come up with?" she asks.

I spent hours reading everything in the papers I could find. Trouble is, I didn't find out too much beyond the basics. He had been stabbed in the back in his own shop. No sign of forced entry. The police only ever interviewed one suspect. "They briefly detained Paul Durr, he was running the food bank at the time. The paper never went into details on why they suspected him."

"Is he back?" she asks, looking around for the ghost.

I shake my head. I haven't seen Lionel since he came home with me three nights ago.

"What happened to him?"

I shrug. "No idea. I'm going to go by the graveyard later. I've found if I shut my eyes tight and cover them with my hands, I can kind of see the ghosts."

Helena stops chewing her gum and stares. "With your eyes closed?"

"Yeah. To tell you the truth, it kind of freaks me out."

She nods, but then changes the subject back to Lionel's murder. "So, we've got unusual activity the Friday before he died. We've got someone questioned for unknown reasons. And that's about it."

I nod. "I wish Lionel was around. I can't hear him, but at least he could answer questions."

"How are we supposed to figure this out?" she asks. "I'm not Nancy Drew and you're not one of the Hardy Boys."

"Maybe we do like you said with Lionel. We form a hypothesis and then we test it."

She nods. God I love the way her hair moves. Is this normal? To get so caught up in what seems like such a small thing. Her hair is jet black and silky smooth. It slides across her shoulders, as if lubricated somehow. Stray strands will sometimes cling to her face and she will idly brush them away as if she doesn't even know she's doing it.

"Yeah, but we don't know enough about him or his murder to form a hypothesis," Helena says.

"Well, we could assume this Paul Durr did it, and go talk to him."

There's silence between us. Did I really suggest we go to a potential murderer and ask him if he killed Lionel Malak? That's great in the movies and all, but I sure as hell don't want Helena talking to a murderer. Don't really want to do it myself.

"Forget I mentioned it," I say, seeing relief on her face. "We need more data. We need Lionel."

———

"Hello, Big Ed," I say when I get to the graveyard. He's walking one of the narrow roads that run through the cemetery when I ride in. His gait is slow and a bit ponderous.

"Well hello, young Mr. Wade." He smiles, but the expression seems put on. He is worried. "Do you mind keeping an old man company for a bit?"

"No, sir," I say as I get off my bike. "Actually, there might be something you can help me with."

He nods and smiles his strained smile again and gestures down the little road as he starts to walk.

We've gone about twenty yards, but he hasn't spoken. "Is everything all right?" I ask.

He smiles that smile again, looking briefly at me. "Reconstructing a life—my Aunty Tilly, that is—can get rather hard on the heart." He presses his hand to his barrel chest.

I think about it for a moment, but don't really understand. "Why?"

He takes a deep breath and lets out a long, slow sigh. "Us humans are messy. I must say, my dear aunt was literally messy, but I am speaking figuratively. We all pretend we got it together. We all put on a good face. But under the surface, we all got our problems. We all got our weaknesses." He stops and looks at me. "Do you know what I'm say'n?"

I lick my lips and nod. "Yes, sir. And how."

He smiles, genuinely this time. "I'm here if you would like to distract me from my own worries with yours."

"I couldn't…"

"You still think of me as a stranger?" he asks.

I nod.

"I understand. That there is a proper and wise caution. I do hope you will change your mind, though. I have enjoyed our little encounters."

I stand there as he continues forward. I am being cautious because I don't know him, but also because him being here just seems a little strange. A detective showing up just when I am trying to figure out why Lionel died.

But that's just a coincidence, right? I don't have to give him specifics or anything. Just find out how you do this.

"If you have a moment, Mr. Lopez," I say, catching up to him. "I was wondering if you could tell me how to solve a murder."

———

So how do you solve a murder? Big Ed Lopez tells me that the TV shows—which I had to explain to him I don't watch—say it comes down to two things: opportunity and motive.

It makes sense. You have to have a reason to kill someone (motive) and the chance to do it (opportunity). Except Big Ed says that assumes we are all perfectly sane and logical. And as he put it, "That sane and logical bit… it's all just a cheap show."

He tells me that there will be a motive and an opportunity, but the motive doesn't have to be something I myself would understand. And he adds, "especially at your tender age." I don't like that. I've seen a lot in my sixteen years.

He goes on and tells me, "What you really have to understand is the victim. Unless it's some random crime, their life, their habits, their friends and enemies—the key is in there."

I find myself relaxing as I talk to him. He is smart and kind and so sad. I think the work he is doing with his Aunt Tilly has made him lonely. I think he really needs to talk about something else besides the picture of her that is forming as he goes through her things.

Which makes me wonder, how do I do the equivalent with Lionel? How do I reconstruct his life, piece by piece, until the picture of it becomes clear? Until someone appears that would want to stab him in the back with a knife.

———

AT DINNER, MY MOTHER IS ALL ABUZZ ABOUT HELENA'S VISIT tomorrow. She prattles on about preparations, what my father is doing—manning the barbeque—what I am doing—vacuuming, setting the table, that kind of stuff. As she does this, I think about Big Ed. What is behind the unusual energy my mom has. What is her "motive." Why did she create this "opportunity"?

"Why did you guys want Helena to come over so badly?" I ask over our empty plates. Dinner was simple, leftover tuna casserole and a tossed salad. The fishy smell still permeates the air.

My father clears his throat and my mother suddenly gets quiet. It seems like a natural question, but as I sit there in the awkward silence it occurs to me that the Truth or Truth game Helena and I play has started to change me. That is a more direct question that I normally would have asked. But I don't take it back. I want to know.

"Well, son," my mother begins, licking her lips. "We like to know who your friends are."

I smile and nod. That makes perfect sense, but doesn't seem like the whole story. "She's a new friend, why the rush?"

My mother looks pointedly at my father who sighs and takes a deep breath.

"It's because she's a 'she,'" he says. "You were different when we talked about her. We just want to get to know her."

I nod again, studying my father. Am I giving him my version of the "look"? So, they are more interested because she's a girl, but that doesn't seem to be all of it either. He shifts uncomfortably in his chair and looks to my mother.

"Aaron… well…" she stammers. My mother never stammers. Part of me is nervous as hell at this, part of me is excited. There is a mystery here and maybe if I start practicing solving the smaller mysteries in my life, I can help figure out what happened to Lionel.

"Mom, Dad," I say looking at each of them. "I wish you guys would just tell me. I can handle it, I promise."

"It's just that," my dad says, taking over for Mom, "the Monforts have a troubled past, and as your parents, it's our job to worry about you."

"Are you talking about her mother?" I ask.

He nods, his eyes flicking away to his nearly empty plate.

"Are you afraid she's mentally unstable or something?" I ask, looking at my mother.

"It… It's not that simple, son. We just… she…" she gets up quickly, her chair sliding noisily on the linoleum floor. "Henry. Talk to the boy." She grabs plates off the table and sweeps into the kitchen.

My father slowly rises and says, "Let's go for a walk." Now I'm wishing I hadn't brought it up.

———

WE START BY RAMBLING THROUGH THE NEIGHBORHOOD, BUT I head us towards the graveyard. I don't intend to go there with my father, I just want to get a glimpse of it. I'm hoping to see Lionel.

The streetlights throw yellow pools of light onto the cement sidewalk and the stars twinkle above us. It's warm, I don't even have to zip up my windbreaker, a really lovely evening. I wish that I was on my way to see Helena in the graveyard, not having an epically awkward conversation with my father.

"We worry about you," Dad finally begins. "It's kind of our job. Every parent has that job, but since you got sick… well, it became that much more of a job for us."

"But, I'm not sick now. I'm good."

"I know," he says, "and we couldn't be happier. The fact that a girl has come into your life is a good sign of your health. That is not lost on us."

I nod, dragging my shoe on the sidewalk, the sound of it echoing off of the houses that surround us. The neighborhood we live in, north of the university, is an eclectic mix. Old, historic houses mixed in with new, modern houses, on the wide and perfectly ordered grid of streets. I can hear Main Street, the sound of cars flowing on it, not far away.

"You just wish I had made friends with a less complicated girl?" I ask.

My father lets out a sigh of relief. "That is a good way to put it, Aaron."

"But, aren't they all complicated?" I ask.

My father chuckles and nods. "That they are, son. That they are. But some are more complicated than others. We just don't want to see you get hurt."

My father's silent and I let it be because we are approaching Main Street, which means the graveyard is not that far away. I want to steer us on to Main Street for the few blocks it takes to get there, steal a glance at the trees and the granite gravestones, see if I can catch a glimpse of Lionel, but it's too far and he'll suspect something for sure.

"We are just friends, Dad," I say. He doesn't reply. "You don't believe me, do you?"

"I am having trouble with that one," he says.

"Do you mind if I tell you the truth?" I ask. "Maybe it will ease your mind."

"I would prefer it, son. You know that."

"We are just friends and I wish we weren't. She's breaking a date to join us tomorrow." I catch my dad staring at me, so I stop and look him straight in the eye. "Honest to god, we are just friends."

He smiles wistfully, his hand coming to my shoulder. "I'm sorry, son."

I feel tears sting my eyes and turn and start walking. My father keeps his hand on my shoulder as we walk home.

14

SATURDAY, JUNE 25, 1977

SATURDAY IS HERE AND BILLY IS NOT A BIT OF HELP WITH MY nerves. I go over to his house in the morning, trying to distract myself from the upcoming event, but he's not useful. He says stuff like, "Shit man, you better brace for impact" or "Shit… I mean… shit!"

It's Billy's usual "shit" laden phrases that just add to my sense of impending doom.

I catch him up on Lionel and tell him about Big Ed.

"How do we do it?" I ask. "I mean, how do we find out enough about this dead guy to reconstruct his life? To understand his friends. To figure out who killed him."

Billy is silent for a long time and looks thoughtful. Hard work for him. "Maybe we don't have to," he finally says.

We're in his messy room and I've been browsing issue 189 of the Incredible Hulk in which he battles the Mole Man. "Huh?"

"Well," he says with a shrug. "The ghost is gone, he disappeared. Maybe all he needed was for someone to care, for someone to know he's a ghost. Maybe that completed his

mission on planet Earth and he got to go..." Billy trails off with
an odd look on his face as he bites his lip.

He grabs a couple comic books and holds them up one at a
time: Fantastic Four, Spiderman, Superman. "This stuff... I
love it, but I know it's not real. Radioactive spiders or gamma
rays don't impart superpowers."

"Yeah..." I say, not having a clue where he is going.

He roots around his "treasure chest." It's really just a couple
of cardboard banker boxes, but it's where he keeps his collectable comic books. It's the one area of his life where he is neat
and orderly. He pulls out a copy of issue number 2 of Ghosts
comic book. It's got an illustration of a scuba diver and chest of
gold with a Spanish conquistador ghost attacking. "This, I
know is fiction. Made up stuff. Right?"

I nod my head.

"But you... you saw a ghost. You and Helena proved it was
real. And that... well that..." he trails off again, carefully
putting away the collectable he got out and then flopping on
his bed.

I kind of see where he's going with this. Lionel calls into
question what's real and what isn't. But I know I'm still missing
something. "Where do you think Lionel went?"

I'm on the floor and he peers at me from his bed, pulling a
big pillow under his chest. "I was going to say heaven, or
maybe hell. But shit, Aaron. What does this mean? There's a
freaking ghost who wants you to solve his murder. There's not
supposed to be any ghosts!" He gets up again and roots around
in the corner of his room. It's a stack of paper and books—I
wonder how he can find anything.

He comes back and sits down on the floor next to me. He's
got the Bible and the Book of Mormon. "No ghosts in here,
only the Holy Ghost."

"No?" I ask, I wouldn't know.

He slowly shakes his head. Billy has been raised Mormon,

it's a big part of his life—not a part I share, but a big part. For him, Lionel raises different questions than he does for me. Billy may be a slob, girl obsessed, and rather compulsive in his use of his favorite expletive, but he's got his faith. It has grounded him in ways that I have often wondered at.

"Shit, man," I say. "I'm sorry, bro."

"And it's not like I can go talk to a deacon or someone about this. They'd just think I'm crazy."

I nod, but don't know what else to say. Billy believes me, that I am really seeing a ghost, and Billy believes in his religion which doesn't allow for ghosts. Shit.

"So…" I begin. "I'm gonna do as you say. I'm just going to leave it alone unless he shows backs up and…" I don't want to continue. I thought this would be the kind of adventure Billy would be all over, but I didn't factor in his faith.

He nods and is about to say something more when the twins open the door and come in. Billy growls at them and chases them downstairs. I quietly let myself out.

———

I'm out front of our house when Helena arrives. I don't work the bookstore on the weekends usually, my dad has employees for that, so after Billy, I was home doing my mother's bidding for hours. There was nothing more to do, and my mother was still fussing, so I snuck out front and sat on the steps.

My breath catches when I see Helena walking towards the house. It's about six, the sun is still pretty high this time of year, the air hot. She's a ways off, but still leaves an impression wearing a powder blue sundress with her hair pulled back. I've never seen her in a dress before.

I'm no poet, but to say she is beautiful is like saying the sun is hot. It just doesn't begin to describe it. Even in the dress she's got that confident, boyish walk. Or, maybe boyish is the wrong way to describe it. It's a confident, direct walk. Like she knows where she's going, knows who she is, knows what's going on. If you saw me walk that way—not that I really can— you might call me cocky.

I stand and start walking towards her, a huge grin on my face.

"Hey," I say as I meet her two doors down from our house. "Ready for the epically awkward extravaganza?" I ask.

The evening light catches in the golden brown of her eyes and I never want to look away.

She shrugs. "Can't be that bad, Wade. It's just food and your parents." She pauses, looking at me, her smile has gone nervous. "It can't be, can it?"

"Truth?" I ask.

She purses her lips and nods.

"They are worried that I'm going to get hurt. They know about your mother and wish that I had made friends with a less 'complicated' girl. They want to check you out for themselves."

She takes a deep breath and slowly lets it out, her shoulders sagging. "Oh, Christ. I should have known."

"Sorry—" I begin, but cut myself off. Her face has gone hard and she stands up straight and squares her shoulders.

"I don't break easily," she says. "I can handle this."

"Yeah?" I ask.

"Yeah," she says. "For you, Wade, I can handle this."

She puts her hand on my shoulder, gently turning me around, and we head for the house. I go docilely. I can barely think. For me she can handle it... for *me*!

———

I KNOW WE'RE IN TROUBLE AS SOON AS I CATCH MY MOM'S face. My mouth is open, about to introduce Helena, but Mom's mouth is open too and her eyes are wide. Her hands are clenched in front of her white apron, which is covering her light pink dress.

I look at Helena and back to my mother. Helena's not wearing any makeup, but she looks way more woman than girl. My guess is that is what has stymied my mother.

The silence is thick and awkward. I want to speak but can't.

"You must be Helena," my father says, stepping in from the living room, his hand outstretched. "I am Henry, and this is my wife Laura."

"Glad to meet you, Mr. Wade," Helena says as she shakes my father's hand. "Thank you for inviting me over, Mrs. Wade," she says to my mother, stepping past me and shaking my mother's hand.

And then it's like the spell has broken. Helena asks something about the drapes (they're blue, and block the light, that's about all I know) and my mother relaxes and launches into the story of how much she went through to get them just right. They move off to the living room.

My father pulls me into a side hug and says, "Relax. We just want to get to know her."

Things go pretty well, all civil and the like, until we are out in the backyard eating. We've got a picnic table in the middle of the yard, not far from the swing set. The sun is getting low and it's still warm.

"So," my mother begins, "how did you two meet?"

I nearly choke on the piece of steak I'm trying to swallow. The question is troubling in two ways. I can't exactly tell them how we met, and even worse, it's the kind of clichéd question you ask a couple and I should have seen it coming.

My father, who is sitting next to me, slaps me on the back and I am able to resume normal swallowing. Helena smiles at me from across the table and says, "Why don't you tell them."

The world suddenly seems small. I am not a practiced liar

by any means. I mean, I got pretty good at lying about how bad I felt when I was sick or during chemo. But not about normal, everyday things.

"We met at the graveyard," I say, my head nodding towards the west. It just kind of slipped out.

My mother goes kind of pale. I wonder if she remembers that incident when I was a kid and saw those ghosts.

My father clears his throat. "Really?"

I nod, feeling my face flush. Since the truth is tumbling out I decide to stick with it, mostly. "I was over visiting Uncle Don's grave." I pause, looking at both of my parents. "I miss him sometimes, you know."

They nod, both looking at me intently.

"Helena here was going by on Main Street in distress. I helped her out."

Helena nods, a small smile creeping onto her face.

"Distress?" my mother asks, still looking at me.

"Yes, distress," I say. "It would be ungentlemanly of me to share more."

"It's okay," Helena says. "I was having trouble with a boy not hearing me clearly, if you know what I mean." She looks pointedly at my mother. "Aaron was kind to me." She shrugs. "Frankly, most boys our age aren't as thoughtful or considerate as your son is."

There's silence then. I'm blushing, I know I am, but my parents seem satisfied. And it's the truth, except we left the part out about how it happened in the middle of the night. I catch my dad's eye and it's clear he knows, but my mother doesn't and seems satisfied.

The rest of the evening goes pretty well, if moderately embarrassing, until the summer sun is finally getting down to the horizon and it's starting to get dark. We're still sitting at the picnic table, a few candles lit for illumination. My parents have been grilling Helena on what she wants to do with her life—turns out she's not really sure—when I see him. Lionel.

He's standing in front of our wooden privacy fence. It's six feet tall and measuring him against it I can tell he's an inch or two taller. He looks kind of dim, but there is no doubt that it is him.

I'm staring, I must be, because my father follows my gaze and asks, "Raccoon? That damn thing is not back, is it?"

"Oh, Henry," my mom begins. "Please don't say it. It ate through half of my flower bed the last time it was here."

Both of them leap up. My father to go get a flashlight, my mother grabs a broom and moves towards the bed of flowers (jonquils, pansies, and peonies) as if ready to defend it.

Helena is watching wide eyed when I lean over and whisper, "Lionel."

Her eyes get even wider and she turns around and follows my gaze to the fence. "What does he want?" she whispers when she turns back around.

I shrug. "No clue."

My father's back out with a big bright flashlight sweeping it over the backyard. "What did you see, son?" he asks.

"I don't know," I say. "Just thought I saw something."

The raccoon search goes on for about ten minutes more before we all move inside. It's after eight and Helena says, "Thank you so much for dinner, Mr. and Mrs. Wade. I really should get going. My father will be off work soon and I'd like to be there when he gets home."

My mother's mouth opens as Helena talks, but when she gets to the part about her father, it closes and she nods.

"It's been a delight," my father says, shaking her hand.

"Walk me out?" Helena asks me, which I gladly do.

We walk in silence until we're a couple of houses away. "Is he still here?" she asks.

I nod. Lionel is walking in the street to the right of me.

"Can you ask him if he really wants us to solve his murder?"

"He's nodding yes," I say.

"Why?" she asks.

Lionel's talking, but I still can't hear him and it's not one simple word, so I can't tell what he is saying. He ends up looking up and shaking one hand. "You want to…" I begin, the thought suddenly not sitting well with me and I'm having a big jolt of empathy for Billy. "You want to go to heaven?"

He beams at me and nods.

"He's stuck here?" Helena asks.

"Looks that way," I say after seeing Lionel smile and shake his head enthusiastically.

Helena sighs and looks around. "This is… Damn. I'm sorry, Wade, but I really do have to go."

"Yeah, okay," I say, shoving my hands into my pockets.

"But, keep asking him questions, see if you can figure out who might have wanted to kill him."

"Okay," I say again.

"We have to help him, don't we?"

I slowly nod and look at Lionel who has a pleading look on his face. "We have to."

"God, Wade, you are one weird kid," Helena says with a small laugh.

"And you're one fascinating woman," I reply as she turns and walks away.

"Monday under the tree?" she calls back. "Where we will dive further into this mystery."

15

SUNDAY, JUNE 26, 1977

LIONEL MALAK WAS A BUSINESS OWNER, NEVER MARRIED, had a few close friends, and went to church religiously, but was in no way devout. He lived in a little house on 900 West, south of the university, that he owned free and clear, having paid it off with a small inheritance he received when his favorite uncle died. His mother is alive and living in Las Vegas, and his father died of a heart attack a few years before he was murdered.

Taking Big Ed's advice, I decide to try to understand who Lionel was. So, after Helena leaves, I go back in and tell my parents I'm tired and want to go to bed. They don't object—they probably think this is some kind of "moody teenager" event.

Lionel follows me, and once upstairs it takes me a while to figure out a way to gather this information. Twenty questions is in order, but I can't exactly be up there all night talking. The folks would begin to wonder. So, I get a flashlight, turn off the lights, get out a school notebook and start writing down yes/no questions and writing down his answers.

Do you know who killed you? NO.

Any idea who might want to? NO.

Did you have any enemies? NO.

I start this way but soon become bored with it. Lionel seems to have no idea who would have a motive, so I change tack and try to piece together a picture of him.

And while asking all these questions, I watch him. How he moves, how he reacts to the questions, what is surprising and what is not. You know, detective stuff.

As I go along, I transfer everything into my diary and tear up the plain paper I write questions on in plain English and throw them away.

Lionel's life was his shop and his work. Something I understand pretty well from my father, and from knowing I'd be happy as a clam to run that little bookstore. Not that I have any idea why clams are so happy.

Lionel only had few friends, but they were close ones. There are three. Two men and one woman. I don't have their names yet, but I think that is going to be next. I need to know who these people are, find an excuse to go talk to them. Maybe they will know something.

While I don't know these people's names, I do know that one of them is not Paul Durr, the man the police questioned. Paul was a client, one of many. Lionel didn't know why they would have suspected him, but I did find out that Paul was in the shop shortly before the murder.

All of this took hours to drag out of him. I eventually fall asleep propped up on my bed.

I have strange dreams. I'm Lionel in my little shop, happy as the proverbial clam, working an old-fashioned printing press. The kind with metal letters you have to work manually, an old movable type press. Roll on the ink. Put in the paper. Press it down. Take the paper out.

In the dream, I find it strangely satisfying. It's mundane work but I'm creating something. Building something.

————

I WAKE WITH A START TO THE SMELL OF ROSES. MY MOTHER is in my room. She's got my diary and is trying to read it.

Her brow is all furrowed as she flips through pages. I rub at my eyes and swallow, my mouth dry and I've got super bad morning breath—even I can smell it. I blink, trying to get my eyes into focus.

"What is this?" she asks, looking at me and holding up the diary. She's in a bright pink robe that in my condition is hard to look at.

"Private," I say. If I had been more awake, I probably would have been more tactful, but I don't appreciate her snooping.

Her lips form a tight line and quiver a touch. "What language is this written in?"

"English."

"This isn't English. Aaron, what is this?"

I am grateful for the forethought to encrypt my diary. It was such a pain at first, but if I hadn't… well, she'd probably know way more than would be good for me at this point.

I swing my legs over my bed and sit there staring at her. She's clearly freaked out, and as I write this now, I can kind of see it. But not right then. Looking back, I think I was definitely having a "moody teenager" event fueled by lack of sleep.

"It's private, Mom. What are you doing in my room? It's Sunday morning." In general, I'm allowed to sleep in during the weekends.

She looks at me again and crosses her arms awkwardly because she's still got my diary open in one hand. "I… You…" she stammers and rushes out.

————

IN THE SHOWER, AS I WAKE UP, I REMEMBER THAT I HAD offered to go to church with Mom. Shit. I rush through and run back into my room and put on some decent clothing. Some nice corduroys and a white button-down shirt. I've got a tie, and think about putting it on, but I just can't bring myself to do it.

When I run downstairs, my mom is gone. It's just my dad sitting at the kitchen table, reading his paper. I see my diary on the table as well as the remnants of breakfast. The smell of scrambled eggs makes my stomach rumble.

"There's still some eggs in the pan," Dad says from behind his newspaper. His tone is even, but I can sense the tension underneath it. "You're too late, your mother already went to church," he adds as if reading my mind.

I sigh, get a plate, and push the cold eggs from the pan onto the plate. They're way overcooked now, but I'm hungry. I take it over to the table across from my father and sit down. My hunger is being fought down by my nervousness. We are about to have a "talk."

If there is a talk to be had, my father is always the one to deliver it. Frankly, I don't know if I'm better off that way. My mom gets much more emotional than my father, but my father can be stone-cold logical in these circumstances, leaving me very little wiggle room.

I take a bite of the cold eggs and swallow hard. I feel the urge to apologize bubble up but force it down. I don't want to start this thing with me babbling on like some scared ten-year-old kid.

After a few minutes, I've eaten about half the eggs—all I can stand—and my dad has slowly folded his newspaper up and is staring at me. His hand delicately touches the diary and he says, "What's going on here?"

"You knew about this. It's my diary, Dad. You encouraged me to write in it."

He purses his lips and nods. "That I did. But what are you writing in here?"

I shrug. "You know… stuff. What's going on with me… that kind of thing."

"So, read me something from it," he says. His voice is so damn even, it's freaking me out. He's worried. He thinks I've lost it.

I grab the diary and flip through it, trying to find a passage that won't get me into further trouble.

I start reading. "'I help out at my Dad's bookstore. I love it. In fact it would be fine with me if I could just quit school and do that. It's simpler. I know my place. I know what to do.

"'With the leukemia, I've missed so much school it's hard for me to fit in and I—'"

"Okay," he says. "That's enough." He lets out this long sigh and actually smiles. "Can I see that page?"

I nod and hand it to him. It starts out like this in the diary "Cinn nne leuqegia".

He looks at it and then back up at me, his smile growing. "What kind of algorithm did you use?"

I smile back, glad that my dad understands. "Alternating letter shifting. Pretty simple."

He nods and gives the diary back to me. "And why did you see the need to do this?"

"I was afraid Mom might go snooping."

He leans back, crosses his arms over his chest, and lets out another sigh. "You forgot about your offer to go to church, didn't you?"

I nod and look down.

"You're going to have to make this up to her," he says.

"Yes, sir," I say.

There is silence then and Dad is fiddling with his paper. "Can I ask you a question?" I ask.

"Yes. Please."

"I have a right to privacy, don't I?" I swallow hard. My parents have given up a lot for me, but I have secrets. I need to keep them.

The smile he gives me is compassionate and for some reason that freaks me out. Why does that question engender compassion? "Yes," he begins, "of course you do. But if you had fulfilled your obligation, gotten up on time, this wouldn't have happened."

"That doesn't give her a right to snoop," I say, my heart starting to beat hard.

My dad pauses, licking his lips. "Actually, Aaron, it's pretty understandable."

"She... I... What?" I stammer. I was not expecting him to take this position.

"Picture yourself as a mother of a child that had a long and devastating life-threatening illness. Your child has been healthy for a good stretch and is now experiencing some rather normal teenage things that you don't understand. Girls, sneaking out of the house, hiding things from his parents.

"But you've given him the benefit of the doubt. He's offered to do something nice for you, so you get up early, make a nice breakfast and await your son's arrival. When he doesn't show up you go into his room to wake him and find him fully dressed, propped up on his bed, with pen in hand holding a book. What do you do? Do you worry about his privacy or, having nearly lost him several times, do you look at the book he's holding?"

My dad is clearly wound up about this. His tone is still even but with each sentence I find myself feeling smaller and smaller.

"Of course, you look at the book," he continues. "And when you do it's written in this gibberish that scares you. It may not be rational, but you fear something else has happened to your son, your only child.

"Your son wakes up and finds you that way. You try to ask him about it. Your words aren't the best you've ever chosen, but you're scared. Your son's answers are defiant and not the least bit illuminating. You feel…" Dad trails off, looking at me. He's silent for a moment. "Tell me, Aaron, how do you think your mother felt this morning?"

I feel the tears just behind my eyes. My dad's damn little speech has given me empathy for her. Something, frankly, I am not interested in. I try to speak, but my mouth just moves in a silent pantomime as I hold the tears back.

I know that my illness has been so hard on them. That even though I am healthy we are all still living with Cancer. I know all this. But I don't want to be reminded. I don't need to know the exact extent that I just hurt my mother.

I stand up quickly, the chair falling behind me and clattering to the floor, but I don't care or look. The tears have found their way out and I feel shame that my father is seeing them.

"Nice speech, Dad," I say, nearly spitting the words out. His eyes are wide now. "I suggest you picture yourself as a son whose father has just delivered that speech to him."

I run out the door, get on my bike, and ride away.

———

My bike is freedom—or at least the symbol of it. No, it's more than a symbol, it is an actual level of freedom. It lets me go places on my own, places my feet couldn't carry me as well or as easily. And it feels like freedom. The wind whipping through my hair, the houses speeding past, the feel of my body warming up with the effort of pedaling.

It's freedom, carrying me away from my father and his criticism. From my house where so much history has occurred…

the good and the bad. And my bike is mine. I bought it with my own money that I earned. I take care of it.

As I ride away from my father and my house, I'm not aware of that freedom stuff, just that I want distance. The warm wind dries the tears on my face and soon I find myself at Billy's house. The big Chevy Suburban isn't parked in the driveway and my brain stalls for a minute before I remember that it's Sunday. They are at church.

I ride onto their yard, step off the bike, and let it clatter to the soft grass. I move to the spigot by the garage and turn it on, swallowing handfuls of water. The ride has left me thirsty. I then go plop down by my bike and my mind just ping-pongs around.

Lionel the ghost... where is he now? Is he here, but I just can't see him in the light? I close my eyes, but don't see him that way either.

This makes me think about Billy and his discomfort knowing that there are ghosts in this world. His faith doesn't seem to have a place for them. And that makes me wonder where they fit in to my own beliefs.

My mother... she is frankly a bit of a mystery to me. My father assures me this is somewhat universal when the male observes the female (or vice versa), but then I think of Helena. I understand her better than my mother. I can talk to her much easier than I can talk to my mother.

With a sigh, I get up and pull my bike up. My legs are a bit jellyized—I rode hard here—so I get on and start riding at a reasonable pace. Church isn't over yet. I may not fully understand my mother, but I do understand that I hurt her. Time to do something about that.

————

WHEN I SLIDE INTO THE PEW NEXT TO MY MOTHER, SHE

doesn't say a word, but her eyes widen briefly. Pastor West is really wound up, his voice echoing over the small church, his cheeks red and his hands stabbing out to point at the assembled citizens of Cedar City.

"But what is the righteous path? How do we know our actions are what god wants for us? What He needs of us?" the pastor says. He holds up his bible and shakes it at us. "It's in here, right?" He pauses, but it doesn't seem like he's really waiting for an answer. "This is the 'good' book. It contains all the answers, right?"

There are some shaking of heads and mumbles of "yes" and "right."

"And how do we sinners know those answers?" he asks, this time tilting forward his ear towards the audience.

I am, frankly, very uncomfortable, and I shift on the hard wood of the pew. I find Pastor West's sermons manipulative and condescending. We are all lowly sinners crawling along and can't tell right from wrong without some god on high telling us every little thing to do. A god that seems to treat everyone as dumb children but then allows the most horrible things to happen in this world. Things like war and murder and... yes, Cancer.

"We read it!" a woman yells out a few pews in front of us.

Pastor West nods solemnly. "We read it," he repeats quietly. "We read it," he says again, his voice getting louder. "We read it!" he yells.

He slams his bible down on the podium, the sound of it echoing through the brick building, the congregation quiet.

He sucks in a deep breath, his large chest expanding. He brushes at his thinning brown hair and grips the front of the podium and leans forward, a large wood cross on the brick wall behind him. "But how do we read it?" he asks quietly. "Do we read it like we read the newspaper or a cheap novel?"

I groan and my mother stabs a look at me. I shut up, but

feel my thoughts hardening against his message. He just said that novels are cheap, that since they aren't the Bible they are somehow worth so much less. Is *The Great Gatsby* cheap? Is *Pride and Prejudice* cheap? Is *Hamlet* cheap? Well… for me, them are fighting words.

"Do we read it like we read the instructions on a TV dinner?" he continues. In fact, he asks about four other questions, his volume rising, his hands shaking out towards us until he finally answers his own questions. "No!" He picks up the bible again, waving it at us. "We read it like it is holy, like it is the word of god, like it is the one thing that can keep us from eternal damnation!

"We read like it is our salvation. Because, you know what? It *is* our salvation. It is not something to be read lightly or once. It is what we turn to again and again, day after day, night after night. We humans… we sinners, we live in a world full of temptation and doubt. This book, this holy word of god, is our only way home. Our only way. *The* only way."

Done, the pastor's big body slumps, his shoulders rolling forward as he steps away from the podium. He wipes sweat from his face with a handkerchief.

The musical director, a plump blond-haired woman, leaps up and tells us where to turn in the hymnal while everyone stands. I'm not paying attention though. I am watching everyone.

My mother is studiously scanning the hymnal, taking a deep breath and preparing to sing. Pastor West looks like he just ran a marathon, his body slumped in a chair on the small raised stage. There's a tall man on the other side of me who is flipping through the hymnal seemingly having trouble finding the right page. A bored girl of about five years is turned around in the pew in front of me, and when I catch her eye, she sticks out her tongue and turns back around. A young couple are holding hands tightly. An older woman has her bible clutched to her chest.

This book, the Bible, has answers for people who believe. It strikes me then, like a ton of bricks, that having answers might be kind of nice. Having a single place to go in a quest for understanding could be comforting. Believing in an omnipotent god in this chaotic world might just be a relief. There's always an answer then. There's always a way forward. It's in the Bible. The word of god.

As everyone sings, I watch them, wondering what that might be like but knowing that it's not for me.

————

PASTOR WEST'S WARM HANDS ENGULF MINE AS HE GREETS MY mother and me as we leave the church. He's standing in the summer sun, sweat forming on his brow. "Good to see you, Aaron," he says.

My mother says something nice about the sermon—everyone always says something nice about the sermon—and then looks at me pointedly.

"Pastor, I was wondering," I begin and suddenly feel nervous. I'm not sure why, and I feel silly about it, but I think I'm afraid if I interact with Pastor West too much, his religion, his belief, might rub off on me. Like it's contagious or something.

And now that I think about it, belief is contagious, isn't it? Belief and ideas spread from person to person just like a virus does. Sometimes that's a good thing—the ideas of basic hygiene transformed our health as a race—and sometimes that's a bad thing—take Hitler and his belief in a master race. With religion, like Pastor West tries to spread, I don't think it's just good or bad, but a bit of both.

"Yes, son?" he says. He has such a kind face, round with a wide, easy smile. He is always so kind.

"Umm… yes… well, we have a swing set that I've outgrown. I was wondering if you might know a family that could use it."

His grey eyes light up like there is suddenly hope for my soul, which makes me even more uncomfortable. I shift my feet on the cement below me.

"What a kind offer, Aaron," he says. "No one comes to me off of the top of my head, but I'll tell you what, I'll think about it. How about we confer on this again next week?"

I look up at my mom and I can see the smile on her face. I really screwed up this week, so I feel like I kind of owe her. "Sure," I say to Pastor West, swallowing hard.

———

AFTER WE GET HOME AND MOM IS WORKING IN HER GARDEN, I go out and talk to her. I know I'm not halfway there to making things up to her yet. She just started the vegetable garden this year. It's a small raised bed with a few tomato plants and one zucchini plant. It's not much, but it's another sign of my health—my mother feeling like she has time to garden.

She's dressed in tan shorts and kneeling on a pad as she pulls weeds out of the soil with her gloved hands.

"I'm sorry, Mom," I say. I dive right into it, because I really don't want to drag it out.

She glances at me and then turns her attention back to the plants. "What are you sorry for, Aaron?"

I take a deep breath and sigh. Here it is, the test. Not only do I have to be sorry, I have to be sorry for the right thing. "I'm sorry that I forgot about my promise to go to church with you. I am sorry for being grumpy this morning." I stop short of apologizing about my diary. I don't care what Dad says, she shouldn't have been snooping in it.

She rocks back onto her feet and swivels so she's looking right at me. She doesn't say anything at first, just looks into my eyes. I have a hard time keeping the eye contact, but I do. She looks down, her brows furrowing before she says, "Thank you, Aaron. I appreciate the apology." With that she turns her attention back to the garden.

I go into the house and hold my sigh in until the patio door is closed. She "appreciates" the apology, not "accepts" it.

My father has taught me to listen carefully to the words people choose. They don't always do it consciously, but there is meaning behind it. And the meaning here is that she's still mad. That I have to figure out something else to do to get into her good graces.

My father looks up from the living room as I hit the stairs going towards my room. I don't make eye contact. I'm still mad about his speech.

16

MONDAY, JUNE 27, 1977

I THINK I NEED TO REVISE WHAT I SAID ABOUT MY BIKE AND freedom. It's not that my bike isn't freedom, it is. And I'm sure when I get a little older it will be a car that symbolizes freedom.

But it's not the essence of freedom. Health is.

Without my health, I couldn't get on my bike and ride. Without health, I couldn't go to church to try to be nice to my mother, or spend my afternoons under a big tree talking to Helena, or be mad enough at my dad to give him the silent treatment.

All these things stem first from being healthy enough to experience them. Health is the real freedom.

———

HERE'S THE THING ABOUT MY DAD AND THE SILENT treatment; he is immune. Or at least he appears to be. If you want to talk, he's always right there. If you want to brood and be silent, he can roll with that.

I hadn't spoken more than a few words since his "here's

how you hurt your mother" speech. When I get to the book-store for my shift, he's there, having opened it up as usual.

He gives me a neatly written list of things to do and I answer with as few of words as possible.

"You know, son," he says as he picks up his leather satchel about to head out the door. "If you're mad at me, I think this will work better if you actually tell me what's bothering you."

I say, "Probably," and get up on the stool that sits behind the little counter and start reading the list. The sting of the empathy he forced on me is still running its course. I don't want to tell him what I'm mad about. He should know, shouldn't he?

My dad shrugs and heads out the door.

———

MY TIME AT THE BOOKSTORE ISN'T VERY ENJOYABLE, BUT I have a smile on my face when I see Helena walking towards me. I'm in the shade under "our" tree on the lawn not far from the Globe replica theatre. She smiles and waves and all my family junk gets swept away like dandelion tufts in a stiff breeze.

"Hey, Wade," she says as she plops down beside me, chewing noisily on her peppermint gum.

"Hey, Helena," I reply, a goofy smile on my face.

She looks at me, her eyebrows coming together. "Having a good day?"

"Am now."

She blinks and looks me over for a moment. "Good to see you too, Wade."

We talk about little things for a while, but not about my family. I don't want to bring that crap into our friendship. Eventually we get to Lionel and the long talk we had on Saturday night.

"You know what you need?" she asks after I tell her. I shake my head. "A Ouija board. You need to do better than yes-no if you are going to get the names of these people or get more complicated information from him."

I nod, it makes sense, I have no idea why I didn't think about it. "I think we might have one at the bookstore. But..."

"What?" she asks.

"Too many questions if I get it from the bookstore."

She nods and pulls at the green grass for a moment, ending in a shrug. "So get a piece of paper, write the letters on it, have him point."

"Wow. Great idea. Next time he comes back, I'll get the names of his friends."

"Well there you go, problem solved. What else can I do for you today?"

She's all smiles and in a good mood, but in a flash of intuition my mood goes a tumbling. "How was your date?" I ask. She postponed it on Saturday and had told me Sunday was "family" day, but she's different.

Her smile actually deepens and my heart flips in my chest. "It was good... But how did you know?"

I force a smile onto my face. "Your mood is a bit effervescent."

"He's nice. Not like Jeff 'the hands' Tate." She leans back onto the tree looking up at the one little cloud in the brilliant blue sky above us and pops a bubble with her gum. "I mean... It's not like he's the best-looking guy I've ever gone out with, or the most exciting. But he's nice. And I'm hoping he's honest too."

I can tell I'm blinking too much as I watch her talk about this new boy. I'm "nice." I'm "honest." I'm certainly not the "best looking."

She looks at me and her face gets serious, her mouth forming a straight line as she pushes up from the tree. "Wade..."

I hold my hands up. "I get it, okay. I really do. You and I are friends, but…"

She nods, "The hormones."

I bite my lip and nod back. "It's a work in progress."

We're silent then, the banging in the Adam's Theatre, the slight breeze, and the cars on the street the only sounds. It's a delicate place we are in. I am so glad to have her as a friend, but I have other feelings too. Feelings she doesn't share. Feelings that I have to somehow keep in check.

She has a smile on her face as we say our goodbyes, but I know my reaction is why she is leaving so soon. I watch her walk away, wondering what's next. With us. With Lionel. With my parents.

———

I've got time, so I ride through the graveyard on my way home. I am glad when I see Big Ed Lopez slowly pacing on the grass near Uncle Don's grave.

"There you are, my young friend," he says as I ride up, a smile on his face. I feel warm inside that he calls me a friend. As adults go, he's different, less like my parents and more like my uncle was.

"Hi, Big Ed."

He smiles, his cheeks pushing up and making his eyes narrow. I think he's glad I called him "Big Ed." "Can you distract an old man from his own cares for a bit?" he asks. I am getting fond of his southern drawl.

I get off my bike and set it down in the grass. "Sure." I have gotten really comfortable being in the graveyard and being with Big Ed. I still have that little nagging question about the coincidence of a detective showing up just when I need to solve a murder, but it's not a very big thing anymore. A kind adult that listens and treats me like an adult is very welcome.

"And what is the nature of your troubles today, Mr. Wade?"

We're walking down one of the narrow paved streets that pass through the tall trees and granite markers of the dead. He's got his hands clasped behind his back and is looking at me.

"Is it that obvious?" I ask.

He chuckles, a brief, deep rumble. "At your age, my friend, it is assured."

"Let's see," I begin, holding up one finger. "My mother is mad at me and I'm mad at my father." He nods, I hold up another finger. "The most beautiful girl I've ever met only wants to be friends." He smiles and nods again as I hold up a third finger. "And I really want to solve this murder."

He stops and sighs. "I am afraid that those first two items are just not things I would be much help with. But I would listen if you want to talk about it. That third item, though, now there I might be useful council."

We start walking again and I tell him what I know about Lionel's murder. One suspect that the police let go. Three close friends. Stabbed in the back while working late at night. A real loner.

"I've learned what I can about his life, like you suggested, but I'm kind of stumped as to how I get people to talk to me about this directly. I'm not the police. I'm not a detective. I'm just a teenager."

He's silent, his gait slow as he walks. He reminds me of Pastor West, at least in his size. He's short with such a broad chest and must weigh 250 pounds. I'm a skinny teenager, it's hard for me to imagine being that big.

"In life, it's best to use what you've got and it's best to stick to the truth when possible—much easier to keep things straight."

I nod, encouraging him to continue.

"If what I've heard about you is correct, you've been ill, right?"

"Yes."

"Well, son," he continues. "If you are willing to use that, I think you've got a great way to get people to talk to you."

He then tells me his plan. It's a good one, all I need now is the names of Lionel's friends.

————

DINNER IS QUIET AND TENSE. I DON'T KNOW WHAT TO SAY TO my mother and I don't want to talk to my father. After eating and clearing the table, I excuse myself and go up to my room as soon as possible.

I use some paper, a ruler, a pen, and scotch tape and make something of a Ouija board. It's a bit more logically laid out though—A through Z in a simple grid with another grid of common phrases and words: "Yes," "No," "The," "I Don't Know," and the like.

Then I wait. And wait... and wait...

No Lionel. I try to read, but my head just isn't in it. Writing this diary is the only thing really helping me keep my head on straight right now. Except it's not on very straight, is it?

TUESDAY, JUNE 28, 1977

NOTHING TO REPORT. NO LIONEL, NO HELENA, AND THINGS still tense at home. Billy and I did hang out for a while and we both avoided the subject of Lionel and what his ghostness means to him.

I have decided to do something for my mom. Something unexpected. Something special. I want to go back to my father's original suggestion, which was she's been through a lot for me and now that I am healthy I should do something for her.

I don't exactly know what that "something" is yet. But I'm getting into the idea. I want to see my mom happy again.

WEDNESDAY, JUNE 29, 1977

I HAVE TO TALK TO MY DAD TODAY. I CAN'T EXECUTE MY plan concerning my mother without a little of his help. It's not a big, grandiose thing. It's just lunch. I want to prepare a picnic lunch and surprise her with it at work.

Her schedule can be a bit unpredictable, being a nurse and all, but I figure I can just show up at her usual lunch time—I know what it is very well. When I was sick at home and she was working, she would always call me on her lunch break.

This is what I need to talk to Dad about. I need the day off from the bookstore.

"Can we talk?" I ask him when I arrive for my shift.

One eyebrow raises and he says, "Sure." He thinks we're going to talk about why I'm mad. How can he not know?

"I need tomorrow off. I want to surprise Mom," I say. My hands are shoved deep in my pockets and I'm not making a lot of eye contact.

"What kind of surprise?" he asks.

"A good one. One she won't expect so she can't be disappointed if I flake out or something goes wrong."

He rubs at his chin and nods. "And you don't care to tell me this surprise?"

"No, I don't. I don't want to disappoint anyone. Best just to do it."

"Sure, Aaron. That sounds good. I'll find someone to cover for you tomorrow."

I'm excited. Seriously, I am. Although I don't really understand my mother, I love her. And, really, how could I understand her? I'm her child. She almost lost me way too many times. How can a teenage boy ever hope to understand that?

And I bet she doesn't understand me either. Maybe I should share some of Helena's wisdom and tell her that it's the hormones that has caused some of my recent behavior. I certainly can't tell her about the ghost.

———

"HE HASN'T COME BACK?" HELENA ASKS. WE'RE UNDER OUR tree again. I'm kind of glad we can meet in the light of the day now. That somehow makes our relationship seem more real.

I shake my head. "And something odd happened Sunday night."

"What?"

"We had been at it most of the night. I was exhausted and starting to fall asleep myself. I thought I was imagining it, but maybe I wasn't. He seemed to, like, fade away right before I fell asleep."

"Fade?" she asks. "What do you mean fade?"

"Well... he's a ghost so he's transparent, right?" She nods so I continue. "Towards the end, he became more transparent, his appearance going kind of smoke-like on the edges. And then, at the end, he was getting so transparent I could barely see him."

Helena stares at me for a while and then pulls at the grass a bit. She looks back up at me and sums it all up beautifully. "Weird."

I smile. It's her word for me and certainly the word for this situation.

We spend the next hour or so blabbing about all kinds of things. But no more about ghosts and neither of us bring up dates. I don't know why she didn't bring it up, but I know why I didn't. I don't want to know about her dates. I want to be able to pretend that there is a tiny part of her that is only for me.

———

LIONEL'S BACK. THE OUIJA THING I'VE DRAWN HAS CHANGED everything. I can have an actual, real conversation with him. It's slow. I still write the questions in regular English in scratch paper, and then watch him as he points at my Ouija papers and I write the questions and answers in the diary properly encoded. It's not fast or anything, but it's a hell of a lot faster than the yes-no game.

Here is our conversation... well the important parts anyway.

———

DID YOU HAVE ANY ENEMIES?
    NO.
    Anyone angry with you, want to hurt you?
    NO... WELL, OBVIOUSLY, SOMEONE WAS ANGRY AT ME, BUT I DON'T KNOW WHO.
    What about Paul Durr? The man the police questioned. What happened that night?
    HE WAS ANGRY, BUT JUST NORMAL ANGRY. HIS BROCHURES WERE LATE, AND HE ACCUSED ME OF

DRAGGING MY FEET BECAUSE OF THE NON-PROFIT DISCOUNT I GIVE HIM.

Do you think he did it?

NO. PAUL HAS ALWAYS BEEN MORE BARK THAN BITE.

You told me you had three close friends. Who are they?

ANN AND JOE EDWARDS, AND VINCENT LONG.

Do you think they know anything about your murder?

I DON'T KNOW.

Do you think they'll talk to me about you? I'm going to tell them I'm doing a makeup paper because of all the school I missed.

THEY MIGHT. I HOPE THEY WANT TO TALK ABOUT ME.

Where do you go when I can't see you?

JUST GONE. GHOSTS GET TIRED, KIND OF LIKE SLEEPING.

What's it like being a ghost?

LONELY.

How is it that I can see you?

I DON'T KNOW.

———

IT'S NOT MUCH REALLY. I'VE GOT THE NAMES OF HIS FRIENDS, some people to go talk to, but it seems like I should be able to get more from Lionel. I mean, I'm talking to a freaking ghost here. He ought to provide some better clues to his own murder.

Towards the end, when I start to ask him about me, things get interesting.

I write, "Why is it that I can see you?"

He replies, pointing to the phrase on the Ouija board, "I DON'T KNOW." But there is something going on. He looks guilty, and he won't meet my eye.

"Lionel," I whisper, breaking my silence, "what do you know?"

He blinks, his eyes briefly meeting mine before they dart away. He looks down at the floor and bites on his lip.

I have an idea why I can see him. I haven't spoken it to anyone. I haven't written it down in this diary. But right then, sitting on my bed with my heart pounding, I ask him, writing it on a scrap piece of paper that I tear up and throw away later. "Is it because of my leukemia? Because I've almost died so many times?"

I hold the paper up and point at the question and whisper, "Is it?"

His eyebrows furrow and he looks like he's about to cry. He points at "I DON'T KNOW" on the Ouija papers, but I don't believe him. His face says "yes."

I just stare at him, suddenly feeling cold, letting my diary drop onto the comforter of my bed.

He holds that look of compassion on his face so long I begin to freak out. What does he know? What can he see?

"Is it coming back?" I ask. I forget myself and don't even whisper. My voice isn't loud, but this isn't that big of a house, there's a chance my parents heard it. My mother specifically. When I was really sick, I could hardly make a sound without her showing up at my bedside.

Lionel doesn't point at the Ouija papers. He doesn't even mouth an answer. He just disappears.

Not like that night he became more and more transparent and then was gone. Lionel gets this look of concentration on his face and then is just gone and I'm left there feeling the weight of the "C" word sitting on my chest like an obese elephant.

19

THURSDAY, JUNE 30, 1977

EVERYTHING IS DIFFERENT NOW. EVERYTHING.

Although I'm still dating everything when it happened, I'm way behind in writing these entries, you'll soon see why. And no, it's not what I thought was going to happen.

Having been sick so much, I've often pondered survival. How I survived two rounds of Cancer—sure I've pondered that, but more the little things. How we survive the near accidents in the car, the falls from the bike, the random virus that takes out a few people, but not most.

Every day we are faced with things that can (and for some will) kill us. Every day. Choking on your dinner. Having a heart attack. A head-on collision. Earthquakes. Fires. Sure, leukemia and Cancer are big and dramatic, but they are by no means the only things queued up to hasten our exit.

When you pull back from the individual—and I mean pull way back—and look at humanity as a whole, it gets even dicier. With genocide and wars and plagues. It's a wonder we've survived at all as race.

So what's my point? Good question. My point is this:

survival should never be taken for granted. Never. I may only be sixteen, but this is one lesson that has been driven home over and over.

When I wake up, I feel thick, my mind is slow, my body is sluggish, as if that obese elephant has really sat on my chest. My pits stink and I'm sure my halitosis could have been lit on fire as I stumble to the bathroom.

What does Lionel know? Can I see the dead because I am dying?

The hot water helps revive me, and as I take stock of myself and my day, I realize that in some ways it doesn't matter. I have this day and I have something to do. Something special. Something for my mother.

So I shake off the fear of the unknowable and the inevitable and concentrate on Mom. She who birthed me into this world and nurtured me for sixteen years, she who worries about me, she whom I don't understand but love.

Maybe this is different for daughters, but there is some inevitable tension that comes in the relationship between a son and a mother. When you're a baby, you need that intense level of nurturing. When you're a kid, you still need some of it, and as you come into adulthood you want it in limited quantities, but it's time to stop needing it.

I'm not sick anymore. I'm getting strong and growing up. I've got to find my own way in this world, and my mother still remembers me as a helpless infant and as a sick boy. The infant part is long ago, but being sick isn't. My last chemo treatment ended seven months ago. We still have to go get regular tests to make sure the Cancer hasn't come back.

I don't want to be that boy that needs his nurse mother for survival. I want to find my own way, I want my mother to worry about me less (because we know she's going to worry some no matter what), and I want my mother to know that I'm okay.

At breakfast I let things stay tense, as they have been since Sunday and the whole church debacle. I don't want to let onto anything. After my parents leave, I get to work.

I dig a picnic basket out of the garage and use some bungee cords to attach it to my handlebars. I go into the kitchen, dig out some crackers, cut up some cucumber and carrots and put them into a Tupperware. I find a nice checkered tablecloth, some napkins, plastic cups, forks, and a couple of paper plates.

I find myself whistling and smiling as I make my preparations. This idea is a good one—she will love a surprise picnic lunch. I'm even grateful to my father for suggesting I do something nice for her.

I change out of my T-shirt and into a navy-blue polo shirt —it has a button. For me, in the summer, this is dressing up.

I pack everything carefully into the picnic basket and check my bungees. I don't want it falling off. I head out on my bike, there are more preparations to make. I need to go to the market for cheese and some apple cider.

This is going to be a good day. I just know it.

———

As I pedal up to our hospital, I'm tired. I had to put some miles in to get from my house to the market and then to here. The Valley View Medical Center is on a hill on the south end of town, near the steep juniper-covered hills that rise up to the Colorado Plateau and Cedar Breaks. Except for this odd tower, it's a low building, one and two stories, and sprawling with lots of glass and some stone walls made of fist-sized rocks cemented together. If not for the ambulance bay, you might mistake it for office buildings.

My mom is a critical care nurse. She takes care of people in the intensive care unit. I sometimes think that's why she has always been so touchy about my health. She's seen way too much reality helping to take care of the sickest of the sickest.

I find a nice shady spot next to one of those stone walls for my bike. It's a hot, crystal-clear blue summer day. I don't want the cider or the cheese to get too warm. I'm sure my mom will still appreciate the effort even if everything isn't perfect, but I want it to be special.

I brush my jeans off, tuck in my shirt, and check the time. It's 12:53 p.m. She tends to go to lunch right around one. My plan is to go in and find her. Tell her I've brought her lunch. I thought of doing something more elaborate, but this seems like surprise enough.

I'm getting ready to head towards the main entrance when I see her. Actually, I hear her first, the delicate bell-like sound of her laughter rings out. I look up from my bike and see her. She's walking with a man that looks familiar and is dressed in blue scrubs and looks happy. Her long brown hair is pulled into a ponytail.

My mouth is open to call to her when they stop. She's facing away from me, but I get a better look at the man. It's Doctor Rogers. He's one of the ICU docs and has been one of my doctors when I've been in the ICU. I've met him on quite a few occasions. He's a few years older than Mom, with grey at his temples and a muscular build. I can't hear what they are saying, but my mother's tone floats over to me. It's an unusual tone. She sounds happy, really happy.

I raise my hand, getting ready to wave and yell to her when it happens.

She puts her hand on his chest, leans up, and kisses him on the lips.

Everything slows down. I suddenly feel really hot and can hear my heart beating in my chest. I taste the remnants of scrambled eggs and for some reason chide myself for not brushing my teeth for this. My mom—who is currently kissing someone besides my father—appreciates good oral hygiene.

She's on her tiptoes kissing him and I half expect one of her feet to kick back like in those old movies of the heroine kissing the taller hero.

Wait a minute. What's going on? Why is my mom kissing Doctor Rogers? Why does she sound happier than she ever sounds at my house? And look how she is kissing him. She never kisses Dad that way.

I hear a fly buzzing about and the sound of cars going by on the street.

"What?!" I yell. The sound comes out strangled and more like a "Wwwwaaaaaa." They stop kissing and Doctor Rogers looks my way. Everything is still slowed down. I can't quite hear him, but I can see him saying her name, "Laura." The way his lips move, wet from kissing her, makes me want to strangle him.

My mother turns towards me, the smile on her face evaporating, her eyes widening as she takes a step towards me. "No! Aaron!" she yells.

I turn and suddenly things aren't so slow anymore. I can hear her calling as she walks to me, but I don't turn back. I get on my bike and pedal away. "Please," she cries. "Wait, Aaron. You don't… I…"

But I'm not listening to her, all I can hear is the pounding of my heart as salty tears run down my face. Despite my fatigue, I pedal hard and fast. I don't know where I'm going, I just know that I have to go.

PART 3

A Boy and a Family

20

THURSDAY, JUNE 30, 1977

(continued)

I'M LYING FLAT ON UNCLE DON'S GRAVE AGAIN. I'VE GOT MY hands across my chest and my feet straight out. I can't lie exactly where he is down there in his coffin, he was a lot bigger than me. But I've got my head where his head is, close to the slab of granite that sticks up declaring the boundaries of his life.

I'm hiding. In a graveyard. Weird, I know.

My dad has driven by a couple of times, the car going slowly down the narrow road that goes through the cemetery. The first time he called out for me, the second time he just drove slowly. When he called I almost got up, almost let him know I was here. It was the tone in his voice—he sounded so scared. My father never sounds scared.

But I didn't move, not a bit. If Dad had gotten out of the car and looked around, he would have seen me. But from a car, from the road, I am invisible.

I've got my bike stashed behind a huge cottonwood tree, so he didn't spot that either.

I feel guilty about that fear I heard. But what am I supposed to do? My mother has a freaking boyfriend! What the hell!? Are they going to get a divorce? What will happen to me?

Whenever I close my eyes, I see Mom kissing Doctor Rogers again. I hear that happiness in her voice. I notice the spring in her step. What the hell?

I mean, I know my parents' marriage isn't perfect. They fight sometimes, they have their troubles—they've had to deal with me and my Cancer. But… What the hell?!

It is hard to describe what I am feeling as I lie here. I'm confused and very afraid. But mostly, I feel alone. I always thought that the three of us were in this together. And if my Mom and Doctor Rogers are… well… Shit!

The sound of tires on pavement brings my thoughts to a clattering stop. Except it's not a car this time, it's a bike and I hear the huffing breaths of the rider.

"Jesus, A," Billy says as he rides up to Uncle Don's grave. "You know you're scaring the living shit out of everyone. Right?"

He's panting hard and I don't get up. I see his round face and red hair framed against the blue sky and the branches of the trees above. His face is red and he looks concerned.

"Sit down, B," I say. "Before you fall down." I sound surprisingly calm. How can I sound calm?

He steps off his bike, letting it fall onto the grass and then flops down next to me.

"Your parents are freaking out," Billy says. "Your mom won't stop crying and your father is gonna wear a hole in the carpet with his pacing." He pauses and then and looks around, his eyes going wide. "Umm… Is he… they… is he here?"

"No," I lie to him. Lionel isn't here, but I've caught a few flashes when my eyes have been closed. No need to freak Billy out. I don't want him to have a heart attack or anything.

"Good," he says, wiping sweat off his brow. I'm still lying

down, I find the disorientation of the perspective pleasantly distracting. "So what the hell is going on, Aaron?"

"They didn't tell you?"

He shakes his head. "Just that you were at the hospital and you ran away."

I snort and slowly sit up. Billy's presence is a dead giveaway to anyone passing by, so I might as well sit. "My mom has a freaking boyfriend." I then proceed to tell him in excessive detail about everything I saw.

"Shit!" he says when I'm done. "Oh my god, Aaron. I mean... Shit! You... I always thought you had the best parents. But... oh... Shit!"

I lie back down, carefully positioning myself above Uncle Don. "Now go, Billy. And don't you dare tell them that you found me."

"What?" he asks, his face puzzled.

I sit back up and look him in the eyes. "Don't tell them where I am. Do you understand me?" I was going to get all fierce with him, scare him into compliance, but then the tears come. They are hot little things sliding down my cheeks, a few of the salty bombs making it into my mouth. I'm not sobbing, thank god. It's embarrassing enough that Billy is seeing me cry like this.

But what else can I do? Emotionally speaking, I don't know which way is up anymore and I have no idea what this all means. My mother with another man...

"They are worried sick, man," he says.

"Good."

"Come on, Aaron. I've got to tell them something."

I wipe the tears from my eyes and feel my face going hard. "You are going to keep this secret, Billy Chadow. I swear to god that if you don't..." I trail off, not finishing the sentence, but from the look on Billy's face he gets the picture. We've been friends a long time, we both know a lot about each other we would prefer our parents don't know.

"But…" he begins.

The tears have stopped and I slowly shake my head.

Billy sits there, his jaw moving silently until his mouth opens and his eyes widen like he's just thought of something. "Okay," he says quickly. "I won't tell them."

He's back on his bike pedaling away so fast it makes me worried what he's up to. I shrug it off and lie back on top of Uncle Don's grave.

———

TIME PASSES ME BY AT AN IRREGULAR PACE. SOMETIMES MY brain is so on fire trying to figure this out (quite unsuccessfully, I might add) then the moments tick by ever so slowly, the leaves in the breeze above me seeming to wave in slow motion, the grass below me gently tickling my neck and arms.

At other times my brain just plain seems to slip out of gear and time flies by, the sun suddenly having moved noticeably in the sky above me. I even doze off a few times.

I'm dozing when the sound of a car racing down the little cemetery road brings me back to full consciousness. Judging from the sun it must be about 4 p.m. I've been here for hours.

The car screeches to a halt right in front of where I am, and I suck in a breath and hold it. Did Billy break down and tell my parents where I am? The car, whatever it is, stinks. It smells of oil and the exhaust is almost thick enough to make me cough. With the car still running, I hear the door open and slam shut, footfalls walking right toward me.

I'm scared to death. I don't want to see either of my parents. But it's not them.

"Get up, Aaron," Helena says, her beautiful face hovering above me like Billy's was a few hours ago.

I lie there blinking. Helena? What is she doing here? My mind is slow, it takes me a bit to figure out that this was Billy's bright idea. Not telling my parents but telling her.

"Get up. Now!" she says, her hands on her hips.

She's wearing the usual jeans but a navy-blue blouse instead of a T-shirt. A bitter thought infects my mind. She was on a date with this new mystery man. That's why she seems mad, because my little crisis interrupted her fun. Suddenly the image in my mind isn't of my mother kissing Doctor Rogers in front of the hospital, but of Helena. My heart thumps in my chest and I feel nauseous.

Helena leans down, her face hard and serious, her voice low, almost a growl. "You get up right now, Aaron. Or I will drag you and throw you into the car. I swear to god."

It's not lost on me that she's not calling me Wade, and that disturbs me, she always calls me Wade. I sit up and look over at the car. It's an old two-door Mercury Comet with faded yellow paint and a few dents in the passenger's side door.

"I'm not going home," I say. I try to meet Helena's eyes, but can't. They are so intense… what is going on?

She stands up. "Good, I'm not taking you home. Now get in the car."

I stand up and slowly brush myself off, looking around the graveyard. It feels safe here. Private. Unless someone is getting buried, there is hardly ever anyone here. There aren't really any problems here either. I mean, everyone is dead. What kind of problems do they have?

And then the thought of Lionel comes up. He's dead and he's got problems. What the hell do I know anyway?

Helena has taken a few strides towards the car and turns when she realizes I'm not following. "Now," she says.

I take a step, but then remember my bike. "My bike," I say, pointing to the tree it is behind.

She sighs and I watch as she marches over to the tree, rolls the bike back, removes the picnic basket and shoves it in the backseat, and puts my bike in the trunk. It doesn't fit well so she loops a bungee cord around the bumper and hooks it to the trunk latch.

I'm still standing there like an idiot. In retrospect, I think I'm still in shock from the whole thing.

She moves around to the passenger's side door and opens it. "Get in, Wade," she says softly. "Please." She doesn't look mad anymore, but worried. I really can't look at her now. I nod and get into the car.

———

SOUTHERN UTAH HAS SOME BREATHTAKING LANDSCAPE. THE earth seems to pinch and fold, producing mountains, canyons, and tilted mesas jutting into the sky. The land rises steeply from the valley, where Cedar City is, up towards mountains on both sides.

We're barreling down the highway south from Cedar City towards St. George. To the west of us are the Pine Mountains and to the east, beyond our sight, Zion National Park. We've come down in elevation from Cedar and the air is hot as it rushes in the open windows.

Helena handed me some food from the picnic basket and made me buckle my seatbelt before we headed out of Cedar City. At first the thought of eating *that* food made me want to puke. The food I had prepared for my mother... The surprise that was supposed to delight her... But soon my very empty stomach wins out and I stuff myself with cheese and crackers and veggies, washing it down with warm apple cider.

It helps. I hadn't eaten since breakfast and had exercised a lot. After eating, I don't know that I feel good or anything, but I'm calm.

"Sorry your family isn't as 'Leave it to Beaver' as you thought," Helena says.

"Thanks." I look around the car. It smells of oil and the black upholstery is cracked and faded. "Is this your car?"

She snorts. "No. This is my dad's car. Our only car."

I blink. That gives me some perspective. This looks like the kind of beater a teenager would have, not the only transportation for a family.

"He lets you use it?" I ask. It's small talk, but way safer than talking about what's really going on. I know Billy must have told her the story.

She shrugs and nods. "If it's important he does."

I stop looking at her and stare straight ahead at the interstate. Not much traffic, a few cars and some semis. So this, whatever "this" is, must be important.

"Where are we going?" I ask. I barely get the question out, my voice breaking at the end. I'm afraid of the answer. Helena, as I have discovered, is fascinating but also complicated. Where the hell would she be taking me given what has happened and how freaked I've been about it?

She pauses, licks her lips, and then glances at me before turning her eyes back to the road. "I… I want you to meet somebody."

She stammered just then. Why did she stammer? Where is she taking me? I mean, I trust Helena. I know that we are friends and all, but if she's nervous about where we are going, then how should I feel?

———

THE BIG OLD BUILDING IN ST. GEORGE HAS A DECIDEDLY institutional look with drab brick walls and small windows. We go through the front entrance, double doors with an awkward roof jutting out over the entryway.

I see a sign on the way in. The Meadowbrook Institute.

And Helena has changed. She's not full of bluster and anger anymore. Her shoulders are slumped and she's not looking me in the eye.

I want to turn and run. Whatever this place is, I don't want to be here. And from the looks of Helena's posture, she doesn't want to be here either. Who in the world can it be that she wants me to meet?

She holds the front door open for me and our eyes meet. Behind the nervousness is steely resolve. I get the impression that if I tried to run she would chase me down and drag me back.

The place smells of Pine Sol and seems too quiet. Our feet echo on the tiled floor as Helena walks to a desk situated in the entryway. It's open and airy, taking up the full two floors of the building with hallways going to the left and the right and a large wooden staircase leading to the second floor.

"Helena?" the middle-aged woman behind the desk says. She's got dark hair and brown skin. "It's not Sunday, sweetie, what are you doing here?"

Helena smiles and nods back at me. "I've brought someone to meet her."

The woman looks me up and down, a frown on her face before she turns back to Helena, her eyebrow raising. "She's doing okay today, it should be fine. But don't let him excite her or anything."

Helena nods and says, "I know the drill, Maria. He'll be fine."

My stomach is doing backflips as this little conversation goes on. Maria hands Helena a clipboard and asks her to sign us in. Helena then waves to me and heads for the stairs.

I hesitate for a moment, my eyes finding Maria's. Her lips are a thin line as she stares at me. I follow Helena mostly just to get away from Maria's gaze.

"What's going on?" I whisper. I'm not sure why I whisper, but this place seems to need it.

"I told you. I want you to meet somebody."

I follow her up the stairs and down a long hallway with lots of doors. I hear different noises now. A TV behind one door, the sound of laughter behind another, a groan behind one. Each door as a nameplate or two on it. "Williams, A." "Pollack, E." "Reynolds, J."

We stop in front of a door with a nameplate that says, "Monfort, O."

Helena pauses, biting on her lip. "I know I haven't explained this to you... I have my reasons for that. But right now, I need you to be on your best behavior. I need you to be your happy and charming self."

She pauses and stares at me. I'm looking from her to the door plate. Monfort. This must be a relative of hers. There must be something wrong with them. This is some kind of institution.

"Aaron?" she asks.

"Yeah... Yeah, sure," I say. "Best behavior."

She grabs my arm, holding it tight enough to hurt, and pulls me back down the hallway a few doors. "This is serious," she hisses. "I don't bring people here. I don't tell them about this. I need to know I can count on you in there."

I blink and then let out a sigh, I had been holding my breath. I'm confused as to what's going on, but it's clear that this is important to her. And even through the shock of my own problems, I am starting to get that. She doesn't bring people here, but she brought *me*.

I straighten up and take a deep breath. "Yes, Helena. You can count on me."

She gives me a small smile and takes my hand, leading me into the room.

———

THE WOMAN LOOKS OLD, WITH GREY HAIR AND STOOPED shoulders. She's facing away from me when I first enter the room. She's sitting at a table in front of the room's one window, sunlight illuminating the jigsaw puzzle she's working on.

She's got a tan sweater on with a blue scarf wrapped around her neck. The room is nice enough. It's got a single bed against one wall, a closet on another wall, a dresser with lots of pictures on top of it, and some framed art on the wall depicting ocean scenes.

"Mama," Helena says, and the woman pauses, carefully puts the puzzle piece she was holding down, and turns.

She's not as old as I first thought, her grey hair seeming somewhat out of place with her face. It's lined, but like someone in their fifties, not in their seventies. Her skin, though, is grey, and her brown eyes dull.

Mama? But Helena had told me her mother had gone crazy and hanged herself. Who is this?

The woman's eyebrows furrow as she looks from Helena to me and back to Helena. "What!" she says, rising from her chair and marching straight up to Helena, her face pinched. "Is it Sunday already? I... I... thought it was Thursday or Friday, but not Sunday.... Did I... Oh..." The woman stammers, her jaw quivering as she talks and stares at her fingers, counting on them.

"No, Mama. Everything's fine. It is Thursday, you were right. You know what day it is."

The woman scratches at her cheek and then her eyes find me. "Oh no... Oh no..." she intones as she backs away. "Not a new doctor. No more test. No more medicine." She backs herself into a wall, her hands pulling at her dull, grey hair.

Helena surges forth and pulls the woman into a hug. "No, Mama. I promise you everything is okay. This is my friend. I brought a friend of mine for you to meet. He's had a hard day and I thought that meeting you might help him."

This woman is Helena's mother. Obvious, I know, but it wasn't until that moment that it dawned on my overworked brain. Helena had told me her mother had hanged herself. I had assumed she was dead. Clearly she is not.

"Hello, Mrs. Monfort," I say, extending my hand. "My name is Aaron Wade and I am very glad to meet you."

Seeing Helena with her mother, imagining what she's been through with her, broke through my myopic obsession with what happened with my own mother today.

Mrs. Monfort disengages from her daughter and looks me up and down again, but doesn't come close. "No, no, too young to be a doctor, and too stupid looking," she says. She turns to her daughter and adds, "Why did you bring him? It's always you and your dad. You don't bring friends." She turns back to me. "Why did you bring him? It's Thursday not Sunday."

"Mama, I thought you would be pleased," she says, sounding like a little girl. "You always ask to meet my friends, and here is one."

The older woman purses her lips, her hands going to her hips as she takes a step toward me. "Very well," she says. "Tell me about yourself and why you deserve to be my precious daughter's friend."

I'm caught flat-footed for a moment, just blinking at her.

"Well?" she asks, taking another step towards me and crossing her arms. I can see a look of pleading on Helena's face.

"My name is Aaron Wade. I'm sixteen and I live in Cedar City and help my father run his bookstore, Cedar Books and Such."

She waves her hand at me and turns to her daughter. "Boring. He's so boring. Why would you be spending time with him?"

"Mother… please…" Helena says.

The older woman turns back to me and says, "What else?"

I search my brain for what she might find interesting about me. Riding bikes—no. Comic books—no. Lots of trivia gathered from constant reading—no. Then I think about what caught Helena's attention and just blurt it out. "I was diagnosed with acute lymphoblastic leukemia when I was eleven."

Mrs. Monfort's mouth opens as I speak, forming a "B," but then freezes for a moment before she slowly nods and takes two steps so she is right in front of me. Her breath is bad, like morning breath to the extreme, and I can see her hand has a tremor.

"Lots of doctors?" she asks. I nod my head. "Awful treatments?"

"Awful doesn't even begin to describe what chemo is like," I say.

I see her take a breath and relax. She takes my hand in hers —they are surprisingly warm—and draws me over to the bed, sitting on it and indicating that I should sit next to her. I do, and she says, "Tell me about the chemo. I want to hear about chemo."

And so I do, in grizzly detail. The more I tell her the happier she seems to get.

THE SUN HAS JUST DIPPED BELOW THE PINE MOUNTAINS as we roar north on the highway, the hum of the tires against asphalt through the open window lulling.

Mrs. Monfort was relentless in wanting to hear about the indignities I'd suffered with my Cancer treatments. Relentless. Most people can't stand more than a few tidbits of it. She wanted everything. To see the scar where my central line was, the scar from the bone marrow transplant, hear about the tiniest side effect of chemo. On and on.

And I gave it to her. After a while it began to feel good to get it out. I didn't forget Helena while I was doing it, worried that it could be way too much for her, but her mother was voracious for it. As if my terrible experiences in the health care system made her feel less alone.

She didn't tell me much of what she had experienced, but I've got to imagine it wasn't that great. Even I know that mental illness is a tough thing to treat and a tougher thing to have.

"Why didn't you tell me she was alive," I finally say, pulling myself out of my reverie.

"What?" she asks, shaking her head and taking a deep breath. She must have been lost in her own thoughts.

"When you told me about your mother, we were doing Truth or Truth. You led me to believe she was dead. She is not." After the shock of it all had worn off, that had started to bug me.

"Really?" she asks. "After all that's happened today, this is what you want to talk about?"

My sadness about my mother is there, but it's abated somewhat. I feel anger welling up, and Helena's half-truth is in my crosshairs. "Yes. Really. I thought we were telling the truth those times."

She glances from the road to me, a half-smile on her face. "We were, Wade. I told you nothing but the truth about my mother."

"But not all of it."

She shakes her head. "No. Not all of it."

"Why?"

She's quiet for a while. The silence is bugging me, like an itch I can't scratch, but I don't say anything. I just stare at her.

She finally sighs and says, "Because no one ever tells you all the truth. Ever. Not about anything real or important."

I scratch my head trying to process her words. All the truth… Okay, I get how that would be too much to tell… there is no time. Even in an hour and a half, I didn't tell Mrs. Monfort the entire truth about my treatments. It wasn't nearly enough time. And my words, though voluminous, couldn't really convey all the nuances. As I mull it over, I realize that what she has just told me was a dodge.

"Okay," I say. "I get that. But you didn't tell me the essential truth. That your mother hanged herself *and* survived was one of the most essential parts of the story."

She's silent again, and I see her blinking rapidly. Surprised? Blinking back tears? I can't tell.

She glances at me again, this time the smile on her face is small and filled with pain. "You need to work on your empathy skills, you know that?"

That hurts, and I open my mouth for a retort and then close it. She's taking a deep breath, and I know there is more to come.

"Because," she continues, "you know, the truth is not a simple thing. Not an easy thing. And neither is trust. That is something that takes time, has to be earned, is delicate." My stomach falls and I'm afraid. "Let's take all that stuff you just told my mother. You left things out… I imagine *essential* things. Things that make you feel guilty or uncomfortable. Things that might paint you in a less than positive light. Things that you might not even admit to yourself."

"I… What?"

"Ohhh… I don't know, but I can guess." She pauses and glances at me, her brown eyes hard. "Do you want me to guess?"

I'm so confused, I haven't had a day be this much of a roller coaster since I was diagnosed, but that vein of anger at my parents, at her leaving out something some essential is still making me defiant. "Sure," I say.

"I think I know you well enough to get this on the first guess." She pauses, licking her lips, I see her hands tighten on the steering wheel. Why the hell did I say "sure"? "I think you've milked this 'I'm a sick kid thing' some."

I'm blinking as I stare at her, my mouth open.

"I think you liked having your mother and father wait on you hand and foot. I think you, at times, played sicker than you were. So they'd fuss over you, bring you your food in bed, buy you that book you were dying to read."

She pauses, the wind and the hum of the tires filling in the gaping silence.

"Am I right?" she asks, but her voice is quiet now. There's no attack, no sense of victory, no joy in it.

I lick my lips and nod. "Yes."

It's true. And it's something I hadn't really admitted to myself, but when she said it, I knew it to be true. I had fought so hard to survive, I had been so dependent on my parents, that I, at times, had played sicker than I was to get what I wanted.

The tears are silently rolling down my cheeks and I sniff loudly. God, how many times can I cry in one freaking day?

Her lips are pursed as she glances at me again. I see compassion in her eyes, but not pity. For that, I am grateful.

"Do you want to know how I knew that?" she asks, her voice sweet and calm.

I sniff loudly again, rubbing my nose on my sleeve. "Why not?" My voice cracks at the end, like that embarrassing six months when my voice changed when I was fourteen.

"Because you're human, Wade. You're a mess just like the rest of us."

She's silent then, and I think it over. Half-truths, things we don't even admit to ourselves, things we don't understand about ourselves. Is this what it was to be human? An essential part of being human?

Helena has lived a different life than mine. While I've dealt with physical illness, she's been dealing with mental illness. While I've experienced what it takes for a body to survive a horrible disease, she's been pondering the failings of the human mind.

She's right, that's for sure. We're all a mess. All of us.

———

MOTHER'S HUG IS SO TIGHT, THAT FOR A MOMENT I'M afraid she's going to hurt me. I smell her rose perfume, but mixed with her sweat and fear, her scent is not sweet today.

Helena and I didn't discuss it. She just brought me home. Our field trip to St. George did what it was supposed to do and while I'm not "ready" to go home, I know it's time.

A quiver passes through my mother and she sniffs loudly. We're standing on the landing in front of our front door. My parents were out the door as soon as I got out of the car. They must have been watching.

"I'm so glad you're okay," she whispers. "Don't ever do that again," she adds, holding me even tighter.

"Sorry," I whisper back. I'm not exactly sorry, but I don't know what else to say. There are things going on here with my family that I don't understand. Things that scare me. But, it was never my intention to hurt my parents. I just needed some space from them.

I can hear my father and Helena talking behind me in the yard. Their voices are low and serious and I can't make out anything they're saying.

The hug finally ends and I get a good look at my mom. Her eyes are puffy and red-rimmed from crying and she somehow looks older than I've ever seen her look before. Frail. It hits me then, the cost they paid for my outing. But that guilt is countered by the anger at what I saw. Who she was with. The secret my parents have kept from me. The lie we've all been living.

My father's warm hand on my shoulder keeps me from saying anything stupid. "Helena wants a moment with you," he says. His voice is even as if he just told me breakfast was ready, as if this was just another day. "We'll be inside."

My mother resists briefly, but lets my father take her in the house, and after the door is closed, I walk down the steps and into the yard where Helena is standing.

She's beautiful, even after this crazy time we've had she's beautiful. But something has changed about her beauty. It's not just the long hair, lovely face, and tantalizing curves. It's her. Who she is to me that is starting to outshine those physical things. Our friendship. Not the kind of friend I've ever had.

I smile. It feels crooked and I hope it conveys some gratitude and some "oh my god, what now?"

"Give me your hand," she says as I get close.

I'm confused, but I hold out my hand. She pulls a pen out of her jeans and turns my hand palm up. She pulls the cap off with her teeth and writes on my hand. "This is my number. I'll be up late, call if you need to. Don't freak out if my dad answers."

The pen tickles as she writes the numbers on my palm in red ink. After the number, she draws a little heart and fills it in.

I should say something, but my mouth is dry and I don't know what to say. "You can handle this, Wade," she says. "You know that, don't you?"

"No," I reply.

She smiles, just a little thing, and adds, "Well, *I* know you can." She glances up at the house and back at me. "And let's face it, this is going to be a bitch. But you can handle it. Just remember that your parents love you, and…" she trails off, her face going dark.

"…and," I continue for her, "I'm lucky to have them."

She sniffs and nods. I don't fully realize it then, but what

Helena did for me today was epic. What she showed to me, what she gave to me… it was not normal in any way.

"Thank you for… I…" I stammer. "Helena, you are the most…" I can't get a coherent sentence out and I feel my cheeks flush red. I want to tell her how amazing she is and how much what she did for me means. I want to tell her how much her friendship means to me.

"Shut up, kid," she says, pulling me into a fierce hug.

I hug her back. And I can't say that I don't notice her femininity pressed against mine, but it isn't that big a part of it. I am expressing my love and affection and gratitude for what she had done. Her minty-smoky scent is even stronger. And I think it is that moment when I grew to truly love that strange smell.

I don't know how long that hug lasted, but it wasn't long enough. Suddenly she's in the car and driving away with a smile and a wave.

I turn and look at my two-story house with its well-manicured lawn, powder-blue paint, and cheery curtains. It's so middle class. So put together. So very orderly.

I sigh as I walk to the front door. It's time to find out what's hidden behind all that neatness. To find out what's beneath it. What kind of mess us humans that live here are.

OPENING THAT DOOR AND VOLUNTARILY WALKING INTO MY house was one of the hardest things I've ever done. Every part of me wants to run away. And it's not lost on me that my parents were probably feeling something similar about the conversation that is to come.

We all want to run away. But we don't. We can't. Not and remain any kind of a family.

And yes, I did run away for a while. But I came back. I opened the door. I walked in.

My mother and father are seated awkwardly on the couch in the living room. They're staring right at me, so I walk in and sit on the wooden rocking chair across from them. The house seems so quiet, so quiet that I can actually hear my steps on the shag carpet.

The rocking chair has a thin pad on the seat, but nothing on the back. It's not comfortable and that suits me.

"You realize," my mother begins, "that you are grounded, of course." There's more than a little anger in her voice and I'm surprised to hear it.

"You can work your shifts at the bookstore," my father says. "But otherwise you are to be here. And you are to answer the phone if it rings."

I purse my lips, starting to slowly rock in the chair. The movement is vaguely comforting. I don't say anything and I see that is making my mother even more uncomfortable. My father seems his usual cool self, but I can see the tension in his shoulders, the stiffness in his back. He's stressed too.

"Do you have anything to say to us?" Mom asks.

My lips are still pursed. Like I'm trying to keep myself from speaking. From throwing accusations at my mother. From saying something amazingly stupid. Is this all they have to say? How I will be punished.

I pretend that I'm my father. All logical and cool. All calm and collected. I take a deep breath and stop rocking, sitting forward in the chair. "You feel the need to punish me. I understand that and accept it. I am sorry for the worry I caused you. But you must realize that the shock I experienced had to come out somehow."

My mother's mouth opens, and she sucks in a deep breath, but my father stops her by putting his hand on her knee. She was about to yell. About to take offense at my "tone."

"Maybe you can imagine what it felt like," I continue, looking directly at my mother, "to see you with Doctor Rogers."

She looks away, red flowing to her cheeks. "I've been thinking about this as best I can. And I can only imagine that you two don't want to be married anymore. That you are only together because of me. Because of my Cancer."

There's silence between us for three breaths, thick and heavy. I can hear the ticking of the little wooden clock on the mantle, it's surprisingly clear. I think we're in shock. I can't believe I said what I said, and I don't think they can either.

That pretending to be my dad got me talking, but I don't know if it was for the best.

And then all of the sudden everything breaks. My mother is yelling, but it's not anger, it's her pain that I hear as she tells me she loves me, that it's complicated, and that I don't understand. I'm crying, great wracking sobs gushing out of me for the family I thought I had but don't. My father is talking rapidly, I don't know exactly what he's saying but it's along the lines that this is not my mother's fault.

And then it's silent again.

———

WE ARE ALL SUCH A MESS. A TRAUMA, LIKE MY FAMILY HAS just experienced, is kind of like a serious physical injury. I took a pretty good spill on my bike when I was ten, before the big-C came visiting. Billy and I had found a nice hill near his home and had set up a ramp at the bottom of it and were jumping our bikes off it.

It's on this little dirt road behind his development. Over and over we go tearing down the hill and fling ourselves and our bikes over that ramp and into the air. When you hit the end of the ramp, you've got to pull up hard on the handlebars, so you come down on your back wheel.

On that last jump, I pulled up extra hard, but my right hand slipped a little bit and the force from my left hand jerked my front wheel hard and to the left. I came down on my back wheel just fine, but when my front wheel connected, it was perpendicular to my back wheel. I went flying over the handlebars and tumbled onto the dirt, my bike rolling over me.

I lay there stunned, looking up at that crystal-clear blue sky we get around here so often. My breath was coming in ragged gasps and my heart pounding in my ears was nearly deafening.

I heard Billy shout as he ran toward me calling my name and saying "shit" over and over again.

As I lay there, I was weirdly calm. I wanted to jump right up and shake it off, show Billy I'm okay, but somehow I didn't have the will.

As it turned out, I had some scrapes and bruises, but nothing was broken. When Billy got me standing, I could hardly walk. I couldn't pretend it didn't happen and was still limping by the time I walked my bike home and couldn't hide it from my parents.

Sitting in the silence, in the living room with my parents, I remember that incident. Our family was in that place where I was on that day, lying on my back, staring at the sky, unsure of how badly I was hurt.

It is clear that my family is scraped and bruised. That we will be "limping" for a while. That this is too much to walk off and hide.

But is anything broken?

As the silence lengthens, I know that this wreck is worse than the one I did on my bike. That this time something is broken. That my family will never be the same.

———

"Helena?" I ask quietly. I'm in the pantry sitting on a five-gallon bucket filled with flour—my mom likes to bake—having just called Helena's number. I'm so glad she wrote it on my hand, there is no way I would have remembered it today and probably didn't have enough of a brain to think to look in the phone book.

"Hey, Wade," she says. "How bad was it?"

"Bad."

"You wanna tell me about it?" Her voice is its husky self, but it's much more serious than usual. It's like she's a different person now that the proverbial shit has hit the fan. I am coming to appreciate the serious Helena.

"I'm grounded, like, forever, and we didn't really talk about 'it.'"

She sighs. "That's not good. Things can't get better until you do. What *did* you talk about?"

I shrug. "My irresponsibility… Actually, there was a lot of horribly awkward silences. And some crying. We all tried to get the conversation started, but it never happened."

She's silent, I can hear her chewing on her gum on the other end. It's funny, but I almost smell her cigarette and gum breath.

"I think they're only together because of me," I say.

"And let me guess? You feel guilty about that."

"Yeah, Helena. I do."

"Well don't," she says, a hard edge to her voice. "They're the adults. They made this choice. And they made it because they love you."

"Yeah… I get that, I do. But it feels…" I trail off, not knowing what to say.

"Like shit, right? It feels like shit, like you are causing your parents pain and that's the last thing you want to do."

"Umm… Yeah," I say. "How… how did you know?"

She laughs, it's thick and deep and lightens my mood just a touch. "Human condition, kid. Human condition. People like you start with guilt, blame yourself."

"You… How do you know all this?"

"Self-defense," she says quietly. "My mom's nuts. I had to learn about what makes us tick to survive. That and quite a few years with a therapist."

I want to say something. I know she's just shared something really intimate. But I can't get any words out.

She laughs, this time it's too high and a bit shrill. "You know, your mom coming at you with a knife does warrant a little talk therapy. You pick up things. Some people point the blame inwards, some outwards. You're clearly the former."

"I... I'm sorry, so sorry."

"Old news, Wade. And tonight's about you. So what else? You haven't told me all of it yet."

I take a deep breath. She's right. "My mother left. She says she'll be back in the morning."

There's silence on the other end of the phone. It's pretty dark here in the pantry, and that is comforting to me, but her silence is making me nervous.

"After she left," I continue, "I asked my dad if she's going to go be with Doctor Rogers. He just nodded and went and poured himself some scotch. He hardly ever drinks and this drink went down fast. But..." I trail off. It's all I can get out.

"I'm sorry, Wade. But this might be a good thing. That they don't have to hide now might be a good thing."

"Oh, but they are still hiding something," I say, my voice too high.

"What?"

"My mother, when she left, said something to my father. She said, 'This is not my fault. I didn't start this. *You* explain it to him.'"

"And did he?" she asks. "Did he explain it?"

"No. I asked him what she meant as he was nursing his drink, staring out the front window to the street Mom had just driven our car away on. He just said I had had enough for one day."

Helena is silent for a while before saying, "You can handle this. I'll be here if you need me."

When she says that, the tears start flowing again. I thank her, make an excuse, and get off the phone. I don't want her to hear me cry. She's seen enough out of me for one day.

And maybe my dad was right. I have had enough for one day, but the day isn't through with me yet.

————

WHEN I GET TO MY ROOM, I'M SHOCKED TO SEE LIONEL standing there. He's got a deep frown on his face that looks even deeper because of his thick, old-fashioned mustache.

I sigh. "What is it?" I whisper.

He goes over to my desk and points at the drawer I keep the Ouija papers in. I sigh again and pull them out and get my diary and start recording his conversation.

"I AM SORRY" he points out on the Ouija papers.

"You saw all that?" I write, thinking he's referring to my train-wreck of a day.

"ENOUGH."

"But, I didn't see you."

"I DIDN'T WANT YOU TO."

I'm taken aback by that. I can't see him if he doesn't want me to? Then what about all those flashes I see in the graveyard. Is the reason I don't see more because they don't want me too?

And then my mind slips back to the last conversation I had with Lionel. After he had told me the names of his friends and I asked him why I could see him.

I write in my diary for a bit, it takes some time to get it out. "Last time you were here you lied to me. You said my illness wasn't why I could see you. I saw your face. You believe that is the reason."

"SORRY."

I write, "I need to know the truth. Is my leukemia coming back?"

I don't have any idea where this courage is coming from to ask this question. My life is in such a shambles now, why in the world would I ask a question like that? But I *need* to know. It's something primal in me. If this fight against Cancer is going to start again, I want to know as soon as possible, so I can...

Wow. So I can... what? What would I do if I knew it was coming back? How would I act? How would it change my life? If it does come back, that would be my "third strike." Each reoccurrence gets tougher to deal with, your odds of survival go down. I don't know if the third time means "out," but the mere thought of it scares the hell out of me.

But I can see freaking ghosts! That changes *everything*, doesn't it?

Lionel is quiet as all these thoughts pass through my mind. He's watching me closely, seeing the many emotions on my face. He's got his hands clasped in front of him, as if he is holding himself back from pointing at the Ouija paper and has a deadly serious look on his slim face.

I look at him and nod for him to continue.

"IT IS COMPLICATED," he points.

"So take your time. Tell me. Please."

He pauses again, his lips pursed. He takes what looks like a deep breath and nods.

"I WILL TELL YOU IF YOU PROMISE TO HELP ME TO FIND MY KILLER."

My stomach suddenly feels heavy. It's clear from that answer that I'm not going to like what he has to say. I feel tears stinging my eyes yet again. How much of this can anyone take?

"I promise," I write in my diary and hold it up for him. "I will do whatever I can."

He nods and starts pointing at the Ouija papers. "WE SENSE SOMETHING ABOUT YOU THAT IS DIFFER-

ENT. THAT YOU CAN SEE US IS EVIDENCE OF THAT. AND WE CAN ALSO SENSE THINGS HAPPENING IN YOUR BODY."

He pauses and points at me. First my thighs and then my chest. That would be the bone marrow in my thighs and sternum, where leukemia would definitely take hold.

"IT'S NOT MUCH RIGHT NOW. WE SENSE TINY DARK PLACES IN THERE. I WOULD GUESS IT IS THE CANCER TRYING TO COME BACK."

I'm staring at him blinking, yet more tears flowing. Part of me is fascinated that he can sense these things. I'm also distracted by his use of "WE." I only see him clearly, is he referring to other ghosts? I close my eyes tight and swivel my head around, but don't catch any flashes of light.

But it's all too much. This day is way, way too much.

"Thank you for telling me the truth," I write. "I would like to be alone now."

I watch as Lionel flies out my window. I think of going back downstairs and calling Helena. But I don't think this is something I can speak of yet.

When I turn off the one small light I had on to illuminate the Ouija papers and my diary, the darkness and the glow-in-the dark stars on my ceiling aren't as comforting as usual. I crawl into bed feeling very, very small, and much to my surprise, quickly fall asleep.

PART 4

A Family and Secrets

21

FRIDAY, JULY 1, 1977

WHEN I WAKE UP, FOR ONE SINGLE BREATH, I'M NOT QUITE with it and I don't remember all that has just happened. I just stare at my sloped ceiling, at the star stickers there. In the morning light, they are inert, but I still like them.

And then I remember. My mom and Doctor Rogers. My hiding from my family. Helena and our trip to see her mother. The dark spots the ghosts see in my body that may be my cancer "trying to come back." The secret my father has yet to tell me.

It's like a tsunami of emotions crashing on me. I am feeling so much, and all at once, that it's just a jumbled mess.

My breathing is shallow and my heart is thumping in my chest. I try to suck in air, but I can't get much in. I feel like I can't breathe, and I panic.

I bolt up in bed and a strangled cry escapes me. It's not much, but my father must have heard me, because he is soon there, sitting on my bed, holding me.

"It's okay, son. It's okay," he says as he rocks me gently.

"I... Can't... Breathe..." I gasp out.

He holds me away from him, his eyes locking onto mine. "You're having a panic attack. Just breathe slow. You're okay."

Except I don't feel okay. I start to struggle, to try to get out of his grip, but he holds me tightly. I'm eyeing the door. I want to escape.

"Aaron! Look at me."

I look at my father and really see him. He looks exhausted, with heavy bags under his eyes. He hasn't shaved and he doesn't look like his normal calm, collected self.

"Stop fighting," he says. "Take slow breaths. I'm right here. You're okay."

My heart is pounding so hard and the adrenaline flowing through my veins makes me want to bolt, but I do what he says. I focus on his grey eyes and ever so slowly start to calm down. He's breathing in this real exaggerated way, slow deep breaths. I try to copy him, and things start to work better. I start to feel like I can breathe again.

———

MY FATHER COOKS PANCAKES FOR BREAKFAST AND MY mother is not home yet. It's weird, having just the two of us at breakfast. A lot of nurses work weird shifts, but my mother has —since I first got sick—managed more normal shifts so she could be with us for breakfast and dinner.

I miss her. Badly. It just doesn't feel right.

"How are you feeling?" Dad asks as he puts a perfectly cooked pancake on my plate.

I pour the syrup on, smelling the sugary sweetness, and cut a piece with my fork. "I'm okay," I say. It feels like a lie, but really, I guess I am okay. I'm alive. I can breathe. No present emergency. Doesn't that qualify as okay?

I scratch my leg where Lionel pointed last night. Where one of the dark spots is they "sensed." It's a silly gesture. It's not my muscles that are involved if there's Cancer, it's the bone marrow. But I feel funny about my leg, as if it's plotting against me or something.

Breakfast is quiet. Just the sound of forks on the plates and the smell of Dad's coffee.

"Where's Mom?" I finally ask as I'm clearing the table and Dad's starting on the dishes.

"She called while you were in the shower. She went in early. We'll see her tonight."

"I want to go see her," I say. "Now."

He turns, the faucet running, soap covering his hands. His brow is furrowed and he doesn't speak but stares at me, his face a question.

"I want to make sure that the thing this morning was just a panic attack," I say. It's a lie, but I can't speak my fear yet.

He nods and goes back to his dishes. He washes a few more and then says, "Okay. Go get ready."

He doesn't think it was anything but a panic attack. And I really don't either. I've had a few over the years brought on by either the diagnosis or treatments I've been through. It has been a few years, and this morning I forgot what they were like in my… well… panic.

He probably thinks I just want to see my mother, and I do. But I am worried about the dark spots Lionel talked about. If I can just figure out a way to get them to take me seriously about it without thinking I'm crazy.

───────

I HATE THE SMELL OF HOSPITALS—ALL MEDICAL FACILITIES, really. That antiseptic tang just puts my nerves on edge. Too many bad memories. Too much pain. And way too much time spent in them.

My dad walks me in through the ER entrance and leaves

me in the waiting room and goes back to find my mother. He's gone long enough for me to get nervous, to worry that they are having a long conversation about me. But, it could easily be that she's just busy.

When she comes out, she's dressed in pale blue scrubs and walking fast, her jaw set, her eyes sharp. I know that look. I've seen it a thousand times before. It's the mother ready to protect her ill child. My dad is a few paces behind her, his hands shoved into his brown slacks.

"How are you feeling, Aaron?" she says as she squats down in front of me.

I grab her and hold her tight. "I'm real sorry about yesterday," I whisper. I mean it this time. The anger is gone and I'm just afraid now.

She hugs me back and when we part I see the tears welled up in her blue eyes. "Tell me what's going on." When it comes to me and my medical "issues," she has a one-track mind.

"Couldn't breathe this morning. I... Well... Dad thinks it was a panic attack. Probably was... but..."

"But what, dear?"

My heart is beating loud again and my mouth is suddenly dry. I've been healthy these last seven months. I've been good. I don't want to utter the C-word. I don't want to cause a panic. But, I've got to know, and I've got to utter my fear to get the test done.

I take a deep breath and sit up straight. "I'm afraid that it's coming back."

My mother's eyes widen. "Any symptoms?" she asks. "Fatigue, strange bruising, fever?" She puts the back of her hand to my forehead.

"No. I just... It's just a feeling."

She bites her lip and continues to look me over. She's feeling the lymph nodes in my neck, searching my arms for tiny pinpoint bruises called petechiae, but she doesn't find anything.

She stands and takes a deep breath, and for the first time in a while I notice my father. He's standing a pace behind her with his arms crossed, a deep frown on his face. Is he worried I have cancer or that I'm pulling something to get the attention away from what I did yesterday? I can't tell.

"Come on," she says to me as she walks towards the big double doors that lead back into the ER. "Let's get you checked out."

I feel a swell of relief and gratitude as I follow her. She has taken me seriously. Thank god.

———

DOCTOR SCHWARTZ EXAMINES ME AND ORDERS A BLOOD draw. He's a short man with balding grey hair who talks very rapidly. I'm just grateful it's not Doctor Rogers, although I keep seeing him walk by. He's on shift too.

My father sits with me in the little curtained area. They made me change into one of those horrible gowns that are open in the back (procedures and all) and I feel vulnerable in the bed with just that gown and a sheet covering me.

Doctor Schwartz is very thorough. He asks me lots of questions and does a more extensive version of what my mother did. I've been through this kind of thing a thousand times.

Dad has been silent during all of this. Too silent. It's making me nervous.

"Sorry about all the drama this morning," I say when I can't stand the silence anymore.

He nods and smiles briefly, but he won't keep eye contact with me. Is it me, or is it that secret he has from when Mom said, "This is not my fault. I didn't start this. You explain it to him"?

In the silence, I think about it. His secret is actually a

welcome distraction from worrying about leukemia. And then it occurs to me. "Do you have a girlfriend?"

He smiles again, but it's one of those tight, pained smiles. "No, son. I don't."

"Did you? Is that what started this?" I ask.

His brows furrow deeply and he gets that faraway look in his eyes. "No. And I owe you an explanation. But now is not the time or place."

I think on that for a moment. And I know he's right. It might, temporarily, easy my discomfort at being here, but it would a terrible place to be for another episode of the Wade Family Drama.

I bite my lip and wait for the test results to come back.

———

BILLY INTONES HIS FAVORITE WORD, SHIT, ABOUT A thousand times as I bring him up to speed. After the hospital, my dad went to the college, and having given me the day off from the bookstore, I called Billy and he rode his bike over.

I know Billy feels strange about Lionel and the whole ghost/religion thing. But I tell him everything and it feels good to get it out. Keeping something like that inside can be poison.

"And what did they find at the hospital?" he asks. Even though the house is empty we're in my room. I'm on my bed and Billy's on the floor. Unlike his, my room is neat. Very neat. I don't like things out of place, it makes me nervous.

"Nothing definitive," I say with a sigh. "My white blood counts are a little high and platelets low, which they are worried about, but it doesn't mean anything yet. The other main leukemia markers, immature white blood cells called 'blast cells' and other things like anemia, are missing."

He pauses, chewing on his lower lip and then running his

hands through his red hair. "So…" he begins, his voice much softer than normal. "What now?"

I laugh. On which front does he mean "what now?" With my family not being what I thought it was? With me and my perhaps returning Cancer? With Lionel and that I promised to solve his murder? My laughter starts out strained and tight, barely there. But as I think on these three things it starts to rumble out of me, the stress of the last day coming out. I laugh hard until my belly hurts and my face is wet with tears.

The whole time Billy is just staring at me with this pinched look on his round face. He's worried about me. His question, of course, was about my health, so I'm sure my laughter seems a little out of place to him.

"Sorry, B," I say when I can talk again. "It's just that… well, it's all a little too much."

He nods and asks me again, "What now?"

I take a deep breath and sigh. "The doctors will confer. Doctor Schwartz will talk to my oncologist in Vegas at the children's hospital. They'll decide what the next step is."

He nods gravely. "Are you scared?"

I feel the laughter coming back, but I bite it down. There is so much to be scared about—family, health, finding murderers. "Yeah," I say. "I'm scared, but…" I trail off. I know it's going to be hard to explain and might make Billy uncomfortable.

He does this tiny little nod and says, "Lionel."

I smile because it's Billy, my best friend Billy, and he knows what I'm thinking without me having to say it. "Yeah. Seeing him… Well, it kind of changes things, doesn't it?"

———

DAD COMES HOME EARLY, AT ABOUT 4 P.M. I'VE GOT MY head deep in Stephen King's "The Shining" in an attempt to distract myself and am sprawled out on the couch in the living room.

I hear his Pinto pull up and my heart starts beating faster. I don't move, keeping my eyes on the page.

When he walks in and I see the look on his face, I'm just dying to run away. He's got dark circles under his eyes and stubble all over his normally clean-shaven face. But that's not it. It's his eyes, they look a bit haunted. My dad is steady as a rock, calm to a fault, he doesn't look this way. Ever.

He places his leather briefcase down and comes into the living room, sitting in the uncomfortable rocking chair that I sat in last night after Helena brought me back. "I guess we need to talk," he says.

I note the page I'm on and slowly close the book, setting it down on the couch next to me.

My father rocks a little, then rubs his hands on his slacks, and then leans back in the rocking chair before tilting himself forward. This is not like him. He's not a fidgeter. How bad can this be?

"Dad," I say, trying to catch his eye, but I don't. "What is it? It can't be that bad, can it?"

He gives me one of those pained smiles and gets up and goes over to the bookshelf by the fireplace. There's a shelf there that doesn't have books but has little crystal decanters and glasses. He pours himself a drink of scotch, and not just two fingers, it looks more like three or four. Drinking this early and this much is also out of character.

He doesn't sit back down but takes a sip of his drink and starts this slow pacing back and forth across our tan shag carpet.

"I've done my best to try to educate you," he begins. "To teach you to think rationally and for yourself. To show you that the world is much bigger than what we see here in Cedar City." He pauses, turns toward me, and gestures at me with his glass. "And look at you. Kids your age would be glued to the TV, not you. You read. You read everything. And…" he trails off with a sigh.

I shift uncomfortably on the couch. TV doesn't interest me much, but not ever having one, I've had very few opportunities to watch it. And I do love books. With all my heart, I do. I know that is the part of me I got from my dad.

He sits down on the couch, the King book between us, and sets his drink down on the end table. It's covered with a white crocheted doily that my mom knitted. "I'm proud of who you are," he says, looking me right in the eye. "I need you to hear that, Aaron. I am very proud of you. You are a thoughtful young man, a hard worker, honest, and you have a very good mind."

I just blink. For my dad, this is effusive. "Thank you."

"And as I tell you what I must," he continues, "I hope that what I have taught you, the larger world I have tried to expose you to, comes into play." He sighs and grabs his drink, taking another sip.

I'm beginning to freak out a bit. This buildup, the longer it goes on, is making me more and more anxious.

But I don't have long to wait. He takes a deep breath and tells me his deep, dark secret.

———

MY DAD IS GAY.

There it is. In stark black and white. My dad is gay.

And not in the "joyous and/or happy" meaning of the word, the way it was used a few decades ago, but in the slang for homosexual.

My father is so scared as he tells me. I've read about people "coming out of the closet," so I know it can be difficult. And for my dad telling me, his sixteen-year-old son, it looks to be the hardest thing he has ever done.

My father is stoic. He's the very definition of stoic, and as he tells me he is everything but. And it is that change in his demeanor that freaks me out at first. He's nervous and twitchy, nursing his scotch and repeating himself a lot.

In this conversation, it's like I'm the parent and he's the child. He seems desperate for my approval. Desperate for me to tell him it's okay. That I still love him. That I understand.

Except, I don't…

Well, I do love him, but I don't understand and it doesn't feel okay.

"I knew when I was young, about your age," he says. "It was confusing. The other boys couldn't stop talking about girls… Not me… I…"

His shoulders are hunched and he's staring at his drink and not looking at me. "I was shy," he continues. "At first I thought it might just be that. This was more than twenty years ago, when homosexuality was more suppressed than it is today. I had no role models, knew no openly gay people, had no basis for understanding what I was feeling.

"And in some ways, it's like that for all teenagers—not understanding what you are feeling. I thought there was something wrong with me. I began to talk like the other boys, pretended I liked girls. That was the way it was supposed to be."

He gets up and pours himself more scotch. He sits back down in the rocking chair. "Growing up in Naperville in the early fifties—attitudes about homosexuality were harsh, full of misunderstanding and hate. In many ways like Cedar is today. Small town Utah is not exactly progressive when it comes to human sexual expression." He barks out a laugh and sips more of his drink.

"Wh… Why?" I manage to say.

His eyes widen and then his brow furrows. I hadn't got out what I wanted to say. He thinks I'm asking him why he is the way he is.

"Why Mom?" I say, finishing the question. "Why did you marry her? Why did you…" I can't say anymore. I don't understand. If he knew what he was (and that is a really terrible way to think about it, but that is what I thought then) why did he get married, and more importantly, why did he have a child… me?

"Fair question," he says. "I was raised Catholic. You know that, right?" I nod. He has some horror stories about going to Catholic school. "It wasn't okay to be who I was. So I changed myself. I… I buried that part of who I was as deep as I could. I pretended to like girls long enough until I believed I did." He shrugs, it's a pitiful thing, his shoulders barely rising an inch until falling lifelessly.

"Do you love her?" I ask. I'm sitting still on the couch watching him, but I feel this nervous energy coursing through my body. I want to shout, to run, to break something. But I don't, I sit there and ask the question with my father's usual calm.

"Yes, yes. Of course I love her. I love her with all my heart. I wish that I were different, that I could be who she needs. I… I tried. For so long I tried. But I can't… not anymore."

"Anymore? What happened?"

"The world has changed, Aaron. It may not be safe to be gay in Cedar City, but in larger cities, it's starting to be out in the open. It's starting to become tolerated, and in some cases, accepted. Don't get me wrong, it's still difficult and different and the bigotry is horrible. But things are moving… finally."

My own brow furrows as I contemplate his use of the word "bigotry." Not applied to different races, but different sexual orientation. It's a brief whisper and I don't pay much attention to it. "I… I don't understand. That doesn't sound right. The world changing is why you can't be who Mom needs you to be? Isn't it normal to give up things to be in a marriage?"

He sighs, gets up, and puts his half-empty glass back on the shelf. "It's not that simple, son. When you change who you are, who you essentially are, for too long... It... It..." He slumps back down into the rocking chair, leaning forward. "I tried... God, I tried for years and years. Your mother and I... we were never as passionate as many are, but it was good for a while." He bites on his lower lip, hard. "It comes out in small ways, terrible small ways, when you suppress something that big. We... we actually get along much better now. You've got to understand, she's my best friend. Our relationship isn't ideal, but we, the three of us, are a family."

There is more to all of this, so much more. I can feel it, like the iceberg lurking beneath the dark waters of the ocean. But I don't want to hear it. I don't want to know about it.

My father isn't who I thought he was. My family isn't what I thought it was.

"You're only together because of me, right?" The damn question slips out my lips. I feel the tears coming, but I am cool and calm in the moment. So cool and so calm that my father probably figures I can handle the answer. That I deserve to know the truth.

"Yes," he says, the room suddenly quiet, the ticking of the clock on the hearth all too loud.

I sit there for two breaths blinking until I can't hold the tears back anymore. I run from the room, my father calling my name, but I ignore him. I run up the stairs and lock myself in my room.

———

READING IS MY SOLACE IN THIS WORLD. IT'S A GIFT FROM MY

father and I love him for it. Books can educate, they can enter-
tain, and most importantly right now, they can distract.

Since locking myself in my room, I've been chugging
through some of Shakespeare's plays. *Hamlet, Macbeth, King Lear,*
all plays with seriously messed up families. Their problems are
so much bigger than mine, but similar. I've got family issues.
I've got a ghost who wants something from me.

The other thing about Shakespeare is its age. The language
is English, but 400 years old. I've got to really concentrate to
read it and look up the archaic usage of some phrases. It's
perfect. It's just what I need, and it's not helping. Not really. It's
nice not to think about all of this, but it is not solving anything.

It feels like my family has cancer. That this sickness has
been creeping under the surface for years, unseen by me, and
when I saw my mother with Doctor Rogers, the first symptom
finally appeared. As I ponder it between the pages of Shakespeare, I wonder what chemotherapy would be like for our
family. Something so terrible it would kill what was wrong but
not quite kill the family.

And then in my more compassionate moments, brief
though they are, I think maybe the problem is me. My lack of
understanding of the situation. But those are brief flickers, like
trying to light a candle in a hurricane.

I'm startled by a knock on my door. It's the third time this
has happened. The first was my father, the second was my
mother. "Go away," I yell.

"Okay," a husky female voice says. "Have it your way."

Helena was not the voice I was expecting. I leap out of my
bed, unlock the door, and rip it open. She's holding a tray with
a sandwich and some milk. Although my stomach rumbles, my
eyes are more hungry for her than for the food.

She walks in without saying another word. I close the door
and lock it behind us. She's wearing her La Familia skirt and
top and has quite a bit of makeup on.

I feel a brief wave of excitement. A beautiful girl in my room… for the first time, really. But that is washed away by my present reality and the firm friendship that Helena and I have built.

She puts the tray down on my desk and looks around the room, her eyes narrow, her lips pursed. "Just as I suspected," she says.

"What?" I ask, a bit confused.

"You're neat. Orderly. Everything has its place."

I shrug my shoulders. It doesn't seem important to me.

"My room," she says, "is quite the opposite. Chaos, but controlled. It may seem a mess, but I do know where everything is." She smiles briefly and adds, "For the most part, that is."

She sits heavily on my bed, bouncing a bit and takes up the large book of Shakespeare's complete works that I was reading. My growling stomach drives me towards the food and I eat quickly as she leafs through the book.

I sigh when I'm done, slumped in my wood desk chair.

"You can go to the bathroom if you want," Helena says, waving lazily towards the door. "They are both downstairs and won't be coming up while we have our little talk."

I nod and make a quick trip. I had been locked in my room for hours and was way past the need for a pit stop.

When I get back, Helena is up and pacing around my room, her arms folded in front of her.

"They told you… everything?" I ask.

She nods, not looking at me, and keeps pacing.

"Lionel… he… he saw dark spots. My leg and my sternum. That's why I wanted the tests."

She nods again but still doesn't look at me.

"My dad… he's… My family… it's…" I stammer, trying to express what I'm feeling, but getting nothing out. It's why she's here. They must have gotten ahold of her.

She finally stops pacing and stands right in front of me, her arms rather than crossed in front of her are more wrapped around her. She seems to be holding herself.

"I'm mad at you," she says, her voice low.

"Mad? What?"

She blinks a few times, a single tear running down her left cheek. "You get news like that—like what Lionel told you—and you don't tell me?"

"It was late. I didn't want to wake you."

"Bullshit," she says, the word tight and bitter. "I told you'd I'd be up late. That I was there for you. I want to know why you didn't tell me."

I scoot back in my chair until it bumps up into the desk. This is not what I expected from her.

"I called you earlier… about being grounded. We talked last night."

She shakes her head slowly, her golden-brown eyes focused on mine, unrelenting. She sniffs and breaks eye contact, moving to the bed and sitting on the edge, her spine erect. "I'm only going ask you one more time. Please tell me why you didn't call me."

I swear to god I don't understand women—or girls. There is a mystery there that is beyond me. What about our relationship made Helena expect I would call her instantly, tell her first? We're friends. Do friends do that?

"Truth or truth?" I ask.

She nods sharply, once.

"I was scared," I say. "I thought of calling you, but hadn't really gotten a grip on it myself. I didn't know what, or if, I was going to do anything about it."

She sighs and nods, but this time slowly, softly. Her head falling into her hands. She sniffs again.

"What are we, Helena?" I ask, my voice unsteady. "That you not hearing this instantly is so upsetting?"

Her jaw moves silently, her head still in her hands. She then slowly raises her head and looks at me with such intensity that I fidget in my seat and regret asking the question.

She licks her lips and smiles a wistful 20-watt smile. "I don't know, Wade. What are we?"

"Friends," I offer. "You've said it a thousand times."

"Does this feel like a normal friendship?" she asks.

I shake my head. "Never has."

I see the tears welling up in her eyes and it scares the hell out of me. I don't know what's going on in that beautiful head of hers. "No... it really doesn't feel like friendship," she says. "At least not *just* friendship. I find myself caring for you more than I want to."

"So what are we?" I ask. We are under the umbrella of Truth or Truth. It's safe to ask these things, isn't it? Safe to hear the truth, right? I almost laugh at that thought. I've been hearing way too much truth lately. Truth is often the most dangerous thing there is.

She shakes her head. "I don't know, Wade. I really don't know. But, please... let me be here with you for this. Let me be part of it." She pauses, leaning forward on the bed. "Can you do that?"

I nod my head, unsure of anything except that I want Helena Monfort to be part of my life.

———

MY LIFE HAS BECOME A SERIES OF PAINFULLY AWKWARD encounters, a new surprise around every corner.

Helena and I talk for a long time. Not about us. Not about what our relationship is or isn't, but about family and ghosts and Cancer.

I don't hold anything back. I tell her all of it... my fears, my concerns, my utter lack of understanding when it comes to my parents.

She is firm on that topic, though. Unwavering. That I have two parents that love me and will clearly sacrifice a lot for me, and that makes me a very lucky kid.

After a long time, but not long enough, she announces that she's got to go. Her shift is about to start.

"Thanks for…" I stammer. I don't want her to go. I don't want to face my parents. "Thanks for everything, Helena."

"Sure," she says, her hands wrapped around her chest again.

We stand there awkwardly in the middle of my room avoiding eye contact. And then she's hugging me. To call the hug fierce is an understatement, she's holding me so tightly. And I hug her back just as hard. I don't know what Helena is to me, but in such a short time she's become so important.

And then she's gone, and I'm left with her peppermint and cigarette scent. I run to the bathroom and then back to my room, locking the door, turning the lights off, and pulling the blankets up all the way to my nose.

It is a long time before sleep comes for me. One thing she said keeps running through my head: *I find myself caring for you more than I want to.*

22

SATURDAY, JULY 2, 1977

LAST NIGHT I DREAMED OF UNCLE DON, HIS BIG STRONG arms hoisting me in the air when I was maybe six. His bright face and blue eyes so joyful. He's tossing me up in the air just a bit, so I feel that brief moment of weightlessness. Like I can fly, free from the confines of the hard earth below.

I'm really too big for this game, but Uncle Don is strong enough to still do it with me. And it seems to delight him so. Or, rather, I think my delight is what is a joy to him. I laugh, and each time he puts me down I ask him to do it again.

I think it was summer and he was over for a picnic in our backyard. Aunt Janis and my cousin Bo are there, but Uncle Don still finds time for me. To toss me in the air over and over until he must have been so tired. But still he did it. Never quitting. Giving me that brief moment of weightlessness.

A banging on my door wakes me up from the dream and I come to consciousness missing my Uncle Don. I don't want to be awake and pull the cover over my eyes to shield them from the sunlight streaming in my dormer window.

"Aaron," my mother says between knocks. "Are you okay, honey?"

As my reality comes crashing back down on me, the question just seems ridiculous. "Fine," I growl, burrowing myself further under the covers.

"It's opening day," she says. "*Romeo and Juliet* at the new Globe Theatre. You don't want to miss it, do you?"

I peek my head out and look at the clock on my bed stand. It's 9:53 a.m. I'm surprised they let me sleep this long.

"Your father is so looking forward to it," Mom adds.

I groan and sit up, rubbing at the sleep caking my eyes. I was out for a long time and do feel a bit better. "All right," I say. "I'll be up in a few."

I sit there for a few minutes pondering my mom's behavior. Are we pretending that none of this happened? That we are still the tidy little "Leave it to Beaver" family toddling off to see a green show and a play? Pretending that nothing has changed?

As I make my bed, a part of me wants that so badly. To just pretend that none of this has happened. That everything is okay. That I am safe and sound.

———

A GREEN SHOW IS KIND OF LIKE AN ELIZABETHAN EQUIVALENT of a warmup act, a kind of a variety show. There is music and dancing and general bawdiness, often performed by some of the actors in the upcoming performance. In the old days, it was all the same troupe, I think at the Shakespeare Festival it's a bit of a mix.

There are four men and four women on the small stage on the lawn of Southern Utah University, with large fur and spruce trees providing shade for the audience that is either sitting on the lawn or standing. There's a mandolin, a flute, a little drum, and a few other instruments. They wear colorful costumes and it's slap-sticky and funny, but I'm not paying much attention.

Billy is there and we're sitting a bit away from our respective families, whispering to each other. I bring him briefly up to speed. He interjects his favorite curse word at appropriate intervals.

"What now?" he whispers when the brain-dump is over.

I shrug. "It's the weekend. We won't hear from the doctors until Monday at the earliest. As far as the family goes... I haven't the slightest clue."

I worry a bit about how Billy will take the "gay" thing. Christianity, in all its forms, is notoriously intolerant of it. I swear him to secrecy before I tell him.

Another part of the green show is women roaming the lawn in period costumes (skirts and bodices that show off a lot of cleavage) selling tarts. "Buy a tart from a tart," one says in an English accent as she passes by. She's practically spilling out of her top and smells of pie and cheap perfume. Billy's eyes follow her hungrily.

"And Helena actually said that," he whispers. "About caring more for you than she wants to?"

I nod. The tart selling tarts has distracted Billy in a rather predictable way.

"Dude," he says, "you gotta make a move."

I just stare at him. With a murder to solve, my family in shambles, and the threat of Cancer on the horizon, he wants me to make a move on Helena. I laugh. I love Billy, and his predictable teenage-maleness is refreshing. Of course it's the girl I should be focused on in his world.

"A move. Like what?" I ask.

He shrugs. "Kiss her, man. Just grab her and kiss her. Find out if there is something there or not."

The thought terrifies me and I'm sure that terror shows on my face.

He bangs his elbows into my ribs. "You gotta know, don't you?" he asks. "I mean, if there is one thing in this world you gotta know, that's it, isn't it? I mean, shit, man——"

Billy is interrupted by one of the tart sellers. "Would you gentlemen like a tart?" she asks.

With our eyes locked, we didn't see her walk up, but as she squats down in front of us, the strange minty scent of her quickens my pulse and I know who it is. Helena.

She's smiling big and pulling some warm tarts out of her basket. "These are broken, I'm afraid," she says as she pulls perfectly good tarts out of her basket and breaks them as she puts them on a napkin and hands them to us. "I can't charge for them."

Billy utters a strangled gasp before going silent. Helena is in one of those cleavage enhancing outfits and the view is… well… it's rather stunning.

"I didn't know you were going to be here," I say. I'm very consciously looking in her eyes. I'm quite sure Billy does not have that much decorum.

"I told you," she says, pointing to the south a bit, "under our tree last week. Remember?"

Last week. It seems like a year ago. But I do remember her telling me that she'd be here working.

"How's it going?" she asks, glancing at my parents and waving. They are looking at us—which they've been doing a lot of.

I shake my head. "Got up late. Hardly a word this morning. Seriously not looking forward to this evening."

"You can handle it, Wade. You believe that, don't you?"

I nod, but there is no enthusiasm.

"You can. Trust me." Her brown eyes and gentle smile make me want to believe.

"Yeah. I can handle it," I say.

Her smile gets wider and she turns to Billy. "Mr. Chadow.

If you ever expect a girl to pay attention to you, the absolute wrong approach is to unblinkingly stare at her breasts for minutes at a time."

"I... Um... Sorry," he stammers, his face going beet—and I mean beet—red.

Helena stands up gracefully and says, "I expect a call from you tonight." She sweeps away selling her tarts. I ignore the green show and Billy and just watch her.

She moves with such confidence and grace. How can she be so young and do that?

"She wants you to call her," Billy whispers. "You gotta make a move, man, you just gotta."

———

THE ADAM'S SHAKESPEARIAN THEATRE IS A BEAUTIFUL replica of the original Globe Theatre, with a stage that is two stories high (great for the balcony scenes), floor seating in front of the stage under the opening in the roof, and covered seating along the rim of the structure, two levels of it.

Before the play starts, there is a ribbon cutting ceremony. The president of the university gives a speech. And then Fred Adams, the man who founded the festival, gives another speech and cuts a big red ribbon that is set up at the front of the stage. It is, frankly, a bit boring until this odd fellow gives the final speech before the show.

He is short with a bit of a belly and bald, a strip of brown hair around his head. He has a huge smile on his face that makes me smile. All the pomp and circumstance is over and it is just him on the stage. At first I think he might be one of the actors, but he is dressed in tan slacks and a tie.

"Ladies and gentleman, welcome to the Adam's Shake-spearean Theatre," he says, gesturing broadly. His voice is a resonate baritone that fills the theatre easily. He has a presence on the stage which makes me think again that he must be an actor.

"Who is he?" I whisper to my father. The man looks familiar, but I can't place him.

"Banquo," Dad answers with a mischievous grin. Banquo is a character from Shakespeare, the ghost that haunts Macbeth. I am going to ask about that when he says, "Just listen."

"My name is Arthur McBride, but my students here have dubbed me 'Banquo,' after Macbeth's ghostly conscious. I have been a student of Shakespeare since I was old enough to read, and it has been my most distinct pleasure to tarry here in your fine city for the last five years working to make this theatre a reality. Helping to bring Shakespeare to the Desert Southwest.

"This is the most realistic reproduction of the Old Globe Theatre in North America. It was in a theatre that looked like this, under similar skies, that William Shakespeare presented many of his plays over four hundred years ago. It is his tradition that we honor here, presenting his works in the same environment that they were first presented in."

He stops, steps forward, and takes a deep breath. "But we have made some minor improvements. The seats, for example, are much more comfortable, and the female parts will be played by women, not boys in wigs." There is a smattering of laughter.

His speech goes on from there, and while I remember some more of it, what sticks with me is his passion. He loves Shakespeare's work and has devoted much of his life to its study. It's almost as if he has become an embodiment of Shakespeare's work, making it his mission to teach the younger generations of its majesty and power.

I am left with that delicious feeling of his passion and joy. I want a life like that, something that I am so passionate about I can spend all of my days with it and be happy.

Two thoughts pop in my head in that regard: Helena and

books. All of my days with those two things and how could I not be happy?

———

THE PLAY IS GLORIOUS, JUST GLORIOUS. FOR A FEW HOURS there, sandwiched between my mother and my father, I almost forget about all my troubles as I watch. In the first act when Romeo first sees Juliet he says:

O, she doth teach the torches to burn bright!
It seems she hangs upon the cheek of night
Like a rich jewel in an Ethiope's ear;
Beauty too rich for use, for earth too dear!

And I think of Helena, how can I not with that poetic description of beauty. As the play unfolds and forces conspire to keep Romeo and Juliet apart, I keep rooting for them even though I know their fate.

The last line of the play sums it up: "For never was a story of more woe / Than this of Juliet and her Romeo." Love, misunderstanding, and tragedy all mixed together in one of the most celebrated works of English literature.

The thoughts of my life that do intrude continue to be mostly of Helena. After seeing her in her "tart" outfit and the new ambiguity of our relationship, I can't but hope for more. Even if it is a tale of woe, I want more with her. I want as much as I can get.

The other thing that catches my attention are the ghosts. Not that I can see them clearly, just the wisps of light seen out of my peripheral vision when my eyes are closed. I notice it first when I blink. And then I start closing my eyes briefly—trying desperately not to draw my parents' attention—and really see them.

It's odd. As the actors move across the stage, the wisps of light, the ghosts, follow them. It takes a bit to dawn on me, but

I soon realize that the ghosts are performing the play too. There is a ghost Romeo and ghost Juliet, a ghost Mercutio and all the others. They know the same blocking the actors do. They time their movements perfectly with the actors.

And once when I look up at the clear blue sky, I close my eyes and see more wisps of light just above us. There is a ghost audience.

When I realize what's going on, that there is a parallel performance and audience of ghosts, I smile the biggest smile. I'm not sure I can explain why, but it is a delight to me. It gives me hope to know that if I am a ghost, I can still watch plays or maybe even perform in one.

It may seem like a small thing, but in that moment, something clicks in my head, that isn't so small. Maybe death isn't so bad after all.

———

DINNER IS QUIET AND OH SO STILTED AGAIN AND I CAN'T wait for it to be over. There is some awkward sitting around and pretending (at least on my part) to read in the living room before my parents head up to bed.

After they do, I'm in the pantry and on the phone so fast it would make you dizzy.

She expects a call, I'm going to call.

A man with a deep voice answers the phone. "Hello."

I'm taken aback for a moment. Who is this man answering Helena's phone? But it only lasts a moment, it's her father, of course. And then there is a whole new terror. What if he doesn't like me? What if he doesn't approve of our friendship?

"Hello? Is anyone there?" he says.

"Umm... Hello, Mr. Monfort," I say, getting my nerves under control. "This is Aaron Wade. Is Helena there?"

"Just a moment," he says, his voice flat and he sounds sad.

What could be sad about someone calling for his daughter? My mind starts racing out of control worrying that so many boys are calling for her that he is tired from having to answer it all the time. That he automatically hates me and doesn't want me near his daughter. I know Helena has started dating someone new… what about that and our "not a normal friendship?"

"Hey, Wade," Helena says when she gets on the phone.

My palms are sweating and I'm all worked up at this point. The uncertainty of it all is driving me nuts. "Hi," I say. It's all I can get out.

"How'd it go with the folks?"

"We seem to have lapsed into eternal, non-communicative silence," I say.

"So… do something about it."

"Like what?"

"Start the conversation," she says. "You're a big boy now. If your parents can't get the ball rolling, you should. Figure out what you need, what you want to know, and start the conversation."

I chew on my lip, thinking about it. It's a good idea, but I cringe when she calls me "big boy." Then the thought flips to her. I want to have a conversation about "us" and if she's not starting it, then I should.

"Umm… I… You…" I stammer. Great start

She laughs, it's rich and thick. "Spit it out."

I take a deep breath and pretend I'm as cool and collected as my father normally is. "I was wondering if we could clarify things a bit. I'm wondering what 'not just friendship' means."

There's silence on the other end of the phone and the steak in my stomach suddenly feels like lead. I hear her shifting around before she says, "I don't know what it means." More silence and then, "What do you think it means?"

"You're the one that said it. I know what I want." My heart is thumping in my chest.

Another pause. "What do you want, Wade?"

"As much of you as you will let me have," I say.

I hear her sigh. "It's complicated."

"I know," I say. "You're dating someone new. I don't care. Whatever you want to give, I'm here. I want it. Just let me know what that is." My whole body is quivering with energy. My voice wasn't exactly steady when I said all that, but at least I said it.

"Is that the truth?" she asks.

"I swear, Helena. I swear."

"It's complicated," she says again.

I give a brief snort. "Ain't that the truth?"

"Can I think about it?"

"Of course," I say. After another pause I add, "But I will admit the waiting is likely to drive me nuts."

She laughs briefly. "Listen, Wade, I should go. We've got family day tomorrow and I've got some things to talk to my dad about before my shift."

"Yeah... okay. I hope your visit with your mom is a good one."

"Me too. Do you think you'll hear from the doctors on Monday?"

"Should. We'll talk then. I'll call you when I know something."

"You're a weird kid, Wade. You know that?" she asks.

"And you're a fascinating woman, Helena."

After she hangs up I slump on the five-gallon bucket like some rag doll. The adrenaline has left me and I am exhausted. It wasn't the move Billy suggested, but it was a move.

23

TUESDAY, JULY 5, 1977

THE REST OF THE WEEKEND IS PURE TORTURE. I DON'T "start the conversation" with my parents. I can't. It's like we're all stuck in a Shakespearean purgatory.

We go through the motions of our lives—eating, talking, resting—and it might look like things are okay, but underneath everything is roiling. Mom probably wants to be with her boyfriend. Dad... God, I don't know where, or with who, my father wants to be. And I'm stuck in this family that isn't what I thought it was. And we are all waiting for the call. From the doctor. About my tests.

Monday is the Fourth of July and we are barely present for it, dutifully barbequing and watching what we can see of the fireworks from our backyard.

The phone call comes early on Tuesday morning. Mom and I are in the kitchen cleaning up from our oatmeal with blueberries breakfast and Dad is checking the oil in the Chevelle.

When the phone rings, my mother jumps. Her blue eyes

find mine and I can see the fear there. We've had way too many bad phone calls for us not to feel some fear.

She picks it up on the second ring. "Hello," she says, wrapping the long curly cord around her free hand. "What?" She nods, a grim look on her face as she listens and my knees turn to jelly. "Yes. I've already gotten the day off." She's nodding now, her face serious. "We'll be there."

When she hangs up, her hand rests on the white phone in its wall holder. Her shoulders are slumped and she's silent. I know it's not great news, but I'm not sure if I want to know anymore. She takes a deep breath, her shoulders straightening, and turns to me. "Doctor Wright wants to see you today," she says with a twisted little smile. "He's concerned about your white counts and wants to do more tests. We've got an appointment at eleven. We've got to get moving."

I nod and say, "I'll get ready." I move slowly towards the stairs. This news is not surprising. We were expecting it. But the reality of it is still hard. One step closer to… To what? To more treatments? To death? To life as a ghost?

I chuckle at the last part. Life as a ghost. What is life as a ghost really like?

———

LAS VEGAS IS OUR "CITY." IT'S ABOUT TWO AND HALF HOURS southwest of us and an hour closer than Salt Lake City. Las Vegas is where we go if we need to fly somewhere, shop at a mall, or go to a major hospital.

Doctor Wright, my oncologist, works at Sunrise Children's Hospital. It's such a cheery name for such a difficult place.

It's a strange place. Las Vegas and the hospital. Las Vegas is this sprawling city nestled in a parched desert valley. So many houses, so many people, so much going on in such a dry, dry place. I hear the Colorado River doesn't make it to the sea anymore, supporting desert cities like Vegas.

The hospital is strange too. It's in the "normal" part of Vegas, away from the strip right across from the Las Vegas Country Club, with its cheery green grass that is grown in defiance of the hot sun.

Doctor Wright's offices are just east of the hospital. We park on the black asphalt and do the "walk." At 105 degrees, the heat is nearly unbearable and hits me like a solid force, like a brick, when I open the door.

My father, who drove, stretches a bit when he gets out and then claps his hands behind his back as he moves towards the two-story building that houses many of the hospital's doctors. My mother smooths her tan skirt and clasps her hands in front of her. She looks back at me, giving me a thin smile, and heads the twenty yards across the crowded parking lot to the door of the office building.

We've done this before, dozens of times. I believe Doctor Wright is good—I'm still alive, aren't I? But it's almost never a good thing when we come here.

I'm frozen, standing still by the car, the desert heat sucking away my nervous sweat, making my mouth dry. It's not lost on me that I initiated this, asking for tests in Cedar after Lionel told me about the dark places he can see in my body. It's because of that we are here. I know that, but I still can't move.

Part of me knows, I think, that the news, ultimately, won't be good. That we are facing another round of treatments. My third strike. It's not my mind that knows, but my body. That's why I'm frozen there, like some damn Egyptian statue. Anubis stuck under the internal glare of the desert sun.

My folks are halfway to the door before they notice. My mom looks back and then my father. They whisper something and she heads towards the door, and air-conditioning, and my father comes back for me.

"I know," he says, gently putting his hand on my shoulder.

"I... I don't know if I can do this again," I say, my voice a little too high, my hands shaking.

"Do what?" he asks.

"Treatments," I say, staring at the black of the asphalt. "I can't do chemo again. I just can't." The memory of the weakness, the pain, the endless nausea come rushing back. The days stuck in my house, unable to see anyone but my parents for fear that my compromised immune system can't handle a visitor. The vomiting, the diarrhea, the barely being able to stand some days.

My father sighs and puts his hand on my chin and gently raises my head until I can see his grey eyes. "Listen to me, Aaron. We don't know anything yet. This isn't about treatments, this is about assessment. We need to know, don't we?"

But I don't want to know now. What good will it do? How many times do we have to beat this leukemia monster back? How many more "treatments" can my body possibly stand?

"Dad... this... why is this happening to us?" I ask. It's the more important question. And it is happening to "us" not just me. If there are more treatments to be had, it will have a huge impact on their lives too.

"I don't know, son. I wish I did. But it *is* happening, and we can't hide from it. We have to deal with it." He takes a deep breath and does his best to put a smile on, but it's not very convincing. "Besides. This time it's probably nothing."

I nod and let him guide me in. But it wasn't "nothing."

———

LIFE AS A GHOST. THAT THOUGHT BEGINS TO BECOME something of a lifeline for me. What is it like, life as a ghost?

I know this is a distraction. I know it may not be the best thing for me to be dwelling on (the word morbid does comes to mind). But the reality of my death is, I think, a lot more real to me than to other people, especially those my age. I can see Lionel, he's a ghost, so isn't it natural for me to wonder what life is like as a ghost?

Tuesday is mostly a blur of poking and prodding that I receive at the hospital after we see Doctor Wright. He doesn't have that much to say, just a tiny smile below his thin grey mustache. They need to know more. That means hours of waiting in the hospital, nearly choking on the antiseptic tang that brings back such bad memories, followed by the aforementioned poking and prodding.

They draw blood. Take my temperature. They poke at my lymph nodes and look at my gums. They do a needle biopsy of my bone marrow by shoving a needle into my pelvis (sheer joy). I'm less a person than an object of study.

My parents are good. They try to keep my spirits up. They offer to take me to Circus Circus to play some games on the way home, but it's nearly dark when we get out and there isn't time.

And the whole time I wonder about life as a ghost.

I'm honestly a little afraid of what it means. Am I giving up? Have I lost the will to fight this disease? And if I have, isn't that a valid reaction to what I've been through? Quantity of life is not the only measure. Quality has to be in the equation. I've been having an amazing summer (in that I'm amazed, not in that it's all been fantabulous) and I don't want to go back to being the "chemo" kid.

I call Helena as soon as we get home. I call her on the kitchen phone, and when I get her, I walk right into the pantry and close the door without a trace of shame. There is an inch-high crack at the bottom of the door and the long curly cord fits there just fine. I see the look my mother gives me and then my father, but I don't care. I need to have private conversations.

We don't talk long. There's nothing really to say. They poked, they prodded, and now we wait for the next phone call.

I'm in a state, a foul mood. My parents are being all optimistic. That since I don't have any symptoms yet, there is nothing really going on. I don't believe it. I know something is going on. Lionel can see it. Lionel is real. And that takes me back to my distraction: What is his life like?

As soon as dinner is over and I've cleared the table, I excuse myself and go up to my room. I don't want the forced cheerfulness or strained silences that keep occurring. I want to be alone.

But when I get to my room, I'm not alone. Lionel is there. I smile. Maybe I can find out what his life is like. Maybe that will help.

———

OUR CONVERSATION IS REALLY LONG. WE SPEND HOURS WITH me writing in my Lionel diary.

A while back, I started recording my raw interactions with him encoded in a separate book. It's a bit time consuming because I have to write the question encrypted and unencrypted, hold up the diary for him to read, write down his answer as he points at the Ouija papers. I then black out the unencrypted question with a sharpie and a scrap piece of paper underneath so it doesn't bleed through.

It's worth it though, I end up with just what I need. I have the raw questions and answers, but I've decided to record a portion of it here in my main diary for clarity.

"I'M SORRY FOR WHAT IS HAPPENING TO YOU," he points out on the Ouija papers.

I nod and thank him.

"I HAVE BEEN WITH YOU ALL DAY. I HEARD SOME CONVERSATIONS YOU DID NOT. BETWEEN

DOCTOR WRIGHT AND HIS NURSE. BETWEEN THE NURSES DOING YOUR TESTS."

My mouth drops open. He was with me? "I didn't see you," I write. "Why didn't I see you?"

He smiles at me. His lips don't move much, but it's more in his eyes. It's a smile full of compassion and it affects me in two ways. It makes me wonder who would want to murder this man, and that makes me even more dedicated to helping him.

"IT TAKES EFFORT FOR ME TO PRESENT MYSELF IN A WAY WHERE YOU CAN SEE ME. IT IS VERY TIRING. THAT IS WHY I AM OFTEN GONE FOR A WHILE AFTER OUR TALKS. I AM RESTING. BUT, WHEN I AM NOT RESTING, I AM WITH YOU."

"Okay," I write. "So go back to your normal mode right now. Let me see if I can detect you at all."

He nods and then is suddenly gone. I can't see him at all. I close my eyes, cover them with my hands. Sure enough, where Lionel was is one of those flashes of light that I can only see out of the corner of my eye. "I see you," I whisper to him.

He moves a little around the room and I take one hand off my eyes and point at him as he moves. I feel this brief moment of happiness. A mystery solved. I can see Lionel because he is doing "something" so that I can see him. That something is tiring. When he doesn't do it, he looks like all the other ghosts do to me.

I mean, it's not like I understand the whole thing, but at least I know why I can see Lionel. It's not just my ability, it's his efforts too.

I open my eyes and whisper, "Come back." And then I can see him again.

"What is life like for you as a ghost?" I write.

He folds his arms, takes a pace to the left and to the right, and then comes back to the Ouija papers. "IT'S NOT SO BAD, BUT I REALLY MISS BEING ALIVE. I MISS FOOD

AND SMELLS AND THE FEEL OF THINGS." He pauses, his hand rubbing at his mustache a bit before continuing. "BUT I DON'T WANT TO BE A GHOST. I WANT TO MOVE ON. AND TO DO THAT..." He stops pointing and looks at me intently.

"I will start investigating just as soon as I can," I write. "I'm grounded right now. Please be patient."

He nods and smiles and we talk for quite a while longer. He doesn't tell me much about "life as a ghost." It's like he's shy to share it, or doesn't like it, or is withholding information intentionally. I can't tell. But, still, it's comforting to me to know. It may mess with my atheistic leanings, but I like knowing that consciousness goes beyond the body.

It's what I've got right now. I cling to it.

24

WEDNESDAY, JULY 6, 1977

I SPEND MY MORNING CLEANING MY ROOM. IT'S ALWAYS NEAT, but I really clean it, going through everything, dusting, throwing out some old broken toys, looking at every book.

It is, I know, an attempt to gain some control of my life. So much is beyond my ability to effect change. This is not, so I go at it with gusto.

As I do, I realize that unless he is resting, Lionel is with me. This is comforting to me somehow.

I take my shift at the bookstore and I'm surprised when Arthur McBride, aka Banquo, walks into the bookstore. I don't know why I'm surprised, he seems a likely customer. I have been pondering him and his passion ever since the theatre opened.

He comes in with a girl a few years younger than me. She has long brown hair, braces, and a good helping of pimples on her face. Banquo has his hand on her shoulder and I figured she must be his daughter.

After the play, I had begun to think back on why the man was so familiar. He had been in town for five years. I had seen him at some Christmas parties at the university, and I think he'd been in the bookstore a time or two. But, I don't think we had ever interacted.

"Anything you want, Page?" he says quietly to the girl, his hand gesturing across the shelves of the store. I am sitting behind the counter trying not to be nosy but being nosy anyway.

She goes straight for the Nancy Drew section, which makes me smile, given what Helena and I are up to. He goes to our section on Shakespeare, which makes me feel a bit self-conscious. He is the expert. I'm worried that we don't have a good enough collection.

I get off my stool behind the counter and walk over. He is thumbing through *Asimov's Guide to Shakespeare*. "Can I help you find anything, Mr. Banquo?"

He looks up and smiles. His face can be rather stern, but when he smiles he really lights up and looks like a young man. I would guess he is in his early forties like my father, but his smile makes him look more like he's in his twenties.

"I'm fine, my boy," he says, looking me up and down. "You're Henry Wade's son, aren't you?"

"Yes, sir." I smell tobacco on his breath, but different than Helena. Not cigarettes, probably cigars.

His smile disappears and his forehead crinkles. It is his version of the leukemia look. He is wondering if I am healthy, if I am okay. "It's okay to ask," I say.

Banquo looks surprised, but then he looks me up and down again and smiles. I suspect he's reevaluating what he thinks of me. "How is your health?"

"Bad news recently," I say.

"I'm so sorry."

I nod and then scan our Shakespeare shelf, thinking over his body of work. "Can I ask you a question, Mr. Banquo?"

"Of course."

"Do you believe in ghosts?" He looks puzzled, so I pull out one of our nice leather-bound *Complete Works of Shakespeare* and flip through it. "*Hamlet, King Lear*, and of course *Macbeth*. They all have ghosts in them. Shakespeare wrote about them and the supernatural over and over. Do you think they are real?"

I know I have good evidence that ghosts are real, but there is a sliver of me that still doubts. A part of me that doesn't want to believe in what my eyes are seeing. It goes against my view of this world. It makes me wonder what I really know.

Banquo, his lips pursed, pauses for a minute and looks me over. "I'm sorry, my boy. I don't believe in ghosts. I believe Shakespeare used them and things like witches and magic to put into stark relief aspects of the human condition. It was just a literary device he used. We can't be sure, of course, it was a long time ago, but I don't think the Bard believed in ghosts."

I nod. I want to tell him about Lionel, about the proof I have. Run this by another adult, but I don't. His daughter walks up to me and asks, "Do you have volume 16 of Nancy Drew? It's the next one and I don't see it on the shelf."

She's got brown hair and warm brown eyes and a nice smile like her father. "Let me check in the back," I say and scurry off.

Shakespeare used ghosts as a literary device. It makes sense, but Lionel isn't a literary device. He's real. Either that or I am totally bonkers and so is Helena.

———

LATER, BILLY COMES BY AND I TELL HIM ABOUT THE POKING and prodding and the usual, awful wait until we know the results. He's good about it all, listening carefully, a neutral expression on his face. He's been through this before, he knows what it's like.

When the store is empty I ask him, "I've got more on

Lionel, do you want to hear it?" Given his previous discomfort, I think it's important to ask him.

He nods but looks down. We're both seated on stools behind the counter. No books to shelve and not many customers, so it's been a slow day.

"Maybe I shouldn't," I say. He's a Mormon, I'm an atheist (I think). We're best friends. I don't want to push him too far.

"No," he says, meeting my eyes. "I want to hear. I've… I've been thinking about this whole ghost thing."

"And…"

"And… so what," he says with a shrug of his shoulders. "There can be a god and there can be angels, and there can be ghosts too. Even if the church doesn't talk about it. Even if it's not in the Bible."

I smile and am glad. It was difficult not having Billy fully with me. I'm so used to it, he's been with me through everything for such a long time. So I tell him all of it, in great detail. The ghost. Helena. My family. Everything.

After it's all over, he says, "We've got to start looking for his murderer." His tone is low and conspiratorial.

"Yeah," I say, nodding my head. "But I am super grounded."

"Did they say for how long?"

I think back. They didn't. "No, but I got the impression it was for a long, long time."

25

FRIDAY, JULY 8, 1977

MY DAYS GROUNDED AND WAITING FOR THE DOCTORS TO GET
back to us have fallen into a pattern. After the folks leave, I do
something around the house to feel like I have some control.
Wash my bike, clean my room, sweep the sidewalk and the
back patio. After I did all that I started cleaning the house too.
It's obsessive, but for once in my life reading doesn't feel like
enough. I have energy and strength, I'm sure as hell going to
use it.

Then I go do my shift at the bookstore. Billy comes by for
the early part of it and Helena comes towards the end.

I then dutifully ride my bike straight home. I want to go by
the graveyard and see if Big Ed is there. I want to ride by Billy's
house or go by the DQ and get some soft serve. But I don't.
Straight home.

Once there I'm tired enough, so I read until the folks come
home, usually sprawled on the couch in the living room. When
my parents come home, I shift to my room. Our conversations
are still so superficial, I can't stand it. We have an awkward

dinner, then it's back to my room and once it's fully dark I chat with Lionel.

This morning that all changed. And how.

The phone rings, it's Doctor Wright's office. It's my mom that takes the call. We're in the middle of waffles and it's almost like time freezes while she's got the phone to her ear.

My dad has a bite of waffle held above his plate, syrup dripping from it. I've got a glass of milk in my hand, my eyes on my mother, my ears perked. She doesn't say much, but the frown on her face grows as she listens, nodding occasionally.

I bite my lip, and hard. I've written that I knew the Cancer was back, but I still had a sliver of hope that it wasn't, that Lionel was wrong, that those "dark spots" he saw were something else.

When she hangs up the phone, she stands there for a moment facing away from us, her shoulders slumped, her hand resting on the white phone. Dad and I are still frozen, still waiting.

When she turns, any doubts I have evaporate. She sniffs and rubs at the tears forming in her eyes.

"The results are in," she says. "He didn't tell me much, just that he wants to see us today. He wants to start treatments today."

And there it is. The dreaded news.

———

I WAS MORE READY FOR IT THAN THEY WERE. Intellectually at least. There's a lot of chaos as we leave. Mom has to call in and get her shift covered, Dad cancels his classes. Mom has me pack a bag in case I'm not fit to travel after they are done with the "treatment."

We've done this before. We all know what to do, but it's like we've all forgotten. We keep getting in each other's ways, forgetting stuff and having to do things twice.

It's the shock of it, I'm sure. And the worry. We know the big-C is back, we just don't know to what degree. That uncertainty makes us weak.

———

I CAN'T IMAGINE DOING DOCTOR WRIGHT'S JOB. TELLING kids they have Cancer. Prescribing them the most difficult of treatments. Watching many of them die. I can't imagine it.

His grey eyes always look tired, they're the color of his short hair and thin mustache. He looks washed out, as if his job has sucked all the vibrance out of him.

"It's remarkable, really," he says, a smile on his face. He's behind his big wooden desk. My mother and I are seated in wooden chairs across from him, and my father is standing, his hands on the back of the chair I'm in.

"I mean that," he continues. "We never catch an occurrence this early. It's remarkable. It gives us a fighting chance, but we've got to hit it hard."

I groan, I can't help it. To hit it "hard" we have to say bye-bye to my quality of life. I take a deep breath and bite on my lower lip to hold the tears back.

"I want to start treatments today. We're going to want to see you every Friday for eight weeks." He goes on detailing the treatment course, the chemicals they will be using, but I tune out.

Eight weeks. The rest of the summer. Chemo hell.

I can't stand it. I just can't stand it.

———

NAUSEA. IT'S A TERRIBLE THING. THIS CONSTANT FEELING

that something isn't right, that never goes away, that sucks the will out of you, that makes food seem like an enemy and keeps the specter of vomiting close.

It sucks. Chemo is all about nausea. Tons and tons of it. Unrelenting nausea. It's always there. It never goes away, not completely.

I hate it. With all my heart, I hate it.

The first treatment hasn't been that bad so far, but it definitely brought the nausea on, and that brought all the baggage of surviving two rounds of Cancer back with a vengeance. I feel a bit weak and dizzy physically, but emotionally, it's like I've been getting chemo every day for a week. I'm depressed, worried that I'm dying, realizing that my nice summer is over. It's back to being the sick kid. Back to my parents taking care of me and worrying about me and having that "look" in their eyes every time I catch them watching me.

The "look." It's subtle, but I've come to know it well.

We're in the chemo room. It's set up with these fancy, dental-like chairs for the patients and hard wooden chairs for the family. There are eight of these setups in the big open room, with two other seats occupied. The walls are a nice light green and there are a few windows that let some sunshine in. The IV is in my arm and the chemo is dripping into my veins, I catch my mom with the look. Dad is talking to me about what we need to reorder at the bookstore. Nothing all that important, he is just trying to distract me. He actually had me laughing, asking me how I enjoyed the latest bodice ripper by Rosemary Rogers. I counter and ask him how he likes it.

I turn to my mom to ask her how she likes it, my mouth open, but freeze when I see the "look." Her eyes wide and a bit vacant. Her mouth slack, her eyebrows slightly furrowed. She isn't here. She is off in the future envisioning my death, or my funeral, or life in our house without me.

I hate it when I see that look. It's only human, I know, for them to envision the future they fear, but I feel terrible when I see them doing it. It makes me scared. If they can see a future without me in it, does that mean something? Logically I know it doesn't, but logic isn't the whole story. It feels true emotionally, and that is hard.

I forge on, though, anything to break the spell. "How did you enjoy *Sweet Savage Love*, Mom?" I say, with a somewhat diminished giggle. "Dad says it's a masterpiece of bodice ripping. Destined to be read and reread hundreds of years from now."

She blinks twice, a frown forming on her face. "What?"

I'm about to go on with the joke, but for some reason I don't. I don't want to fall into all the same old patterns, counteracting the "look" by pretending there is nothing wrong. Putting on a brave face when I'm scared to death. Us doing everything we can to avoid the conversations we need to have.

I'm not the kid I was last time we did this.

"I'm scared too, Mom," I say, all humor gone from my voice.

She blinks a few more times and nods and then forces a smile on to her face. "Oh… No.. no… You're going to be fine, Aaron. You heard Doctor Wright, we got it early, we're going to beat this thing."

I take a deep breath and glance at my father. He looks dead serious and I'm not sure what's going through his head. I was hoping for some encouragement on this path, but there is none there.

I reach out my hand to her. She hesitates and then takes it, squeezing it hard. "Mom, I need something from you and Dad. It's important." She nods and I can feel a slight tremor of fear in her hand. "As a family, we need to speak the truth to each other. No more pretending things are okay when they are not. No more hiding the truth, even if it's a hard truth and we don't want to hear it."

She lets go of my hand and wraps her arms around her chest.

"The truth is," I continue, "we don't know what is going to happen. We're going to fight, as hard as we can. But we don't know what the result will be."

She purses her lips, tears forming in her eyes, and she nods. She fumbles in her purse and pulls out a handkerchief, blotting at her eyes. She then abruptly stands, her chair scraping against the linoleum of the chemo room floor. "I need some coffee, either of you need anything?" She doesn't wait for an answer but rushes out of the room.

————

WE HUMANS ARE SO COMPLICATED, AREN'T WE? MY NEED for the truth was not exactly what my mother needed right then. She needed something different. She needed to believe that I would be all right.

"You've got to understand," my father says after my mother has been gone for twenty minutes. "There's got to be hope."

I'm confused. "I didn't say there wasn't hope. That there wasn't a chance. I just said it wasn't guaranteed. We all know that."

He nods, rubbing at his chin. "I know that, son. But there is a big difference between the meaning of what you said and how it feels."

"So what do I do? Go along with the delusion, swearing that I'm going to live forever until the day I die?" I feel my face flushing with anger. "What good is that? How can it help to deny the basic truths of this world we live in?"

Dad takes a deep breath and sighs, rolling his shoulders and stretching his neck. "All I'm advocating, son, is empathy. You should certainly be truthful, but consider others' feelings regarding the truth. Find a way to—"

"To allow others' delusions?" I ask, my voice too loud. Others are starting to stare. "To encourage my mother to live in a fantasy land regarding my health, like you and Mom had me in a fantasy about our family?"

My father's face hardens, and he leans back from me. "It's complicated, Aaron."

I snort. "No doubt. I'm sure you had a brilliant reason to lie to your son about who you are and what kind of sham marriage you have, staying together only because you got a kid with Cancer."

My father's face doesn't change, he's a stone, hiding what he is feeling from me. It seems to me what was going on had something to do with the chemo—or at least I hope it did. I am starting the conversation that I needed to have with my folks, that Helena encouraged me to start, but it was coming out all twisted and wrong.

I am angry at them, but a lot more angry at what is happening to me.

Without any resistance from him, my anger dissipates and I start to feel embarrassed. This is not the time or place for this. "I... I'm..." I stammer. "Can you please go check on Mom? I'll be fine by myself."

He nods sharply and leaves.

26

SATURDAY, JULY 9, 1977

I'M A DUMB-ASS. I CAN BE SO STUPID SOMETIMES. AS I THINK on it, the chemo has to be partially to blame... it has to be. Those chemicals mess with your body in such a profound way your emotions end up all over the place.

New rule. Don't start any heavy discussions the day of or the day after chemo. Just try to get through those days one single breath at a time. If your life is only about your survival, that's not much of a life. But some days (i.e. chemo days), it has to be enough.

Case in point, me and Helena.

She came over on Saturday, early in the afternoon. The chemo was hitting me pretty hard and I was all nauseous and burbley. My mother and father were there and supportive, but we still had all this distance between us. My mom was bruised from my stating the "truth" and my father was just quiet. We were all adjusting.

One day, healthy and having a good summer. The next day, a nauseous wreck.

"You want me here, right?" Helena asks. She has shorts and

a T-shirt on, her longs legs stretched out in front of her as she slouches in a chair on the covered portion of the patio. Mom has made us lemonade and the glasses, covered with condensation, sit on a little metal table between us. I have been kind of quiet, so I think that's what inspired the question.

"Of course," I say, doing my best to smile through the yucks.

She slides her chair around so it is facing me and takes my hands in hers. They are warm and a little rougher than I expect. I like the feel of them. "I know you feel like shit," she says. "But I need you to talk to me. Tell me what's going on. What I can do?"

"Don't have a magic wand handy, do you?"

She smiles and shakes her head. "No magic cures here. Fresh out. I used my last bit of magic to turn Jeff Tate into a frog."

I smile, but it's weak and halfhearted. "I'm scared."

She nods. "So am I. We all are."

It's a simple word, "we." In this circumstance, it's an honest one. Although "I" am the one with cancer, it is "we" that have to deal with it and, indeed, survive it. It's not just happening to me. I get that intellectually and for the most part I get it emotionally. But not then. I felt horrible and I had had enough of people wanting me to be empathic with them. I was the one with the goddamn leukemia.

"It's different for me, though," I say.

"What?"

"It's different. You're scared because I might die, but I'm the one whose white blood cells aren't being produced correctly. I'm the one that got pumped full of poison yesterday. I'm the one who feels like throwing up every single waking second."

She leans back, letting go of my hands and says, "I get that."

"No," I say, my voice rising. "I don't think you do. I don't think any of you do." I say the last part to our sliding glass door. My parents are sitting inside talking at the kitchen table. I'm sure they can hear me.

"Calm down, Aaron," Helena says.

"No. I will not calm down," I say, sliding my chair back and standing up. "I'm the one," I yell at my parents who, judging from the shocked looks on their faces, can definitely hear me. My hand goes to my stomach, the activity is making me feel worse. "I'm the one with the goddamn Cancer. I'm the one." I then turn to Helena. "Do you get that? Do you understand?"

Even though she's got her arms crossed and her jaw set, I can see that she's scared. She's still sitting but is leaning as far away from me as she can.

I swallow hard, tasting that terrible metallicy tang that comes from the chemo. It, like the nausea, is a near constant companion, reminding me over and over that I am sick, that these treatments are hell, that I may not survive.

"I get it," she says, her voice low and dangerous. "You're the only one here having an experience that matters. Your pain is worse than mine or your parents, so ours don't count. Your suffering is all that you can see right now, not anyone else's."

She rises abruptly and turns her back to me and walks to the gate leading to our front yard. A moment later I hear the tires of her father's car squeal as she drives away.

27

SUNDAY, JULY 10, 1977

I HAVEN'T APOLOGIZED TO ANYONE YET. I JUST CAN'T. I'M starting to feel better today, but still not very good. I'm mostly tired and the obligatory chemo mouth sores have arrived right on time. I was up tossing my cookies in the night. My body knows the shit they put into me is poison, thus the nausea and vomiting.

My mom is there helping me when it happens. Handing me a towel, getting me a glass of water, doing those little things that do help. She looks tired in her pink robe and so vulnerable.

At breakfast I have a little juice with my pills, but I'm scared to have anything else. I almost tell them I'm sorry. I know my fit yesterday wasn't fair or right. But I don't. I decide that maybe actions are better than words in this case.

"Can I go to church with you?" I ask my mother.

She's surprised. I know she is. My first offer to go to church was to do something nice for her because I was healthy. Now that we are in treatments again and I've been such a dumb-ass, it seems I should work even harder to find nice things to do for her.

"Are you up for it?" she asks, giving me her appraising, nursely look.

"I don't feel great, but yeah, I think I can manage," I say.

She nods, a brief smile on her lips. My dad is staring at me, he's trying to figure out what I'm up to, but he doesn't say anything.

AS I SIT ON THE HARD PEW AMONG THE PARISHIONERS AT our small Lutheran church, I ponder what's going on. All these people share a set of beliefs that revolve around sin, redemption, how to live your life, and what happens when you die.

They believe something. They all think they *know* what happens after our bodies are done with us. This, presumably, gives them peace of mind, helps them deal with the inherent cruelty of our biological lives.

In the middle of Pastor West's sermon, feeling like I want to throw up, I suddenly get it. Why religion is so successful—just looking at it in terms of its popularity. It would be a relief to "know" what's going to happen to me when I die.

I then look around and wonder if Lionel is here. He's something I don't have to believe in. When I proved to Helena he existed, I proved to myself that he existed. I am not imagining it. Lionel does not require belief. He exists independent of anything I think.

I *proved* Lionel exists. Proved.

Something clicks in my head and I look at my mom and smile. She looks back at me and smiles too. She probably figures I've had some kind of religious epiphany or something. Well, it's an epiphany, just not religious.

I know what I need to do, after the appropriate groveling and apologies, of course.

28

TUESDAY, JULY 12, 1977

OUR TABLE IS MORE FULL THAN USUAL. BILLY AND HELENA are here and so is Lionel. I've got a plan. It took some doing to arrange.

Step 1: Apologize for my dumb-assery. After church on Sunday, I apologized to my parents and told them the truth—that I was struggling with the news and the chemo. I then waited until pretty late and called Helena from the pantry and told her the same. She wasn't all that keen to accept it until I told her my plan.

Step 2: Arrange for all parties to be present. I talk my parents into letting Billy and Helena come over for dinner, since I'm all grounded and stuff. I then arrange for Lionel's presence next time I saw him.

Step 3: Be nervous as hell. It's a big leap I am about to ask my parents to make, but I've got to do it. I've got to clear out the junk and start living my life—especially now.

I clear my throat as everyone is about done eating. Mom made meatloaf and mashed potatoes with gravy. Usually one of my favorites, but my stomach is still kinda chemo-ized and I mostly just ate the potatoes without any gravy.

"I have a confession to make," I say, rubbing my sweating palms on my jeans. Helena catches my eye and nods and Billy bites his lip. Parental trust is not the teenage norm. But my situation and relationship with my parents is not normal.

"First of all, I want to apologize again for being so... you know." I feel the heat of shame on my cheeks. While there was some truth to what I said—I am the one with the Cancer—it was mostly self-obsessed BS. This is hard for everyone. "I am sorry. This has not been easy, not for any of us."

My mom smiles and says, "Thank you, Aaron. We appreciate your apology."

"And now to the confession." I take a deep breath and let out a long sigh. Dad has got his arms crossed and Mom is a little blinky and appears to be nervous. "I need you two to keep an open mind as to what I'm about to say. I can prove it and am prepared to do so, but you need to be open and give me the time to do it."

"What is going on here?" Dad asks, his brow furrowed.

"I've... I..." I stammer, looking desperately at my friends for help. Billy looks away, but Helena gives me a nod.

"Something extraordinary has happened to your son," Helena says to my parents. "It's time you knew about it."

"What? Aaron, what is this?" Mom says.

"I have something I need to do, something important," I say, swallowing hard. "I made a friend, a very unique friend, and he needs my help. I want to introduce you to him so you understand. So you let me help him."

"Is someone else coming over?" Dad asks.

"He's already here," I say.

"Well, I'm just confused," Dad says. "Frankly, Aaron, you're not making much sense."

How do you tell your parents something like this? I don't

want them to think I'm crazy. I want them to believe me. I want them to let me help Lionel.

"Just spit it out," Billy says. "There is no other way."

I nod, looking at everyone seated at the table with me. Mom, Dad, Billy, Helena. I then close my eyes tight and cover them with my hands and see Lionel standing behind my parents. He's nodding towards me slowly and he gives me a thumbs-up.

When I open my eyes, my folks are seriously staring at me. They're all worried so I figure it probably doesn't matter and just tell them. "I see ghosts. There is one named Lionel with us right now. I can prove it."

———

I EXPECTED NOISE, LOTS OF IT. YELLS OF DISBELIEF OR CRIES of worry. That's not what I got.

"What?" Dad says.

"Ghosts?" Mom says.

I nod. "I can only see one ghost clearly. His name is Lionel Malak."

Recognition blooms on my father's face. "The printer who had a shop near the bookstore? The one that was murdered?"

I nod, my mouth dry, the scent of the meatloaf making me nauseous.

"Ghosts?" Mom asks again, slowly shaking her head. She seems distant, as if caught up in an old memory.

"I… I thought you were sneaking out at night to see Helena," Dad says, looking at Helena and then me.

"I was. But to see Lionel, too. It's got to be dark for me to see him easily."

"I… Oh…" Mom stammers.

"Is this true?" Dad asks Helena.

"Yes, Mr. Wade. He proved it to me. "

"My…" My mother says as she stands, her hand brushing at her face. "I…"

My father surges up. "Laura, what is it? What's wrong?"

She looks at my father, her eyes wide and says, "Ghosts. There… there's no such thing as ghosts."

"I can prove it, Mom," I say. "Just give me a chance."

"I… I think I need to lie down, Henry. Can you help me upstairs?" Mom says.

He nods and puts his arm around her, gently guiding her. She's acting like she's drugged or drunk. Something is clearly wrong.

———

I'VE GOT THE NERVES, BAD. HELENA, BILLY, AND I ARE sitting in the living room. I'm in that uncomfortable rocking chair again.

After my father took my mother away, we stared across the dinner table at each other for a few minutes until Helena told us it was time to clean up. We took care of the kitchen, quietly and quickly, and ended up in the living room. Waiting.

"Is he still here?" Billy asks, his eyes narrow, as if squinting will help him see the ghost.

I close my eyes and cover them with my hands. Lionel is pacing nervously across the shag carpet of the living room. Somehow that helps calm me some. I tell Billy.

"Should you go check on them?" Helena asks.

I shake my head. It's an adults-only thing that's going on up there. I don't think I'd be welcomed.

Helena gets up and starts perusing one of the bookshelves. My dad calls it his "essentials." It's got everything from Homer to Dickens to King. Books that are already classics or ones he thinks are bound to be. Actually, Stephen King is there because of me. I'll occasionally suggest a new author for the essentials and we'll have great big debates about it. After King released *Salem's Lot* I was able to make a convincing argument that he belonged there, even though it's only his second novel.

She's got Tom Sawyer open when my dad walks into the living room. He's pale and looks a bit lost.

"Your mother won't be joining us," he says, his voice a bit shaky. And that scares me. My dad is not a shaky voice kind of guy.

"Is she okay?" I ask.

"It's just… she will be, Aaron. She just needs to rest right now."

"But… I need to prove this to her too. That I can see Lionel."

The smile he gives me freaks me out. It's more of a crazy smile than a happy smile, all lopsided with a bit of a tremble. I might have expected this kind of look after I proved I could see Lionel. Not before. "Oh, she already believes you, son," he says.

It's like the air just got sucked out of the room. Helena is frozen with the book halfway back to the shelf. Billy is blinking and chewing on his fingernail and I'm leaning forward in the rocking chair.

My father takes a deep breath, straightens up, and squares his shoulders. "Now, let's get to this," he says, his voice back to normal. "Prove to me that ghosts are real."

———

IT TOOK MORE THAN LIONEL TELLING ME WHAT FINGERS HE had held up to prove things to my father. It took a lot more.

He ended up moving us all back into the kitchen while he setup one of the "essential" books in the living room for Lionel to read and convey to me. It took me getting my Ouija papers and us turning all the lights out so I could see him clearly and easily.

I had a little penlight that I used to record what he pointed out into the diary. It was eerie, I must say. My dad standing in the doorway of the kitchen watching us, making sure none of us was sneaking into the living room and looking at the book. Helena sitting next to me leaning towards me, as if closeness might help her see what I was seeing. Billy sitting across the kitchen table from me, leaning away, continuing to chew on his fingernails. And Lionel going back and forth to the living room and back into the kitchen. He, for one, seemed happy, a smile on his face as he floated through the wall as he went back and forth getting me a few words at a time. (I think he was avoiding walking through my father, which I appreciate).

When it was done, we turned the lights back on and I handed my diary to my dad. He picked up what I had written and read it.

"Tired?" he said. "Well, I should think so. And now I will tell you all about it, since you have treated me so well. I am the spirit of the Petrified Man that lies across the street there in the museum. I am the ghost of the Cardiff Giant. I can have no rest, no peace, till they have given that poor body burial again. Now what was the most natural thing for me to do, to make men satisfy this wish? Terrify them into it! haunt the place where the body lay! So I haunted the museum night after night. I even got other spirits to help me. But it did no good, for nobody ever came to the museum at midnight. Then it occurred to me to come over the way and haunt this place a little. I felt that if I ever got a hearing I must succeed, for I had the most efficient company that perdition could furnish. Night after night we have shivered around through these mildewed halls, dragging chains, groaning, whispering, tramping up and down stairs, till, to tell you the truth, I am almost worn out. But when I saw a light in your room tonight I roused my energies again and went at it with a deal of the old freshness. But I am tired out—entirely fagged out. Give me, I beseech you, give me some hope!"

I didn't recognize the passage, but the humor of it being

about a ghost was not lost on me. Dad took it and came back with a collection of Mark Twain short stories, which I hadn't read. The story title is, quite simply, "A Ghost Story." He sits down at the table with us and goes word by word over the book and my diary. At the end he closes both, leans back and sighs.

"I have no explanation for this," he says.

Billy is blinking too much. He hadn't seen proof of Lionel before, he had taken my word.

"It's real, Mister Wade," Helena says.

Dad nods and rubs at his chin and then looks at me. "Without your mother vouching for this, I still wouldn't believe it."

I'm scared and excited. There's another secret in the family, but this one is about ghosts. My mother believes me without any proof. Why?

"And I assume there is a reason you're choosing to tell me this now," he continues.

I nod, but don't speak. There's just too much whirling around my head. Too much for me to come up with a coherent sentence.

"Can you tell me what it is?" he asks.

I nod again and take a deep breath. I'm wishing either Helena or Billy would speak up, but it is not theirs to do. They are here to support me. I sit up straight and square my shoulders, pretending again I have my father's unflappable calm (well, nearly unflappable, as I am learning).

"Just like that ghost in Mark Twain's story, Lionel needs help," I say, my heart thumping loudly. "He needs to know who killed him. He… he wants me to find his murderer."

Dad sits there blinking, his jaw slack for the longest time.

"We have a plan," Helena says, a gentle smile on her face. "We're going to interview his three closest friends. We'll tell them it's for a paper Aaron is doing, makeup work for missing so much school."

"He won't be doing this alone," Billy says. "One of us will be with him the whole time."

"We'll be real careful, Dad," I say. "We're not going to go out and accuse people of his murder. We're just going to do some interviews. Lionel will be with us too. I... We... Please, Dad. Please. I need to do this. Lionel is my friend, he is suffering not knowing who killed him and why."

My dad takes a deep breath and says, "No." With that he gets up and leaves the kitchen.

"Lionel is the reason we caught my leukemia so early," I call after him, but he doesn't turn around.

We hear his footsteps on the stairs, undoubtedly to check on my mother.

"What now?" Billy asks.

I feel my cheeks flush again, but this time it's not shame, it's anger. I told the truth. I proved something amazing and all I got was a one-word answer from my father. I deserve more.

"We're going to do it anyway," I say.

29

WEDNESDAY, JULY 13, 1977

Vincent Long reminds me a bit of Lionel Malak. He's whip thin and tall—just like Lionel. He looks different, though, with his short black hair and a few days' growth of beard.

"We went to high school together," Vincent says, taking a drag on his cigarette and blowing the bluish smoke up towards the ceiling. We're sitting in the Cedar City Diner on Main Street. "I hated him at first, he had this aloof air that I thought was about him thinking he was better than everyone else, but it turns out he was just shy."

We're in one of the tall-backed booths with red vinyl covering it. Mr. Long is drinking coffee and Helena and I have Cokes. Billy is at the bookstore covering for me—Helena picked me up from my shift early.

I'm taking notes in my diary as he talks. He may look a bit like Lionel, but he sure seems to be more of a talker.

"Lionel put together the school yearbook starting his sophomore year in 1958. He just had this eye for detail, and he was so damn meticulous." Mr. Long stubs out his cigarette and looks at me. "Why are we doing this, again? Talking about Lionel, I mean."

"It's an assignment for English. I've missed a lot of school and am trying to make things up a bit over the summer."

He nods, his dark eyes locking with mine. I'm afraid he doesn't believe me. "What's your name again, kid?"

"Aaron Wade, and this is Helena Monfort."

He nods, his chin ending with it tilted up as he gazes down at us. "How did you know Lionel?"

"My dad runs Cedar Books and Such. I work there. Lionel's place was just a few doors down," I say, trying to step around his questions. The truth is I didn't really know Lionel when he was alive. I had met him, I knew who he was, but he kept to himself.

Mr. Long sips his coffee noisily and fiddles with the stub he just put in the ashtray. Helena is mostly quiet, watching the two of us. She's sitting in the booth next to me, her nearness something of a distraction. She was the one that came up with meeting these people in a public place—safer that way. Vincent Long works at a local garage and is dressed in a dirty denim shirt with his name embroidered on the pocket. He smells of oil, and grease is imbedded under his fingernails.

He takes a deep breath, letting out a noisy sigh. "I miss the shy little bugger," he says. "Crying shame what happened to him. Crying shame. Never harmed a person in his whole life, and someone ends up shoving a sharp piece of metal in his back."

"Do... do have any idea who would want to do it?" I ask. He has been reminiscing about Lionel for a while, but I didn't expect it to be this easy to get him talking about the murder.

He scratches at his scraggly beard and shakes his head. "He had that big job he was working on for the food bank the night it happened. I had been there earlier helping box up some of the brochures."

"Was he all right then?" Helena asks, leaning forward. "Was anything unusual?"

He snorts. "It was Lionel, things were always unusual with him. He was an odd bird, if you know what I mean. But, no. It was all the norm for him. He was stressed, being behind on the job, which he absolutely hated—and is why I was over lending a hand. He knew Paul Durr, son of a bitch that he is, would be raising a ruckus."

"Do you think he did it?" I ask, my voice low.

Vincent bites his lip, his eyes going distant for a moment. "I thought he might have. You know, it's a weird thing. Paul's got this big fancy mission and yet he's such a dick. You'd think the people doing the supposed nice things in this world would be nice themselves."

"But you don't think he did it now?" Helena asks.

"Nahhh," he says, sipping more coffee. "He's an asshole, but he's not a murderer. I got a hold of him after the police let him go. I was sure he did it and wanted a piece of his flesh. I cornered him in his office in the food bank's warehouse. Little chicken-shit about peed his pants when I got a hold of him—I was none too gentle in my questioning. Turns out Paul's all bark, no bite, if you know what I mean."

"Yes, sir," I say. "I know what you mean."

"Do you have any idea who might have done it?" Helena asks.

"Believe me, I want to know. I want to know bad." He leans close, his eyes searching our faces. "You two fancy yourselves as Nancy Drew and one of the Hardy Boys?"

"What... No..." I stammer, feeling the flush of blood on my cheeks. "It's my... my extra credit for English."

He leans back and laughs loudly. "Bullshit." I'm blinking too much and I know it, and Helena is fidgeting in her seat. I didn't think we'd be this easy to see through. "But, relax, okay. Your secret is safe with me." He takes a scrap of paper out of his back pocket and pulls a pen from the front of his overalls and writes on it. "You find out who did it and you need some help, you call me. Here's my home number and my work number."

"Thank you," I say, making sure I can read his sloppy writing.

"And if you want to make a friend for life, call me when you crack this case. I want to be there to see the son of a bitch that done this get dragged to jail. Lionel may have been a weirdo loner, but he was a good guy. He was my friend." Vincent rubs at his eyes to stop what I think are tears forming there.

After he leaves, Helena looks at me and says, "Well, it's not him."

I nod and say, "I'll consult with Lionel tonight, see what he thinks."

————

As we're driving down Main Street from the diner back to Cedar Books and Such, we see my dad going into the bookstore.

"Shit!" I say. Billy is in there, behind the counter, but how long will it be until my father finds out I'm not there.

"He didn't see us, Plan B," Helena says, taking a sharp left onto 65 North Street and then pulling up in the parking lot behind the bookstore. The stores facing Main Street are not all the same size, so behind them is an irregular sized parking lot that fills out the space between the buildings that face Main Street and the ones that face the other roads on the block. On our way to the bookstore, we pass what used to be Lionel Malak's print shop. I see the sign on the back door hasn't been replaced. "Malak Printing and Signs" it says.

I don't have but a moment to look at the sign before we're past it and Helena's got me in front of the bookstore's back door. She lets me out and leans over and says, "Stay calm. It's all part of the plan." She then drives off. I stand there for a moment watching the yellow Comet go, trying to calm myself.

We did plan for this. My father's return to the bookstore from the university isn't exactly on a set schedule.

I slowly open the back door and breathe a sigh of relief when the bell doesn't ring, Billy disabled it and oiled the hinges earlier.

I can hear Billy and Dad talking out front as I slowly close the door behind me, pulling it ever so gently shut. I ease open the door to the storeroom (which wasn't all the way closed and also had its hinges oiled) and use my foot to slide a box to disguise any noise I might be making.

The storeroom of the bookstore is a place I love. It's about density. There are more books here per square foot than in the main part of the bookstore. There's a desk in one corner, where my dad does the business stuff, but most if it is strong metal shelving with box after box of books. New books we haven't unpacked yet. Overstock we've got to ship back. One whole shelf that is our supply of Shakespeare books—Dad buys a lot of them when they are on sale and saves them for the tourist season. Books that are on order neatly laid out and visible with a receipt on each one that we are waiting for the customers to come in for.

There are also cleaning supplies, stock for the rest of the store (like stationery and diaries and tourist stuff), but it's mostly books.

I fumble around a bit more, making noise intentionally, and come out with a box I prepared before I left. It's got a few Bach's, a complete works of William Shakespeare, the new *Time* we just got in with Jimmy Carter on the cover, and the feather duster.

"Hey, Dad," I say when I get out there with the box. My heart is pounding loudly, but I do my best to act normal.

"How have sales been today?" he asks.

I glance at Billy and he's rubbing his chin awkwardly with this thumb and index finger—he's signaling we made two sales while I was gone. "Six customers," I say, adding the four that I rang up before I left. I don't meet his eyes for long and start putting the books on the shelves, dusting as I go.

Dad takes Billy's place behind the counter and Billy walks over. "Shit!" he whispers to me.

I give him a small grin and nod. We had prepared for this. We had planned for this. We had been hoping not to need it.

"Same time tomorrow?" he asks in a normal tone.

"I'll be here," I say. "Thanks for hanging, B."

"Any time, A," he says, heading out the door.

It's quiet then, Dad's looking through the receipts for the day and I'm shelving the books and magazines and doing more dusting. Dad is crazy about us keeping the dust off the books. "Dust is no friend of a book, so it's no friend of mine, " he says all the time. Fastidious is the word. It seems to come naturally to me, I am that way too. My father and I have a shared hate for dust mites and that scent that infects books that have those mites chomping on them.

"How are you feeling today?" Dad asks when I end up back at the counter with my empty box.

"Good," I say. "I mean, not as good before chemo started back up, but not bad. I haven't wanted to puke every waking moment today."

My dad nods and then gets an odd look on his face. He leans over the counter and sniffs me loudly, his eyes narrowing.

"Is there something you want to tell me, Aaron?" he asks, leaning back and crossing his arms.

"No, sir," I say. It's the truth, there is not a thing I want to tell him.

"How's Helena today?" he asks.

I'm taken aback. How does he know? The sniffing? I lean

over and smell my shirt—button down dress shirt, can't wear T-shirts while on duty—and get a whiff of Vincent Long's cigarette smell. Dad thinks it was Helena.

"I'm... She..." I stammer, feeling that heat of shame on my cheeks again. I can't believe that I've been caught already. He doesn't know what we were doing, but he knows I was with Helena.

He smiles and shakes his head. "You really ought to take her out to dinner or something."

"What?" I ask. I'm confused.

He leans forward, putting his elbows on the counter, our heads almost at the same level. "If you two are sneaking off in the middle of your shift, the least you can do is take the girl out. Buy her some food."

My mouth is open, my eyes are blinking, and my cheeks feel like they are on fire. He thinks we were sneaking off to make out or something, not go interview a potential murderer. "But... She... I..." I stammer some more. My mouth and my brain just don't seem to be connected.

Dad sits back up and laughs. "Think about it."

I nod, taking the empty box into the back room. I get the box cutter and break it down and put it on the low shelf we keep empty boxes on. Folks that are moving sometimes come in and ask for them, we like to oblige them if we can.

I pause and take a few deep breaths. Helena and I out on a "date." I had never thought of the idea, but now that it's in my brain it begins to take over like some freaking virus. A date with Helena. She had said she's not sure where we are in our relationship. I've told her I'd take whatever she wants to give and don't care if she is seeing that yet-to-be-named other boy.

A date with Helena. I get this cheesy picture in my mind of candlelight and soft music. She's wearing a dress, I'm wearing a tie. We're sitting at this little round table and the waiter brings fancy dishes with silver metal covers. With a flourish the waiter removes them revealing an exquisite plate of surf and turf. Helena leans over to me, a smile on her face, her hand reaching to mine—

But I'm grounded. The thought rudely derails my little fantasy and heat comes back to my cheeks, but this time it's anger.

I stomp back into the bookstore. "I'm grounded you know. So... umm... thanks for putting a thought in my head I can't possibly act on."

I stomp back into the storeroom and fumble with an unopened box of books. This is usually one of my favorite activities. It's a little like Christmas every time—I never quite know what I'm going to find. I've got the box cutter in my hand, but it's shaking. Asking Helena out on a date never occurred to me. There are other hurdles besides being grounded. Like getting her to say yes, not having a car (or a driver's license, haven't gotten around to that yet), having no idea what to do or say on a date.

But the thought of it... My god, I can think of nothing else.

"I'm sorry, Aaron," Dad says from the door to the store-room. "I wasn't thinking when I said that." He pauses and then smiles. "But I'll tell you what. I'll talk to your mother, see if we can have a special dispensation for this."

I'm staring at him, box cutter in hand. "Th... Thanks," I say, and then look down. I can't meet his gaze. There's guilt (letting him believe what he wants to about how I got smelling like cigarettes), surprise (that there might be some relief from being grounded), and desire (I can't tell you how much I want to do this but barely dare to hope it can happen).

"I'm going to try hard on this," Dad adds. "Cause... you know... every man should have a shot at the woman of his dreams."

I can't help it, I'm staring at him again. Is Helena the "woman of my dreams"? Well... yeah. Duh! The romantic phrasing, though, had never occurred to me. Another thought that occurs to me is that this is one of my dad's "just in case you don't live long enough" things. He had fought hard to let me go to Disneyland with Uncle Don when I was twelve. It was during my first remission and my mother and father couldn't go, but Uncle Don had a haul out to Anaheim and thought it would be fun to take me along.

He was going to fight for this because he didn't know if I would live long enough to have another chance at a date with a girl. With the "woman of my dreams."

"How you feel about her is obvious to anyone with eyes," Dad says. "I'll do what I can, but there will be some conditions if I can get your mom to agree."

"Conditions? Like what?"

He smiled. "Just the usual. Knowing where you're going, when you're going to be back. And… and you and I will have to have a man to man talk first."

I nod, it still feels like a dream. Date. Helena. Woman of my dreams. "Sure, Dad. Thank you for this." I'm biting my lip now and he's smiling a real smile.

"We're not there yet, but I'm going to do my best."

30

THURSDAY, JULY 14, 1977

HELENA AND I DON'T GO OUT INTERVIEWING POTENTIAL murderers today—we still need to interview Ann and Joe Edwards—I'm a bit spooked by the close call we had yesterday.

Lionel didn't have much to add last night to what we got from Vincent Long. He did say that he believes what Vincent said and that we should trust him.

"What do we know about the Edwards?" I ask. Helena is leaning against the counter of the bookstore, I am sitting behind it. Her cigarettey-minty scent is in full force as she chomps on her gum.

"They're local business owners, just like Lionel," she says, snapping out a little bubble with her Wrigley's. "They have been married nine years and run the bakery two blocks down." She lazily waves to the north. "They've got weird hours—arising at an ungodly time to start baking bread—and seem to keep mostly to themselves. No one's got anything bad to say about them, but no one's got anything particularly good to say either. Except that their éclairs are to die for... a fact I can heartily attest to." She grins, a hungry smile on her face. Which makes me think of what Dad said about taking her out.

I straighten up on the stool. I had been slouching a lot today. And not just the normal teenage slouch, but the chemo slouch. I don't feel particularly bad, but my energy is complete shit and I can't get that metallic chemoy taste out of my mouth. It's driving me a little nuts, to be honest. And there is one more component to the fatigued slouch—I didn't sleep very well. Lionel and I talked briefly, and after that, as I closed my eyes and tried to sleep, thoughts of Helena—a date with Helena— plagued me like a batch of hungry mosquitoes up at Navajo Lake in the middle of summer.

"You keep looking at me funny," she says.

"You're beautiful," I say, the words slipping out accompanied by a flush of heat on my cheeks. "I... What I..." I stammer.

She laughs, straightening up and shrugging. She's got on jeans and a form-fitting blue shirt. The shrug makes me want to stare at her chest, but I don't, I look away. I remember what she told Billy when he was staring at her in her tart outfit at the green show. *Mr. Chadow. If you ever expect a girl to pay attention to you, the absolute wrong approach is to unblinkingly stare at her breasts for minutes at a time.*

But god did I want to stare.

I take a deep breath, meet her eyes, and slowly say what I was trying to say. "You're beautiful, so beautiful it's hard to look away."

Now Helena's cheeks flush red and she looks down. "Thank you."

"I... I was wondering about something," I say. I'm already embarrassed, my heart is beating a loud rhythm in my ears, what is there to lose at this point? My dad was right, I don't know what's going to happen to me, time seems to be less on my side than most people.

"What?" she asks, her brown eyes meeting mine.

"Can we go out sometime? I mean, provided I can get permission and you want to. I mean... only if you want to. I don't have a car and I can't drive, but maybe you could borrow your dad's car. I'm sure my father would drive us, but that would be—like—so embarrassing." I'm rambling and I know it, my eyes wandering the bookstore and avoiding hers. Maybe since I actually got it out, I can't stop talking. Maybe I just keep babbling because I am afraid of her answer. "It doesn't have to be anything big, just the two of us at dinner. A movie if you like. I mean if you want to, I know that what we are, beyond friends, is not exactly well defined, but why can't we just have a meal. If it's just as friends, that's fine with me, if it's—"

She puts her finger on my lips and I look at her. She's not smiling, her face is actually rather serious and my heart flutters and does a backflip and I swallow. "Shut up, Aaron," she says, but her voice is soft, almost a whisper.

"I... Well..." I stammer, her finger still pressed to my lips. It's not much in the scale of these things, but it somehow feels intimate to me. Not a kiss or anything, but she's touching me.

"Shhh."

I nod, my cheeks feeling like they are on fire and she slowly takes her finger away and licks her lips. I swear I'm going to die soon if she doesn't say anything, but I keep my mouth shut and stare at her like some love-struck fool (which I am, of course).

She bites her lip and says, "You know that it's complicated, right?"

"I don't care," I say. "I meant what I said." I was referring to our recent phone call where I told her I would take whatever she would give, no questions asked.

She's looking at me hard, her eyes searching mine. "You really don't, do you?"

"No."

"That is not normal, you know. Most boys get jealous so easily."

I shrug. I don't understand why. Maybe it's the leukemia and all the life I've missed because of that. Maybe it's that we have a solid friendship already. Maybe it's because I'm some kind of mutant, emotionally transformed by the repeated infusions of chemicals in my brain.

Her eyebrows furrow as she continues to study me. I know she's looking for signs of jealousy, of me not telling the truth, but it's not there for her to find.

"Okay," she says and then nods. "We'll do it."

My smile is huge and my whole face feels warm. The most beautiful girl in the whole town just agreed to go out with me. What is there to not be happy about? Now, if only Dad comes through and lets it happen.

———

WE CHAT SOME MORE, HELENA LEANING AGAINST THE counter casually, me sitting up on the stool, real straight now, but not about anything that important. Not the date that she has agreed to. Not the ghost. Not my Cancer.

I almost feel like I'm not really in my body, like I'm looking down and witnessing it all. She is just so damn beautiful it *is* hard to look away. It's hard to look at her too. I feel these things I've never felt before.

I feel equal measures of excitement and fear. I feel so lucky that she's there, just chatting with me, but I am also afraid of when it will end. She will leave and my life will not be as bright.

Does every boy at some point feel this way about a girl? If not, I feel sorry for them. And do girls ever feel this way about boys? And because of my father, I wonder if boys feel this way about boys and girls about girls. All joyful and terrified at the same time. I hope they do.

"Gotta go, Wade," she says straightening up and pulling her long black hair into a ponytail. She's got a pink whatcha-ma-thing (I honestly don't know what they're called) that holds her hair in place. It's an unusually girlish touch for her. Her colors tend to blues, greys, and black. She's not a bright color kind of a girl.

"Yeah," I say, trying and failing to seem casual. "Thanks for… you know…"

She laughs, and shakes her head, her newly placed ponytail swinging gracefully. "You're a weird kid, Wade." With that she turns to leave.

"And you're a *beautiful* woman," I call after her. She shakes her head and gives me a wave without looking back. I'm not sure if she caught that I swapped "fascinating" for "beautiful." The truth is she's both.

31

FRIDAY, JULY 15, 1977

CHEMO DAY. SHIT.

First a drive to Las Vegas. Then waiting. Then the obligatory poking and prodding. The checking of the blood to make sure the chemo hasn't hit me so hard I can't take more. They've got me on some new drugs, so they are watching my blood levels like a hawk.

I'm a bit distracted by my new haircut. It's a short buzzcut that Mom did with the clippers, the kind of haircut I used to get at the beginning of the summer when I was a kid. The kind of haircut a boy that is getting chemo and expecting his hair to fall out gets. I lean into the distraction, feeling the scorching Vegas sun on my scalp as we walk into Dr. Wright's office, feeling the suddenly overwhelming sensation of a slight, dry breeze on my head, each hair feeling a much different sensation and my brain letting the unusual signal through.

As the nurse draws blood, I rub my free hand on my head enjoying the fuzzy, tingling feeling. It's new and it's not horrible and it's something that doesn't begin with a capital C.

The blood draw is kinda useless, though. My mom had

drawn blood on Thursday morning and had it evaluated at the hospital. As the nurse is drawing my blood, I ponder this, because it's not normal.

We've done it for years when I've been in treatment. Mom brings a little kit home with her, draws my blood on the way to work, and has the results by dinner. I don't even have to go to the doctor's office, we do it at the kitchen table. I've come to accept it, but it isn't normal.

It makes me think of Doctor Rogers and Mom, which makes my stomach clench up. Maybe she can do this because she has the head of the ER as a boyfriend. I kinda freak out a bit, all this stuff is still unresolved, still unspoken, still hanging in the air.

"You okay, dear?" Nurse Wendy asks.

I look up from my blood flowing into the vial and smile at her. She's real nice, like pretty much everyone is at Doctor Wright's office. Nurse Wendy was around for my last adventure in chemo-land, so I've seen her quite a bit. "I'm fine. Just... you know..."

She smiles with her mouth but her eyes are sad. The "you know" is that if my blood levels are good, I will be toddling over to Sunrise Children's Hospital to do my time in the chemo room. "You know" is more than enough at this point.

"You're a fighter, Aaron," she says. "You're going to kick this."

I do my best to smile, but I don't feel it. The terminal nature of our adventure on Earth makes me a little less than optimistic. As Jim Morison said, "None here get out alive." And this is my third strike with the mighty leukemia.

So yeah, as you can tell I'm on the pessimistic end of the pendulum. I have days like that, and this has been one.

32

SUNDAY, JULY 17, 1977

FINALLY STARTING TO FEEL HUMAN AGAIN. I COULD DESCRIBE the nausea and puking. I could detail the low energy and the goddamn metallic taste that won't go away. I could go on and on, but that would be boring and depressing. Suffice it to say that after several chemo days in bed or in the bathroom, I am starting to feel human again. And I'm in a mood.

At breakfast, I'm poking at my oatmeal—plain, don't think I can tolerate anything fancy—and look at my parents. My dad has his head in the newspaper as usual, the crackle of the pages turning loud in the silence. My mother has dark circles under her eyes and is staring out the patio door into the backyard.

The sky is heavy and it's raining. This is not some lovely monsoon that sweeps in for an afternoon, comes down hard, and is then gone. This is a big storm that looks like it's here to stay, bringing a blanket of grey with it.

The patter of the rain, the clack of spoon against bowl, and the crinkling of the newspaper are the only sounds. Everyone lost in their own thoughts, hiding in their own worlds.

Enough. I've had enough.

"I can't take this anymore," I say.

The newspaper comes down and my dad is staring. My mom straightens and puts her hands in her lap and looks at me too.

"What is it, son?" Dad asks.

"This," I say, waving my hand around the table. "Us. All the things that have been secret. All the things we don't talk about. I can't take it anymore."

I think my agitation is partially chemo related, but if so, then I'm glad for it. The silence went on too long. The conversation was being avoided by everyone. It was too damn much.

My mom crosses her arms and takes a deep breath, like she's bracing for impact or something. Dad licks his lips and won't look at me.

I almost laugh. This is my family. We are courteous and kind, but we stuff a lot down and never talk about it. Hope that if we pretend it's not there long enough, it will go away.

But it doesn't, does it?

"Perhaps it would help if you would be more specific," Dad says.

I blink a few times, take a deep breath, and let it rip. "One," I say holding up my index finger. "You and Mom and how you're together just to care for your sick child. Two, your sexual orientation." I had done some reading since my dad revealed his preference for males and hope that I said that right. "Three, I can see ghosts and Mom believes me for reasons unstated. Four, I'm on my third occurrence of Cancer, and we know how the odds go. Five, I laid everything out about Lionel and wanting to help him and you shut me down with one word and we haven't discussed it since." I pause and take a deep breath, all the fingers on my right hand pointing skyward. Was there more? If so, I couldn't think of any of it.

The rattling of the rain on the roof is now the only sound.

It's not enough. Mom swallows hard and Dad is now the one staring out into the backyard.

"It's Sunday," I say quietly. "I would appreciate it if we could talk about some of this."

————

I BELIEVE THAT THE REALIZATION OF MY TRANSIENT NATURE has given me courage. Courage to ask Helena out. Courage to "start the conversation" with my parents. Courage to actually hear what they have to say.

In some ways it's a shame. I wish I had had the courage when I was well. But as in all things in life, even Cancer has its gifts. The gift of courage and a sense of urgency.

"Let's start with the 'no,'" Dad begins. "That one is easy. I said no because the idea of you trying to track down a murderer is unacceptable because of its inherent dangerous nature. Even if you were healthy, I would have said no. The other night I didn't elaborate because I thought the danger part of it obvious and your mother needed me."

We have relocated to the living room. I am once again in that somewhat uncomfortable rocker across from my parents sitting on the floral-print couch.

I take a deep breath, considering my words, trying to meet my dad's logical tone. "We had a plan," I say. "I thought I explained it. We were going to interview his closest friends. That's it. No accusations, just some simple questions in a public place. Lionel would be along and watching, maybe able to see something we couldn't."

My mom's eyes widen just a touch. "Is... is he here?" she asks, looking around.

I do my closed and covered eye routine and look around. I see the now familiar flash of light out of my peripheral vision. "Yes he is. I think he's with me most of the time now."

My father clears his throat, steering things back to the original question. "I did hear your plan, son. And while I appreciate the care, a person clever enough to commit a murder and get away with it could see through your ruse."

I have a huge lump in my throat remembering how easily Vincent Long had seen through our "ruse."

"But don't we have an obligation as humans to reduce the suffering of others when we can?" I ask Dad.

"Of course we do," Dad says. "But we have to consider the potential cost to ourselves as well as the benefit to the other party."

I open my mouth up to speak and Dad holds his hand up, stopping me. I lean back in the rocking chair, the wooden dowels pressing uncomfortably into my back.

"The potential cost to you," he continues, "of finding a murderer is too high. You must agree."

Dad was in "logic" mode. I had to meet him there. Mom was just watching us, her head moving back and forth like someone watching tennis.

"I think you've underestimated the benefit," I say. "Not only can we relieve Lionel's suffering, we can potentially save lives."

"Lives?" Dad asks.

"Yes. This person, this murderer, is probably still here in Cedar City. They killed once, they might kill again. We can bring peace to Lionel and maybe save a life or lives."

Dad pauses, his eyes distant, clearly thinking, and then a small smile finds his lips. "You've made some good points," he says. "And I'm proud of how clear and articulate you are. But the answer is still 'no.' We cannot have you putting yourself in harm's way, especially now."

I sigh. I am determined to do this thing, to help Lionel. I'm disappointed because I will have to continue lying to my parents. It's my life, shouldn't I be able to decide what risks to take? I know I'm a minor and all, but my circumstances are not exactly normal.

I'm about to launch into another topic when nausea hits me hard. Like a big wave smacking you down, it crashes on me and sends me metaphorically tumbling. Then it sends me literally running to the bathroom where my meager breakfast comes back up.

My mom tends to me with what appears to be a practiced ease. She's a nurse and this is round number three, so she knows what to do. But I know it's not easy for her, she looks tired all the time now that I'm back in treatments.

As I squat on the tiled bathroom floor panting and sweating a bit, the acid from my stomach having wreaked havoc on the back of my throat, I ponder my mother.

I have established that I don't really understand her. But I do know that she worries. I do know my illness is sometimes harder for her than it is for me.

So, I have a realization while sitting there, my mother in the doorway in case I need something. When it comes to Lionel and his murder, it's better this way. Better that it be done covertly and without my parents' consent or knowledge.

My disease asks enough of her. It's not reasonable to ask her to endorse her ill son looking for a murderer.

I smile briefly, proud of my revelation. But it only lasts a moment and then I'm puking my guts out again.

———

I LIKE PASTOR WEST. I DON'T AGREE WITH HIM theologically, but I like him. He makes a visit to our house around 4 p.m.

I've spent most of the day in my room after the puke-a-thon and have recently relocated to the living room couch. I'm thumbing through the collection of Mark Twain short stories.

The one Dad had Lionel look at when I was proving I could see him. But I'm not getting much reading done. I feel like I'm running a bit of a fever—it was only half a degree when my mom checked—and I feel all fluey and gross.

On days like this, hydration is the name of the game. That and staying sane. We haven't had any more serious conversations. Everyone is in "take care of Aaron" mode, including me.

"How are you doing, Aaron?" Pastor West asks after he lowers his bulk into the rocking chair. I'm sprawled on the couch with flannel pajamas on and a quilt over my legs—I've also had the chills on and off all day.

He had spoken quietly to my parents for a few minutes before coming in to talk to me. I ponder what to answer and decide to go with the truth. "Terrible," I say, but I do add a smile.

He gets up and looks at the rocker and then at me. "Do you mind if I slide this a bit closer?" The rocker is on the other side of the room from the couch under the big picture window.

I shrug and he relocates himself.

"Are we about to have a theological discussion?" I ask. I am curious about his need for closeness, which I suspect is about intimacy.

He smiles and brushes at his thinning brown hair. "If you would like, but that was not the main reason for my visit."

I take a sip of my chamomile tea.

"I just wanted to tell you that I've found a home for your swing set." He smiles and nods towards the backyard. "Joe and Ann Edwards, they run the Sunrise Bakery, not far from your bookstore. Perhaps you know them."

I'm suddenly hot and I throw the quilt off and sit up. Joe and Ann Edwards. Two of Lionel's close friends. My heart is thumping hard and the pastor's sweet-smelling cologne is making me feel nauseous again. I swallow hard, trying to force the nausea down. I don't want to have to run to the toilet and miss this.

"I… I didn't know they had kids," I say.

"They didn't," he says. "It's quite tragic." He leans back in the rocker, his eyes distant for a moment. "Ann's sister, Ellen, recently died in a head-on collision that also killed her husband. They left behind a child, Silvia. She's six and will be coming to live with the Edwards soon."

I belch loudly and excuse myself. I don't feel well at all but it's clear this is important. "When did this happen?"

Pastor West takes a deep breath and continues. "This happened about nine months ago. Silvia went to live with her other aunt—Ann's other sister Kim—up in Salt Lake City. But that hasn't worked out very well. Kim is… well… she's got some problems, not exactly the stablest person in the world. I think it was obvious to Ann early on that they would need to take the child, but it's taken them some time to work things out. What with the bakery and all."

Nine months ago was when all this happened. I struggled to remember how long ago Lionel died… Did I even know? Could this be related?

Another wave of nausea hits, I really can't take his cologne, I think it's Aqua Velva. I cover my mouth, mumble an "Excuse me," and run to the downstairs bathroom and slam the door behind me. I throw open the seat and kneel in front of the toilet.

I have the dry heaves, but nothing comes out. This is worse than actually puking. It doesn't last long, though.

When I get out of the bathroom, Pastor West is gone and the rocking chair is back in its place. I go back to the couch but can't read and can't rest either. I need to talk to Lionel. I need it to be dark.

———

LATER IN THE AFTERNOON, I TRY CALLING HELENA, BUT she's not home. It's family day for her, so I didn't really expect to reach her, I just want to talk to someone about this.

I opt out of dinner, Mom brings me some broth in my room, which I do manage to get down, and I wait for darkness. Usually I love the long days of summer, but I want it to be dark. Lionel and I need to have a conversation.

I don't feel good, but I have this nervous energy, so I slowly clean my room a bit more while I wait. Comics in their correct place, the collectables in little plastic sleeves. Check. All my books properly dusted and protected from the dreaded dust mites, especially the collectables (I've got a signed first edition of *Jonathan Livingston Seagull*). Check. My wooden desk all straightened up. Check. The blue carpet is a bit dirty, but I don't get the vacuum, I don't think the folks will be too happy with me cleaning right now after the pukey day I've had.

And then it gets dark. Finally. But I don't pull out my Ouija papers. My parents are still awake and I don't want any questions. I do, though, pile up the pillows on my bed so I can lean comfortably against them, get out my diary and start doing yes/no questions with Lionel. I whisper real quietly and find that he can hear me just fine.

"How long ago did you die?" I whisper.

He holds up eight fingers and my heart begins pounding again.

"Eight months ago?"

He nods.

"Did you know about Silvia and Ann's sister's death?"

He nods, a sad look on his face. Of course he knew, they were close.

"How did Ann take it?"

He scrunches his face and see-saws his palms back and forth.

"So not good?"

Lionel shakes his head.

I pause, considering. I really need the Ouija papers so we can have a real conversation, but I just can't risk it. I know in my gut that this is related to his murder, but I don't know how. I also need to talk to the Edwards, but I am so seriously grounded, and after today's conversation about solving murders, I know they will be keeping a closer eye on me.

"I think they are involved," I whisper. "The Edwards, I mean."

His eyes widen and he shakes his head rapidly, his bottom lip sticking out a touch. He doesn't agree, but the idea obviously makes him uncomfortable.

His mouth opens to speak, and then I think he remembers I can't hear him and he closes it. He looks around the room, his eyes wide like a caged animal. He then opens his mouth to speak again, but closes it, looking so frustrated. He waves at me and then disappears.

I FALL ASLEEP ON TOP OF MY FLUFFY ROYAL BLUE COMFORTER and wake up when it's close to midnight and find a blanket has been put on top of me. My parents must have checked on me, I'm betting on my mom. I use the bathroom and am wholly grateful it's for a normal use of the commode. After I get out, I listen carefully—all is quite in the house.

I walk quietly downstairs, grab the phone and take it into the pantry, closing the door behind me. It smells like flour and tea, which my stomach doesn't rebel at. The phone has lit numbers so it's easy to dial Helena.

"Hello," she says, picking up on the third ring.

"It's me," I whisper.

"Oh. Hi 'me.' What's up?"

"It's the Edwards... At least I think it is. There is something

there, I just know it. We have to go talk to them. We have to."
My voice is rushing out, my whisper getting a bit loud. I don't
want to wake the folks up.

"Okay, okay. Slow down there, cowboy. You're not making
any sense."

I take a deep breath and tell her of my conversation with
Pastor West. Of how Lionel died a month after Ann's niece was
orphaned. Of how uncomfortable Lionel got when I brought
up the possibility of their involvement.

"Why do you think they're involved?" she asks. "There's not
a real connection here. Ann's sister dies and a month later
Lionel does. I don't get it."

I take a deep breath, getting ready to explain it, but realize I
can't. "I don't know either," I say. "It's a hunch. I know something is going on here. We need to talk to them."

Helena is quiet for a while, I can hear her breathing on the
other end so I know she hasn't hung up.

"So we'll go talk to them," she finally says.

"How? I'm super grounded."

"I have an idea but need to think it through. When do you
think you'll be back at the bookstore?"

"Ummm... Well... I had a bad day today, so definitely not
tomorrow. Maybe Tuesday, Wednesday for sure."

"Wednesday it is then," she says. "I'll see you then."

33

MONDAY, JULY 18, 1977

I can handle food today, but only the bland and the boring: plain oatmeal, dry toast, a banana. I've got that fluey feeling again but not much of a fever. This symptom could be from the leukemia or it could be from the chemo or a combination of the two. It's not that bad, my nausea is only mild and for me on chemo, that's a good day.

My mom takes the day off from work—I told her I was well enough to be on my own, but she insisted. In some ways it's kind of nice. We linger at the breakfast table and talk, the plain oatmeal left in my bowl congealing into an unappetizing mass of glueish substance. I clear it from the table and then we sit. I'm sipping chamomile tea and Mom is drinking coffee.

"You know, I'm really sorry about the craziness," I say after the chitchat has died down for a while.

She smiles, it's somewhere between rueful and compassionate. "It's not your fault that you have leukemia."

I nod. "Yeah, but not just that. The whole teenage thing..." I don't elaborate, I know she knows what I mean. The sneaking off, the running away after seeing her and Doctor Rogers all kissy, the pushing on the wall of silence and secrecy that surrounds our family. And even by mentioning it, I realize I'm doing it again—pushing on the wall.

Mom looks hard at her coffee, it's a nice tan color, she takes lots of cream but no sugar. It's warm in the house but she's still got on her big fluffy pink robe. "Henry told me to expect this," she says, still not looking up. Henry is my dad, it's a little odd for her to use his first name with me.

"What?"

She looks up and meets my gaze, a thin smile on her face. She's still got those dark circles under her eyes which makes me worry. "He told me that if I stayed home you would want to talk about one of the five things you brought up yesterday."

"I… Well…" I stammer, rolling the conversation back in my mind. I hadn't actually asked to talk about those things, but I was building up to it. She had beat me to the punch. "We don't have to."

My mom is beautiful. Maybe all sons think that of their mothers, but I think on an objective scale that she must be considered beautiful. She's got long brown hair and piercing blue eyes with well-manicured eyebrows above them (that women plucked their eyebrows sure freaked me out the first time I saw my mom doing it, not to mention the curling of eyelashes). She has an oval face with high cheekbones and expressive lips. All of this arranged symmetrically in a way that seems to be pleasing to the eye.

I know her face well, and as I study her reaction I see a variety of emotions at play. The fatigue from the last few weeks as represented by those dark circles I've mentioned. A shyness in the way her eyebrows twitch and her lips purse. An appraising gaze as she studies me, maybe having a hard time seeing me change in the ways I've changed recently. And then I see fear in those eyes. She's scared. Of my Cancer, of course, but maybe at bringing these things out into the open, of wondering how I will take it. And most of all, fear of the future.

I'm taking a breath to speak again when she says, "No. It's time. We do need to talk about some of these things."

"Thank you, Mom."

Her lips form the briefest sneer before she says, "Don't thank me yet. You haven't heard what I have to say."

My exhausted body dumps a pitiful amount of adrenaline into my bloodstream as I feel the fear from that statement. My heart races a bit and I feel my blood pressure rise.

"But not right now," she says, getting up. "I need a shower and I need to get dressed." She looks out to our backyard. "And I need the sun for this conversation."

———

MY FEET SEEM TO BE DRAGGING AS I COME BACK DOWN THE stairs from my room. I took a shower, got dressed, and tidied up my room. The whole time one thought going through my head: *What have I done?*

Sure, I was getting what I asked for, starting those conversations that Helena urged me to start. But what would I find when the dark corners of my family were suddenly illuminated? My mother and her boyfriend. My mother believing me about ghosts. My third occurrence of leukemia.

The realization I had, felt deep in my gut while I made my bed, was that it couldn't possibly be good stuff. I had gotten so upset I found out about the secrets, that my family wasn't it the "Leave it to Beaver" family that I thought it was. Was I ready to find out what it really was? Was I strong enough?

When I go downstairs and into the kitchen, Mom is already out on the patio, the sliding glass door open letting in the warm air of the morning. It's about 10 a.m., a pleasant time to be outside this time of year. Mom's sitting at the table with two glasses of iced tea. She is wearing capri pants made out of a light denim and an old white button-up shirt. Next to her glass of iced tea are a pair of gardening gloves and the kneepad. She's getting ready to pull weeds.

She doesn't seem to notice me and I find myself staring at her. She doesn't seem shy or nervous now. Her back is erect and she's gazing out into our yard with a blank expression.

I take a deep breath and walk out, sitting in the white metal chair next to her. It affords me a good view of my old swing set, which makes me think of Pastor West and the Edwards.

"Where shall we start?" Mom asks, taking a sip of her tea, leaving a pink stain from her lipstick on the rim.

I blink and stare. It's one thing to ask to be treated like an adult. It's a whole other thing to be treated that way. She is asking me to lead, to start the conversation, to solicit the information I want.

Before the swing set got me thinking about Lionel, I think I would have asked about her and Dad. But, honestly, I don't know if I'm ready for that yet. "Can we talk about ghosts?" I ask.

She bites her lip briefly and then scoots her chair so she is facing towards me. I do the same.

"Why not."

———

I'VE SAID A BUNCH OF TIMES HERE THAT I DON'T understand my mother, that it's my father that makes more sense to me. Today I gained understanding for her and lost some for him.

"I saw ghosts when I was young," she says, an expression on her face that kinda looks like a smile and kinda looks like a frown at the same time. "It's that simple. That's why I believe you."

And there it is, short and sweet. I can't speak.

"I was young when I could see them. It started around four, ended around six. There you go."

Something's not right. That weird expression on her lips, that fearful look in her eyes. It's the truth, but not all of the truth. She doesn't want to tell me the whole story.

"What did your parents think?" I ask. It may sound strange that I didn't refer to them as "Grandma" and "Grandpa," but I never knew them. They both died when I was very young. I think I might have met them as a baby, but I have no memory of them.

She blinks and her nostrils flare briefly. "You have to understand, this was Tallahassee in the forties, it was a different world." Her eyes meet mine briefly and it is clear that she's scared, that these are hard memories.

"Tallahassee is more Georgia than Florida. It's the South." Her voice is slipping, some of the southern accent that you usually never hear in her voice bleeding through. I know this happens to her sometimes when she is scared. "Mama had a paddle, about this thick." She holds her thumb and forefinger about three quarters of an inch apart. "It was four inches wide and had a few large holes in it, looking when I was young like some odd piece of swiss cheese."

She takes a deep breath and drinks some tea and then looks at me. In her eyes is the question, "Are you ready for this?" I don't know and I'm glad she doesn't actually ask.

"Mama believed in paddling. It was the way we were raised. Don and I got the paddle when we were bad. She would whack us good on the b-hind and we would cry. It worked well for me, but not so well for your Uncle Don." Her accent is full-blown southern now. It's strange to hear her this way, maybe it's the memories doing this to her.

"Tallahassee is older than Cedar and bigger. Lots of ghosts wandering around. There was one of a little girl named

Adeline that was around my age, four, when I met her. She was haunting the house next to ours, and when I saw her, I thought she was just a normal little girl. She had this pretty little white dress on that never seemed to get dirty and her brown hair was made up so nice in these big curls."

She pauses, her eyes looking out at our backyard, but far, far away.

"Adeline and I played and played. She told the strangest stories and—"

"Wait. You could hear her?" I ask.

"Yes. I could hear her and see her, just fine."

"In the daylight?"

Mom nods and then continues. "But no one else could see Adeline. At first my mama thought it was cute that I had an 'invisible friend.' But then I started saying some of the things that Adeline had told me. Like that time Pa was drunk and slapped her hard after Don and I were in bed."

My heart's pounding. "Leave it to Beaver Land" is far, far in the rearview mirror. I miss the innocence of it.

"Ma was real religious, Southern Baptist, and prayed a lot. She was so mad when I asked her about it, I got the paddle right then and there and didn't understand it. Before long I began to understand what Adeline was. What the other 'see-through folk' I came across were. I'd find things out. I would sometimes tell Pa or Don and it would get back to Ma. She would use the paddle on me, but not in the normal way. She would beat me with it hard on the b-hind and the back of my legs. It would leave bruises, horrible bruises. I would have trouble sitting for days."

The summer light doesn't seem so bright anymore and I take a sip of tea so I don't have to say anything. I never thought I would find out something like this. Ever.

"She thought it was the work of the devil," Mom says. "When the paddling got bad, I started ignoring Adeline, although it broke my heart—and hers. I stopped talking about them, and after a time, I stopped seeing them."

She takes a deep breath and smiles at me, like she is trying to tell me that all that stuff was in the past and she is okay. But her eyes make it clear she isn't okay.

"I... I'm sorry that happened, Mom," I say.

She shrugs and gives me one of those fake smiles again.

"That's why you freaked when I saw those ghosts when we were at the cemetery when I was four?"

She nods but doesn't say anything.

It's silent for a while, only the jangle of the ice cubes in our glasses and the sound of a car passing out on our street.

"Now, I have a question for you," she says, her southern accent gone. "And I need the truth from you."

"Sure, Mom. Sure."

"You're still looking for this ghost's murderer, aren't you?"

"OH MY GOD! WHAT DID YOU TELL HER?" HELENA ASKS ON the other end of the phone. I was once again in the pantry late at night sitting in the dark talking to her. I had filled her in on my mom's ghost history. When Billy was over earlier, he had had a similar reaction, but it had involved liberal use of the word "shit."

"I told her the truth," I say.

"What... Wait... You did not."

"I did. I had to, after what she had told me."

There's silence on the line and I'm afraid I've lost the connection, but I can hear her breathing.

"What happened?" she finally asks.

"We came to an understanding," I say. I'm being deliberately vague. I'm kind of enjoying her surprise and want to draw it out.

"What? That you never leave the house again in your entire life?"

I laugh. "No. That I tell her everything we are doing. Everything we are planning. Everything we learn."

"You're shitting me."

I shake my head. "Nope. Mom's part of our little gang now."

"Wait," Helena says, "back up. Back way the hell up. Start from the beginning and tell me everything."

I take a deep breath and tell her.

———

WHEN MOM ASKS ME THAT QUESTION, I CAN'T TALK. I TRY to drink some tea to buy some time but end up aspirating a bit of it and having one of those awful choking/coughing fits. I thought that would get me out of answering but it doesn't. After it is all over, she repeats the question, this time with a serious look on her face and her arms crossed in front of her.

"Yes," I answer.

She nods. "Thank you for telling me the truth."

I look at her closely. She doesn't seem to be freaking out. Her arms are uncrossed, and she looks kind of relaxed. "You're not mad?"

She shakes her head. "I am worried, though."

"Well... I..." I stammer. "There's good reason... I mean, I have to do this. I—"

She smiles and holds up her hand, cutting me off. "I heard your arguments for this when you told your father and I understand where you are coming from."

"Okay..."

She takes a deep breath and lets it out slowly.

"I also realize that you have a thick head, just like your father."

I nod, but don't say anything. The proverbial cat is out of the bag and I'm not sure if saying anything else will make it worse or better.

"But I will make you a deal."

"A deal?" I ask.

She nods and smiles. It's not a real smile, but better than when she was talking about her childhood, so that's something. A breeze comes up and plays with the stray brown hairs that halo her face and have escaped her ponytail. "You tell me everything you know, everything you've planned, and keep me in the loop on what you find out."

I wait for more, but she takes a drink and stares out into the yard. "Um… that doesn't sound like a deal."

"Oh…" she says as if startled from a dream or something. "You do that, and I will handle your father."

This is making me *very* uncomfortable. The breeze is warm and I'm sweating, the sun is starting to get kind of intense. The iced tea glasses are sweating too, covered in cool droplets of water. I bring mine to my forehead.

"Are you okay?" she asks.

"Fine. Just a little hot."

She gets one of those pinched motherly looks on her face and hustles me into the kitchen out of the sun. I am a bit disoriented. I'm used to my father taking the lead on things. For him to tell me he's going to "handle" my mother. It's a strange role reversal.

"Why are you doing this?" I ask. "Aren't you worried about the risk like Dad is?"

"Of course I am. But I would rather you have an adult you can call on than to be doing it all on your own in secret."

"And Dad?"

She shrugs. "For now, we don't tell him."

I sip a little more of the tea. There's no sugar in it, so it's got a bit of a bite. It's the way I like it. "Are you and Dad okay?" I ask quietly.

She gets a weary expression on her face and rubs her eyes. "Yes, Aaron. We are okay. Even in the best of circumstances marriages can be challenging."

What she doesn't say is, *These aren't the best of circumstances.* Far from it, really.

"There's something you should understand about your father," she continues, looking at me. I give her a nod. "He's not comfortable with my emotions. Not the strong ones, at least."

I shake my head. "I don't understand."

"It's not unusual at all. But I bet you've noticed that women —your Helena, for one—express their emotions more often and with greater strength than you do."

I smile remembering when I met Helena, her screaming at Jeff Tate out on Main Street in the middle of the night.

"I'll let you in on a secret," she says, leaning close to me. I can smell her rose perfume, which for some reason doesn't trigger my chemo-nausea and never has. "Having emotions and letting them out is not a sign of weakness."

I just blink, my mouth opens a bit. My mother's treating me like an adult. She's confiding in me. She's telling me secrets of the female gender. I love it. It's scaring the hell out of me.

"I'm stronger than he thinks," she says, her arms crossing over her chest.

I remember Helena saying, *Just don't treat me like I break easy, okay?* I think back to my parents' relationship. My father seems to want to handle the difficult things. He wants to protect my mother and me from harm. That's natural, isn't it? I ask her about it.

"Your father does his best to protect me from certain things. And I appreciate that, I do." She takes a deep breath and lets it out in a sigh. "But when it comes to you, I don't want to be protected."

Our glasses are almost empty, so I get up and get the pitcher out of the refrigerator and pour us both more. Mom thanks me with a pinched smile.

I sit back down and tell her everything I know. About the night Lionel Malak was killed. About the interview we had with Vincent Long. About what Pastor West told us about Joe and Ann Edwards. About how Helena is cooking something up for Wednesday.

She takes it in quietly, nodding occasionally, asking for details a few times. She's not this wall of coolness like my dad. I can see emotions pass across her face: surprise at the timing of Lionel's death and Ann's sister's death; revulsion when describing the details of his murder; happiness when I talk about Helena; fear when it's all over.

"You're scared," I say.

She snorts, it's almost a laugh. "Of many things, son."

"Of this?"

She shakes her head. "Not really. As long as you aren't out there accusing people of murder, I'm not too worried."

I don't believe her. "Mom…"

"Okay. I'm worried. But I still think it's better this way." She's quiet for a moment and then asks, "Is Lionel here?"

I do my closed and covered eye thing and look around the kitchen. I catch a flash of light out of the corner of my eye by the stove. "Is that you, Lionel?" I ask, and the light moves. I open my eyes. "He's right there." I point at our white Whirlpool stove.

She bites her lips, takes a deep breath, squares her shoulders, and starts addressing the stove. "Hello, Lionel. I am sorry for what happened to you. We met a few times, but I don't know you well, so I don't know how you're going to take this."

She pauses and I'm just agog. Really. My mother is talking to a ghost. Holy Shit.

"I appreciate your need to have peace. To understand why you were killed. But listen to me now. This is my boy you have enlisted to help you." Her southern accent is starting to slide back in. "My boy. He is the most important thing in my life. If this thing you two are doing puts him in danger... if he is hurt... Well, I will hold you responsible for that. And, believe me, just because you are a ghost doesn't mean that I won't find a way."

She slowly rises and walks out the sliding glass door, grabs her garden gloves, and starts weeding the herb garden with a fierceness that scares me.

————

HELENA'S SILENT ON THE OTHER END OF THE LINE. I HEAR the click of a lighter and then a deep inhale.

"Well?" I ask.

She laughs, but it's a quiet, dry thing. "It's official," she says. "I love your mother."

I laugh with her and feel warm inside remembering what she said to Lionel. "She's pretty great, isn't she?"

"That she is." She's quiet for a bit and I hear her heavy inhalations as she smokes. "So, I guess I should tell you what I have planned for Wednesday, so you can keep her in the loop."

"Okay."

"It was going to be a surprise, but..."

"The suspense is killing me," I say.

"Please don't talk like that," she says, her tone suddenly serious.

"Like what?" I ask.

"You said, 'the suspense is *killing me*.' That last part is just an expression, I know. But damn it, Aaron, it felt like someone punched me in the gut when you said it."

I take a breath to defend myself when I remember what my mother said. *Women—your Helena for one—express their emotions more often and with greater strength.* "Sorry," I say, and I am. "I sometimes forget there is an elephant in the room."

"A big fucking elephant that stinks and steps on everyone's toes."

"Yeah… I know. Believe me, I do."

She's quite again. "This whole thing scares the shit out of me, Wade."

I smile because I'm "Wade" again. "So, what about Wednesday?" I put some energy in my voice. I'm changing the subject, because I don't want to go there right now.

"Yeah, Wednesday," she says, and I'm glad she's going along with the shift. "Tell your mom I'm going to sweet talk your dad into letting me take you to the bakery. Good chance we'll run into the Edwards. Public place, we'll be safe."

34

WEDNESDAY, JULY 20, 1977

MY MOTHER IS LAUGHING MORE. IT'S A WEIRD THING, WE'VE got a secret. I can't say I'm entirely comfortable with keeping this from my father, but I am enjoying the change in my mother.

It's not huge, she just seems happier, a little less tense. A while back when my father suggested I do something special for her, I thought I knew what he meant. Like bringing her lunch at work—that was a disaster—or going to church with her, which was nice but not like this. This is special. There's a piece of my life, of me really, that I only share with her.

I've had things like this with my dad for years. Like the pinewood derby which he's helped me out with a few times. The bookstore—Mom doesn't do much there, it's more our thing. Books, for that matter, my mom reads but that passion I have for all things bookish came directly from my father.

I still feel a bit of guilt over this, but every time I have a little private conversation with her and see the conspiratorial grin on her face, that guilt gets plowed down. I know she's doing this to keep me safe, but this feels more like friendship and I really like that.

———

Tuesday drags by. I'm well enough to work a shortened shift at the bookstore. Billy comes and hangs out and I fill him in. But it's not until Wednesday's shift when that little bell on the door rings and I look up to see Helena walking in that I feel good.

My body has shucked off the worst effects of the chemo and I feel almost normal. Well, it's rather my new normal at this point. Not much energy, a touch of nausea here and there, and that damn metallic taste in my mouth, but I'll take it. "Normal" has definitely changed.

"Good morning," I say to her. "Welcome to Cedar Books and Such. We have the town's best collection of books and other fine items. And if you are looking for anything related to Shakespeare, well, go no further. We've got the best selection in all of Southern Utah."

She laughs as she approaches and smiles broadly. There's an older couple digging through the Shakespeare section and they look up briefly at our exchange, their brows furrowed.

Helena looks beautiful. She's got on a long taupe-colored skirt that flows around her tanned legs and above that a light-yellow blouse. It's not the usual jeans and T-shirt outfit she's worn most of the summer. Looking at what I can see of her legs, I've got to wonder why she doesn't wear skirts more often (or shorts, for that matter).

"You look great," I say, meeting her smile with my own as she makes it up to the counter. "What's the occasion?"

"I'm celebrating," she says.

"What?"

"My father got a raise at the warehouse. It's not a lot, but it will definitely help us out."

"That's great. So, you got to do some clothes shopping?"

She twirls, the skirt picking up and I see her legs just past the knee. "Goodwill special," she says. "You'd never know, though. They're in great shape, practically new. I have no idea why someone would give them away."

I keep a smile on my face as I think of one big reason why someone would. Namely the former owner dying. Now, I know Helena doesn't break easy, but I see no reason to dim her brightness, it makes me feel warm inside.

"Is he here?" she asks, her tone low.

I nod. "I talked to Lionel last night. He said he'd be with me all day.

We chat and she helps me dust until my father comes in just before 2 p.m. and then she starts working her charm. It doesn't take much really, she's in such an effusive mode, how is a boy (or a man) to resist. We are soon off, walking towards the Sunrise Bakery. Helena grabs my hand as we walk and I feel…

Oh my god, I can't even explain it. Her hand is warm and a little bit rough. She gives my hand a good squeeze as we pass by where Lionel's shop used to be—it's a place that sells lotions and stuff now. I mean, I'm sure that for most boys my age, this wouldn't be a big deal. But for me, it's like the whole world has changed.

Maybe it's just a friendly gesture. Maybe she's just in a great mood. I don't care. I love it. I cherish the feeling as we walk together, hands clasped, down Cedar's Main street in the hot sun of a July afternoon.

I just love it until we come across Tyson.

He's tall and wiry, taller than Helena and a lot taller than me. He's got blond hair, down to his collar, long enough to attract disapproving looks from adults and whispers of "hippie," although he doesn't look like one. He's got a motorcycle helmet under his arm and parked at the curb is a Kawasaki. I don't know much about motorcycles, but it's big and fancy with a black gas tank and gleaming chrome.

"Hey, Hel," he says, his voice deeper than it looks like it should be.

That moment when she sees him is the moment she lets go of my hand. The day, suddenly, is not so bright. I hate that he calls her "Hel" instead of "Helena."

"Tyson," she says, the smile gone from her face.

"Is this little pipsqueak him?" he asks, his long chin gesturing to me. I'm scared. He's bigger, a couple of years older, and isn't currently having poison pumped into him once a week. But I want to get between Helena and him. I want to protect her.

"Yes," she says.

He shakes his head and sighs. "You've got to be fucking kidding me."

Now I'm just mad. His eyes, a light blue color I'm sure girls would call "dreamy," snap from Helena to me and back to Helena. I don't like him. I seriously want to hurt him. I want to feel my fist connect with that sharp chin of his.

Helena takes a breath and steps forward. "Go fuck yourself, Tyson." He takes a step back, resting his gloved hand on the handlebar of the motorcycle. I don't blame him. When Helena is mad... well, she certainly does express her emotion with "greater strength."

"You had your chance," she continues. "More than one, I might add. But you tried to lock me down. You tried to control me. I..." There's more, but she looks back at me, her brown eyes are practically sparking, and then back at him. She then takes a deep breath, walks back to me, grabs my hand, and drags me towards the bakery.

This time, her hand in mine doesn't feel the same, but I'll take it none the same.

―――――――

JOE EDWARDS KIND OF LOOKS LIKE A BAKER. HE'S GOT THIS
puffy look to him like freshly risen bread. If I had to guess, it's
from eating too many of his wares. But I know enough about
life to know that is a shallow assumption. I've been puffy, kind
of like that before, and it was from steroids, not pastries.

He's got a little brass bell on his door, just like we do at the
bookstore. He looks up from behind a glass display case full of
pastries when we walk in and smiles. "How can I help you?"

I've been in here before. I formally met him once with my
father at a Chamber of Commerce mixer where people stand
around eating finger food and blabbing. I can't say that I liked
it very much. I just don't really have that much to say about
"business."

"Do you have any coffee brewed?" Helena asks with a
smile.

Now that we're here, this is not what I want to do. I want to
talk to Helena about Tyson. I want to know the details. I don't
want to do this.

"All day long," he says. "For here or to go?"

"Here is good." She looks to me. "What do you want?"

"Umm… tea if you have it. Peppermint would be good."
My stomach isn't doing so good. I keep picturing Tyson, how
tall he is, how old he looks, how he called me "pipsqueak."

"Coming right up," he says. "Sit where you like."

There are three small tables at the front of the shop, most
of it is taken up by the actual bakery, which you can see beyond
the glass counter full of sweets, breads, and treats. It smells like
bread and sugar, with a hint of something else—maybe vanilla.
I like the scent of it, but rich food is generally not a good idea
right now, I'm on the infamous chemo dieting plan.

We sit at a round table, the chairs are padded and have
twirling iron on the backrest. It reminds me a bit of that

rocking chair in our living room. The one I seem to be always sitting in when it's time for an uncomfortable discussion. Helena tosses me a smile, but I can see it's forced. I've got to think she's still feeling our recent encounter with Tyson.

"Here you go," he says bringing out our drinks in white ceramic coffee mugs. He's got a white apron on with tan stains and traces of flower. He's got big hands and short blond hair. I see a few traces of grey as he leans down. "Anything else I can do you for?"

Helena looks at me pointedly. Now? She wants me to do this now?

"Umm... Mister Edwards, I'm Aaron Wade," I begin, swallowing hard, trying to get my head back in the game. "You might not remember me, but my father, Henry Wade, he runs the bookstore. This is my friend Helena."

Recognition lights up his face and he smiles. I relax a little, he's got a great smile.

"Yes, of course, it's been a while. I owe your father a call about that swing set and I understand I have you to thank for that."

"Happy to help, Mister Edwards."

"So, what can I do for you, Aaron?"

"I... I..." I stammer, then look to Helena. "We..." I just lose my whole train of thought. "Umm..."

Helena smiles up at him. "Aaron here is a little shy to ask, but we could use your help on a school assignment?"

He stands there, looking a bit uncomfortable and scratches his head. "School's not for a few more weeks, right?"

I feel my cheeks flushing. I don't want Helena to do my talking for me, so I jump back in. "I've missed a lot of school from being sick. There's something I need to get done this summer."

"Oh, okay. Hope it's no math or anything. That I can't help

you with, but ask if you need to know anything about bread, I'm your man."

"It's about… well…" I'm still all stammery, but at least I'm talking. "I'm doing kind of a biography of someone that you might have known."

His brow furrows. "Oh. Who?"

"Lionel Malak."

The color drains from his face and he licks his lips and swallows. "Sad thing that. Horrible, really."

"It's kind of a tribute," I say. "We're gathering people's memories of him and I'm going to put them all together. It's a tough assignment, but I've gotten so far behind in English."

He crosses his arms and sighs, looking back to the counter. There are no other customers in the bakery. "That was a bad time for us," he says. By "us" I assume he is also referring to his wife Ann and the tragedies in her family. "But we're getting past it all now. Finally. Lionel was my friend, I loved him like a brother, but I would appreciate you not talking to my wife about this."

"Do you have a few minutes to talk to us?" Helena asks.

He glances back at the counter and with a sigh, sits down. He's a big man and for a moment I'm sure it's him, that he's the murderer, and here we are alone in his store. I glance out the huge windows that front the store. The sun's still shining out there and cars and people are moving by. Nothing will happen right here, I assure myself.

"How well did you know Mister Malak?" I ask.

"He was a brother to me. That's how well I knew him. I miss him every day." His eyes get a bit moist and I don't feel threatened anymore.

"What was he like?" Helena asks.

"He wasn't a simple man and he was mighty hard to get to know. He had this front he put up to all his customers. It was like pulling an eye tooth to get past it." He pauses, his eyes defocusing as he stares out to the street. "It wasn't me. It was Ann. We all met because of our businesses. We needed menus and business cards, he needed bread and loved our cupcakes. Ann was fascinated with him, but I couldn't be bothered."

"What did she find fascinating?" I ask.

"His sense of humor. It was so dry it might just blow away in the breeze like a maple leaf in fall. If you weren't listening, you'd miss most of his jokes." He smiles as he remembers. "Like this one time when I was over at his place picking up some flyers, and I thanked him, telling him they were just what I needed. He looked back at me with the straightest damn face and said, 'Well, Joe, I'm sure a man like you needs a lot.'"

I'm just looking at him. If there was a joke, I missed it.

"It sounded like 'needs,' but it was K-N-E-A-D-S. A man like me 'kneads' a lot. I'm a baker."

I laugh a little and so does Helena. It's more of a pun than a joke.

"It was the delivery. He said it like the most normal thing. It wasn't until I was halfway back to the shop that I got it. I told Ann and she couldn't stop laughing about it. She started doing 'knead' jokes with me all the time after that." He scratches at his eyebrow where his skin has a dusting of flower. "That was about ten years ago. I think that's where it all started. That stupid joke." The smile on his face slowly fades until his puffy features are slack.

"It's such a shame what happened to him," I say quietly.

He nods, his face still sagging. "Sometimes life just keeps punching ya. It doesn't give up. Doesn't stop. You know what I mean?"

I nod grimly. "I do."

"I bet you do, Aaron. How is your health, by the way?" It's a small town, everyone knows everyone's business.

"I'm back in treatments," I say. It's really the most diplomatic way to tell someone your Cancer has come back.

"Oh, hell… I'm so sorry. Really I am."

"Thank you, Mister Edwards, I appreciate that. You've given me some good stuff about Mister Malak. Can I ask you another question?"

He nods but doesn't answer. I can't quite read his face. There's sadness and agitation, but I'm not sure what else.

"Do you have any idea who would want to hurt him?"

His eyes narrow briefly as he looks at Helena and me, then they relax. "Not a clue. Not a one. Except for bad jokes, Lionel didn't hurt no one. Not a soul. He'd even capture spiders and take them outside. He was one of the gentlest men I've ever known." He yawns and stretches. "Well, I've got to finish up a few things. Been up since three, and I've got to get things ready to hand off to Alice, the lady that closes up for me."

"So you and your wife go to bed early as bakers?" Helena asks after darting me a quick look. I don't know what she's getting at.

"Yup. Up at three, down by eight. It's our schedule. Why?"

"That means you and your wife were in bed asleep that night, right?" Helena asks.

He looks puzzled and then recognition dawns on his round face. "That night" being the night Lionel was killed.

"Of course. Why do you ask?"

"Oh… no reason. Just part of Aaron's assignment is asking how people found out, and I was just trying to find a way to ease into it."

He looks at me, his eyes narrowing again. "Well, that's a hell of an assignment you've got, son."

I nod, a knowing smile on my face. "I know."

"I remember it vividly. Both Ann and I were in the shop here when the sheriff came in and told us. He had a lot of questions for us." I'm about to ask another question, but he gets up and yawns again. "Now, if you two will excuse me, I've got to get moving. And, please, don't talk to my wife about this."

I nod and reach for my wallet.

"No need, son. This one's on the house."

After he's gone, Helena's eyes are wide and she nods to the door. There's something she wants to say.

————

WHEN WE GET OUTSIDE, HELENA IS LOOKING AROUND AND I open my mouth to speak and she whispers, "Not here," and starts walking back towards the bookstore.

There are so many questions. I look around for Tyson or his big hulk of a motorcycle, but I don't see either. She doesn't take my hand this time, she just walks up Main, takes a quick right on 65 North and ends up leaning against the old brick of Lionel Malak's former print shop.

"You okay?" I ask. I would prefer a more direct question about Tyson, or even about Joe Edwards, but the obvious agitation on her face forces that question.

"Fine," she says. She's not, it's totally obvious.

"Do you want to talk about it?" I ask, again being vague.

Her eyes are sharp as she searches my face. "You treating me like I break easy?"

"No... I..." I stammer. Yes, of course I was treating her that way. I have a moment of 100 percent empathy with my father being scared of my mother's strong displays of emotions. I don't know what's wrong. I'm afraid it's about me. She keeps staring. "Sorry about that," I add.

She nods once, her arms crossed, her eyes constantly looking towards Main Street.

"Tyson?" I ask.

She bites her lip. "He wasn't what he seemed."

"Was he the one you were excited about a few weeks ago?"

She blinks twice, her eyes meeting mine briefly, and says, "That he was."

"I'm sorry."

Her eyes come back to mine and stay there. "Do you mean that?" she asks, her voice low and a bit husky.

I shrug. "Well, yeah. You're in pain, I hate to see it."

The smile on her face I can only categorize as rueful. "You are the weirdest kid, Wade."

"What? Why?"

"You tell me you don't care if I date someone else," she says, "that you just want to spend time with me." I nod. "You meet my ex and instead of being jealous or crazy, you feel empathy for me."

"Well, to tell you the truth, I want to hit him on that pointy little chin of his." She laughs. "And I'm insanely jealous of his height and apparent health and that…" I trail off, I feel the bite of jealousy, and I am ashamed of it.

"Go on, please."

"Truth or Truth?" I ask.

"Always."

"He's older, taller, and better looking than me. I… I have no idea why you're hanging out with me." She gives me a "what the hell are you talking about" look. "Really, I don't get it. I'm this short, scrawny, sick kid. Why are you even spending time with me?" That pipsqueak comment Tyson made is a poison in my mind.

She smiles wide enough to show off her teeth. "I'm very glad to hear all this, Wade. Thank you."

"What are you talking about?"

"It just shows that you are human, just like the rest of us. I was beginning to have my doubts." She laughs and I can't help but smile.

We chat a little more about nothing much and then she grabs my hand and we go back to the bookstore. The sun is warm and bright again and I am as happy as I've ever been.

———

"WOMEN LIKE TO SEE SOME VULNERABILITY IN MEN," Lionel points. It's dark and we're in my room. I pulled out the Ouija papers to talk to him. We have been discussing the day.

"Really?" I whisper.

He nods and then points some more. "ASK YOUR MOM SHE WILL CONFIRM."

I always thought men were supposed to be all John Wayne or James Bond, tough and invulnerable. I think about what Lionel has said and whisper, "Some?"

"ALL THINGS IN BALANCE, MY FRIEND. TOO MUCH VULNERABILITY IS AS BAD AS TOO LITTLE."

I nod and think about that. I could see that if I shared every last fear I had, it would be off-putting—I've got plenty of fears.

"Did you learn anything from Mister Edwards?"

He shakes his head, his narrow face falling. He's got a similar slack look on his face as Joe Edwards did when we talked. "IT WAS HARD. I HAVEN'T SEEN HIM SINCE I DIED." He rubs at his face and I swear he's about to cry. Can ghosts cry? "I MISS HIM AND ANN HORRIBLY."

"From what he said, I don't know if we'll get a chance to talk to her."

The expression on his face is so complex, I have trouble reading it. It's a bit wistful, a bit fearful, and a whole lot of sad. "THAT MAY BE FOR THE BEST."

"What?"

"I DON'T KNOW IF I COULD BEAR IT."

I watch him closely in the dim light and point my little flashlight down into my comforter so I can see him better. Ghosts, or at least Lionel, glow. There's no other word for it. I think it's why I see them better in the dark. Because of this I can see his face clearly. There is something complex going on there. With Vincent Long and Joe Edwards he was easier to read—sad was the predominant emotion. With Ann Edwards, the sadness is there, but there is something wistful there too.

"Is she special to you, Lionel?" I whisper.

He looks at me, as if he forgot I was there, a surprised look on his face. "I'M TIRED. I SHOULD REST NOW AND SO SHOULD YOU."

He slowly fades away and I'm left here wondering what he's not telling me.

35

THURSDAY, JULY 21, 1977

TODAY FOR BREAKFAST, I AM UP TO HAVING A FEW blueberries on my oatmeal and some margarine on my toast. It's a good day in the food department and both of the parents seem to be cheerful.

"Your mother and I have discussed it," Dad begins after noisily folding up his paper, a little grin on his face. "We think it would be okay for you to take Helena out."

I must look silly frozen there, my mouth wide, a triangle of toast halfway to my mouth.

My mother laughs and my father's grin turns into a huge smile.

I manage to unfreeze my jaw. "I... Well... Thank you!" I hug my father and then my mother.

"There is a condition," he says.

I sit back down. That introduces the element of fear. Fear of the condition, yes, but much more fear of the actual "date" with an actual "girl." That girl being the most amazing Helena Monfort who recently dated the tall, handsome, older Tyson, and really could date just about any boy she wanted.

"It's not that bad of a condition," my father says. I guess he thinks the horror on my face is about that.

"Condition?" I ask, I'm trying to fight my way back to reality.

"You and I have to have our little talk that I mentioned, and I will be your chauffeur for the evening."

My mind is a whirl. The last thing I want is for my father to drive us, but, honestly, that is not the bulk of my concern. Now that we have approval, I have to formally ask for the date. Think of a place to take her. Figure out what to wear. I've never been on a date. What if she's changed her mind and says no? Which would be worse, a "yes" and having to figure all this out or a "no" and dealing with the rejection?

"Are you okay, Aaron?" Mom asks, her warm hand on my shoulder.

"Fine," I mumble. I am most definitely not.

"We're thinking next Wednesday," Dad says. "You should be pretty recovered from your chemo by then, and we need you in early on Thursday so you can have a good night's sleep before we go to Vegas."

"Wednesday," I repeat and nod. It barely registers. That's less than a week.

"Well, I've got to go," Dad says as he gets up, patting his mouth with a napkin. "Talk to your girl and let me know if we're on for next Wednesday."

My girl. It sounds so strange. Helena isn't "mine," not by any stretch. But she is something so special to me.

I don't know how long I'm sitting there, thoughts whirling around in my head, but my mother finally says, "Would you like to talk about it?"

I look at her and can see in her eyes, this would be another "special" thing I could do for her. But I can't, at least not directly. "Do... do women like to see some vulnerability in men?"

She looks surprised, I'm sure that's not quite what she expected. She purses her lips, her eye searching my face. "Umm... I don't know if I would put it that way."

"What way then?"

"I think we like to know our men. We like to know what they are thinking, what they love as well as what they fear. Their strengths and their weaknesses. We want to know them. And, I guess, that might feel like vulnerability from a male perspective, but it's not. Letting these kinds of things show takes great strength."

I stare at my mom, she's becoming this whole other person to me. I really can't believe it, but she is acting like my friend more and more.

I thank her for the answer and force myself onto a different track. I update her on our time with Joe Edwards.

"What's next?" she asks after I'm done.

I shrug and finally get that bite of toast in my mouth. It's cold now, but since it's got margarine on it, I consider it a bit of a victory. "I don't know. Lionel was so strange about Ann Edwards."

My mother looks down, suddenly all demure. "I think they were having an affair," she says, her voice quiet. I have this realization about mom and Doctor Rogers. She feels guilty about it. Even with the strange circumstances of her marriage and my father's knowledge and tacit approval, there is still guilt.

"Why do you say that?"

"Well, without what you told me, I wouldn't have put it together. But I remember seeing Lionel at the bakery this one time. It was last spring, a particularly warm day, and I glanced in. He was sitting at one of the tables watching her as she took care of a customer. His look... well, it was like she was the only person in the world."

I take a deep breath and sigh. I'm not happy about this

complication. If this is true, why didn't Lionel tell me? How am I supposed to help him if he doesn't tell me everything?

———

THURSDAYS FOR ME ARE NOW BITTER SWEET. I FEEL PRETTY good, low energy and metally mouth aside, but I know what's about to come on Friday. Another punch in the gut by the mighty chemo monster. And this Thursday is complicated by a huge case of the nerves. I have to ask Helena Monfort out for a date. Officially.

And don't get me wrong, I want to, but I somehow doubt I am strong enough to hear the answer. Either answer. My day is a blur until the bell to the bookstore rings and she walks through the door. My heart leaps and I feel myself beginning to sweat.

She's back in jeans and a T-shirt—I honestly miss the skirt —and looks upset.

"Tyson?" I ask as she comes behind the counter and sits next to me on a stool.

She slumps against the wall and lets out a long sigh. "Asshole," she says.

"You want to talk about it?"

She shakes her head, but then says, "He was beating on my door in the middle of the night drunk. My father had to chase him off."

"I'm sorry," I say. I don't know what else to say.

She shrugs and says, "Talk to me. Distract me."

So I update her on my conversation with Lionel and what my mom said about a possible affair.

"Men do get weird when they have feelings," she says and then looks at me with a grin. "Except you. You seem immune."

I just blink, I can't speak. How wrong she is. I have feelings,

I have something to ask her, and I know I am weird right now. So weird.

"What's wrong?" she asks, sitting up on the stool and looking at me, her hand touching my shoulder.

What happens next, I can only chalk up to a little thing I've come to call chemo-courage. I really should call it Cancer-courage, but that just doesn't feel right. In that moment with Helena, time seemed to slow down, and the fact that I would be hooked to an IV for four hours tomorrow, that the treatment would kick the shit out of me, that I was in treatment because I was on my third strike with leukemia. All of those things give me courage.

And here's the thing about courage, if there is no fear, then what you are doing is not courageous. I am sweating, I can feel a bead of sweat tickling its way down my back. My hands are shaking and I can barely speak.

"Will... I... Helena... you..." I stutter and stammer, the look of concern growing on Helena's face. This is my first time doing something like this.

Helena seems to figure something out because the look of concern transforms into one of restrained amusement. Her brown eyes are bright and her pursed lips holding back a smile. "It's okay, Wade. I won't bite, I promise." I have to imagine I'm not the first boy who sounded like an idiot trying to ask her out.

I scratch at my shirt, wishing I didn't have to wear long-sleeve, button-down shirts at the bookstore. It feels like it's strangling me.

"Will you...? Can we...?" I close my eyes and take a slow, deep breath. I calm a bit, just enough, and ask her, keeping my eyes closed. "Will you go out with me next Wednesday?"

In some ways I'm glad I can't see her. I can hear her breathing, smell her tobacco-mint breath, feel the warmth of her near me, but I can't see her face. Whether she's amused or devastated or bored.

"Open your eyes, please," she says softly.

When I do, the look on her face is none of those. It's... hmmm, how to describe. She has a small smile on her face, her eyes are bright, but her eyebrows are a bit furrowed, making it look like there's some concern, some worry.

"Yes, I will go out with you."

The rest of my breath comes whooshing out of me and I sag on the stool feeling exhausted. It's like I just rode my bike hard for miles, this feeling. How can asking a simple question do that to you?

"Thank you," I mumble.

She chuckles and gets up. "I better go. I hope tomorrow is not too bad." I watch her as she walks to the door wondering if my face has the kind of look on it that Mom saw on Lionel's face when he watched Ann Edwards. I get what she was saying. When Helena is in the room, she kind of takes things over for me.

She looks back and smiles. "Call me this weekend, okay?"

"Yeah, of course."

36

SUNDAY, JULY 24, 1977

THE LAST FEW DAYS HAVE BEEN A BLUR OF PUKING AND feverish sleep. I'm not sure what's happening, but this chemo seems to be knocking me down hard. Maybe I've just forgotten how hard this really is. Maybe something really is different, I can't really tell. There's not much to say, though. It's been all about survival, boring stuff really.

"You've got some visitors," Mom says on Sunday afternoon. I'm up in my bedroom propped up on pillows trying to read *Sleeping Murder*, Agatha Christie's last novel, and even in my exhausted state I notice the sparkle in my mother's eye.

"I feel… uuuck," I say.

"I think you'll want to come down," she says, a smile playing at her lips. That gets my attention, she hasn't smiled in days and the circles under her eyes are getting darker.

"Why?"

"It's Pastor West and the Edwards. They've borrowed a truck and they've come to get the swing set."

My heart is suddenly pounding in my chest and I'm more awake than I've been in days. "Here? Now?"

She laughs. It's a small thing, but I'm glad to hear it. Then I remember Pastor West's visit last week and his cologne. I wrinkle my nose and put my hand on my stomach. "I don't think I can handle his cologne."

"We talked after what happened last week. He's not wearing any. Neither are the Edwards." She pauses and smiles again. "I thought you and I and Mrs. Edwards could have a little tea while the boys take the swing apart and load it up." The smile on her face is positively mischievous. "Does that sound good?"

"Yeah," I say with a smile. "That sounds great."

———

Did I already mention how much I love the change in my mother? I bet I have, but I just have to say it again. Parts of our relationship becoming a friendship is awesome. Really. I wonder if this is what it is like when you grow up and are away from the house for a while. Do your parents become more like friends? I'm sure they always worry about you, but maybe they become mostly friends. It gives me something to hope for past these sick teenage years.

Ann Edwards is lean and sinewy, very different from her doughy husband. She's got shoulder-length black hair with a noticeable amount of grey sneaking in. By the time I put some clothes on and make it downstairs, Mrs. Edwards is sitting at our kitchen table and Mom is pouring tea.

"There you are," Mom says, a small smile on her face. "Aaron, you remember Ann Edwards, don't you?"

"Of course," I say, extending my hand to her. Her grip is weak and her hand is moist. Her hazel eyes look sad and she's got dark circles under her eyes like my mom. "I'm glad Pastor West found a good use for the swing set."

"Thank you," she says slowly, forming the words with what

appears to be great deliberation. "Silvia will be most grateful too, I am sure."

I sit down across from her and my mother sits between us. "We are so sorry for your losses," Mom says. "I can't imagine what you've been through, losing your one sister and your other sister's medical issues." Mom is being tactful, those "medical issues" being mental in nature.

It makes me think of my trip to Saint George with Helena to meet her mother. What Helena has been through with her unstable, knife-wielding mother. Physical illnesses are difficult, like the big-C, but I can't imagine how hard it is to cope with mental illness.

"Thank you," Mrs. Edwards says, bringing her cup to her lips and blowing on the steam. The smell of mint is strong, Mom has served mint tea to us all, and I am grateful for it. My stomach isn't doing well at all and the mint is helpful. "And I'm sorry to hear about your…" she adds, looking at me.

"My relapse," I finish. Mrs. Edwards nods sharply and bites her lower lip. "It's okay to talk about it." Past Ann Edwards I can see Joe Edwards, Pastor West, and my father eyeing the swing set. I feel a brief pang of longing for the time when I was young and healthy and my mother had to yell at me to get off the swing.

"You are very brave," Mrs. Edwards says.

I shrug. "So are you, and kind to take in your niece."

She tries to smile again, but the attempt seems to be in vain, it's a twisted little thing. Her smile conveys only sorrow. I find myself wondering what Lionel saw in her, but maybe that was a happy time then. Maybe the burden of what has happened has changed her. How could it not?

No one talks for a bit, the clanging of tools against metal from outside and the sipping of tea really the only sounds. It's awkward.

"When does Silvia arrive?" my mother finally asks.

"We are driving up to Salt Lake tomorrow to get her," Mrs. Edwards says.

"What a big change to your household," Mom says. "If there is anything I can do, please don't hesitate to ask."

"Thank you," she says.

It's all so awkward. I am trying to think of an excuse to go back to my bedroom—I could fake a puke attack—when my mother takes a deep breath and straightens up.

"So much tragedy for you in the last year," Mom says.

Ann bites at her lower lip again and nods. That lower lip biting seems to be a nervous habit.

"Did you know Lionel Malak well? So terrible what happened to him."

I am watching Mrs. Edwards closely. When Lionel's name is mentioned, her eyes look even sadder and I can see them mist up. She doesn't cry, but it looks like she wants to. She takes a sip of her tea to, I believe, try to cover up her reaction.

"Not the kind of thing we see in our town," Mom continues. "It makes me worry about Henry and Aaron at the bookstore if there is some crazy person running around."

Mrs. Edwards reacts to the words "crazy person." She jumps, just a bit, as if there had been a loud noise or someone had yelled.

"And they never caught the perpetrator," Mom says, her forehead wrinkled in concern. I have to wonder how much of it is put on. I had no idea my mom had so much Nancy Drew in her.

"Are you okay, Mrs. Edwards?" I ask. She's gone a bit pale and is blinking too much.

"I'm sorry," my mom says, leaning towards her. "Have I upset you?"

"No... No..." she says, holding her hand up. "I am fine. It's just... Well, you are right. There have been too many tragedies.

I hope that is all behind us now. That we can just go about our lives in peace."

The way she says it makes me believe she hasn't had much peace in her life lately.

———

LIONEL MALAK IS FURIOUS WITH ME. IT'S STRANGE SEEING A ghost flush red with anger, but I guess it is possible. It's dark and we're in my room. I excused myself early from dinner, I couldn't eat much anyway.

"WHY DID YOU AND YOUR MOTHER FEEL THE NEED TO UPSET HER SO?" he asks, pointing at the letters on the Ouija papers so quickly I can barely keep up.

I'm really not in the mood. I meet his anger. "Why didn't you tell me you were having an affair with her?" I hiss back.

He folds his arms, his gaunt face looking suddenly petulant. "LEAVE HER BE. SHE DIDN'T DO IT."

"But you did have an affair with her, didn't you?"

He folds his arms across his slim chest, takes what appears to be a deep breath (he's a ghost, not sure why he would need to do that), and slowly nods.

"Did her husband know?" It's an important question.

"HE DIDN'T DO IT."

"That's not an answer."

His eyes dart up and to the right, he appears to sigh, and then he shakes his head "no."

"So he didn't know... Maybe he found out, maybe—"

Lionel is in my face and I swear to god I can almost hear him speak. Maybe it's my imagination, but I hear him shouting "no" in a reedy, strained voice.

My heart is pounding, this is feeling less like a friendly conversation with the afterlife and a little more like a haunting. "I think you should leave," I say, I don't even bother to whisper.

He steps back, blinking as his jaw moves. If he is still speaking, I can't hear him. "I'm trying to help you," I whisper. "But if you aren't willing to consider the Edwards, to be honest with me, I think you just have to learn to live without knowing."

I swing my legs out of bed and stand up. I feel dizzy, spots swimming in front of my eyes. I make my slow way to the bathroom. Lionel does not follow.

37

MONDAY, JULY 25, 1977

I'VE GOT A COUGH TODAY. IT'S NOT BAD BUT IN MY condition it is worrisome. Leukemia is all about the immune system. My body is producing some crappy white blood cells which don't work very well. On top of that, the chemo kicks what's left of my immune system in the teeth.

I didn't sleep well last night. After my encounter with Lionel, I lay awake in bed thinking it over. Murders are most often done by someone the victim knows. Murders are often crimes of passion. I am beginning to believe that Joe Edwards did it after he found out about Lionel's affair with his wife.

But what do I do with that information? Tell the sheriff? He's not going to believe me, and even if he did, there is no proof. And the accusation itself could cause lots of problems. Because if he is a murderer and I accuse him, that puts me and my family in danger. If he isn't, then that creates a rift in our small town.

And then when I finally sleep, I have a nightmare. I'm in a big abandoned building, some kind of factory. It's got red brick walls and high ceilings. It's dark, with only a crescent moon sending silvery shafts of light through the high square windows. I hear a scrape of foot against bare concrete, I see the shadow of a person with a long thin knife in their hand. A knife like the one that was found in Lionel Malak's back. I run and hide, but I keep hearing the scrape of a foot, seeing the knife-wielding shadow.

I wake up with a start, sucking air deep into my lungs and coughing it out. I had heard a sound, like that scrape of a foot against pavement like in my dream. I look around, rubbing at my eyes, feeling my heart thumping in my chest. It's my mother. She's sitting on the edge of my bed, a concerned look on her tired face. I think the creaking of my box spring when she sat is what woke me up.

"You don't look good," she says, holding the back of her hand to my forehead. "You've got a fever."

I rub at my face some more trying to come back to reality. I look over at my clock, it says 8:52. I never sleep this late. Something must be wrong.

"Don't move," she says and gets up and leaves the room swiftly.

I groan. This is not good. My lower back hurts, my chest is tight, and my head feels like it's not screwed on properly. Not good at all.

If I was a normal, healthy person, this level of sick would not be a big deal. Could be a twenty-four-hour bug. Easy. But I am not normal and neither is my immune system. Any kind of infection like this is a big deal. I could tell by my mother's demeanor.

She comes back with a glass of water, a thermometer, a mask over her mouth and nose, and her kit for drawing my blood.

I take the water and drink it down. I'm very thirsty, but when she goes to put the thermometer in my mouth, I shake my head.

"What?" she asks, her blue eyes shading towards sapphire. I don't know if this is a real thing, but when she's so concerned that the lifesaving nurse part of her takes over, her eyes always seem darker.

"We need to talk first," I say. I know what's coming and it's all about survival. There may not be time later.

Her eyebrows furrow as she considers. There seems to be a bit of a battle between nurse-mom and friend-mom. She bites her lip and grabs my arm. "You can talk while I draw some blood."

And I do. I tell her about my talk with Lionel, and I don't leave anything out. I tell her of my suspicions of Joe Edwards and that Lionel confirmed the affair with Ann Edwards. "What do we do?" I ask when I am done.

She pops the thermometer in my mouth and says, "Right now we focus on getting you better." Her voice is a tad muffled behind the mask. I hate it when the masks come out. It happens any time I get sick when the big-C is visiting. My parents wear them, and visitors—if I'm lucky enough to have them—do too.

And then a thought comes crashing down on me. It's Monday, Wednesday is just two days away. I have to be well enough to go out with Helena. I just have to be. I mumble "date" around the thermometer.

"We'll see," my mother says. Friend-mom is definitely on vacation.

Her forehead crinkles as she studies my face. "And I'm going to have to bring your father in on the whole Lionel Malak murder thing."

"Buuut..." I say, the thermometer really starting to annoy me.

"No buts, Aaron. We have a suspect and a motive. I don't know what to do next, we need him."

I nod and smile. She said that *we* have a suspect. Looks like friend-mom is still in there a bit, but I am very worried about my father's reaction to Mom and me keeping secrets from him and going directly against what he said.

She takes the thermometer out and I swear I can tell there is a frown under the mask. "99.5. It's not much of a fever, but it is a fever."

I sigh and lie back down, I know what's coming.

"Stay in bed. I'm going to run your blood over to the hospital. I'll be back."

I nod, I am sure the disappointment about this is showing clearly on my face.

"We've been through this before," Mom says from the door. "We'll get you better."

"By Wednesday?"

"We'll try," she says, but I know the odds are stacked against it. When I get sick, especially with the double whammy of leukemia and chemo, I don't get well quickly.

I throw the covers over my head and groan.

———

WHAT I AM ABOUT TO SAY WILL PROBABLY MAKE ME SOUND like a grumpy old man, but what the heck. Life is hard. It is. For everyone. At least for everyone I know.

My mom and dad in their barely-there marriage, my mother probably really wanting to be with her boyfriend, my dad... well we haven't really talked about it and it feels awkward anyway. On top of that they've got me and my multi-part dance with the C-monster.

Look at Helena, she's the "lady of the house" and has had to deal with some of the harsher realities of mental illness. She also has had a terrible time with boys.

Lionel Malak is dead and we may have found his murderer,

but he can't face it. Not even in his death does "life" get easy for him.

Even Billy doesn't have it easy. He's chubby, terrible at sports, has never had a girlfriend, and gets teased a lot. He wrestles with the dichotomy between his faith and the world he lives in. That and he longs for Barbara Bach in a way that can't be comfortable.

Everyone has their challenges. Everyone. We all seek to escape these kinds of difficulties, but it just seems impossible. There is so very much about this life that is completely out of our control.

So my days as a bedridden sicky have begun. And my life has gotten even harder. Monday passes slowly. I'm not sick enough to sleep that much, so I stay in bed and read. I have my mom bring me *The Lord of the Rings* and read it for the fifth time. I need something that is reliably distracting.

Billy comes over in the afternoon. My mom lets him visit for a whopping twenty minutes. Even with the mask, she is extra vigilant. Billy is worried. He's got this little line between his eyebrows. It's a subtle thing, I don't think he knows he does it, but when he's got something that is really bothering him, it's this bit of tension that shows on his face.

"Joe Edwards?" he says slowly, scratching at a pimple on his forehead. I filled him in on all the latest. He also brought me a pile of comics to read while I'm down. Some Doctor Strange, Silver Surfer, and The Avengers. Stuff I haven't read in a while.

"He had a reason to do it," I say.

Billy bites his lip. "What do we do?"

I'm heartened that he used "we" just like when my mom did. "Not a clue. I have no idea how we prove it and Lionel is MIA.

Billy gets quiet. He's sitting on my desk chair, he pulled it up next to my bed. That line between his eyebrows is deeper and his eyes aren't focused.

Here's the tough thing about being sick. What it does to other people. They think about your mortality. They worry about what is happening to you. They get feeling all helpless and don't know what to do to make things better.

With Billy, I know he is worried about me. He's been on this whole adventure, so he knows how serious a cold can get.

"Don't worry, B," I say with a smile. "I'm going to kick this thing's ass and we'll be back to normal in no time."

His face stays in the worried configuration for half a minute before a smile flicks onto his face. "I know, A. You'll be up in no time."

I'm not telling him because I have this great faith in my ability to get better. I'm saying it because it hurts to see my friends and family like that.

———

"You don't break easy, right?" I ask Helena. It's about seven and she is sitting on the same chair Billy was, dressed in her La Familia outfit, her face made up.

The last time I saw her like this was in the graveyard. Now in real light, I can see how old she looks in the makeup she has on, even with the mask she is wearing over her nose and mouth. It's really quite stunning. She looks like she's at least twenty. So mature. So beautiful.

"You know it," she says.

I nod and hand her my diary. "Then I need you to do something."

Her brows furrow as she looks at my writing. "This is encoded or something, right? Because if it isn't, I've got a major problem."

"Yeah," I say quietly. "Time to teach you how to read it."

She puts the diary down and stares at me, her mouth a thin line. "Why?" she asks, her voice low and cautious.

"Truth or truth?"

She nods slowly but doesn't speak.

"I'm afraid. I—" A coughing fit cuts me off. I'm feeling worse than I did in the morning. Some of that could be the normal nighttime sicky stuff. But it could also be something else. Judging from my mother's face last time I saw her, she seems to think I'm getting worse too.

"I've written a lot," I begin again. "About Lionel and the clues we followed. About my family and what we're going through. And... And about you and how I feel."

She's blinking a lot now, a light blush of red on her cheeks. I'm not sure, but I think her eyes are a bit moist too.

I take a breath, a shallow one, I don't want to start another coughing fit. "I need you to take care of these if something happens."

"You're going to be fine, Wade. This is just a little bump. This—"

I hold up my hand. "Truth or truth, Helena. Please." We started this game together when we first met. I need someone I can lay it all out for. And she doesn't break easily, right?

She swallows hard. Now I'm sure there's moisture in her eyes. I hate this, but she's the only one I can imagine being able to handle this right now. Being strong enough. She shifts uncomfortably in the wooden chair and looks away, but I watch her face. She bites on her lower lip, sniffs, and blinks a few times.

"I need you to do this. I don't know who else can..." I trail off, a tear is now running down her cheek and I feel sick to my stomach (sicker than normal, that is).

She sniffs again, straightens up, and turns to me. "Okay. How do I read this thing?"

————

TEACHING HELENA IS ACTUALLY QUITE FUN. SHE'S QUICK and picks it up pretty fast.

"It's a letter shifting algorithm," I say.

She looks at me blankly. I guess if you haven't read about these kinds of things those words don't mean much. I have her get a piece of paper from my desk and I write out all the consonants.

BCDFGHJKLMNPQRSTVWXYZ

"When I write, I shift letters in the words in a particular way." She nods. "I cooked this up myself and I think it is unique. I shift only consonants, I alternate how they are shifted, and I reset at the beginning of every sentence."

She's looking confused, but I expected that. So I show her.

"So if we are starting a sentence with the word 'Helena,' we are going to shift only the consonants in a +5, -5 pattern. So 'H' plus 5 turns into 'N', the 'L' minus 5 turns into 'F'." I look up and she is nodding.

"So the 'N' would be plus five." She leans over and I allow myself a glance at her cleavage, which is well displayed in her La Familia blouse. I take this as a good sign that I'm still alive. She runs her finger along the paper with all the consonants, her face close to mine. Even with the mask I can smell the cigarette-mint scent that is so her. I don't want the moment to end. I want her close as much as possible. "So that's 'T,'" she says, sitting back in the chair.

"Right," I say, feeling rather flushed in my cheeks and hoping she doesn't notice. "So 'Helena' transforms into 'Nefeta.'"

Helena flips through my diary and says, "Okay, I see 'Nefeta' in here a bunch of times. Is my name always Nefeta?"

I shake my head. "No, it depends on where the name falls, whether it's plus 5 or minus 5. Remember the algorithm resets every sentence, so in the middle of a sentence it might be 'Bereha.'"

She flips through the diary some more and nods. "Okay, I see those here. And so Billy would be either..." She leans close again, her finger running along the paper. I try to soak as much of her in as I can. I feel excited by her presence and sick at the same time. I feel happy to have her near and am scared of what the future might bring. "'Hifrs' or... Wait, when you do minus five from 'B' what happens?"

I gently take her finger in my hand, which was pointing to the 'B,' and guide it to the 'Z' and then backwards from there. Her hand is warm and I feel even flusher than I have. "You just wrap around, so 'B', goes to 'Z,' 'Y,' 'X,' 'W,' and ends up 'V.'"

She nods. If this nearness thing is affecting her, I can't tell. Her brain seems fully engaged. "So that would be 'Virf...' The 'Y' would wrap the other way?" she asks.

I nod.

"So it's 'Virff'... Oh, wow, two fs. 'Billy turns into 'Hifrs' or 'Virff.'"

"You go it."

She leans fully back in the chair staring at the diary, her brow furrowed. "But... This ain't easy to do. I mean... every word."

"It takes some time," I say. "I was slow at first, but I don't have to think about it much now."

She snorts. "Yeah, but you're smart. I'm..."

"Smart, Helena, you're smart."

She shrugs, still looking at my diary. "I get Cs in school. I don't read constantly like you."

"That's knowledge not intelligence," I say. "You get Cs in school because you are busy keeping your household afloat. You could get As if you had the time."

She looks at me, all shy like. It's not an expression I'm used to seeing on her face. "You're not bullshitting me, are you?"

I shake my head. "God, no. I don't know many kids that could pull off what you do at your age. You work. You take care of your father. You help skinny kids try to solve murders." She smiles at that. "You picked up my crazy diary encryption in five minutes. Believe me, I know you're smart."

"I don't know..." she mumbles, shaking her head, still looking down at the diary.

"I can prove it," I say, getting out of bed and moving towards my bookshelf. A wave of dizziness passes over me and Helena is there beside me holding my arm. "Just got up too fast," I say, but she keeps a hold of me. I pull out my first diary, the one that I started this all with and hand it to her.

She looks confused. "What..."

"Read it. This starts the night before we met. I gave you a five-minute lesson, I bet after a day or so you won't need to use that list of consonants, you'll just be able to read it."

She nods solemnly at me and holds my arm while I make my way back to bed.

"You're smart, Helena. I know it, it's time that you did too."

She looks like she's about to cry and I feel bad about it, my mind racing trying to figure out if I did something wrong. She doesn't sit back down, but stands there holding my diary to her chest like it's something precious.

"I better get to work," she says, turning for the door.

I want to say something, find out if she's okay, if I did something wrong. But before I can get a word out, she's leaning down next to my bed and kisses me on the cheek through her mask. "Thank you, Wade."

And then she is gone. It's a long time before I can get to sleep.

38

TUESDAY, JULY 26, 1977

THIS IS NOT GOOD. I WAS AWAKE MOST OF THE NIGHT coughing, my mother attending to me each time. I feel bad about it. She's not getting any rest either.

My dad comes in before he leaves for school, he's got the "Aaron's sick" pinched look on his face, a mask covering his nose and mouth. There's something else in his eyes too, and I feel a spike of fear. I'm sure Mom has told him about our continued investigations of Lionel's murder.

"Hey, pal," he says, sitting on my bed. He's got tan slacks and a long-sleeve dress shirt on.

"Hey, Dad."

He purses his lips as he looks at me. I saw myself in the mirror a little bit ago. I look like hell.

"Doctor Rogers will be coming over shortly."

I swallow hard, getting the gunk out of the back of my throat. I'm confused, why would Mom's boyfriend be coming over?

"We think it's better not to have you around other sick people if we can avoid it," he says.

My mind is sluggish. Doctor Rogers is coming over to examine me. He's the head of the ER as well as being my mom's boyfriend.

"Are you okay with that?"

A coughing fit delays my reply. "Does it have to be him?"

"I know it's confusing," Dad says. "But he's good at what he does, and because of his relationship with your mother, he's willing to bend the rules a bit and do this."

It makes sense. "I don't have to like him, do I?"

My dad smiles broadly, even through the mask I can tell. "No, son. You certainly don't have to."

He leans down and kisses me on the forehead before standing up and saying, "I'll be home just as soon as class is over."

My father isn't much of a kisser, and the mask was in the way. It just makes it clear that things aren't good.

———

DOCTOR ROGERS HAS WARM HANDS AND COOL BLUE EYES. I've been examined a thousand times by doctors, he is efficient and direct. I thought I would feel awkward, but I'm really too sick to care that much. I am rapidly getting worse.

He feels the lymph nodes at my neck. He has me take my shirt off and listens to my heart from the front and then my lungs from the back. That's when I notice his warms hands. It's a small thing, but I really appreciate it. Cold hands on your sick body is no fun at all.

My mom stands in the doorway watching, fidgeting with a notebook gripped in her hand. It's the "Aaron Notebook," the one she keeps with my vitals, notes on how I feel, when I throw up, stuff like that. I think of it as the "puke journal."

When Doctor Rogers pulls a mercury thermometer out of his bag and swabs it with an alcohol pad, my mom rushes up and shows him the notebook. I watch closely to see if there is anything out of the ordinary in their interaction, but it's all business. He sticks the thermometer in my mouth and looks at the notebook, his index finger running down a line of figures.

He's handsome, more so than my father, I think. You would probably say my father is "bookish." Doctor Rogers is, on the other hand, athletic. He's over forty with grey decorating the temples of his short black hair. His face is square and his body is obviously strong.

I manage to not cough while the thermometer is in my mouth, but after it's out, I have a whopper, getting gobs of green out onto a tissue. There's a box of tissues on my bed and a trashcan right next to it. My mom must empty the thing ten times a day.

When I can look around again, they've left the room. I hear them talking out in the hallway.

"I'd like to hear," I croak, the mucus in my throat making it hard to talk. They seem to ignore me. "Hello!" I say as loud as I can, which is just a louder croak. I've never been comfortable with these conversations happening without me. But I've never said anything about it before. It feels good and it feels scary at the same time.

The talking stops and it's quiet for a little bit. My mother then comes in, her arms wrapped around her chest, followed by Doctor Rogers. He glances at her and now I see it, the relationship there. It's not the look a doctor would give the mother of any old patient. It's a look filled with concern and a bit of trepidation.

"I was just telling your mother," he says, "that you need hospitalization and IV antibiotics."

I groan. I hate hospitals. God how I hate them. No privacy. No rest. Nothing to do but lie there and be sick.

Doctor Rogers comes and sits on the edge of my bed. He's

back to being a doctor, and I have to admit he has a good bedside manner. "Your body can't fight this alone, Aaron."

I nod and look at my mom who is studying her feet. I'm not all there, but I put it together, her look and his trepidation. "So what's the argument about?" I ask.

My mother looks up, surprised, and then takes a deep breath and says, "I want to take you to the children's hospital in Vegas. Doctor Rogers feels you need intervention now."

I look at my mother and ask, "Do I get a say?"

She blinks, her eyebrows furrowing, her bare feet scraping at my blue shag carpet. "I... well—"

"I want to stay in Cedar," I say, not waiting for her answer.

"Why?" she asks, her blue eyes finding mine. She looks so scared, it makes my stomach flutter.

"Because here I—" a coughing fit takes over and Doctor Rogers's warm hand is on my back, his other one handing me tissues. Quite despite myself, I am starting to like him.

"—this is my home," I choke out. "Friends. Family. Better."

I don't think I'm being very coherent. I want to tell her how if I'm here, my friends will visit, and that will help me get better. That if I'm here, it will be easier on my family. But it seems to be enough, my mom nods, giving Doctor Rogers a look that conveys a whole book of emotions. It's not much of a look, really, a widening of her eyes, her head leaning forward, her lips parted as if to speak. But it says, "I'm counting on you to save my son."

As Doctor Rogers wraps me in a blanket and lifts me up in his strong arms, I feel for the guy. If this doesn't go well, my mother will never forgive him.

As we leave my room with its pitched roof and glow-in-the-dark stars on the ceiling, I close my eyes. I see a flash of light out of my peripheral vision and I know Lionel is back. That Lionel is with me. And I find comfort in that. If I am going to die, maybe he will be there to help me.

PART 5

A Boy and a Ghost

39

SUNDAY, JULY 31, 1977

I WAKE UP IN THE ICU, THE BEEP, BEEP OF MY HEARTBEAT ON the monitor pulling me from the inky depths. My eyes are sticky and I can't open them. I have vague memories, of riding to the hospital in the backseat of Doctor Rogers's car. Of a large nurse with round glasses and black hair. Of endless coughing. Of a long conversation with Lionel Malak. Of other ghosts gathered in a large group.

That brings me back. Lionel and I had a talk. Well, "talk" doesn't really encompass the scope of it. It was an argument and I remember him yelling at me and… It's not quite in focus, but something happened. A lot happened.

I try to speak, but there is something in my mouth and my throat hurts horribly. I'm intubated, not for the first time. My heart is thumping, I hear the beeps on the monitor speed up and I try to calm down. The tube is pushing air into my lungs, and I hate the feeling, so helpless and out of control.

I feel an IV in my left arm, so I slap my right hand on the bed, as I force my eyes open. The bright white of the fluorescents hurt, so I shut them again and bang my hand a second time. My head is elevated and I get a glimpse of a person in the room.

I feel a warm hand take mine. I crack my eyes open and try to focus, but I can't see very well. Long dark hair and a round face.

"Just stay calm," she says, her voice is anything but. "I'll get someone." I feel her hand letting go of mine and I squeeze it as hard as I can. It's Helena. I don't want her to leave.

"Okay, okay," she says. "I'm here, Wade. I won't leave you." I give her hand another squeeze and feel tears leaking out of my eyes. Which, in this case, is good. I can see her a bit clearer. She's got on a big long-sleeved T-shirt and sweats, her hair loosely pulled back, and she looks exhausted.

"Can I get some help in here?" she yells.

I want to tell her there's a button to call the nurse, but that damn machine is still pumping air into my lungs like I'm some kind of blowup doll or something.

"Somebody!" she yells, louder, a hysterical edge to her voice.

I calm down some now that I know there will be help soon. I'm alive and Helena is here. That much, at least, is all good.

My mother rushes in, she's a mess too. Her brown hair flat and lifeless, the dark circles under her eyes as big as I've ever seen them. She rushes over to me and Helena makes to let go of my hand, but I hold her even tighter.

"He won't let go," Helena says as Mom tries to stand where Helena is.

I see a look on my mother's face. It's hard to read, maybe one part jealousy and two parts hope.

"Just stay calm, Aaron," she says, her lips devoid of their ever-present pink lipstick. It's odd seeing her this way. "I'll be right back with Doctor Rogers."

I give her a nod.

Helena shifts her hand in mine, I think she's just trying to get it more comfortable, I was probably squishing her fingers. "Don't worry," she says. "I'm not letting go."

And there it is. Right there. That moment. The thing to live for. This fascinating and complicated woman (let's face it, she's not a girl) by my side, not letting go.

I give her hand a gentle squeeze, looking into the depths of those golden-brown eyes. She's got a grimace of a smile on her face and—for her—looks like hell. But I don't care what she looks like. I only care that she's here, that she's my friend.

I feel tears spilling out of my eyes and Helena follows suit. She brushes at her face with her right hand, only making it more obvious that she is crying. Her smile gets broader, but still has that grimacey crying look.

It's strange, but right then I don't want the moment to end. Not ever. Me and Helena, connection and hope. What more could I want except for the damn tube out of my throat?

40

TUESDAY, JULY 26, 1977

(continued)

THINGS CAME BACK TO ME AS I FINISHED MY TIME IN THE hospital. Strange things. Scary things. Lionel Malak and his band of ghosts. And yes, I'm a little out of order here with these entries, having jumped back from waking up five days ago. But it took time to remember it all, to get well enough so I understood what actually happened.

So indulge me as I flip back in time.

My little cold had settled into my lungs and my poor immune system couldn't handle it. It went from a chest cold to bronchitis to pneumonia lickety-split.

Pneumonia boils down to an infection of the lungs that results in fluid building up. The lungs being an apparatus to breathe, you can imagine that fluid down there is really bad.

Nurse Iona, the one I mentioned earlier with glasses, black hair, and ample proportions, was on shift when I came in. She has this ease to her as she goes about doing her job. She moves slowly, but efficiently. It's a slow/fast kind of thing.

She is an ER nurse—just like my mom—and looked

familiar although I would not have been able to tell you her name. When I first got there, she helped me into the awful hospital gown in a little curtained-off area in the ER.

"Don't be ashamed, sonny-boy. I seen plenty a white b-hind in my days here." Iona is black, quite a rarity in Cedar City, Utah. She gave a husky laugh after that.

She gets me into the hospital bed, hooks me up to an IV, and leaves me there alone.

I'm not alone for long. I think my mom was trying to call my dad, but it gave me time to think. It is getting harder to breathe. I've had pneumonia before and know what that fluid in the lungs feels like. It's a weight there that never goes away, a heavy weight on the chest, an impossibly phlegmy cough.

So I think about my family and Billy and Lionel and most of all Helena. I still feel the sting of Tyson calling me a "pip-squeak"—and compared to him I am—but it came to me that I would gladly be called names daily by older, stronger, hand-somer boys if I could just be well and have more time with Helena.

Just a friend. Fine. I don't care. I just want to be in her pres-ence. I just want to experience as much of her as I can.

"He's in love," a male voice says with a southern drawl. The voice is quiet and I can barely hear it, like someone had whispered from far away. I can hear the comings and goings out in the ER. The beep of monitors, the sound of footfalls on the boring white linoleum floor, the talking of doctors and nurses and families.

But this is different. The voice sounds far away, but it "feels" close.

"Can we help?" another male voice asks. This one is thin and reedy, a bit nasally.

"Not by ourselves," the first voice says. "We need every last spirit we can get."

"But… should we?" the second voice asks. "Is it our place?"

I push myself up in bed, looking around, trying to find the source of the voices, but I can't see them. My face feels so hot from the fever, but also because I know they are talking about me. I hack up some more green goo, afraid that I might have missed what the voices were saying.

"Everyone should get a chance at love, Lionel," the first voice says, and a chill passes up and down my spine. I know this voice. I had several interesting discussions with him in the graveyard. "Even you got a chance at that," he adds.

"Big Ed?" I ask. "I… Wh… What is going on?" I'm confused. Big Ed Lopez, the detective I met at the graveyard, the one who is dealing with his Aunt Tilly's estate, is talking to Lionel Malak. How can that be? Can he see ghosts too?

"Hold on, Aaron," Lionel says. "We're going to try to help." As he speaks, his voice gets distant and I know he's gone.

I lie back down and soon my mother is there, the permanent look of worry on her face.

———

I'M IN THE ER MOST OF THAT FIRST DAY. THINGS MOVE SLOW there, one emergency getting displaced by another. My mother is there and then my father. Nurse Iona is there a lot checking my vitals, scribbling on my chart, smiling and being so very nice to me.

I got to really like it when she came in. She didn't have the freaked out look of my mother or the statue-like look of my father. I could tell from her face that it was serious, but she had a quick smile and a smoky laugh, while she moved slowly but went quickly.

It got so I studied her, so fascinated I was with how she moved. Not fast, but she seemed to use the minimum number

of steps, her hands only needing to do things once. Very efficient, but not hurried at all.

"In case you're wondering," she says after some time of this
with a twinkle in her eye. "I am taken." She holds up her left
hand, a ring on her finger. It is a simple silver band.

"What?" I ask, puzzled.

"Well, the way you watch me boy, I am start'n to think
you're fallin' in *love*."

I turn beet red. My parents had stepped out and I am so
grateful for that. "I… Well… No… There is a girl… A friend…
we…"

Iona's laugh is rich and encompasses her whole being. From
her eyes to her cheeks to her belly, she laughs with such an
abandoned joy I can't help but smile myself.

"I'm just mess'n with you," she says as she leaves the room.
I'm left wondering how she can be so calm, can laugh like that,
in the middle of the chaos that is the ER.

After that things became a blur and then I started hearing
voices again.

———

HERE'S WHAT THE BLUR OF BEING SERIOUSLY ILL IS: THE
beeps and mechanical sounds of the hospital that never go
away. The smell of antiseptic and the stronger, less pleasant
smell of your own biology. Voices nearby talking about you as
if you aren't there. Flashes of faces, the squeezing of hands, the
poking and prodding of nurses and doctors.

I remember hearing Billy's voice at one point, the deep bass
of Pastor West, and then seeing the worried face of Helena.
But I was only dimly there. I was starting to hear the voices of
ghosts again.

Well, I don't think that last part is normal. But as my fever got worse and my lungs filled up, I was less and less in this world and more someplace else.

I've mentioned that I'm an atheist. That means I don't believe in an anthropomorphized, omnipotent god. It doesn't rule out the possibility of life beyond the body. Well, I am sure for many atheists it does, but with a literal interpretation of the word it most certainly does not.

"How do we do this?" I hear a voice say. An old lady's voice.

"Why him?" another asks.

"No one did this for me when I was sick."

"Maybe it would be better for him to go. That body... my god, it's been through so much."

"But he's so young. Look at his mother, I don't think that she would survive."

"Did you see his young lady? Now for that I'd gladly be alive, even in that beat-up body of his."

"Yes, but we've never done anything like this before. Should we?"

"Can we?"

"We must try."

There are many voices, I can't tell them apart, but somehow, I know they are ghosts. They have this different quality to them, this sounding like coming from far away, but I know they are very close.

"Enough," another voice says that I know is Big Ed Lopez. "You all stop your yammer'n. You want to try this, stay. You don't want to try this, go. And in either case shut your traps and listen up."

I squeeze my eyes shut. My mother, father, and Helena are there in my little ER area. Another bending of the rules for my mom. You are only supposed to have one guest at a time back there. And while their voices have a more "real" quality to it than the ghosts, I am drawn to the voices of the ghosts.

With my eyes shut tight I start to see them too. Not just flashes of colors, but the transparent look of ghosts. And right at the end of my bed, I see Big Ed Lopez. His short, barrel-chested body, his bright brown eyes, his short black hair shot with grey.

I am so confused. "When did you die?" I say aloud.

I hear my mother's surprised voice saying something, but I ignore it.

Ed looks right at me, a deep frown forming on his face. "We haven't much time, people." There are other ghosts there. Kids and adults. Old and young. Fat and thin. I would guess about twenty ghosts are arrayed around my bed. Not all of them are within the confines of the curtain, but I can see them on the other side of the curtain too.

Ed walks right into my bed and gets close to me. "I died ten years ago, son."

"But... I... those talks we had. In the graveyard. During the day. I..."

He smiles. "A bit of trickery, I am afraid. I was there to help you along for our friend Lionel."

And Lionel is there right next to Big Ed, his gaunt face pinched. "And you did help me," Lionel says in his nasally voice. "I know who killed me now. I am sorry for getting so upset with you, it was... well it was mighty hard to come to grips with."

"Joe Edwards?" I ask. My mother's voice is becoming higher in pitch. I am sure this conversation I am having with my eyes squeezed shut is freaking her out, because she knows I'm not hallucinating, that I'm talking to ghosts, and the reason has to do with how sick I am. But I can only focus on one thing at a time.

Lionel's eyes get so sad. He doesn't answer but shakes his head.

"Who then?" I ask.

"You all can chew that fat later," Big Ed says, holding his hands up.

"But..." I say.

"Son, I know you got questions," Big Ed says. "I promise you they will get answered. But you must be patient. I..."

A coughing fit hits me and all I know for a time is that wracking pain. When it's over I can't see or hear the ghosts anymore.

———

IT'S LIKE A BAD DREAM, REALLY. BEING SICK, SEEING AND talking to ghosts, coughing my lungs up, having a harder and harder time breathing, burning up with fever. It's the worst dream ever.

My body is fighting for survival and I'm just kind of along for the ride. There are moments of relief, a cool cloth on my head, the sweet sound of a calm, compassionate voice (Iona, I suspect), and this comforting warmth that flows around me, but they are so brief and then I'm lost to the battle that is being waged.

And then, all of the sudden, the pain is gone and I am standing next to Big Ed in that hospital room in Cedar City, Utah. I recognize it as the ICU. There's a little more space than the ER and a lot more equipment. The curtained area is dominated by the hospital bed and there is a person in there hooked up to a ventilator. The hiss of that machine and the beep of the heart monitor produce a strangely comforting rhythm.

Big Ed has this wistful smile on his face. He's got his jeans, button-down western shirt, and shiny cowboy boots on, just like I remember. But he's a bit transparent, not like when I saw him in the graveyard, but like when I saw him with my eyes closed in the ER.

He's silent as I look around and look at myself. I'm in jeans and a white T-shirt. At first, I'm really glad to be out of the hospital gown, and then I notice the silver cord that connects with my belly button. It snakes from there to the person in the hospital bed. It dawns on me what's going on.

"Am I dead?" I ask him.

"Not quite," he says, shoving his hands into his pockets. "Not while that there beeping continues."

I nod. I'm not scared, I'm actually relieved. All the pain and nausea is gone. I feel good for the first time since my treatments started. Actually, in some ways, I feel better than I can remember feeling. I'm not tired. I'm not hungry. I don't even have the smallest itch. All I feel is this vague sense of well-being.

"Am I going to die?"

His eyebrows do this little dance on his forehead. "Most likely."

"We talked earlier, didn't we?"

"That we did, son."

"What were all those ghosts doing around my bed?"

"We were try'n to help you."

I look around the room again and notice my mother. She's flopped in a grey armchair, her eyes closed, her hair flat and lifeless. I feel something then, a sharp pang of guilt. My illness has been so very hard on her.

"It didn't work?" I ask.

He shrugs. "Things just aren't that cut and dried. You are alive, if barely, so we might'a had a part in that."

I walk over to my mom and look at her. Her head is resting on the back of the chair at an uncomfortable angle, and she's slumped down with her legs awkwardly dangling out.

"She's a mighty good mother, that one," Ed says.

"I will be sorry to leave her," I say. The pang of guilt that hits me is potent, but doesn't last long. I keep feeling this sense of peacefulness, this calmness. I was, for all intents and purposes, a ghost. But it didn't scare me at all.

I turn back to Big Ed. "Are you going to tell me now, how I could see you in the graveyard?"

He looks surprised, as if my question is the last one he expected. Like maybe he expected me to ask him how I survive this. But right then, I'm just so peaceful, and so worn out from the fight, that I don't want to survive. I'm ready to die. But I am not without curiosity.

"With a little help from my friends," he says.

"I don't understand."

He sighs and shrugs. "Things are different over here. It was an experiment, really. It took ten other souls lending me their energies so that I could appear solid to you. But, even then, only you could have seen me. And we couldn't do it for long and we all ended up exhausted."

"But why? Why not just tell me you were a ghost?"

"You needed a friend," he says with a kind smile. "A ghost would have brought up other questions. And we were doing it for Lionel. He's had such a time with how his life ended."

I thought it over some. "And your Aunt Tilly and cleaning out her house. Was that all lies?"

He shook his head. "That was the god's honest truth. Just ten years earlier. I came here to deal with her estate. I died of a heart attack sorting through that woman's endless junk. I've been here ever since, for some reason, even though my bones got dragged back to be buried in Texas."

I don't really like it, but at least I understand.

We stand there for a bit, in a thick silence. I look from Big Ed to my mother to my... my body. It's strange to think of it as my "body," but it certainly doesn't feel like "me" at this point.

"What now?" I finally ask.

Big Ed smiles and shakes his head. "I don't know, son. It's not like there's an instruction manual or anythin'. But I do know that it comes down to you livin' or dyin'. You can't stay like this for very long."

———

I WASN'T A GHOST FOR LONG, BUT I DID REALIZE THAT IT CAN be quite boring. My mom slept, slumped in the chair. The heart monitor beeped, the ventilator whooshed, and the sounds of the hospital going about its business surrounded us. But that was it. Just me looking around and Big Ed standing there patiently.

"Aren't you going to try to convince me to survive? Tell me I have so much to live for?" I say. It comes out rather sarcastically.

"Well, that there would imply that it's your choice," Big Ed says. "But I don't know that it is."

I don't like that thought, not one bit. But I understand it. Leukemia had not been my choice. This pneumonia that is killing me was not my choice. My Uncle Don dying when he did was not my choice or his.

"So what do we do?" I ask. "I mean, if I have no choice, if what I want doesn't matter. What do we do?" I hear a tinge of the hysterical in my voice. Just a touch, but enough that I know Big Ed caught it.

"What you want matters, son. All I was say'n was that it's not the only factor. It could, though, be the deciding factor."

"What?"

"The ghosts and I, we gave you our best, we poured all the energy we could into you, but you just kept get'n worse. Made me suspect you might not want to keep fightin'. I sent them away to rest until we can determine this."

I walk back over to my mother, that silver cord floating along with me, passing through the hospital bed as if it wasn't there. My mother's beauty is still apparent, but it is masked, nearly occluded, by her fatigue and worry. I try to touch her face, but my translucent hand passes right through her. She moans and shifts her position. "Maybe it would be better for her if this ended now."

Ed snorts out a laugh behind me. "You got shit for brains, boy?"

"What?"

"There ain't no mother on god's green earth that would want to see her child die." His face goes from complacent to angry, red blossoming on his round cheeks. He walks to me, grabs my arm, and drags me through the back wall of the ICU room.

His grip on my arm is strong, but it doesn't hurt. It's this numb, barely-there sense of touch.

We pass through a hallway, I catch a glimpse of an exhausted-looking Doctor Rogers down the hall at a nurse's station. I feel the tug of that silver cord, pulling me back toward my body, but Big Ed's grip is stronger.

He pulls me through another wall, things going dark briefly, and into a waiting room. It's a small room, maybe ten by twelve, lined with grey armchairs, a few small tables, and filled with people I know.

I first notice Billy. He's chewing on his thumbnail and slowly pacing the length of the room, his red hair disheveled. His mother is sitting in one of the chairs, her eyes never leaving her son.

Pastor West is there, his spine erect, a bible open in his lap. His lips are moving as his finger traces the words on the page.

Next to him is my father, his face no longer a stony mask. His eyes are red rimmed, he's obviously been crying, and he hasn't shaved in a couple of days. Seeing that feels like someone just ran me through with a sword. My stoic father reduced to this is more than I can take.

I turn away from him and notice, sitting on the other side

of the room by herself, Helena. She's got grey sweatpants on and a Cedar High sweatshirt. She's sitting loosely in a chair, her brown eyes way too wide, she almost looks catatonic. Her eyes are red-rimmed, like my dad's, and she's got dark circles under them like my mom.

"I... I..." I stammer, the emotions that are hitting me are so strong I can't even talk. I feel guilty for what they are experiencing, but I also feel their love. I feel a tiny slice of happiness that these are my people, but that is overwhelmed by the fear that I will never get to talk to them again. I feel a longing to touch Helena so strong that I don't know how to bear it. I want to talk to her, to speak to her, to see those faraway eyes come into focus.

"Still think they'd be better off if this ended now?" Big Ed asks, his voice barely above a whisper.

I shake my head. "No."

"Are you ready to fight?"

I don't answer right away. I nod towards Helena and Big Ed walks me over, his grip still tight on my arm, that silver cord is taut now and trying to drag me back to my body. She's not moving, she's barely blinking. Seeing her that way just rips my heart out.

"She loves you, boy," he says.

"I... Wait. Are you sure?" I look at Big Ed and there is a frown on his face, but his eyes are smiling.

"Look at her. It's as plain as the nose on your face. You don't grieve like that if you don't love."

"But... It's been so complicated. She has so many boys after her. She has such a complicated life and so do I. We... I..."

"My god, boy. I swear you do have shit for brains."

I turn back to Helena and look at her again. I hate seeing her that way, god how I hate it.

"And you love her," he says.

I nod. Of that I have no doubt.

"So, son. Are you ready to fight?"

I straighten up. "Yes. I am ready."

————————

I'VE HAD SOME TIME TO THINK ABOUT MY EXPERIENCE AS A "ghost" with Big Ed Lopez, and I think "ghost" is the wrong word. I think "spirit" is a better word.

That transparent body that I walked around with, the one that was connected to my physical body with that strange silver cord, was my spirit. The part of me that is not flesh and blood. What we call ghosts are just spirits without a body, but really no different.

I knew who I was. I had my memories. I could move about, but without the body, the flesh and blood, it was a hollow experience. But, most importantly, it still was an "experience." I was conscious. I was "alive."

As I look towards the future, that does bring me comfort.

After viewing my loved ones and the pain my illness was causing them, Big Ed took me back to the ICU and my body. That silver cord is taut and dragged me back until we got close and he could finally let me go.

Lionel is standing there at the end of the hospital bed looking rather sheepish.

"I'll go gather the troops," Big Ed says, "and give you two a moment."

Lionel's shoulders are high, his stiff arms shoved into the pockets of his smock. He looks nervous and like a child that knows they did something wrong.

"I'm sorry I got so mad," Lionel says, his eyes downcast.

I shrug. "Are you going to tell me who did it?"

His nostrils flare and his mouth twists before his eyes meet mine. "Ann."

I think back to the tea Ann Edwards, Mom, and I had in our kitchen. How she was twitchy and nervous, her skinny face and hollow cheeks. I look closely at Lionel and I can see the two of them together. They are much more similar than Joe and Ann. They're both tall and angular, and a bit nervous. Joe is calm and round, nothing like the two of them.

"Why would she do that?" I ask. I can see them together, but I can't see her killing him. I can see Joe Edwards exploding in a jealous rage, but not Ann, the woman that loved him.

"Silvia," he says, his voice low.

Silvia is Ann's niece, the girl they took my swing set for. She is probably with them right now after losing her mother to an accident and after her aunt (Ann's sister) had mental health issues and had to give her up.

It's still not adding up for me, but he is not being very communicative. "How do you know?"

Lionel makes a real show of chewing on his lower lip as he paces around the room. He's not watching where he's going and ends up walking through the bed and the curtain. His hands finally come out of his pockets as he starts to speak. "We were in love. She was going to leave Joe, but when her sister died, it all changed. She changed. She knew her other sister, Kim, wasn't really up to the challenge, but let her try anyway. Joe and her had never had kids, had never wanted kids."

He pauses, searching my face. I nod, encouraging him to continue. "She cut it off with me then. Said she had to get her marriage right, said she thought little Silvia would need her. Said we couldn't even be friends anymore."

I'm shaking my head, I still don't get it. Lionel's eyes are wide, too wide, and his face looks even more gaunt than usual. There is something that looks like mist forming at the edges of his ghostly body and he looks a bit out of focus.

"But she couldn't stay away. After two weeks she was back

in my arms, but so full of guilt. Ann was making a go of it with Joe for Silvia, but the cracks were already showing."

He's even more out of focus now. "Are you okay?" I ask.

He shakes his head, little staccato movements back and forth. "I remember some things from that night. The presses were running, loud. The smell of the ink filled the air. But right before it happened, I smelled lavender."

"Lavender?"

He nods slowly, shoving his hands back into his pockets. "Her perfume. I am sure of it. It was her."

I slowly roll it over in my mind. She tries to break it off with Lionel, but can't. She wants to stabilize her marriage so she can care for her orphaned niece. So she kills Lionel so she can truly end the affair. It doesn't add up. "But why would she resort to this?"

He sighs. "You're too young to understand. Passion makes us do strange things." He's looking at me but is blinking a lot. He's holding something back.

"That's not all of it."

He chews on his lower lip some more. "No. The three sisters, Ellen, Kim, and Ann, had a difficult childhood. Their father was... well... he wasn't a kind man. They have all struggled with depression. Ann herself has been diagnosed as bipolar. She had been prescribed medication for it."

The way he said "prescribed medication" tickles something in my mind. "She wasn't on it when she killed you, was she?"

He shakes his head. "She hates the pills. She says they make everything grey."

Lionel goes silent and I let him as I ponder it all. It's too much for me, really. Way too much. From what Big Ed has said, I'm going to have to fight to survive, but what am I going to do with this?

"I'm going to have to tell someone this," I finally say. It's so clear to me. So simple.

Lionel's eyes get wide. "No. Please. She's back on her meds, I've been watching her. Silvia needs her, Ann won't do anything to screw that up."

"She killed you, Lionel. I don't think she should be caring for a child."

His mouth twists and that fuzziness of his ghostly body disappears. I see a flicker of red run along the edges. I'm beginning to suspect that ghosts' emotions are sometimes visible. "No!" he shouts, his face twisting into an ugly mask. "You cannot. You must not."

"I have to, Lionel," I say. "Please understand. What if she goes off her meds and hurts Silvia?"

The red flicker along the edges of his ghostly body is growing darker and thicker. It's like a red fire is engulfing him. "You will not tell anyone," he says, taking a step towards me.

For the first time as a spirit, I feel fear. Lionel is not rational. Lionel is desperate. Lionel wants to hurt me to protect Ann.

His eyes flick around the little ICU area. From my mother still slumped in the gray chair, to the bed with my struggling body, to me, to the silver cord floating placidly in the air between us.

"Um... Okay..." I stammer, putting my hands up and backing up to the foot of the hospital bed. "You're right, Lionel. Ann would never hurt Silvia. I don't know what I was thinking."

Lionel's face twists again, his mouth disappearing beneath his mustache. "I can't take that chance," he says softly.

He's not looking at me anymore, but the silver cord that connects my spirit to my body. Why is he focused on that? The red around Lionel starts flickering and condenses into a solid red hue that hugs him. His right hand starts to change and I gasp. His fingers melt together, his hand becoming a solid whole, the color sliding towards silver. The bottom end of his hand becomes a fine edge and now it looks like he has a crude butcher's knife for a hand.

His face is clenched and his eyes are focused on his hand, not me or my silver cord. I suddenly know what he means to do.

Ghosts like Lionel are spirits without a body. I am a sprit with a body. That silver cord is what connects my sprit to my body. Lionel wants to sever that cord, detaching my spirit from my body. Lionel wants to kill me.

I'm sure of it. To stop me from telling anyone that Ann killed him, he will kill me.

Something snaps in me. I don't want to die. I don't want the last look on my friends' and family's faces to be what I just saw in the waiting room. I don't want my mother to wake up when my heart stops and the monitor squeals out an alarm.

Big Ed told me I would have to fight for my life, but I had no idea it would be something like this.

Just as the edge of Lionel's knife-hand finishes forming, I rush him. I don't know what will happen, I am acting like I have a body when I don't, but what else can I do?

I hear a chirp of surprise when I run into him, my shoulder connecting with his chest. It's a strange feeling, or rather mostly a lack of feeling. I feel the contact, but it's this numb barely-there sensation like when Big Ed grabbed my wrist.

My momentum carries us through the curtain and out in front of the ICU nurses' station. It's a curve of a counter with stacked charts on metal clipboards. Nurse Iona is there as well as another nurse and Doctor Rogers.

"That sweet boy just can't die," Iona says to Doctor Rogers. "We can't let him die."

"It's out of our hands now," Doctor Rogers says with a sigh. "We are doing everything we can."

We slide past them and through the counter. There's a young blond nurse there writing on a medical chart. We end up on her, or rather she is inside our spirits. I feel a tingle as we pass through her and she bolts up, steps away, and shakes her head and hands.

"What is it, Mandy?" Iona asks.

"Just felt a chill… A horrible chill," she says, still shaking her arms.

Iona crosses herself and says, "The spirits, they are sure restless tonight."

Our momentum has stopped. I feel my cord tugging me back to my body, but I seem to be able to resist it. Lionel reaches over me, his arm with the knife on the end rising to take a swing at my silver cord.

I stop resisting the tug of the cord and am rapidly pulled back to my body.

I see Lionel's hand slice through empty air (and the counter that forms the nurse's station) as I slide back to my body.

"If man is done with that boy," Iona says, her arms crossed over her chest, "then I say we pray."

I end up through the curtain and in the middle of the hospital bed (and my body). Lionel is rushing towards me, his knife-hand leading the way.

I look around, reflexively, but there is no help for me here. My mother, still asleep, can't help me. My father and friends in the waiting area can't help me. I'm not sure if I can even help me.

As Lionel comes flying through the curtain (literally), his knife-hand outstretched, I react instinctively. I hold my hands up and catch his wrist as the knife is speeding down towards the belly button of my body, to the place where the silver cord emanates.

And I catch his wrist, that dull sensation of touch again, and am face to face with Lionel.

"Don't do this," I say. "Please. I don't want to die."

"For Ann," he growls. "I must protect her."

It's this strange moment. I'm face to face with the Lionel, his teeth bared, his eyes too wide, a layer of translucent red surrounding him. I can feel his arm pressing down and I don't know if I can keep him from cutting my silver cord, keep him from killing me.

And in the moment, I think about relationships. Yeah, weird, I know. But it's just a flicker of a moment that the thoughts tumble through my head. I think about how passionate I feel for Helena, how I long to be close to her, how I want to always be with her, how I would protect her from the pain of the world if I could.

I'm losing the battle with Lionel, he is forcing his hand closer and closer to my cord.

And then I feel two things. Empathy for Lionel and what he is trying to do—his passion has twisted into this strange form where he is willing to do horrible things to protect Ann. I also feel a fierceness I've never felt before. I am not fighting just for my own life, I am fighting to protect my family and friends from losing me. I am fighting for myself, but I am fighting for them too. For Mom and Dad and Billy and Helena.

"No!" I shout, and feel a strength surge through me. Lionel's arm starts to rise and surprise flickers across his face.

That surprise doesn't last long, it soon turns into a look of triumph. "Sorry, kid," he says as he suddenly goes out of focus, looking more like smoke for a moment than a person.

In that moment, his wrist passes through my arm, and then the knife is traveling towards my silver cord. There is nothing I can do to stop it.

———

MY FATHER ONCE TOLD ME THAT IT'S NOT IMPORTANT HOW *long* you live, but *how* you live. When he said this, he was sitting on the edge of a hospital bed at Sunrise Children's Hospital in

Vegas. I was eleven years old at the time and was in the midst of my first chemo treatments. I remember his face, it was so serious, his eyes so earnest.

"Quality over quantity, Aaron," he said. "Always choose quality over quantity."

I was in the hospital because I had spiked a high fever a few days earlier, which meant an infection, which meant my leukemia and chemo-compromised immune system would need help.

I was only eleven and was just trying to get my head wrapped around what was happening. I think this was my father's way of telling me that I might not have a long life. That I had to do my best with the life I was going to have. It was an obtuse way to say it, but I know that is what he was getting at.

As Lionel's knife-hand speeds towards the silver cord floating lazily above my body, I have a silly question run through my head. How do I make my last moments of quality? Even if it's only a second or less. What can I do to live this, right here, right now, to the best of my ability?

I think of running away, but my cord is rooted in my body, that's where the vulnerability is and I can't run from it. I think of running through the walls to the waiting room to get one last look at Helena, but I don't want that blank stare to be the last thing I see.

And suddenly it all seems funny to me. Here I am a ghost already worried about the last time I see Helena or finding the right thing to do for my "last" moments. But if Lionel severs my chord, I will be a ghost just like him. I will still be "me" just without the body. All this worry about endings just seems ridiculous.

So I laugh right out loud. A belly laugh that rises up from deep within. And I am laughing at Lionel in his desperate attempt to control the situation. To stop me from telling someone about Ann Edwards murdering him.

Lionel's hand is moving quickly, solid again, so I don't laugh much before it strikes the silver cord, but I see his knife-hand slow just a touch. And when it passes right through the cord without me feeling a thing, I laugh even harder.

This Shakespearean tableau just strikes me as so funny. Me, the young man trying to "survive." Lionel, the crazy ghost desperate to save his murdering lover from justice. All the living so worried about this process of "dying" which, since I am currently a ghost, doesn't seem like all that big of a deal.

Lionel curses when his knife-hand passes through the cord again. I laugh.

This time he doesn't take another swing, he stares at his knife-hand with a look of intense concentration on his face. The knife becomes this buttery silver that matches the silver of my cord. It doesn't have the glow of the cord, but it looks much more like it.

His eyes meet mine and I stop laughing, a chill running down my spine. There is no sorrow in his eyes, no regret, just the grimmest of determination. *This time*, his eyes say, *this time it will work*.

And I believe that look.

His eyes flick away from me and back to the cord as his hand rises up high. This is it, he is going to do it this time.

"Stop!" a deep voice yells just as Lionel's knife starts its descent. It's Big Ed with about a dozen ghosts arrayed behind him. He has stepped through the curtain and I can make out the glow of the other ghosts dimly behind him.

I see Lionel's face clench, but he doesn't stop, his silver hand, sharp as a knife, comes crashing down on my silver cord.

———

MY LIFE DOESN'T FLASH IN FRONT OF MY EYES. AND IF IT did, I don't think it would have taken very long. A normal childhood sequence for the first eleven years and then a blur of treatments and hospitals and feeling like crap. If my life had flashed before my eyes, I would have wanted this summer to be the bulk of it. Starting out in health, sneaking to the graveyard at night, the wonder of Helena and seeing the ghost of Lionel, even all the madness with my family. I would have taken it in all again and savored it to the level it deserved. The smoky-minty smell of Helena. The earnestness of Billy as he tells me to "make a move." The sweetness of my mother becoming my friend. The sparkle in my father's eyes as he urges me to ask Helena out.

Time seems to slow as the knife arches down. My mother moans and shifts in her chair. Snippets of Iona praying float to my ear, *Jesus, please, please watch over this fine young man.* The stern look on Big Ed's face as he rushes towards Lionel, his large hands outstretched.

And then the knife contacts with the cord right where it exits my body's belly button and…

A sharp, slightly melodic, clink rings out like glass against glass as the knife connects. A flash of the brightest light emanating from the point of contact. That light flowing down the cord to me and up through Lionel's arm to him. A surge of energy, like I'm being electrocuted. Screams. Lionel flying backwards away from my body and I am flying towards it, the silver cord reeling me in like a hooked fish.

The scream of my heart monitor, a flat line displaying. My mother bolting upright and screaming. "Crash cart! We need a crash cart in here!"

Big Ed's face close to mine as I fly towards my body. "Fight, boy! Fight!"

And then I'm in my body and the real battle begins.

———

BEING BIOLOGICAL IS HARD. THIS IS SOMETHING I'VE learned well in my five-year dance with leukemia. It's hard being in a body. But I never felt it like I did when my soul was reeled back into my body after Lionel tried to sever the silver cord.

I went from feeling so light to feeling so dense. From this airy freedom, to feeling like I had been buried alive. From ease to suffering.

Remembering it now, it feels like a horrible nightmare. Which is probably accurate, because I wasn't "awake" in the normal sense, nor was I fully unconscious.

I feel this crushing pressure on my chest, like I'm caught in some great vice. I vaguely feel the respirator pushing air into my lungs, but it doesn't counteract the pressure.

It's too much. I can't do it. I can't be in this bag of flesh and bones. I want to be free of it again. Free of the pain. Free of the struggle. Free.

And then things change. I feel a fire in my chest and I'm vaguely aware of my body convulsing. They must be shocking my heart. And right after that I feel this beautiful sensation. It's hard to describe, but it feels like a warm honey-colored light is engulfing me. The pressure on my chest eases. I calm down some.

"Fight, Aaron. Fight now. Find your way home." It's Big Ed's voice that I hear in my head. It travels down with the honey-colored light. His voice is sweeter than I have ever heard it.

I can't see anything. I feel the fire in my chest again. I hear Big Ed telling me to fight. The warmth engulfing me intensifies.

And I fight.

I fight for just one more breath, just one more moment in the sunlight, one more smile from my mother, on more hug from my father, one more look at Helena.

I seem to be locked in this epic battle in this nightmare

state. I can't describe it to you in concrete terms, because it wasn't like that. It was my will, that warmth, and whatever the doctors were doing to me fighting against the cold and the darkness.

It seemed to last forever. Until I woke up with the tube in my mouth and Helena by my side.

41

FRIDAY, JULY 29, 1977

I'VE DECIDED TO STOP WRITING THIS DIARY. IN FACT, IT'S now fall, the leaves have changed, and I'm back in school and I am just coming back to this. The story, as I've written it here, is unfinished, and I just can't abide by that. There is a little more to tell, so here goes.

This entry is dated in July because that is where I need to start to finish things up. I'm going to go back and finish this. And then move on. Frankly, I don't have time to write in my diary right now. There's a life to be lived.

But, anyway, back in July, a few days after my last entry, I am still in the hospital. I'm getting frequent visits from everyone that was in the waiting room. Billy and some of his family (the twins tag along quite a bit, much to Billy's dismay), Pastor West, and, of course, Helena. She doesn't have that catatonic look in her eyes anymore, and she always holds my hand when she sits with me.

It's become this thing for us. Just the simplest of human contact, but I love it. There are things we haven't said yet, I think we're both waiting for me to be a bit better, but our hands seem to bridge that gap. It may not have been said, but we both know it.

It's late, Helena just got off work from La Familia and is sitting in a chair next to my bed, my hand in hers. She's got warm hands, and they are bigger than mine. Her being taller than me doesn't bother me anymore. She's here, and such "manly" concerns about being dominant physically are ridiculous now.

The lights are off and we've lapsed into silence. It's way past visiting hours, but everyone knows me and they always let Helena in no matter what time it is.

I'm still weak as a newborn bird, hooked to an IV, but I'm getting better. I've also got a private room, which is another luxury of having your mother and her boyfriend work at the hospital.

I've got my eyes closed and I see him. Big Ed Lopez. I haven't seen or heard from a ghost since Lionel tried to sever my silver cord.

"How you doin', son?" he asks, a smile on his kind face.

"It's Big Ed," I tell Helena. I had told her everything as my memory came back. She sits up straight and looks around.

"I'm good," I say. I keep my voice low, I don't want to attract any attention. "I'm alive. I think I have you to thank for that."

He shrugs and shakes his head. "We did what we could."

"That wonderful warm sensation. That was you?"

He nods. "It was us, all us ghosts."

"Thank you. I… I…" I try to speak but am overcome with a wash of emotion. I'm so grateful to be back, to have time with my family. I blink back tears and I feel Helena squeeze my hand.

"Thank you, Big Ed," Helena says. "Thank you for giving Aaron back to us."

The smile on Big Ed's face is huge. Helena's charms extend

even beyond the shuffling off of the mortal coil. "Tell your young lady that it was our pleasure, and that it wasn't just us. It was your efforts, the doctors and nurses, and especially her giving you somethin' to fight for."

I convey his message and she blushes. We haven't done anything but hold hands at this point. We haven't said words like "boyfriend" or "girlfriend." But she is my girl and that doesn't really capture it after what we've been through in the last six weeks. Words fall short.

"How is Lionel?" I ask.

Big Ed sighs, his eyes briefly downcast. "That boy, he's in a mighty bad place. We are doin' our best for him." Big Ed must have seen the distressed look on my face because he adds, "Don't you worry, son. He won't be bothering you again."

"I'm glad to hear that."

Helena squeezes my hand and gives me a questioning look so I catch her up on the conversation.

"And now it's time for me to get my old hide outta here," Big Ed says.

"Will I see you again?" I ask.

He purses his lips and shakes his head. "I don't think so, son. We'll be keeping our distance. I feel like it's time for you to be in the land of the livin'."

And it was. I haven't seen or heard from a ghost since.

42

TUESDAY AUGUST 9, 1977

I'M FINALLY HOME, BACK IN MY OWN BED WITH THE SLOPED roof and the glow-in-the-dark stars. I can't tell you how good it feels to be surrounded by my own books, have my own bathroom, to be in my own pajamas.

I'm weak, very weak, and I've lost a ton of weight (weight I didn't need to lose), but I am alive and that is no small thing. I got a look at myself in the bathroom mirror as I was getting ready to get in the shower this morning. My ribs stick out, my shoulders are sharp and bony, and my hair is all gone. What little there was started falling out while I was in the hospital and I had Mom get the clippers and do a Telly Savalas on me. Better to look like Kojak all at once than to slowly watch my hair fall out and deal with it being everywhere like a dog shedding.

It's shocking. I look like one of those pictures of holocaust survivors. Not quite that bad, but it's freaky. Seeing my body makes it clear just how close things got. The human body is a miracle, it can take an unbelievable amount of punishment and survive. But it can't take an unlimited amount and I know we were right there, on the hairy edge of that limit.

I stare a little more and worry about Helena seeing me like this. I know I was a "pipsqueak" and now I'm something even worse. She's healthy, with curves in all the right places. I'm a bag of bones.

After I get out of the shower, my parents are sitting on my bed waiting for me. At first I'm a little mad, I had to fight with my mother to let me take a shower alone, and I think they're there making sure I don't fall or something. But when I see their faces, I know that's not it.

My mother has this clenched look, her brow furrowed, and her arms crossed. My father looks even more serious than usual.

"What's going on?" I ask.

"Sit down, son," Dad says, patting my bed next to him.

"What is it?" I'm starting to freak. I seriously can't take any more bad news.

"It's about the Edwards," my mother says, with an unconvincing smile. Mom looks better than when I was in the hospital, but she still looks so very tired. I worry about her.

At Helena's urging, I told them everything. They know about Ann really being Lionel's murderer.

"Did... Did Ann do something?" I ask, afraid she's had another psychological break, like the one she had when she buried a knife in Lionel's back.

"She's in jail," my father says.

Back in the hospital, when I told them what I knew, we were all stumped on how to act on it. Sheriff Thompson wouldn't buy "a ghost told me" as evidence. We couldn't think of a way to get real evidence. "What happened?"

"She confessed to Lionel's murder," Dad says.

"What... How...."

"It was your father's plan," Mom says. "We were able to

convince Sheriff Thompson that Lionel and Ann were having an affair. That Joe Edwards had motive to kill Lionel because of the affair. It took some doing, but your father convinced him to bring both the Edwards in and question them together."

I'm confused at this point. They convinced the sheriff that Joe did it, which I certainly believed when I found out about the affair. How did that get a confession from Ann? And why were they so serious? That Ann was in jail seemed like a good thing.

"Ann cracked," Dad says. "When it all came out, when the sheriff made it clear that Joe had motive and a serious investigation of him was going to happen, she cracked and confessed."

"That was your plan?" I ask.

Mom nods. "We knew that she cared for Joe and wouldn't want to see him take the blame for her actions."

I let out a huge sigh and smile, but the smile is not reflected on my parents' faces. "This is good, isn't it?" I ask. And then I think about it a bit and my smile erases. "What about Silvia?" I feel for Ann's niece suddenly having another home ripped away. I know that I couldn't have survived to this point without my family.

My mom is blinking and my dad is suddenly studying his fingernails.

"What happened?"

Mom purses her lips. "It's... We... Henry, you tell him."

"I wasn't quite honest with you," Dad says, still looking at his hands. "Ann isn't in jail anymore."

"What!" I look around, afraid that she's here. That she wants revenge. That she will hurt us, or worse yet, Helena. I stand up and my father grabs my hand.

"She's in the morgue," he says.

I blink and slowly sit back down.

"She hanged herself with the belt she was wearing the same night she confessed."

The words hang in the air like a physical presence. I know that Ann was mentally ill. But I don't understand mental illness. It makes people irrational and unpredictable. Ann took her own life once her deed was discovered and that seems so foreign to me given how hard I just had to fight to live.

I take a deep breath and slump against my father. He puts his arm around me in a gentle hug. I am suddenly feeling beyond exhausted.

"What about Silvia?" I ask.

"We don't know," my mother quietly says.

After that, they leave me so I can take a nap. I lie there in my bed for a long time. It's still light outside and I can't see the glow of the stars on my ceiling, but I stare at them nonetheless.

I think about the ghosts, Big Ed and Lionel, and wonder how Lionel is doing. I wonder if Ann is with him now, if they can finally be happy. But then I think of Joe Edwards and Silvia and then I am sad. Even if Ann and Lionel are happy, Joe and Silvia still have a long road in front of them.

I don't understand this world. I don't. It's illogical, capricious, and confusing. Later when Helena comes over, we talk about it for a long time while we hold hands.

We come to the conclusion that it's not the kind of thing you can understand. I find that both comforting and disquieting at the same time. Comforting, because I can give up trying to figure it out. Disquieting because this life is so far out of our control.

43

WEDNESDAY AUGUST 31, 1977

A MORE NORMAL ROUTINE HAS BEEN ESTABLISHED. I RESUMED chemo last Friday, which is good in as much as it means I am healthy enough to take it. I've gained a few pounds and am tolerating the nausea better than before the near-death thing. Not that I'm any less nauseous, it's that I'm still riding the high of being alive. And since you can't feel nauseous if you're dead, I'm much more willing to make friends with it.

Don't get me wrong, it still sucks, but because of my attitude, my suffering around it is less. School's been back in session and Helena has been bringing me homework to do every day. There's hope that after chemo ends everything will look good and I can spend most of my junior year actually in high school.

But that's all small stuff. Tonight is the night Helena and I finally go out. I wake up early (like 5 a.m.) and having nothing better to do, I go through a few of my assignments (English and history, putting math off), do my homework, and then clean my room.

I am just a mess of nerves and keep myself busy. My mom

comes in to check on me at 6:30. She's in her pink robe with her fuzzy bunny slippers yawning.

"What's going on, Aaron?"

"Date," I say. "First Date." I'm dusting my books—for the second time this week. They don't need it, but I do.

She walks over, yawning again, and takes the blue feather duster out of my hand and puts her hand on my back, guiding me to the bed. She sits down and pats the bedspread (which was perfectly made until she sat—I'll have to remake it).

I sigh and sit down.

"Don't wear yourself out today," she says slowly.

I look into her blue eyes. Is she in mom mode or friend mode? I can't quite tell, but I decide to assume it's a friend.

"I've never been on date," I whisper, my head down.

She chuckles quietly and whispers back, "This isn't a normal date."

I look up and she has a bemused smile playing on her lips. I still can't tell if she's Mom or Friend. Maybe it's gotten to the point that in most circumstances, she is a bit of both.

"What?" I ask, still not following.

She chuckles again. "In the history of boys and girls going out, has there ever been a lead up like this?"

I ponder it briefly. Meeting in a graveyard. Proving to her I can see ghosts. Becoming friends. Her taking me to see her mother when I was freaked out about my parents. Trying to find a murderer. Almost dying and waking up with her by my side. I smile and nod, her right eyebrow arching up.

"If you think about it," she says. "This is hardly your first date."

After Mom leaves, I do calm down some. I pull out my diaries and read all the parts I've written about Helena. I'm trying to understand her better. I don't think it helps much, but I do enjoy it.

———

"YOU LOOK GOOD, KID," DAD SAYS FROM THE DOOR TO THE bathroom. I'm straightening my tie in front of the mirror, trying to find if there is a configuration that looks good and doesn't feel like it's choking me.

I've got on my best tan corduroys, a white button-down dress shirt, and a thin black tie (my only tie).

I look at my watch. It's just after six… It's not time to leave yet. My mom did help to calm me down, but now that it's time for the *"DATE"* (capitalized, in quotes, and underlined) I am nervous again. My mom is right, it's not really our first date, but it is our first *"DATE."*

"I'm early," he says. "We haven't had that talk yet."

My dad is dressed in his usual tan slacks and button-down shirt. School is back for him full-time and he's there a lot more.

"Talk?"

"Yeah," he says, his smile turning nervous. "Back when you were grounded, it was one of the conditions of the date. That you and I have a talk about women."

I groan, step away from the mirror, and say, "Where are we having this talk?" Something about my father's nervousness makes me suspect it's not here.

"You ready?"

I take another look at the mirror. My tie being straight won't hide my lack of hair, my pale complexion, or that I am a serious pipsqueak, so I nod and we leave.

———

HE DRIVES ME TO THE LUTHERAN CHURCH, PASTOR WEST'S church. It's Wednesday so there is no one here. He gets out of the Chevelle and walks in without a word or a glance back at me. I'm seriously puzzled. My dad doesn't go to church. My dad doesn't believe in god.

The door is open, which I'm a little surprised by, and he walks right down to the front of the church and starts pacing in front of the pews.

It's not a big church, a rather plain rectangle, with wooden pews, an aisle in the middle, a podium up front, and a large, rather plain cross hanging on the wall behind it.

"What are we doing here, Dad?"

"Why is this a holy place?" he asks.

I shrug. I didn't think he thought it was.

"Come on, Aaron. What makes it holy?" He stops his pacing and stares at me, his hands shoved deep into his pocket.

I look around at the cross, the single stained-glass window over the entrance that shows the crucifixion. Pews stuffed with hymnals. I turn slowly around taking it all in. "It's not any of this," I say, referring to what I see.

"What is it, then? What makes this a holy spot?"

I take a deep breath and let it slowly out. This is a test. I know it. But, I know from experience that what my father is looking for isn't a particular answer, he wants me to think.

I bite my lip and stop my turning when I'm facing him. He's an atheist and so am I, for us god doesn't make this place holy. That only leaves one thing. "The people that come here. The way everyone treats this place."

He smiles and nods. His skin crinkles around his eyes as he smiles, accentuating the crow's feet growing there. My dad looks older than he did at the start of summer. Really, we all do. "Exactly. It's how we approach something, how we treat it that makes it holy. Makes it sacred."

I nod. It makes sense. Holy or profane, the way we interact with something makes it that way. In a profane way, Barbara Bach is holy to Billy. That thought makes me smile.

He takes my hand and pulls me to the front pew, sitting down. I sit next to him, but he doesn't let go of my hand.

"When it comes to women," he says, his voice hushed. "We men must treat them as holy, as sacred."

I'm confused and I'm sure it shows.

"Two things you need to keep in mind," he continues. "First, that women are miracles. We men provide a little genetic material, but they are able to form another life in their womb. Sacred, no?"

I nod, not really enjoying all this talk about reproduction and wombs.

"Second, for most of the history of this planet, and way too often even now, men treat women poorly. As objects to do with as they please."

I lick my lips and tug at my tie. It's suddenly feeling very hot in here.

"So, it is your mission," he says, his hand on my shoulder, "to treat Helena with the respect she deserves. To not take her for granted. To not assume you can take what you want. To let her take the lead as your relationship progresses. And to always, always respect her."

I blink. My homosexual father just gave me a lecture on how to treat women. At first that feels discordant, as if he has no right to lecture on the topic. But then I think of my mother, who is still married to him despite of his sexual orientation. And then I wonder if he's had a lack of respect in his life because of who he is. Things that I don't see, and he's certainly not going to talk about.

"She *is* sacred to me, Dad."

He nods. "I know. I just didn't want to let this go unsaid."

His hand is on the back of my neck and he pulls me close, kissing me on my bald head. He's done that more since I lost all my hair. I like it.

"I sure hope I don't screw this date up," I say.

"Just be honest, treat her with respect, and listen carefully," he says. "That's all you need to do."

"That's it?" I ask.

"Son," he says. "That will put you ahead of most every other boy."

I think back to when Helena and I met. Her screaming at Jeff Tate out on Main Street because he didn't know what "no" meant and I know he's right.

We sit there for a time in the silent church, my stomach and my thoughts churning. There is so much I don't understand, and with my father there that leads me back to him.

"Can I tell you something?" I ask, my quiet voice sounding echoey in the empty space.

"Sure, son. Anything."

"I… I've been doing some reading… and… um…." I just don't know how to get it out.

"It's okay, Aaron. You can tell me anything."

I swallow hard and feel bad because I figure he doesn't know what's coming. "Well, I like girls… I mean… you know…"

"You are attracted to women," he offers.

"Yes. And you are not."

He nods, his head down.

"So… I don't understand it, but I've been doing some reading and males liking males and females liking females is not new or anything, and it happens with animals, and…"

Now he's staring at me, his grey eyes hooded behind his glasses like he's ready for it to be bad. Real bad.

"…and I don't have to understand it to love you."

He lets out a sigh and hugs me tight. I don't have to understand my mother to love her and I don't have to understand my father to love him. We are all different, but we are all people. We are a family.

"Thank you, son," he whispers, his voice thick.

"And if you have a boyfriend… well, I would like to meet him."

He pushes back and holds me at arm's length, searching my face.

"Really?"

I nod. I'm scared, it didn't exactly go well when I met my mother's boyfriend, but I'm so over family secrets.

He smiles widely. "Well, I don't have a 'boyfriend' right now, Aaron, but I appreciate your being open."

And then we chat there in that holy space about simple, secular things and I feel this closeness to my father that I didn't know was possible.

———

IT'S NOT HELENA THAT OPENS UP THE DOOR TO HER HOUSE, it's her father. He's a rough-looking man with short black hair, a scar on his cheek, thick hands, and a broad chest. My breath catches in my throat when I see him. We haven't met.

"You must be Aaron," he says opening the door.

I swallow and nod, hating my tie again, and walk in.

"She's primping," he says, walking into a small living room and plopping down in a beat-up recliner the color of mud. There is one single lamp lit in the room throwing yellow light on the stack of newspapers on the end table next to the chair.

"It's nice to meet you, Mister Monfort," I say, finding my voice.

He nods, his mouth a thin line as he looks me up and down. I can almost hear him thinking "pipsqueak." He's a strong man, which isn't surprising, his work at the warehouse would require it. As I study his face, I can see traces of Helena in the brown eyes and the prominent cheekbones.

"She's all I got, you know," he says, casually, just throwing it out there like he's talking about the weather or something.

"What?"

"Helena. She's all I got." He licks his lips and rubs his calloused hands together. I can hear the scrape of skin against skin, it seems way too loud.

"Yes, sir," I say. I don't know what else to say.

"She's mighty fond of you, boy."

"Umm… I am very fond of her too, Mister Monfort."

He's staring at me, blinking, leaning forward in his chair. It's like he's trying to look inside of me to see if I'm going to take his daughter from him or hurt her. Trying to determine if I'm worthy of "all he's got."

"So, this cancer thing," he says, slowly easing back in his chair. "How bad is it?"

I hear footfalls above and wish Helena would get down here. "It's bad," I say. "This is my third round with it."

He bites his bottom lip, a gesture I've seen Helena do many times, and nods. "You gonna make it?"

I shrug. "I hope so."

He smiles, it's a small thing, but it makes him look handsome, more like I expected Helena's father to look. "Hope is a good thing, ain't it?"

I nod.

"Can never have too much hope."

I hear footfalls on the stairs and then Helena is there. She smells of perfume (some kind of flower) and has a light-blue dress with a white sweater on. Her hair is swept back from her face and held in place with barrettes and she has a smile on her red lips. She is the most beautiful sight.

"Are you boys getting along?" she asks, her gaze going from me to her father and back to me. Mister Monfort is standing staring at his daughter.

"Yeah," I say. "I'm glad to finally meet your father."

"Daddy," she says, going to him and kissing his cheek. His face lights up and he is truly handsome. He doesn't seem like a worn warehouse worker anymore. He seems more like a handsome movie star suffuse with confidence. "What were you two talking about?"

"Hope," I say. "We were talking about how important hope is."

————

HELENA INSISTED THAT WE HAVE DINNER AT LA FAMILIA. I suggested The Coal Creek Grill, a nice steak house just east of town, but she wouldn't hear of it. It had to be La Familia. I didn't understand until we got there.

My father is the chauffeur, we sit in the backseat the short ride over holding hands and not talking.

"Here we are, kids," Dad says, pulling us up right in front of the turquoise-colored door. He's looking back at us, a big grin on his face. I let go of her hand and say, "Just wait." I get out my side and run around to her side and open the door for her. Her forehead bunches briefly but then she smiles widely and takes my proffered hand.

"You kids have fun," Dad calls from the car. "I'll be back at nine."

He pulls off and we're standing in the La Familia parking lot, our hands clasped. There are Christmas lights on the front of the rather plain brick building. That and the colorful door are their festive decorations.

I take a step towards the front door, but she doesn't move. She nods her head to the side and pulls me around to the back of the restaurant.

Fran Diego herself greets us at the back door. "It's all ready, amigos," she says. Fran is the owner of the restaurant. She's a plump fifty dressed in the same kind of skirt and blouse that Helena wears when she works here.

I throw Helena a questioning look, but she just squeezes my

hand and pulls me forward.

We walk into the kitchen. It's crowded and hot, three dark-skinned men working at steel counters and a fryer and stove. I see their faces light up when they see Helena, but it doesn't bother me. It's my hand she's holding.

"Hola, chicos," she says as we pass through. Their enthusiastic greetings echo back.

Fran leads us past a long stainless-steel sink and to a door. I figure it leads to the restaurant, but it doesn't. It leads into a storage room. It's a fair size, maybe twelve feet on a side, with big metal and particle board shelving all around. On the shelves are sacks of flour and beans. Huge cans of green chilies, napkins, and the like. But it's what's in the middle of the room that is important. A small round table with a white tablecloth, two chairs, and a wine bottle in the middle of the table.

In the wine bottle is a white taper candle burning brightly. Helena squeals with delight and gives Fran a big hug telling her, "Gracias, mi amiga. Gracias."

Fran beams at both of us and says. "I'll leave you two alone now. Enjoy."

She closes the door behind her, muffling the sounds of the kitchen and we are alone. Candlelight, Helena, and a private place for just the two of us.

I swallow hard, step forward, and pull a chair out for her. She smiles and sits as I scoot the chair in and go to the other side. I'm frankly speechless because of what she's done. She arranged this for us. For our first date. I'm quite nearly overwhelmed. I find that my emotions are much stronger since my little dance with the afterlife, both tears and laughter are close.

After I sit, she holds out her hand, resting it on the clean white tablecloth palm up. I put my hand in hers and let out a sigh.

This is no normal date. This is Helena and I. We who met

in a graveyard. We who have dealt with ghosts and solved murders. We who can't stop holding hands.

I know it seems mundane, this always holding hands. It's tame. It's old fashioned. It's the most innocent of physical intimacies. But I love it.

She held my hand when I woke up in the ICU with that tube down my throat, and I hope she'll be holding my hand until we're old and grey, our hands wrinkled, our knuckles swollen by arthritis.

Our evening is magical. Fran brings us our food, never saying a word. It's like the world is just us two. We talk about Lionel and Big Ed Lopez. We talk about her mother and her fears of the same thing happening to her. We talk about my cancer and how uncertain the future is. We aren't like some couple on a first date that don't know anything about each other. We know each other so well.

We laugh. We have a few awkward pauses. We sip our sodas and stare into each other's eyes.

At the end, when we both know my father is waiting and it's time to go, I say, "I love you, you know." I don't know how it happened. I'm just so relaxed it just slips out.

Her eyes go wide and she blinks. I hold my breath and am afraid I've said too much. It's a first date, these aren't the kind of things you say.

But then she's standing and yanking on my hand and then we're inches apart and I'm looking up into her amber eyes. They're so big, so deep, and I see a sheen of tears on them. My heart is thumping in my chest sounding like some huge bass drum.

She then lets go of my hand, puts both of her hands on the sides of my face. She's so serious and I dare not say another word. And then she pulls my head towards her, leaning down a bit, and kisses me.

It's not a long kiss, but it's Helena and it's my first kiss. Her lips are wet and so soft. I smell the salsa on her breath, and the tobacco and mint smell below that. Her lips are firm and feel amazing against mine.

After it's done, she's standing in front of me crying and laughing at the same time. I'm dizzy and don't really understand what she's going through. But then I feel the tears on my own smiling face and I get it. This kiss is something I didn't think would ever happen. That I would meet someone like her and feel like this.

It's surprising to me, but she must feel the same way.

"So, I guess this means that you love me too?" I ask, the biggest smile on my face.

She laughs hard, nods, wipes the tears from her face and then she's kissing me again.

———

I DON'T KNOW WHAT THE FUTURE WILL BRING. BUT THIS IS the end of the story. That first kiss with Helena in the storeroom of La Familia is the perfect place to stop.

I do have one more thing to say, though.

Cedar Breaks National Monument is not far from here, just forty-five minutes up on the top of the Colorado Plateau. It's this sandstone bowl that has eroded in the most fascinating way. Large salmon colored towers of rock, called hoodoos, populate the land like sentinels in the most mystical of temples.

It is just rock and water and time. The power of erosion. But it's not the kind of place you would ever imagine seeing on this planet. It's magical and powerful and surprising. It's holy.

It's the higher-altitude, smaller cousin of the better-known Bryce National Park, but I like it better. Fewer people and I love the spruce and fir forest up at its 10,000 foot elevation.

On the edge of this canyon grows the bristlecone pine tree. It's a twisted little tree, that dangles on the edge of the canyon with lots of wind, little rain, and the inevitability of erosion pulling it down.

Bristlecone pines are also the oldest living things on the planet (well, there is some debate on that, but for me they just must be the oldest). They live over two thousand years. I myself have stood in front of one of these twisted ancient trees marveling at the beauty of Cedar Breaks below them. These trees live in the harshest of circumstances, but somehow live the longest.

I've been fascinated with them since my father told me all about them on a family trip to Cedar Breaks when I was six years old. The branches and bark twist as the tree grows. It looks stunted and twisted but is so very tough.

I've come to look at myself and my life a bit like that. The winds of leukemia have twisted my life and stunted my growth. I stand on the edge of a precipice in harsh conditions always in danger of falling.

But the view. My god, the view.

I don't know if I have another week or another sixty years, but I do know that I will be like the bristlecone pine tree on the edge of Cedar Breaks. I will be holding on and fighting for my life as long as I can.

And I'm not silly enough to think my efforts, my will, determines my survival. Makes a difference, yes. Controls it, no. So much is out of our control, isn't it?

So, enough of this time spent writing, there is a life to be lived. Helena's waiting downstairs, we've got plans. She'll be there to hold my hand and I'll hold hers just as long as I can.

EPILOGUE BY HELENA MONFORT-WADE

June 2017

I said no to writing this epilogue a dozen times. I told the editors, Tamara and Jin, that Aaron's words should stand alone. That the summer of 1977 and all we went through was served just fine by his diary. But they wouldn't give up. They said that people would pester them endlessly if they didn't know what happened to Aaron and me.

So here I am, finally writing it. But first a warning. Aaron did his best to end this in as close to a "happily ever after" as he could. Kind of a realistic happily ever after. And if you are okay with that ending, there is no need to read further.

You can imagine for yourself what happened to us in the last forty years.

If you are a pessimist, you might imagine that the Cancer (I'll capitalize it just like Aaron did) got him and he didn't survive until the end of 1977. That his parents were devastated and didn't recover. That I couldn't deal with the loss and slid into drug addiction.

Or maybe you're an optimist. You might imagine that the summer of 1977 was the last we ever saw of Cancer. That

Aaron went to college and took over the bookstore. That we were married a few years later and had a passel of kids. That Aaron eventually took up writing and his works equaled that of his hero, Stephen King, and that if I told you his real name you would recognize it and be amazed.

I will tell you this, that the truth is somewhere between those two extremes. So, take a moment and imagine what happened. If you are satisfied, close this book. If you would like to know what really happened to us, join me on the next page.

Okay, I'm just going to rip the bandage off.

Aaron Wade died on December 31, 1979. I hate New Years now. The holiday is absolutely ruined for me.

While he overcame his "third strike" with leukemia and we had nearly two good years, it came back with a vengeance in late summer, 1979. There were no ghosts to warn him this time and the leukemia got into his central nervous system. It affected his mind. It wasn't pretty.

But those two years... they were so precious. I wouldn't trade them for anything. And I did what he wanted, I held his hand every chance I got and was holding it when he took his last breath.

I won't go into the end, the horrible ending Cancer can afford you, but I will talk about some of the highlights of our two good years. I think Aaron would have wanted that.

After that first date, our relationship progressed rapidly. No boy had ever treated me like Aaron did, and with his condition, taking our time didn't make any sense. We were in love, in this silly, sloppy way that I had never imagined possible. Aaron took the advice his father gave him in that church before our first date and was an absolute gentleman, but the only thing to wait on was his health.

I remember walking down the hallway of our high school hand in hand on his first day back to school. He was finally healthy enough to attend class, his hair growing back in. He had this huge grin on his face, he was so damn happy to be there. No one was ever very happy to be in high school, but he was. He drank in every surprised look of every boy that saw me with him. It delighted him to no end, and that delighted me, so I made a good show of it with the public displays of affection.

Our lives fell into a pattern for the rest of 1977 and part of 1978. School, work, and spending as much time together as we could. He would go get his tests every three months down in

Vegas and they always came back clear. It really started to feel like he was going to be fine, like we would have a normal life.

In the spring of 1978, I graduated from high school a year ahead of Aaron. I stayed living with my father and worked more. Aaron tried to get me to go to college, but I wasn't interested. I think that hurt him, he loved learning and books so very much.

In fact, that was one of the two areas we had problems with that year. I was content to serve Mexican food at La Familia and spend as much time with him as I could. He wanted more for me. The other area we had issues with was my smoking. As soon as he and our relationship seemed stable, he started harping on me about it. Well, "harping" is not the right word. He really just went about educating me about the effects of smoking. Relentlessly.

One day in early 1978, we were sitting in the high school cafeteria having lunch. Billy Chadow was there and few of our other friends. Aaron plopped a book in front of me that had this odd picture. It was this pink fleshy looking stuff with these awful grey areas marbled through it. Like rotting ground beef or something.

"What is this?" I asked him.

"What your lungs will look like if you don't stop smoking soon."

This was like the fifth time he did something like this around the smoking. When Aaron got something in his head like that, he just wouldn't let it go. I lost it and we ended up having a screaming match in front of the whole school.

He took Cancer personally and couldn't understand why I would be doing something that was known to cause it. I was seventeen then, I didn't understand the power of addictions like I do now.

That was our first fight.

He was at La Familia with a dozen roses when I got off shift that night. He said, "I love you and want to keep you as long as I can."

I lit a cigarette in front of him, flipped him the bird, and walked away, convinced he was like every other boy that had tried to control me.

But he never gave up. Not on me—that night he ran after me with those flowers and insisted on walking me home. After a few blocks we were holding hands—it wasn't intentional, just habit—and I couldn't stay mad at him.

He kept on me about the smoking, but never did it again in a public place. For him I tried to quit smoking that year, but it didn't stick.

Aaron turned eighteen on May 15, 1979. He took me up to Cedar Breaks to celebrate and rented us a little cabin in nearby Brian Head.

He took me out to see those bristlecone pine trees of his that he talked about. The park is at 10,000 feet and because of the spring snow, the park was closed to vehicles and we had to rent a snowmobile and then snowshoe through the gorgeous, snow-covered red- and salmon-colored rocks. He told me the story of his father taking him there when he was six. He told me that he too may be stunted and twisted, but he was still here. That he would fight for the beauty of life as long as he could. He told me that I was what he fought so hard to live for.

That night at dinner in a nice Brian Head restaurant, he kept looking at his watch. In fact, he was so nervous about getting us there on time for the reservation that he drove me a bit crazy. But it was a nice dinner and after desert he started looking at his watch every thirty seconds.

"What is with you?" I asked.

He looked at me, blinked a few times, and said, "Just five more minutes."

I shook my head, I didn't know what he was talking about.

"And I'll be eighteen," he said, looking at his watch again. "I was born at 8:33 p.m."

I still didn't get it, but when the five minutes were up, he took a little jewelry box out of his pocket, got down on one knee in front of me, and asked me to marry him. This was his first act as a legal adult.

I blubbered and cried and said yes. Of course I said yes. There was clapping around us as I pulled Aaron up and kissed him, but I didn't see any of them. All I could see were his happy blue eyes.

We got married on June 21, 1979, in a lovely ceremony in the Cedar City Cemetery. Aaron insisted. He wanted Big Ed Lopez to be there for it and Lionel too. It was summer solstice, the same day two years earlier where Aaron had proved to me that he really could see Lionel. Despite all the craziness of his near-death experience, he said he owed the ghosts his life and that they had brought us together. How could we do it anywhere else?

It was the talk of the town, believe me. In a small town like Cedar, the tongues wagged. No wedding was ever talked about as much as that one. About fifty uninvited people showed up just to gawk.

Aaron didn't care and I didn't either. We were married by Pastor West right in front of Aaron's Uncle Don's grave (he wanted to do it on the grave, but I put my foot down on that).

Billy and his whole family were there. Aaron's parents. My parents—my dad brought my mom up for it, she had a good day and enjoyed being out of the care home. Fran and a huge gang from La Familia were there too.

I got to wear white and Aaron was dressed in a tux. Billy was his best man and I had Aaron's mom Laura as my maid of honor.

At the end of the ceremony when we had a brief quiet moment, Aaron leaned over and whispered, "Do you think

Lionel and Ann Edwards are here? Do you think they are happy now that they are together?"

I had to smile. He was such a romantic, he even wanted the murderous ghosts to have a happily ever after.

We had a huge party at La Familia afterwards and that night I moved in to Aaron's little room with the glow-in-the-dark stars on the ceiling.

We had a few good months until the headaches started and the diagnosis hit. It wasn't perfect—Aaron's fastidiousness clashed with my sloppiness—but we were in love.

After the diagnosis, he went down fast. He fought hard, so hard, but it wasn't enough. I said I wouldn't talk about this, and I won't, but there is one thing I should mention.

When it was clear how dire his diagnosis was, we tried to get pregnant. Actually, I asked, then begged, and then we fought. He didn't think it was a responsible thing to do—father a child he might never see. I told him that if he wasn't going to make it that I needed (desperately) something of him when he was gone.

I had almost lost him already so there was a sense of realism from everyone around the Cancer moving to his brain. He eventually agreed to do it for me and we tried. As much as his energy would allow, we tried. But it didn't work. I feel bad about dragging him to a fertility specialist in Vegas when he was fighting Cancer, but I was desperate. As it turns out Aaron was sterile. One of his treatments along the way had done it. This wasn't a surprise for any of us, and that just made me feel worse.

I lost it that day and cried in the backseat of the car the whole way home. It was Aaron's father that drove us to the appointment. When we got back to the house, Aaron left the car without a word. There was so much he endured so grace-fully, but my grief wasn't something he could be present for.

"There's still hope," Henry, his father, said after Aaron was gone.

I snuffled and nodded. "I know."

"We have to hope," he said, his eyes so sad I started crying again.

And we did hope. Every day we hoped he would start to get better. Every day Aaron fought like a champion to stay alive, to stay positive, to enjoy the moments he had.

And then one day that fight ended. I was holding his hand.

———

Life has its strange twists and turns, as it has for all of us that were there with Aaron in the late seventies. I thought I would update you on us all. Where we are now, what has happened to us in the post-Aaron era.

Pastor West stayed at the Lutheran Church for two more years. And then in what must be called a cliché, he fell in love with Lisa Collins, his secretary, and ran off with her. Last I heard, he's at another church up in Oregon.

Billy Chadow married a lovely woman of Asian descent in 1981. He met her on the campus of Southern Utah University. They are still happily married with six kids and five grandchildren. Billy became an accountant and now runs one of Cedar's biggest accounting firms. He still loves comic books and I'm sure he still has a place in his heart for Barbara Bach.

Henry and Laura Wade were divorced in 1980. It was probably the most civilized divorce known to man. Henry kept Cedar Books and Such, and Laura kept most of the proceeds from the sale of the house. In 1981, she moved to California, where she remarried a few years later. I think there was too much of Aaron here for her then. Henry kept teaching for a few more years but hired someone to manage the bookstore and wasn't there that much. I think there was too much Aaron there for him. It was "their" place, after all.

He eventually moved to Las Vegas to teach at a college there. He retained ownership of the bookstore until the early nineties and would be in town pretty often.

Henry and Laura have both been retired for a few years, and while I wouldn't call them best friends, they still do talk from time to time. And Laura has told me that when they do talk, they usually talk about Aaron and that is actually a good thing now.

And now we're down to me. I took Aaron's death hard. Real hard. At first, I was mad at him and then I was mad at god, and during that time I would gladly be mad at anyone that got in my way (more so than my teenage norm).

I told you that our wedding was a big deal for a little town, so was the funeral. Aaron was buried next to his Uncle Don right where we met, right where we got married. That spot holding so much of him, of us, was not something I could bear.

Reading Aaron's words has been hard, it has brought me right back to all that happened and has made his loss seem so real again. The tears that I thought I long ago left behind on this have come back in force. I told Aaron so many times that I was strong, that I didn't break easily, that I could take it, but his death broke me. A loss like that *should* break you, otherwise what kind of person are you, what kind of love did you experience? Aaron's death broke all of us.

After he died, I moved back in with my father. I worked at La Familia and drank too much. Way too much. Six months later it took Aaron's parents, Billy and his family, Pastor West, and my father staging an intervention to get me off that path. I went into rehab and got some counseling and started going to AA meetings. Actually, it took a lot of counseling to get my head straight.

Aaron's mother, Laura, and I became very close. We shared

a grief. Aaron was her son, he was my love. She took me on as her mission and wouldn't stop until I was cleaned up and on a better path. No matter how I yelled and raged at her, she wouldn't stop. I think she transferred all her maternal energies from Aaron to me. I was her daughter and she was my mother. I don't think I would have made it without her.

I ended up moving to Sacramento where Laura had landed and going to nursing school there. We still talk several times a week and she is still a mother to me.

There are just too many loose ends to wrap up quickly here. And I think "loose" ends is a good way to put it, illustrating how our lives intertwine, tangle, and fray. My own mother died a couple of decades ago and I felt so bad for being away from Cedar, for not seeing her but once or twice a year, but Laura was a mother to me again then and helped me come to terms with it. She really is my mother, ever since I was seventeen.

It's been a long, long road getting over Aaron. Actually, that's not true. I'm not over him, and while I wouldn't trade our time for anything, the ending still hurts. I still feel short changed by how little time we had.

I'm fifty-seven now. I've been married twice more, have a son and a granddaughter, and I'm still not quite over the boy I met in a graveyard in 1977 that could see a ghost.

After a long time away, I am back in Cedar City. I'm on my own now. I divorced my second husband, and my third died of a heart attack a year ago. Aaron was the only man whose name I took, and maybe that wasn't fair to my other husbands. I don't think I really understood why I did it at the time, but I think I was just holding on to part of him. I wanted to see the Wade at the end of my name even if it did hurt for the longest time.

My father's been retired for a while and he is at the point where he needs a little help, so I'm back in the house I was born in.

I am still nursing and I guess I have Aaron as well as his mother to thank for that. It was the nurses that made Aaron's time in the medical system bearable. The nurses were the ones that nurtured, that cared about the quality of his experience, not just his survival. They (and Laura) inspired me to want to do the same, and I have for nearly thirty-five years.

My granddaughter is coming out for the month of August this year. She's going to stay with my father and me. I spent a lot of years trying to distance myself from 1977. But now that I'm back, now that Aaron's diaries have been turned into this book, I feel the need to remember.

I'm going to tell Stella, my granddaughter, all about him. I'm going to walk her by the old Wade house. Take her to where La Familia used to be (it's a Greek restaurant now). I'm going to show her the Adam's Memorial Shakespearean Theatre, the tree Aaron and I used to meet under on campus, and the place where Cedar Books and Such used to be (it's still a bookstore but has a different name).

The theatre that they opened in 1977 is no longer in use. They've replaced it with something bigger and more modern across the street. Word is that the Adam's is going to get torn down one of these days. I hate it. Aaron was so excited about the theatre and what it would mean to Cedar, and indeed the Utah Shakespeare Festival has grown as has Cedar City, but I really hate that they're done with that theatre.

I haven't been able to walk into the bookstore yet. I've only been there once since Aaron died to see his father, Henry. I lost it. Completely. After that we'd meet at other places. Too much of Aaron in that bookstore. Maybe with Stella and all the years in between I'll have the courage to walk in.

I'm going to take her to the graveyard and show her where her grandmother was first married and where the first man she loved is buried. I've driven by a few times but haven't stopped.

In the early days I would go, I would stroll the narrow roads under the cottonwood and firs and cry and talk to Aaron as if he was a ghost, as if he was there, needing to believe he could hear me. Ghosts are real. I know that, but I have no idea if Aaron was a ghost then. In my heart, I know he's not there anymore. It would be a terrible shame if he was there all these years later.

And I'm going to take her up to Cedar Breaks and out to Aaron's bristlecone pine tree. I'm going to let her gaze on its twisted trunk and limbs and tell her all about Aaron. About how we can be like the bristlecone and endure so much. How, if we love with all our heart, who we are endures long after we're gone.

Stella is seven. I think she's old enough to absorb some of this. I hope so. And in any case, it will do me good to remember the good times and the passion Aaron and I shared.

The last word Aaron said before he lapsed into a coma was, "quality." It started as a long conversation about quality versus quantity, an idea his father had talked to him about early on in his Cancer journey. About how we all had limited time, so we had to make the best of it. In the end, we shortened it to the one word. When things were tough one of us would say "quality" to the other.

After he said it, I squeezed his hand as his eyes fluttered closed. He took his last breath five hours later and I was still holding his hand.

God, he was such a weird kid, but I loved him so.

Helena Monfort-Wade

June 2017

Cedar City, Utah

AFTERWORD

This book has taken a very long time. Much longer than my first novel, even. I drafted it at the end of 2013 and the beginning of 2014 and then things got intense with my mother's care and then she died on the last day of 2016, and then...

Well, I had a backlog of books to get out that were in a similar state and I was not sure if I was going to write anymore. My mother had dementia and her last few years were very difficult. Dealing with her disease, all of her things, her finances... it was an honor to be there for her, to try to give back some of the gift she gave me in bringing me into this world, but it was so very hard. At the start of 2017, I didn't know if I wanted to be so busy, to add all the time writing and producing and marketing books on top of my day job.

And this book. It deals with family, a boy growing up in the seventies in a high desert town with a mother he had a complicated relationship with. Laura Wade is not my mother, but I did grow up in a high desert town (Arizona not Utah) and my family wasn't exactly normal (in different ways than the Wade family). So I wasn't sure that I wanted to do anything with this book.

My wife, Aleia, is my first reader. That means I read my stories to her first, before anyone else sees them. She's often cooking with me sitting in the hallway, reading to the wonderful sounds and smells of her amazing culinary creations. It's become something we both love, a way for us to share this strange thing I take so much time doing.

In early 2017 when we were still numb from what we'd been through, Aleia wanted me to read to her so I pulled this manuscript out. I hadn't looked at in nearly four years and... well, it was good. I had enough distance that it really seemed like I could see it a lot more clearly than most of my books and it was good. Really good.

Spending those many hours reading to her, cleaning up the manuscript, immersing in Aaron's life was healing. Not completely, but I could start to breath a bit deeper and I remembered why I love to write so much and I knew I had to get this book out. It still needed work. I had to get the location right. I needed to review all the medical stuff and make sure it worked for the time period. But I **had** to get it out.

This book is why I kept writing, why I am still writing. This book helped me come back to myself after a very difficult time.

I hope you enjoyed it. And I hope you have family in your life (biological or chosen)—they are what makes this precious life worth living.

Robert J. McCarter

August, 2019

P.S. Cedar City and the Utah Shakespeare Festival are wonderful. Aleia and I discovered it sometime in the 90s when we were exploring the stunning beauty of southern Utah. Cedar is close to all those parks and does an amazing job with the plays. We got to see a play there for the first time in a while in 2018 while we were there doing my last bits of research to finish this book.

If you are in the area, do check it out. Highly recommended. And there's a nice bookstore right on Main Street. When I walk in, it feels to me like Aaron and his dad used to run the place, like Helena and Billy used to come visit. Like all of this really happened.

ACKNOWLEDGMENTS

So many people to thank on this one.

First off, my wife Aleia, without whom this book would not exit.

To my mother, who I dedicated this book to. Our relationship was not simple or easy, but she always loved me and she valued family above everything. I love her and I miss her. I think she would have liked this story.

Unlike many of my books, I am very aware of the inspirations for this book:

- John Greene's *The Fault in Our Stars*. I really love this book and it inspired me to take on a YA (young adult) tale of a kid with cancer. I did have to add a dash of fantasy because it's me.
- *Super 8*, the movie. I really like the sweet, tentative connection between Joe and Alice in the midst of all

the sci-fi madness. Aaron and Helena are older, but I wanted to capture something of that sweetness.

- *Joyland* by Stepehn King. It's a coming of age story with a young man a few years older than Aaron that takes place in the seventies with a dash of the mystic, the kind of balance I tried to achieve here.
- *Shuffled Off.* Yup, I just mentioned my own book. The idea for this book came to me as a title, a bit longer one than the finished title: *A Boy, a Girl, a Ghost, and a Graveyard.* Well, it just had to take place in the ghost world I started with *Shuffled Off.*

It was all these components (and more, I am sure, that I am unaware of) that created this story.

Thanks to Jordyn Redwood for reviewing the medical details for me to make sure I got late 1970s leukemia and treatment right.

As always, thanks to Dianna Cox for her proofing and making sure I don't do anything too terrible.

And a big thanks to my team of beta readers: John Bifano, Elizabeth Fitzekam, Roni Hornstein, and Eliot Schipper. Thank you for your time and your input and making this story better.

And finally, thanks to you, dear reader. Thank you for spending your precious time with Aaron and Helena.

BOOKS BY ROBERT J. MCCARTER

A Boy, a Girl, and a Ghost is my fifth novel in my "ghost world" and I have some shorter works too. Below is a brief description and then a bit about my other works.

A GHOST'S MEMOIR

The "A Ghost's Memoir" series are modern-day first-person ghost stories (i.e. the ghost is writing the story of their time as earth-bound spirits):

Shuffled Off: A Ghost's Memoir, Book 1

Sometimes death wakes you up…

"The wry humor and raw emotional truth of JJ's journey will have readers rooting for him from death to eternity." – *Kirkus Review*

Drawing the Dead

Life and death are not that far apart…

"You've GOT to Read This Book!" – *Amazon.com 5-star review*

(Just like A Boy, a Girl, and a Ghost, this novel focuses on the living interacting with the dead)

To Be a Fool: A Ghost's Memoir, Book 2

Who wants to rest in peace?

"Though there are moments that bring tears, you will also be taken

on a startling ride through a unique vision of the afterlife" –
Goodreads.com 5-star review

Of Things Not Seen: A Ghost's Memoir, Book 3

A question of faith, a matter of love…

"A Deep Tale of Ultimate Triumph" – *Amazon.com 5-star review*

For more information go to ShuffledOff.com

———

WALTER ANCHOR, GHOST DETECTIVE

Like the Ghost Memoir books, these stories are first-person ghost stories about Walter Anchor who is trying to solve is own murder.

Case 1: "Detecting Haley"

Case 2: "The Ghost Brides Gift"

Case 3: "A Long Hard Fall" (coming soon)

For more information go to RobertJMcCarter/WalterAnchor

———

OTHER BOOKS AND SERIES

I write in a lot of different genres, here are some links where you can find out more or go to RobertJMcCarter.com/books for a complete list.

Wood and June versus the Apocalypse

The apocalypse has never been this much fun!

"Funny, Sweet, Different, and Incredibly Well Written!" – *Amazon.com*
5-star review

Neutrinoman & Lightningirl: A Love Story

Superheroes… falling in love… saving the world.

"Delightful, Charming. Surprisingly Romantic." – *Amazon.com 5-star*
review

Seeing Forever

A life worth living?

"In this quiet but far-reaching thriller, author McCarter explores the essence of what it means to be human… Sci-fi as it should be: engaging, moving, and grand in scope." – *Kirkus Review*

————

SHORT FICTION

I am a finalist for the *Writers of the Future* contest and my stories have appeared or are forthcoming in *The Saturday Evening Post, Pulphouse Fiction Magazine, Fiction River, Andromeda Spaceways Inflight Magazine,* and numerous anthologies.

I have two short story collections out:

Life After: Stories of Life, Death, and the Places in Between

A Matter of Life and Life After Death

Anomalous Readings: Thirteen Curious and Confounding Tales

Explore the curious and confounding…

For more information on my shorter works, go to
RobertJMcCarter.com/stories

www.ingramcontent.com/pod-product-compliance
Lightning Source LLC
Chambersburg PA
CBHW030915050726
47498CB00003BA/756